Rocks That Float

# Rocks That Float

by
Kathy B. Steele

John F. Blair, Publisher
Winston-Salem, North Carolina

*The paper in this book meets the guidelines*
*for permanence and durability of the Committee on*
*Production Guidelines for Book Longevity*
*of the Council on Library Resources.*

JACKET IMAGE
*The Leaky Boat*
by Dennis Bale, 2002   www.elabsinned.com

Library of Congress Cataloging-in-Publication Data

Steele, Kathy B., 1950–
Rocks that float / by Kathy B. Steele.
p.    cm.
ISBN-13: 978-0-89587-318-7 (alk. paper)
ISBN-10: 0-89587-318-4
1. Divorced men—Fiction. 2. Neighborhood—Fiction. 3. Geologists—Fiction.  I.
Title.
PS3619.T434R63 2005
813'.6—dc22
2005017014

DESIGN BY DEBRA LONG HAMPTON

To
John and Katie

# Rocks That Float

# Chapter 1

## *Carolyn*

CAROLYN DAY SELLS HOUSES.

She is in a particular hurry to sell property to this prospect. Carolyn Day wants to get this man out of her Lincoln Town Car, wants his hairy buttocks off her leather interior, wants his impatiently jiggling denim-covered knee away from her burled dashboard, but first wants his earnest money.

"Here's one on Dillehay Pond," he says, not asking to look at the house, just mentioning it.

Jimmy has found the house at 602 Randleman Road by looking through Carolyn Day's *Multiple Listings Service*, a catalog of houses for sale printed monthly and distributed to real-estate agents. Bored, Jimmy pulled the MLS book out of her open briefcase and has been flipping the pulp pages as she drives him from condo to condo, subdivision to subdivision. It is the size of a phone book, and that worries Jimmy. He wants this chore done. He had thought that buying a house would be like shopping for jeans, just a matter of looking for the 34 X 32 on the leather label. He shakes his head at the hundreds of tiny photos, wondering who has to stand out in the street and shoot such pictures to make a living. Post-its mark the homes Carolyn is showing Jimmy. He notices they are all within a few pages of each other, then realizes the catalog is organized by price. Jimmy is surprised that his affordability category is about halfway into the book, while the little Randleman Road house on Dillehay Pond is in the first ten pages.

Carolyn resents his intrusion into her briefcase. "The Randleman Road address would be an investment property," she says. Her eyes dart to her black slim-line case. She wants so to close it. To slam it, even. "A *rental* home," she concludes. This is why she prefers dealing with women. Women know what they want in a house. A woman customer would talk stain-grade molding and granite countertops and bubble tubs, and a woman would not have pulled anything out of her briefcase. Flattening her lips, Carolyn massages them with her Nutmeg Glimmer, letting glycerin soothe her dry flesh. She allows herself a muted smack at the end of the ritual. "And I guess you know, I guess everybody knows, that Dillehay Pond is polluted."

"I've spent some time on Dillehay Pond," he tells her. "I did a sampling project there a couple of years ago. I pulled up over two hundred sediment samples, four cores, and God knows how many water samples. We ended up with a stack of lab printouts tall enough to sit on. There's stuff in the sediments that sounds like a battery recipe—cadmium, zinc, mercury, lead, copper. But it's tied up in the bottom sediments. It's not going anywhere, and it's not hurting anybody."

"You don't want to live there, though."

Why on earth not? he wonders. He remembers Dillehay Pond as fishing-pond peaceful, one of his favorite work sites. "Why on earth not?" he asks out loud.

She smiles patronizingly at the windshield. "You'll want to be in a neighborhood with other professionals like yourself. And you'll want a property that will appreciate in value."

Jimmy knows he is being addressed with all the respect of a child strapped into a backseat restraint device. He has been too passive, led through vacant condos and still-lived-in homes by a woman he doesn't much like, imprisoned in Carolyn Day's car doing what Carolyn Day wants in order to make Carolyn Day some money. He admits to himself that he has relinquished control of the morning, but he is determined to take back the afternoon. "That's got to be my decision," he states, looking directly at her.

She nods but doesn't look at him, using driving as her excuse, busily checking all three mirrors. "Of course." She manages to appear preoccupied with a lane change. "I plan to show you everything in your range. You'll have lots to choose from."

Jimmy notices that not one hair moves when she nods. On her head, between bright gold earrings, sits a sculpture of fine wire.

"Tell me about the Dillehay Pond house."

Carolyn guides the car into a left turn, letting her fingertips touch just as lightly as possible, insisting that the power steering do the work. Her bracelet, crowded with gold charms accumulated over many birthdays and Christmases, jangles as the wheel slides obligingly through her fingers.

"That particular house is owned by a bank," she begins, surprising Jimmy. He thought he had caught her in ignorance. "They remodeled it completely. New wiring, plumbing, heating, and air. Insulation. Put a good deal of money into it to attract an investor. The bank wants to move it, not own it. Typical foreclosure situation. And foreclosure is a common situation in the Valley."

"The Valley? Is that the name of the subdivision?"

"The Randleman Road houses are not a subdivision." Carolyn tries to smile, but it doesn't work. "Those are some of the last of the mill houses, what used to be an entire town a long time ago, built for the workers at the Dillehay Mill," she drones, trying to mimic a tour guide's monotone, hoping to make it sound as dry as a history lesson, irrelevant to home buying. "That whole area of the county is called 'the Valley.' It's the Stone Bowl Creek Valley. A century ago, it was a major textile center."

Her words make the map appear in his head, the location map he included in his final report, ingrained in his mind because he prefers hand-drafting to computer drafting. Computer maps are too angular, too reluctant to show the gentle curves and arcs that nature carves. Stone Bowl Creek's route from the Carolina Piedmont across the fall line he had drawn as a thin blue wiggle, a wiggle that suddenly became a bigger splash of blue that was Dillehay Pond, widening from the wiggle to the dam. From the black perpendicular that was the dam, Dillehay Pond waved upstream like a pennant flag. Below the dam, the blue wiggle took the discharge from the dam to the Savannah River. The crumbling castle that had been the Dillehay Mill was a tiny black square on Jimmy's map, identified in the legend as "Abandoned Mill Site (presumed source of contaminants)." Upstream were four more black squares.

And then the word *rental* catches up with him. "Rental potential might not be a bad idea," he announces. He turns to Carolyn. "Remember, I'm only assigned to Muldoy Chemicals. I still work for KDR out of Columbia. They put me in charge of this restoration project at the Muldoy site, and that's probably gonna run about three years. If I could live in the house while I'm here and then have it to rent out, that might work for me."

Amused, she smiles. "Let's stop for lunch and discuss what your options are. You probably want to distinguish between investment property and a home."

"Is it empty?"

The smile disappears. "I believe so," she says, suddenly vague.

"Well, if it's empty, can't we just go look?"

"Of course we'll look. We'll go on to the Carlton Drive house— that's the one I told you has that big workshop? And then we'll go see the one in Buffett Place, the one with the pool. And then we'll scoot by the little Valley property on our way to the new condo complex I want you to see. Brand new. You can design the layout because it's just going up."

At his job, Jimmy coordinates well drillers and lab techs and college interns and computer jockeys. He knows how to supervise. "Well, you get no argument about lunch. Let's get a sandwich somewhere and then go to the Randleman Road house."

"That's perfect," Carolyn Day lies. Very slowly, very cautiously, she guides the Town Car through a wide U-turn, making sure she just misses the ditch, making sure it looks like a lot of trouble and a major reversal of plans.

She takes Jimmy to the Randleman Road house down Valley Road. She is lucky; she catches every red light. At each stop, she licks her Nutmeg Glimmer and sighs impatiently. She drives slowly past the empty shopping center, past the flea market, past the abandoned houses. As they near the tiny SaveMore store in Walthourville, she finally comments.

"Now, there's a rumor that they might build a big new Publix out on the New Highway. I'll try to find out about it, because I doubt you could find what you need here, in this little store."

"What town is this?" Jimmy asks.

"This is Walthourville. It's the county seat." She sighs, settles into her seat at yet another stoplight. "We're on 209—County Road 209. It's called Valley Road. This is the route you would take from Muldoy Chemicals every day. I hope you have better luck with lights than I do."

Jimmy remembers tracing 209 onto his map. Valley Road parallels the length of Dillehay Pond, in fact follows the length of Stone Bowl Creek. It began as a dirt road through the Valley, was paved when the mills operated twenty-four hours a day, and now is just a road through the Valley again. Truckers and travelers take the highway, the four lanes built by federal money.

Carolyn Day hopes for a train, but when she makes the right turn that takes them across the tracks downhill to Dillehay Pond, her luck runs out. She stops anyway, looking up and down the empty tracks. Bumping over the rails, she explains. "I always stop, just to be sure, you know."

"This track ever used?" he asks.

"Oh, yes," she assures him. "Trains go through the Valley all the time, taking coal to the power plant and hauling pulpwood to the paper mills over on the Georgia side of the river." She pauses to let him imagine the sounds of a train. "I wonder if these people ever get stuck back here when the trains come through."

"Probably happens." Jimmy tells her what she already knows.

"Well, you'll want to keep that in mind. I mean, what if an ambulance needs to get down here? I'm surprised it's legal, leaving people stranded like that."

Jimmy is unfazed, accustomed to the trains that rule downtown Columbia, cutting the university campus in half, drowning out speech in the Capitol. To his left, Jimmy sees a curve of concrete rise above the tracks, linking Valley Road to the New Highway, showing no concern for the few people marooned in the few mill houses left between the ramp, the tracks, and Dillehay Pond.

Engineers had been commissioned to design a highway connecting the airline hub of Atlanta to the pleasures of the Carolina coast, so the asphalt rises and crosses the Stone Bowl Creek Valley without touching down, marching on concrete stilts across Valley Road, across Southern's tracks, across the trickle that is Stone Bowl Creek below the dam. At Valley Road, a complex intersection ate twenty-eight acres of the old mill town, burying Hamilton Street, St. Luke Street, and Kimbrough Street, burying the cross streets, Coleman Road and Butterfly Road, blocking Tuttle Street, which had once led cars over the dam. In the long shadow beneath the highway, blackberries and smilax and scuppernong tangle between the curbs of what had been Cemetery Road, the route to the centuries-old Lamplight Cemetery, now a saddening square of chain link caught in the peripheral vision of highway travelers. One block of nine houses had not been in the way of the engineers' plans. Carolyn Day drives down that one block, looking left and right at the house numbers. Jimmy looks straight ahead at the pond spread out before them, right there at the end of Randleman Road.

Carolyn Day's car is as long as the house. "I bet the mosquitoes are bad out here," she warns.

Jimmy jumps out of the car. Carolyn takes two minutes. In her briefcase, she finds two printouts, complete with color pictures, on the houses she plans to take him to after he gets this little place out of his system. While he looks through this tiny house, she will spread these out in the kitchen so he can see the difference between a mill house and the houses she wants to sell him, houses with prices ten times higher and thus commissions ten times larger. She puts the printouts into her shoulder bag and slides the MLS catalog back into her briefcase, which she closes and locks. At the last Brokers Board meeting, there had been discussion of abandoning the printed version of the MLS catalog in favor of protected access online. She decides she will describe this snooping client to support that plan.

When the perfectly sealed car door finally opens, she is startled by the noise that has taken over Randleman Road. Down the sidewalk marches a flock of singing children.

"Yankee Doodle went to town . . ."

The girl in front, who looks too old to be playing parade, holds a small American flag high over her head. Both hands grip the broom handle that is her flagpole. Her forehead is pinched in effort. Behind her, a younger boy who is doing most of the singing beats a spoon on the plastic top of a red Folgers can. And behind him trail five preschoolers, four boys rattling tambourines made of paper plates hung with buttons and one tiny girl with another Folgers can. She stops to rattle her pebble-filled can, runs to catch up, stops again to rattle.

"Riding on a pony . . ."

Carolyn closes her car door and activates the remote lock held in her hand. Happily clapping time, Jimmy stands just off the curb, leaving the sidewalk for the seven children. They cross the street in front of Carolyn Day's car, squeezing between the chrome of her grille and the black-and-orange sign warning, "Road Ends." Despite herself, her eyes follow them, and that's when she notices the lady on the porch watching the parade.

"Stuck a feather in his hat . . ."

Down the street, Carolyn sees people on every porch except the one with the For Rent sign and the one that has collapsed. All are watching, smiling, clapping like Jimmy is doing. Carolyn hurries up the steps, anxious to get the key out of the lockbox and get this waste of time over with so they can move on to serious properties. Jimmy watches the kids to the far end of the block, where a man leans on a cane and sings louder than the children.

"And called it macaroni."

The children then cross the street again, high-stepping and jingling and drumming right up the steps of the last house on Jimmy's side of the street. They settle on the stairs, no longer singing but just as noisy. A woman bends over them with a bag of cookies. Jimmy can hear her laughing, even though the boy still beats a rhythm. Screen doors slam one by one as the porches of Randleman Road empty.

"Must be a day-care center down there," Jimmy comments, but Carolyn Day is already opening the front door, using her shoulder, making it look like work.

Framed in the doorway, she turns and nods. Then she speaks, enunciating carefully so that it seems like an attempt at a whisper. "I think you're right. And you want to be careful of buying in a neighborhood where zoning laws aren't enforced."

Jimmy walks around to the side of the house, the side on the pond. He sees the dock, thirty feet of grayed planking, and he is sold. Carolyn is inside the house doing a quick walk-through to find something wrong, looking up for a roof leak, looking down for a sag in the floor, aiming her laser device at walls to measure the pitifully small square footage. At the back door, she looks out and sees Jimmy at the end of the dock, his hands in his pockets, staring at the pond. "Shit," she says.

The Dillehay Pond project had been primarily a boat and Jimmy. KDR owns two boats, one a thirty-footer with a little cabin under the bow big enough for sleeping uncomfortably if you have to, the other a little fourteen-foot inboard. The little one is used more often, since KDR secures contracts to study rivers and streams and ponds a lot more regularly than contracts to study the coastline. So the little one looked like hell when Jimmy pulled it out of the metal storage building outside the KDR office.

He had first towed it to a car wash and hosed it off, just to get a good look at the damage. Raccoons had lived and loved in the boat, and that required some cleaning up and the replacement of a couple of floating cushions. The blue carpet was permanently streaked with pumpkin-colored clay. Jimmy knew it on sight, the sand-studded clay left behind on the Carolina coastal plain by an Eocene shoreline. On the bow next to the boat's official registration number, clumsily applied stick-on letters spelled out *Little One*. Jimmy chuckled, wondering which of his KDR buddies had taken the time to name the boat but hadn't invested a minute to disconnect the battery. It was dead, and the connections were corroded. Jimmy replaced all the cracked rubber hoses and had a mechanic tune up the Mercury engine but forgot to do anything with the trailer. One of the tires blew out on a hot stretch of I-20. He left *Little One* on the shoulder, hoping someone would steal it, and spent the rest of that day tracking down a trailer tire. He was smart enough to buy two.

So it had taken two days just to trailer the boat the eighty-three miles from KDR's parking lot to Dillehay Pond. And that was a typical situation in Jimmy's life. Being a field scientist requires more mechanical and logistical skills than scientific knowledge. Jimmy's one of the company's few field people, since most of the KDR geologists prefer to graduate to desk jobs. They sit in front of terminals and do groundwater modeling, or they write environmental impact statements, or they oversee projects. Jimmy likes being muddy.

Jimmy is looking for a new place, a place away from Columbia, away from reminders of his ex-wife, a place as different from their shared house as possible. Dillehay Pond, sparkling with memories of a job gone well, of a time when he could go home at night and tell his wife about the belted kingfisher that had perched on his boat and swallowed a carp, seems somehow both remote and familiar.

Jimmy knows Carolyn is watching him. He shouts, "Is the dock part of the property?"

It's obviously part of the property, thinks Carolyn. Just five feet of vetch and sandspurs separate it from the three risers that climb to the deck. From where Carolyn stands, the dock looks like an extension of the deck. "I don't know," she tells him, not shouting, hoping he will have to strain to hear. "I don't have a plat for this property. I had no idea we were coming here."

"Well, I'm pretty sure it must be part of the lot, but find out, okay?" Then he drops to his knees and swings his head over the dock. He rocks back on his haunches long enough to pull his Swiss Army knife from the pocket underneath the Lee label, then rolls forward again to stab at the pilings.

Carolyn licks her lipstick, sorting through her extensive repertoire of sales techniques. She could remind him that his electronic gadgets would be safer in one of those gated communities along the Columbia highway, or warn him that Randleman Road is the jurisdiction of Osmond Vause, Osilo County's erratic sheriff, proud of his low arrest record and empty jail, currently at battle with the state because he refuses to allow lottery tickets to be sold anywhere in the county. She could tell Steverson that the pond he's admiring could disappear. State Representative True Padgett is obsessed with Dillehay Pond, wants to fill the entire thing in, ostensibly to bury pollution but actually to end the county's unemployment problem, accumulate votes, and keep his name in circulation. Carolyn dismisses both options. Steverson doesn't look like the type to worry about theft. He might just like the idea of an oddball sheriff—more local color to chuckle over. And he has studied the pond, so he'll recognize the congressman's backfill project as the type of insane idea that only political rhetoric and access to tax dollars can breed. And she doesn't want to be included in the back-woods folklore she imagines him telling his city friends: "The lady who sold me the house says the sheriff wants everybody to call him by his first name and doesn't like to arrest people. And the congressman wants to turn the place into Love Canal!" Nope. She doesn't want redneck jokes associated with her ivory-and-gold-embossed business cards.

Carolyn quietly closes the back door. She pulls her cell phone from her shoulder bag. She does not dial the listing agent. Instead, she dials Carolina Federal. "Hello, hon, this is Carolyn Day. Put Mr. McAvoy on, would you?"

Carolyn was raised in the canons of trust, of virtue as reward, taught at the folding table in Sunday-school class, engraved in the plaster molds of Vacation Bible School, heard over sizzling marshmallows at Camp Saviour-in-the-Mountains. She believed in accrual. *Cast thy bread upon the waters: for thou shalt find it after many days.*

For sixteen years, she worked hard at her marriage. While her husband accumulated enough air time to upgrade to first class, Carolyn shopped for disposable diapers, kept the washer churning, and arrayed the refrigerator with a magnetic alphabet. She enrolled in cake-decorating and stir-fry lessons, worked as a part-time school librarian, hung wallpaper, served as treasurer of the PTO, and twice found the Yard of the Month sign standing in the deep mulch around her Formosa azaleas. She was there to applaud when her children received their honor-roll certificates, when her husband was named Jaycee of the Year. *All her household are clothed with scarlet.*

In fact, no benefits accrued from hours of childbirth or years of care giving. Benefits, she was stunned to learn, had been appropriated by her husband, who announced in the sixteenth year of their marriage that he had bought a condo with a Jacuzzi, and that he would be moving there to live his life. *Wherefore? Because the Lord hath been witness between thee and the wife of thy youth, against whom thou hast dealt treacherously.*

Divorce nullified the covenant, nullified the canons, nullified her. Carolyn memorizes Bible verses like she collects charms for her bracelet, rattling them when she wants to, assigning her own meaning to the verses as she assigns commemorative significance to the gold baubles at her wrist. Always, a verse pops into her head suited to the moment, providing comfort or explanation or validation. But the words did not raft to the top of her marital crisis. She reread the onionskin pages, straining the old words through her new life the way she had once filtered beef stock through cheesecloth until she had a perfectly clear consommé. *And the vessel that he made of clay was marred in the hand of the potter; so he made it again another vessel, as seemed good to the potter to make it.*

Carolyn became a convert to the creed of addition, joining the congregation of those who tallied and balanced. She first made sure that the house was hers. *Whoso keepeth the fig tree shall eat the fruit thereof.* Then she made sure that the kids were his. *Whatsoever a man soweth, that shall he also reap.*

The trauma of the divorce was too much, she told the family-court judge; she was mentally incapable of caring for three children. "I'm seeing a therapist," she whispered in the quiet courtroom, looking and sounding like a danger to herself and to the community and particularly to helpless children. "Please," she begged, "you can't allow me to have custody." *For every man shall bear his own burden.* The father must be given sole custody. He would have to find room in the condo with the Jacuzzi for fourteen-year-old Jennifer's twelve-speed and twelve-year-old Zack's skateboards and eleven-year-old Matthew's GameBoy. *Better it is that thou shouldest not vow than that thou shouldest vow and not pay.*

She dutifully attended the court-ordered therapy sessions every Monday morning, which she enjoyed immensely, an entire hour of talking about herself. *In the house of the righteous is much treasure.* Five days a week, she drove to the university's Salkehatchie campus, speeding past the USC-Osilo County campus, where she might have found herself in class with a friend's teenager. She added accounting courses to a transcript dormant for eighteen years, until the credits added up to a degree. After that, she drove to evening classes at the technical college, where she gained her real-estate license. It was amazing how many hours were in the day, how much could be accomplished, without soccer practices and gymnastics events to sit through, without laundry baskets full of blue jeans, without suits to pick up at the cleaner's, without a two-page grocery list and a coupon file.

For seven years, she had worked hard as a real-estate agent. She had added to her life, added credentials, income, a car registered in her name, an office with a brass nameplate on the door. She had seen her name in the paper as vice president of the chamber of commerce. *And they gave the money, being told, into the hands of them that did the work.*

"Hey, Mac, this is Carolyn. How are you? How's Myrtice? One of these days, she's got to tell me how she grows those tomatoes. Were those Beefsteak or Better Boy? I didn't see you at the chamber breakfast—everything okay? Well, good, I was worried. Listen, I've got an idea. I have a client, a young man just divorced, looking for what you guys would call a bachelor pad. I think that little mill house you-all have had on the market for a couple of years might just appeal to him. I was wondering, if I steer him your way, is there a bonus in there?" *The hand of the diligent maketh rich.*

The cell phone is back in the soft brown leather of her bag when Jimmy opens the back door. She leans on the white Formica, looking comfortable, looking patient. "I called the bank, and they'll fax me a plat," she tells him. "But they won't budge on the price. They have too much in it, they said. I spoke directly to Mac McAvoy, the bank president," she says dolefully, shaking her head. Then she smiles. "But Mac assured me that the dock is part of the property. He says it should be in good shape, that they replaced it when they remodeled the house."

Jimmy scans the kitchen. "Hey, this place is cool."

"Everything you see is brand-new. All the appliances still have the warranty tags attached. Built-in microwave."

Two strides take Jimmy through the galley kitchen. "It's like an apartment," he says with a smile.

Carolyn nods happily. She points. "Two bedrooms."

He steps quickly through one small and one tiny bedroom, finds the narrow bathroom. "Is there just one bathroom?" he calls.

"Just one bathroom to clean," she promises. "Perfect for you."

He is at the back door again. "I think I'll screen part of the back deck in."

A sale, an addition to her account, and she can get back to dealing with wives and moms who sit gratefully in her accommodating car and walk admiringly through dozens of homes. "I'll get the contract to Mac today," she promises. And I'll get this man out of my Lincoln today, she promises herself. *Where no oxen are, the crib is clean.*

Chapter 2

# *Jimmy*

So Jimmy Steverson becomes the new person on the pond, the first new surname on a Randleman Road mailbox in a generation.

Jimmy's KDR pals help him move in. Carl backs the yellow Ryder truck around the house, directed by Mike. Mike, who spends most days looking into the gray gloom of a computer's face, is enjoying himself. He invents elaborate hand signals to direct Carl.

In the side mirror, Carl watches Mike's hands form what looks like a bird flapping its wings. "What the hell is that?" he yells.

"Means edge away a little bit. You're too close to the house."

Carl pulls the truck forward, straightens his path, and backs again. Mike spreads his arms wide, then brings his hands together as the truck closes in. Jimmy is on the deck laying boards down the stairs for the dolly. "When his hands close," he hollers to Carl, "that means you can run over him."

"I oughta speed up, then. Get that chore out of the way. Now, what does that mean?"

Mike's left hand is held up palm outward—the traditional *Stop*—while his right hand seems to be pushing something up. "Means *Stop* and *Raise the back gate.*"

"Raise the back gate? You have to open up the back like a garage door, jackass."

"He doesn't get out much, Carl. And he's used to doing everything from a keyboard."

Carl and Jimmy stand aside, arms across chests, offering no help as Mike fumbles with the latch and finally sends the truck's door upward on its tracks. He is more adept with the lever that operates the mechanical lift. Carl and Jimmy watch Mike raise and lower it several times until Carl decides to put everyone to work.

"Okay, Mike, quit playing and get the dolly out."

Mike rides the lift back up and looks around.

Carl grins. "The orange thing with the wheels."

Jimmy and Carl are lost in amusement at the sight of a grown man discovering a dolly. Cautiously, Mike rolls it a few inches. "What does it do? Does it fold out?"

"It's remote controlled," Carl says.

The sofa goes in first, Carl at one end, Jimmy at the other, Mike gleefully operating the lift.

"God, Jimmy, this sofa's gonna eat up this living room. I think your apartment was bigger."

"It was."

They edge the sofa under the front window, the only place it fits. Through the window, they see Lakeishia Mims's Volvo wagon pull up, the seats filled with people and the back filled with aluminum-foil-wrapped mounds that promise food. Lakeishia, KDR's business manager, steps out and checks the house number, then checks an index card in her hand. Louis, their geochemist, is sound asleep in the front seat. Will and Jamil, KDR's other two geologists, climb out of the backseat and go to work hauling coolers. Lakeishia stares at the house, looking worried.

"Lakeishia doesn't like your house, Jimmy," Carl says. "I bet you we're gonna have to listen to one of her lectures. You know, where she says shit like, 'If you divide your 501(c)(3) by your 401(K), you'll see that your P/E ratio doesn't add up to a hill of beans.' "

"You're the boss, Carl. Tell her to shut up."

"Jimmy, you might need to hear it. You sure 'bout this place? You're a long way from everybody, from the office."

Jimmy wonders if Carl means this as directive or advice. Carl is in fact Jimmy's boss, according to the KDR staffing chart, but he has never had to exercise the authority. Jimmy hears from him only when he goes overbudget. "I'm fifteen minutes from the well site at Muldoy."

"And about a century away from everything else. Have you looked up and down this street good? Looks like a Norman Rockwell painting of hell."

"Well, I don't really care much about Randleman Road. I moved here to be on the pond."

Jimmy opens the door for Lakeishia, who greets him with instructions, as always. "Jimmy, if you don't have your refrigerator plugged in, get it done now. We're bringing in food. And we'll need a table."

"The fridge came with the place, and it's running."

Lakeishia, holding a hubcap-sized platter, gives him an extra second before repeating herself. "And we'll need a table."

"Table's on the truck still."

"Get it off the truck first, then."

Lakeishia heads to the kitchen. Jimmy and Carl obediently head to the truck. They shove the mattress and box springs aside to clear a path to Jimmy's kitchen table. Carl carries it, legs up, to the deck, where he turns it upright to stand in the shade of the house.

The influx of food and six-packs and four more people turns moving into Moving Day, a party. Platters of sandwiches, buckets of wings, bowls of pasta and potato salads, bags of chips, a plate of brownies, stacks of paper cups and plates cover the table. Once the food is organized, Lakeishia corners Jimmy. She likes him, appreciates his honest expense-account reports, respects his ability to get accurate bids from drillers and suppliers. "What I want you to do, Jimmy, is start photocopying your receipts and giving me just the copies. Your originals are always muddy or wet, so they don't file well. Also, you need to rethink this house." Lakeishia doesn't see this as a change of subject. To her, life and job are part of the same investment package. "This property will see no appreciation, and in your asset-allocation situation, this house is your primary investment."

Jimmy is not offended. Lakeishia routinely offers her financial expertise to the willy-nilly geologists and distracted chemists around her, always with the air of a kindergarten teacher advising on crayon selection. She is indirectly responsible for Jimmy's ten percent ownership of KDR. Carl encountered Lakeishia at a meeting, learned that her transcript included science courses, and recruited her relentlessly, desperate for someone who understood that mercury is a contaminant and Mercury is a planet. Unable to match her salary, he lured her with ten percent of the company and signed over another ten to Jimmy at the same time, out of fairness.

Lakeishia is not done. "And I'm guessing that you bought this place outright with the proceeds from your first house. Which leaves you without mortgage interest to deduct on April 15. So you might want to consider setting up a home-equity line of credit."

Carl interrupts, hoping to give Jimmy a chance to bite the sandwich he'd already been holding for ten minutes before Lakeishia's commentary began, while he answered questions about why he'd moved here, who built the pond, whether there were any bass or cat in it, whether he was going to buy a boat, when they could come fish. "According to Jimmy, he didn't actually buy a house on Redneck Road. What he did was, he moved to the pond."

"To the pond!" toasts Mike, holding a Corona bottle high.

"To the pond!" is the ragged echo that becomes the refrain of the evening. Anyone pulling a beer from the cooler is obliged to yell, "To the pond!" and the group obligingly answers.

Just after midnight, Mike pulls the last item off the truck, Jimmy's rope hammock. Mike becomes drunkenly obsessed with hanging it. The only tree on the lot, a water oak, conveniently planted itself just far enough from the deck to allow the hammock to swing between the oak and one of the four-by-fours supporting the deck. Lakeishia, who has stayed sober in order to drive, watches the five guys mill about in the dark, searching for the hammock's hooks, looking in toolboxes for a drill, trying to find an extension cord, pausing to shout, "To the pond!" She jokingly asks, "How many drunk geologists does it take to hang a hammock?"

"How many are here?" asks Carl.

At two in the morning, the hammock is hung and toasted—"To the hammock!"—and the party ends.

Jimmy is up by ten. The noise of the shower wakes Carl, who eats leftover wings and heads grumpily back to Columbia in the Ryder truck. By eleven, Jimmy is picking up beer cans. His trash can is full, so he stuffs three trash bags under the deck, trying to get his new home respectable enough for his parents' visit. When they drive up in their new Saturn, Jimmy is connecting the propane tank to his grill.

The new car serves as a distraction for the first few minutes. "We needed something smaller," his dad explains. Jimmy admires the car as long as possible, but ultimately his new house becomes the topic of conversation.

His mom retrieves a shopping bag from the trunk, then seems uncertain where to go. She points to Jimmy's porch. "Up here?" she asks.

"That's me. Y'all come on in."

She explains the shopping bag. "I brought salad and dessert."

"I'm grilling chicken."

His mother heads inside to refrigerate the salad, but his dad stops on the front porch. "Just painted," he notices.

"Yeah, the bank completely renovated it."

His dad lingers, looking up and down the street. "Kind of the best-looking one on the block." Jimmy knows this is meant to remind him that when one invests in real estate, one buys in the best neighborhood, not the best house in the neighborhood. "So you bought this, right? Not leased? You're temporary down at that plant, aren't you?"

"I bought the house, Dad. I'll be at the Muldoy well site for about three years."

"Then what?"

"Well, then KDR will assign me somewhere else, I guess."

"No, I mean, then what about the house?"

"Well, I don't know." Jimmy shrugs. "Come on out back, look at the pond. I've got my own dock."

In the few minutes they have been on the porch, his mother has begun unpacking. She has opened a box of towels and is stocking the bathroom. "Jimmy, there are no sheets on the bed. Where did you sleep last night?" Jimmy and his dad laugh. "Well, then, where are your sheets?"

"All the boxes are in the little bedroom."

In the chaos of the party, Jimmy had thought that neatly stacking the boxes in the extra bedroom was an accomplishment. He figured when he needed something, he'd open the appropriate box. But with his mother here, he is forced to unpack. His dad produces a pocket-knife and slices open boxes while Jimmy gets his mom her bottled water and his dad a Diet Coke. For the next several hours, they hang clothes, make the bed, plug in telephones, and put books on shelves, until his dad finally says, "We need to get that chicken on the grill."

On the deck with the grill going, Jimmy finally forces his parents to walk the dock and admire the pond.

His dad says, "You're gonna get a boat, I bet."

"Yeah, probably a bass boat with a trolling motor."

"Already got you a hammock up, I see."

"Yeah, the guys got that up last night."

"Looks like you're camping out here. Like a fishing camp, or a summer camp."

"Well, I guess that's one way to look at it, Dad. That I'm camped here while I get the Muldoy wells in."

His dad nods. "This shouldn't be anything permanent, Jimmy. This really isn't the kind of neighborhood you want to be in forever."

"Well, I don't really care much about Randleman Road. I moved here to be on the pond." It sounds familiar when Jimmy says it. He remembers making the same defensive statement to Carl.

"You can hear the highway traffic from here," his dad points out. "But it's not too bad. And nothing ever kept you awake anyway."

While his dad bastes the chicken, Jimmy listens. Against a background of tires on pavement, he can distinguish a truck's engine and the rattling of a loose hubcap. Abruptly, the frogs begin their evening chorus.

"You won't be here long, Jimmy," his dad says. He speaks reassuringly, as though he is talking to a hospital patient.

Sunday is Jimmy's first day alone in his new home. He wakes to a display of light and shadow on the clean eggshell paint of his bedroom wall, light dispatched from the sun, bounced from the undulating surface of Dillehay Pond, cut into dancing stripes by the branches of his water oak. It reminds Jimmy of a Chinese woodcut he had been forced to describe in an art-history class. He stretches, grateful for the sheets his mother put on the bed, then watches the light show slide down the wall. He can measure the movement—a minute to pass from the top of the light switch to the bottom—and so he imagines he can feel the planet rotate. He wonders, had he been a Mesa Verde resident watching a sunbeam angle through the doorway in his adobe walls, would he have deduced that his home, and not the sun, was moving? Jimmy rolls over, looks out the window at the bright surface of the pond, searching for something blinding enough to bleach a memory, a conversation with his ex-wife.

"Plato's cave prisoners, remember?" Gwen had asked. "That's what we are. We can look up into the stars, but we can't interpret them any more than Plato's guys could figure out what those shadows were on the roof of the cave."

From a worn textbook, the relic of a lit course, Jimmy and Gwen read Blake aloud to one another, first as a lark after too much wine, then night after night in front of the fire, arguing that research was futile, that human perceptions were limited, that science was a trade, that science was a religion. They would fall asleep there, the only warm spot in the old farmhouse, the brick-sized textbook forgotten until one of them rolled over on it.

A rooster crows, and the sound rescues Jimmy. He sits up, listening, unsure he has actually heard such a sound. A second crow, more robust than the first, tells Jimmy there are at least two chickens on Randleman Road. Under the impression that roosters crow at dawn, he checks his clock, sees the digital 10:42, and gets up.

# Chapter 3

## Mayme

Miz Mayme is the bread baker.

Jimmy knows his next-door neighbor's name by hearsay and her baking by aroma. Several times a day, Miz Mayme's ovens send warm currents by to visit. First, the yeast signal makes his nose itch, followed shortly by a sweet scent that draws pictures in the air of fat brown loaves. His neighbor's early-morning baking has replaced his alarm clock.

Jimmy has lived on the pond one month. Tonight as he comes in from work, he finds one of his aluminum folding chairs set up on his porch. In it sits one of those fat brown loaves he has conjured many times. It's still warm, busily steaming up the plastic bag that protects it.

An hour later, showered and changed, he's knocking on her door, trying to make the screen rattle enough to be heard. A fan set on high and a TV tuned to *Wheel of Fortune* send noise through the screen, as though meant to accompany the bread smell. "Hello? Miz Mayme?" A silhouette appears in the kitchen door. "Miz Mayme? I'm Jimmy

Steverson. I live next door. I just dropped by to thank you for the bread."

The silhouette moves into the light and becomes a tall woman, taller than Jimmy. "Well, come on in here," she says as she unlatches the screen. "Glad to meet you. Glad to get somebody new on the pond." Her words are friendly, but there is no smile. She gestures toward the sofa.

"Well, thank you." Jimmy sits, and Miz Mayme settles into a rocker. "That bread was delicious. I had it for supper."

She nods but still offers no smile.

Several rocks and nods later, Jimmy continues. "Yeah, I had three slices right off the bat, just put some honey on it. Then I toasted some and scrambled some eggs."

She nods. She rocks.

"Anyway, it was great. So thanks."

"You renting the place?"

"No, ma'am. I bought the house."

She nods.

Jimmy worries that he shouldn't have addressed her as *ma'am*. He had put her into his grandmother's generation before seeing her, largely because of the way people hollered for "Miz Mayme" from porch to porch. But except for the gray hair in the tight ponytail, he sees no evidence of age.

"I work for a company out of Columbia, a consulting company called KDR, but I'm assigned to the Muldoy Chemicals plant right now."

She nods again.

"And the pond seems like a nice place to live," he continues.

"I've been here forty-some-odd years," she offers. "Saw a lotta work going on at your place, back before you moved in."

"Yeah, they tell me the whole interior was redone."

Miz Mayme nods. "I reckon when the bank took it from Orene, they had to do something, 'cause that old lady hadn't been able to do nothing to that house in thirty years. That was Orene Connell used to own that house. Orene borrowed on the house 'cause of her boy. And then he run off and left her with them payments."

Jimmy had never thought about the previous occupant of the house. It seemed new to him, reeking of carpet glue and paint and sawdust. The newness was its appeal. The house reminded him of all the apartments he had lived in as a bachelor and had nothing in common with the 1892 farmhouse he and his ex-wife had tried to restore. Now, he learns that the house has a history, and a sad history at that, and he is uncomfortable hearing it.

"I tried to check on her every day," continues Miz Mayme, relentlessly telling Jimmy a story he doesn't want to know. "And then one night, I didn't see no lights come on, and I sent my son-in-law over to see about it. And she had done had a stroke. And then she got put into the nursing home, and then she died, and then the Medicaid people put a lien on the place."

Jimmy knows the story following the lien. The lawyer explained it in great detail at the closing, placing documents one at a time before Jimmy, papers that told the tale of the government's lien and the bank's purchase of the lien and the lawyer's title search that cost Jimmy two hundred and fifty dollars. But he had never heard the name Orene Connell before today.

"Had Mrs. Connell lived there a long time?"

"Before my time. She was one of the old mill people. Now, the only real mill people here would be Fairy Etta and Cone, across the street there."

Applause erupts from the TV; Jimmy can picture Vanna White clapping. "Well, I don't want to keep you from your show, so I'll just get going." Hoping to make a quick yet polite exit, he stands. "Just wanted to say thanks and to get to meet you."

She nods. "Yeah, I know you get going early in the morning. I see when your lights come on. Come on in the kitchen before you get gone."

Jimmy follows her into what she calls the kitchen. He wouldn't have called it that, could not have produced a noun that fit the large space that is half of Miz Mayme's house. White spackling scars the ceiling, tracing the line of the bedroom wall that had been knocked out to make the original kitchen wider. The sleeping porch wall had been removed, too, making the room deeper. Lined along one wall are the remnants of a standard everyday kitchen—the original sink with its exposed pipes, a stove, a refrigerator. To his right, in front of the window, stands an array of cooling shelves, crudely constructed. Unpainted one-by-ones climb each wall ladderlike, supporting bridges of pipe. Four layers of grills, an assortment rescued from abandoned appliances, sit precariously atop the pipe. They display just-baked loaves and rolls. A box fan sits on a chair, humming and blowing warmth out the window. Three more stoves stand across the room side by side, one an ancient white porcelain model, one a chipped avocado green, and one brown. They are needed only for their ovens, so across their unused tops rests an old door. And on that door is an amazing collection of jars.

"Here," Miz Mayme says, handing him a shoebox.

"Thank you," he answers automatically. Though he holds a warm shoebox in his hand, he remains fascinated by the jars, whose contents are in motion. "Is that your yeast?" he asks.

"Sourdough starter," she nods. "It's like yeast, sort of. Get it started with yeast, then all you gotta do is feed it ever' so often."

Jimmy counts. She has twenty-four jars—mostly old coffee and mayonnaise jars. Behind the rows of jars stand two lamps, one a gooseneck desk lamp, one a ginger-jar lamp with the shade askew, both set to send light and warmth to the grateful and busy creatures in the jars. Jimmy thinks of an array of aquariums in a pet store. "What do you feed it? Sugar?" he guesses.

She nods. "Sugar and potato flakes. Once a week, at least. What I ain't using stays in the refrigerator, kind of resting up, in a couple of big old pickle jars. I got a extra refrigerator out on the sleeping porch, just for the jars. Then I take it out and pour a little bit into all these here jars, and I feed 'em. These here I just fed this afternoon, so I can use 'em in the morning."

Jimmy knows exactly what he is looking at, knows he is watching a simple biological process, knows that the stirring within the jars is gas bubbling up as *Sacchromyces cerevisiae* multiply and secrete enzymes that turn sugar into carbon dioxide. Still, the contents seem magically motile. Illuminated as they are, they look like lava lamps without the color, with only the color of bread.

Atop each jar lies a scrap of cloth, pinked squares ready for a quilt. Jimmy lifts the red plaid covering one jar and sniffs. "Smells just like beer," he says. "Even looks a little like beer, with all this foam on top." And he can hear it, a popping Rice Krispies sound.

"You come by anytime," Miz Mayme offers. "I always got bread. I usually give away the loaves and rolls that don't come out so pretty. They still taste just as good. Shoot, that's how the bolenos got started."

"Bolenos?" He remembers the shoebox and opens it. Resting on waxed paper are half a dozen sweet, crusty bolenos. "You make bolenos?"

"Well, yeah, hon. That's what I make mostly now. Used to make 'em just to use up the dough scraps after I made the cloverleaf rolls. Made those little lumps, rolled 'em in sugar and cinnamon for the kids. Shoot, ever'body started wanting 'em, so that's mostly what I do now."

To Jimmy, there in the warm kitchen with its bubbling jars and cinnamon scent, Mayme's bread baking seems like a wholesome hobby that brings in pocket money. In fact, baking is how Mayme survives, how she has survived for the three decades that Royce Boulineaux has been missing.

Mayme told their daughter that her daddy was dead. Everyone else said he had run off. Everyone else was right. Seven months after Royce disappeared, an envelope appeared in the mailbox. Inside was a fifty-dollar bill. In December, a package came. Inside was a doll. Mayme put it under the tree for seven-year-old Sandra. Days or weeks or months would pass, and another envelope would arrive. There was never another package. Most of the envelopes contained a twenty; once it was a hundred-dollar bill; once it was a ten and eleven ones. Mayme kept all the envelopes, her only connection to the blue-eyed man she had met at a VFW dance when she was seventeen. On an area-code map torn from the phone book, she kept track of the postmarks, kept track of her Royce. She told no one about the envelopes from a ghost. Mayme expects one every day, though the last one came three years ago.

Every day, Mayme stands at the mailbox, her left hand curled around the top, her right holding the latch, and she talks to Royce. She opens the box and leans over to peer into the metal tunnel, her pipeline to Royce. Every Sunday, she cleans her mailbox. Every spring, she paints it.

"You didn't know I make the bolenos?" she asks Jimmy.

He looks into the box again, inhales the cinnamon scent. Bolenos sell in shoeboxes, three dollars a box. Jimmy worries that he should offer to pay her, but that seems inappropriate. "God, I love these things. I buy these and take them back to the office in Columbia. Everybody up there loves them. Anytime anybody's going through Osilo County, going to Hilton Head or wherever, they bring back bolenos. Last time I went into the office, I took six boxes of these things up there."

She nods.

"Well, thanks."

She nods.

He is back on his own front porch before he wonders about the name. When he first heard of bolenos, he was on the north side of Osilo County doing some Vibracoring. He needed a strip of tubing for the little Briggs & Stratton that produced the vibration that let him ease PVC pipe down into muck and draw it back up filled with core. He pulled into a garage and presented the cracked length of black rubber to the mechanic. The young man sighed. "Well, the computer ain't gonna help me find this in stock. But lemme root around a little bit. I know we got something that'll do. Listen, you go on and sit up front. There's coffee up there, and bolenos. I'll holler when I find it."

The mechanic had drawled the word as *bowl-ee-nose*. Until today, Jimmy had assumed it was a Spanish word, like *burritos*, some local culinary phenomenon like Charleston's benne wafers or New Orleans' beignets. He learned you could buy bolenos all over Osilo County, at the Kountry Kookin restaurant, at the Chicken Strut, at the BP station, at the volunteer fire department, always in waxed-paper-lined shoeboxes with "$3" crayoned on each end.

But tonight, from his front porch, he squints at Miz Mayme's mailbox, painted a bright blue enamel. Carefully stenciled in red is the number 604 and below that the name Boulineaux. Jimmy pretends he is back in his French 201 audio lab and reads the name aloud, his lips a kiss and his tongue a curl. Then he says it Osilo County-style, lips barely open, vowels all long, picturing nuggets of bread in shoeboxes. The syllables roll slowly out of his mouth like bowling balls: "Boleno."

# Chapter 4

## *Bonus*

BONUS WOOTEN IS COMMANDER of the Osilo County VFW post.

Jimmy meets Bonus the day the funeral procession drives through Bonus's yard. Bonus is notified by phone, as always, by the Reverend Young Botham.

"Morning, Mr. Wooten. This is Reverend Botham. How you and Pontoo doing?"

"We're doing fine, Young. You-all okay?"

"We are blessed with health and thankful. Mr. Wooten, I will need you to open your gate tomorrow afternoon. About three o'clock."

"The gate will be open, Young."

"The congregation thanks you, Mr. Wooten."

"No problem, Young."

Only Bonus uses the reverend's first name. Because it sounds odd when spoken aloud, like a foreign name, most people avoid it. Bonus likes the name, likes having an opportunity to speak it, because it has an Asian ring to it, like the names of his faraway in-laws. Bonus brought home two wives, one from Korea, one from Vietnam. Kwan-Sook died of tuberculosis. Nguyet was riding her bicycle to the SaveMore when she was hit by an eighteen-wheeler. Twice a year, Bonus sits at his kitchen table and writes letters to his Korean in-laws and his Vietnamese sister-in-law. He does this on Christmas, to fill the day, and on the birthdays of his wives, to mark the day. He hopes they can read what he writes. He always encloses a money order.

Bonus hooks the red leash to the red collar around Pontoo's neck, and the two head out. Pontoo would be safe running free on the dead end that is Randleman Road, or in the adjacent lot Bonus bought and fenced in, but Bonus enjoys the ritual. When Pontoo lifts his back leg against a tire and squirts a stream, Bonus feels his own leg wanting to lift, too, wanting the long-gone days of feeling a warm, strong spurt instead of a dribble. Lately, it takes him so long to empty his bladder that he sits on the toilet to get it done. He thinks of Korea, squatting to pee because he was scared to stand up, holding it until dark, he and the other boys joking about wet boots.

Pontoo stops at the empty house at 603 to sniff the rotting steps. Bonus figures a possum must be living under there, because Pontoo is fascinated. At 601, Pontoo pauses in the driveway to lift a leg and water a back tire on Fairy Etta's '79 Oldsmobile. Bonus leans on his hand-carved cane and watches, nodding in admiration at the sound of urine hitting rubber, then climbs the three steps to Fairy Etta's porch.

"Fairy Etta, it's Bonus out here." He talks softly through the screen, not wanting to wake Cone if Fairy Etta has managed to get him to sleep. He hears an answer from the kitchen.

"Step on inside, Bonus. I'm feeding Cone."

Bonus knows there is no place for him to sit in Fairy Etta's kitchen, arranged to accommodate Cone's wheelchair. Bonus moved their refrigerator out to the sleeping porch and ran a copper tube up through the floor for the icemaker. Fairy Etta has pushed the rock maple table against the wall. Covered with a hemstitched white cloth, it holds a row of plastic jugs with prescription labels. Bonus maneuvers around the wheelchair so Cone can see him.

"How you doing, Cone? I tell you what, you got a pretty lady here feeding you lunch. I think you got it made." He lays a hand on Cone's shoulder. "Fairy Etta, Young Botham called me just now."

"When is it?"

"Tomorrow, three o'clock."

"You gonna let everybody know?"

"I'm gonna walk the other side of the street, but you'll have to let Vivia know."

Fairy Etta pushes a spoon into Cone's mouth. "I'll step over there once I'm done here."

Bonus finds Pontoo waiting on the porch. The two set off to let the other side of the street know about the reverend's phone call. The boy in Orene's house isn't home; Bonus can tell because his pickup isn't in the driveway. He finds Miz Mayme out back hanging sheets on the clothesline. Bonus lets Pontoo off his leash, and the dog heads to the pond.

"You're gonna have a wet dog, Bonus," Mayme warns.

Pontoo noses through the tall grass at the edge of the pond, laps the water to get the feel of it, then walks cautiously in. He swims out a few yards, returns, runs out barking, runs back in.

"How you doing, Mayme?" Bonus asks just to be polite. He is watching a great blue heron sail up the pond as though following its own reflection.

Mayme nods.

"Come by to tell you Young Botham called."

Mayme nods. "When is it?"

"Tomorrow, three in the afternoon."

Mayme nods.

"Can you tell that boy lives in Orene's house?"

"I'll try. That boy works some long hours. You gonna get to the rest of the street?"

"Well, I'll go over to see Miz Charlie Mae. But I kind of try to stay away from MaryBeth."

Mayme nods. "I'll talk to her."

"Watch Pontoo?"

Mayme nods.

Mayme's backyard is a mix of fescue, rabbit tobacco, and sand-spurs. Miz Charlie Mae's backyard is a garden. Azaleas nest under arching dogwoods, little islands floating in emerald green centipede. An ancient camellia obscures most of the back wall of the house. The stair railing is being displaced by a wisteria thicker than the posts it is strangling. Knocking loudly at the back door, Bonus yells, "It's Bonus, Miz Charlie Mae." He hears footsteps. "I'm at the back! Back door, Miz Charlie Mae!"

On Miz Charlie Mae's TV, rabbit ears spread to pick up SCETV, on which a nature show is displaying a polyphemus moth. On the kitchen table, a clock radio whispers poetry, Garrison Keillor reading a selection for *The Writer's Almanac*. When she finally hears Bonus, she goes first to the front door, then to the back door, where she spends a minute looking for the deadbolt key.

"Did I call you, Bonus?"

"No, ma'am, Miz Charlie Mae, you didn't. How you doing?"

Her eyes have the confused look of someone just waking up, the lost look of a scared child, the same innocence Bonus sees in Pontoo's eyes, all there in one pair of brown eyes that have watched eighty-seven years pass. "You know, I usually wait 'til I need you to come over, and I didn't think I called."

"No, ma'am, you didn't call. I need to tell you that Young Botham called me."

"Oh, lordy, Bonus. Who passed?"

"I didn't think to ask, Miz Charlie Mae, 'cause I don't really know anybody in that church."

"Last time, it was Murdis Grandberry. She used to take in ironing. Her two little girls would swim with us in the pond. You know, the coloreds weren't supposed to swim in the pond, but it was all right if they were swimming with white children. Nobody said anything, you know, if they were with white children."

"I'll find out who it was, Miz Charlie Mae. It'll be about three o'clock Friday. That's tomorrow. Long as I'm here, what you got that needs opening?"

"I got a few things."

Bonus steps into the kitchen and goes right to the china hutch. Beneath the shelves of pink-flowered plates and cups and saucers, Miz Charlie Mae has arrayed the things her stiffened fingers cannot open. Bonus opens the ketchup bottle and peels away the foil seal. He opens a Tylenol bottle and pours the capsules into a waiting Ziploc sandwich bag. He does the same with containers of Centrum Silver vitamins, calcium supplements, dry-roasted peanuts. "How 'bout in the fridge, Miz Charlie Mae?"

"I'm not sure, Bonus. Let's look." She opens her refrigerator to learn what is inside.

Bonus pulls the plastic rings that prevent Charlie Mae from opening her half-gallon jug of milk and quart of orange juice. He tests the tops on jars of mayonnaise and mustard and pickles. He points to her two six-packs of Budweiser. "You still doing okay with cans?"

"I can open the cans with this little thing, looks like a toy. Looks like the toy shovels you buy children at the beach." She shows him the red plastic utensil that helps her pull the ring tops on cans.

"Well, that looks handy," Bonus says, admiring the gadget he gave her.

"I do miss my beer bottles, though. I like beer in a brown bottle."

"I know you do, Miz Charlie Mae." Bonus knows it well. She has told him dozens of times. "Now, what else you need?"

"Bonus, I don't need a thing. I got what I need in this world."

"Your yard's looking good. Everything okay there?"

Miz Charlie Mae smiles. "My yard's my pride, Bonus. You know that. I can't do much out there myself anymore, but I have this man that comes."

Bonus knows about the yardman. He hired him. "You made a chess pie lately?"

"Well, Bonus, let's look in the icebox and see."

Jimmy and Carl huddle in front of a computer screen all day, watching Jimmy's well data map the plume of contaminated groundwater. They quit at seven and head out for steaks and beer. Jimmy gets back to Randleman Road at midnight, pulls off his jeans, and sleeps in T-shirt and boxers. Too tired to be awakened by Mayme's bread-baking scents at four, he is startled by his alarm at five. He heads back to Columbia for a meeting with the DEHP geologists, who will study his maps and tell him where they want more wells. Jimmy has ninety minutes in his pickup to wonder why he hadn't spent the night in Columbia, to worry that he should be living there. The DEHP meeting ends at noon. He has a foot-long slaw dog with Carl and then has another ninety minutes to wonder why he lives so far from KDR's offices, from DEHP headquarters, from Curly's Famous Hot Dog Stand.

Jimmy has learned to anticipate and appreciate his first sight of the pond, right after he bumps over the tracks. On cloudy days, the water pulls down the gray of the sky and looks oddly solid, until a slap of wind leaves a hand print. At night, he expects streaks of light from the barbecue place to lay a phantom bridge across the pond. On this sunny afternoon, the pond should be a shattered mirror. What he sees instead is the broad side of a Winnebago RV parked in front of the Road Ends sign. As Jimmy turns into his driveway, the door to the RV swings open and a man climbs down.

Bonus hollers as soon as Jimmy opens his truck door. "You Jimmy?"

Jimmy steps out of his pickup. "Yeah. I'm Jimmy Steverson." When he turns to reach behind the driver's seat for his briefcase, he sees a long black vehicle that could only be a hearse enter Randleman Road and turn slowly, ceremonially, into the fenced lot between the two houses at the far end. As Jimmy watches, one car after another follows, disappearing between the two houses.

"Jimmy, I'm Bonus Wooten. I live down at the other end of the street. I come by to tell you 'bout the funeral."

Jimmy walks to the sidewalk, carrying his briefcase. "Where in the hell are they going?"

Before Bonus can answer, a door opens. Vivia Wardlaw steps cautiously down her four steps and stands on the sidewalk directly across the street from Bonus and Jimmy. Then she turns her back. Next door to Vivia, Fairy Etta wheels Cone onto their porch and turns his wheelchair to face the door. Then she steps onto the sidewalk, nods at Vivia, and turns her back to the street.

"So what's going on?" Jimmy asks, a question directed more at himself than to Bonus. He is sure he knows the answer. He can see the people in the cars, and they are black. He sees his neighbors, their backs turned, and they are white.

"Hop up here in my Winnebago, Jimmy. Let me tell you what we do about these funerals."

"No thanks." Jimmy turns to go into his house, swallowing disgust. When he gets to his steps, he sees Miz Mayme come out, stand on the sidewalk, and turn her back to the street.

"Jimmy, hon, you got to look the other way," she says quietly.

"I'm trying to tell him, Mayme. He don't know what we're doing."

"I believe I do, and I don't like it." Jimmy has climbed his steps and is opening his door. His peripheral vision catches a white-haired woman and the young woman who keeps kids in the house down the street. They stand on the sidewalk opposite the gate being used by the funeral procession, their backs turned, their hands folded respectfully, heads lowered.

Inside, Jimmy throws his briefcase on the sofa. "What kind of hellhole did I move into?" he asks his living room. He leans over the sofa to see through the window, unable to resist watching. He sees Bonus turn and face his RV, head down, hands folded. The funeral procession continues, car after car.

Seconds of silence tick off before Bonus is sure the last car has turned in. He climbs into his Winnebago, gracefully executes the complicated turn required by the narrow asphalt of Randleman Road, then backs into his yard. He closes the double gate behind him. Still watching, Jimmy sees Vivia and Fairy Etta climb their porch steps and close their front doors. Mayme heads to Jimmy's front door. Jimmy ignores her knock.

He concentrates on installing the new geochemical-data software his boss dropped into his briefcase. Forty-five minutes later, Jimmy feeds it a spreadsheet of data—TDS and pH and hardness—and watches to see how the software handles it. He experiments, turning the same data into different pictures. His focus on his work displaces the images of his bigoted neighbors, but the sight of the Winnebago reappearing at the end of the street reminds him.

He closes the folder he is working in, inserts a CD, calls up the maps it holds. When he has the Walthourville 7.5-minute quad on the screen, he zooms in on Dillehay Pond. He finds what he's looking for, a dot labeled "Cem" just below the dam. Apparently, an old cemetery is trapped within a no man's land bordered by the dam, Stone Bowl Creek, and the New Highway and its access ramp.

Once again, Jimmy leans over the sofa and watches. The shiny black hood of the hearse peeks around the edge of the abandoned house behind which it had disappeared. Slowly, the vehicle turns into Randleman Road. Several seconds later, a car appears, then another. As Jimmy watches, he realizes that Bonus has twice moved his RV, allowing the funeral to enter and exit. In the same way that his software manipulates data, he reconfigures what he has seen, his neighbors with their backs turned to the black mourners on their street. They were all dressed for a funeral. Even Cone in his wheelchair wore a tie.

Jimmy leaves his house and knocks on the Winnebago's door.

"Glad you came on out, Jimmy," Bonus greets him. "Climb on up here." Bonus looks comfortable in the swivel chair that is the driver's seat.

"Your name's Bonus?"

"Bonus Wooten. I'm at the other end of the street, number 607. I was hoping to tell you 'bout this funeral so you'd know how we do things here."

Jimmy has to work to put his answer together. "You can tell me how you do things, but I may do things differently, Mr. Wooten."

Bonus was a drill instructor back when heatstroke was an acceptable part of the weeding-out process and can size up a young man in seconds. He surprises Jimmy by laughing. "It's like that old saying about the right way, the wrong way, and the army way. This here's the pond way. Get on in here so we can keep the AC inside, where it belongs."

Jimmy climbs the three steps, closes the door, and sits in the passenger seat, a captain's chair identical to the driver's seat, as comfortable as a La-Z-Boy.

"Over yonder behind us is an old cemetery, the Lamplight Cemetery. Vodelia Kaye—you met her yet?—she says it might be the oldest black cemetery in the state. Goes back to slave times. Vodelia's big in the historical society, so she knows all that stuff. Anyhow, the highway kind of wrapped around it. Like the dam, sort of. Vodelia says old man Hammond Hutto—guy who built the pond and the first mill back in the 1800s—he put the dam where it is because he wouldn't mess with the cemetery. Now, when the New Highway went in, the highway department set up a trust fund to maintain the cemetery, and they said they'd come escort people in to visit the graves, but they said no more funerals. Declared it officially inaccessible."

"No more funerals? So this funeral is illegal?"

"Yeah. Now, Osmond—Osmond Vause, he's the sheriff, you met Osmond?—he says if we don't see it, that's fine with him. So we just turn around so we can say we were looking the other way. Which is true."

"How come you come outside on the sidewalk, then? Why not just stay inside and really not see it?"

Bonus laughs again. "Now, we're getting to the pond way. Well, see, for the funerals to get to the cemetery, back long time ago, they had to go right through the mill town, right down Cemetery Road. And people didn't ignore funerals back then. They'd take their hats off, bow their heads, you know. Anytime a funeral was coming through, people would come out on the sidewalk and stand. So that's what we do. We come out on the sidewalk and we stand. We just have to look in the other direction."

On Tuesday, the KDR staff spontaneously moves from office to bar in jubilation at wrapping up an environmental impact statement. On Wednesday, they convene at the Pig's Rib to celebrate the survival of Hump Day. On Thursday, they show up at Louis's apartment to celebrate Will's Ph.D. Jimmy is a long stretch of asphalt away, learning to cope with the new phenomenon of empty evenings.

On this Friday night, he is glad to let the road take him away from the well site, is looking forward to a shower and his bass boat. He goes in his front door and is out the back door in only minutes. When the summer darkness finally falls, he is up where the pond begins to narrow into the stream that feeds it, too far away to see even the lights at the barbecue pit. He is on his back, down in the bottom of the boat, his feet propped on the bench, looking up.

Buzzing on beer and weed, Jimmy floats on one dark surface and squints up at another. How did they do it? he wonders. He is looking at the same clues Galileo had, the same things Copernicus saw, but even with downloaded photos from the Hubble, it makes no sense to him. Jimmy fumbles for a line from Blake, something read on one of those nights by the fireplace. He paraphrases into the night, "We can only compare what we're capable of perceiving." A green heron squawks, a faraway dog barks, and Jimmy tells the darkness more of what Blake knew about a scientist's limitations. "If we had only three senses, we could not invent a fourth or a fifth." He knows he does not have the lines right, closes his eyes tight, trying to squeeze the verses out, reluctant to lose these relics of his marriage. He can feel the brick hearth hard on his shoulder, remembers the ragged sleeping bag they shared, wants the words back, too, to speak aloud into the dark present.

Jimmy wakes, swats a mosquito off his face, grabs the gunwales in surprise when the boat rocks, surprised to find himself afloat. His boat is snagged in an overhanging sycamore. The trolling motor pulls him silently away from shore, where he can see the lights from the New Highway, orienting him.

At home, he turns off the AC and opens the windows, listening for the whippoorwill, for the barred owl, wondering if Gwen remembers the Blake nights, if she can still recite the lines. He eats breakfast on the deck, spots a hawk perched in his water oak, scans the pond until he finds what the hawk is watching, a family of wood ducks sheltering under his dock.

The weekend looms long. Twice, he has convened a crowd for fishing and grilling and drinking Saturday into Sunday, but this week his e-mail invitations were declined. He learned that Carl and his wife have bought horses and a trailer and will spend their Saturday in a barn, that Louis is engaged, that Jamil is studying for his certification test, that the highway between Dillehay Pond and Columbia is not a road but a barrier.

His work caught up, Jimmy is restless. He starts three books—an old T. C. Boyle, a new Jonathan Kellerman, a biography of Newton. He washes his truck, listens to *Car Talk*. He makes his weekly phone call to his parents. After lunch, he tries television, but he hasn't had time to order a satellite dish, so he has little to choose from.

He clicks the remote, and the room is silent. The house he shared with his wife was never silent. They sawed and hammered. They argued about what CDs to play, laughed at SNL. Gwen required background noise—a drill, the Cuisinart, *Headline News*, NPR.

Jimmy throws the remote, is disappointed when it settles silently into the carpet. He stares at it for a few seconds, thinks about driving into town to rent a video, and is startled by the sharp, quick raps at his door. Bonus Wooten stands on the other side of the screen, using his cane to tap on the doorframe.

"Wonder if you'd help me haul the tombstone."

Jimmy squints as though his eyes will help him understand what his ears have not. "What?" he asks Bonus.

"Man that makes the tombstones won't deliver them down to the cemetery. So Young called and asked if I'd let 'em leave it at my house. I got it in the bed of the pickup. It's a little old flat piece of marble. I just need another hand at lifting it."

Jimmy tries to make sense of a request involving tombstones and pickup trucks. "You mean down at the old black cemetery? That place where the funeral went?"

"Yeah. Now, Young could get some of the men of the church to do it, but you know, I don't think they oughta risk it." After several seconds, Bonus assumes that Jimmy hasn't understood. "You know what I mean? I mean, if a state trooper glances down off the New Highway and sees a couple black guys fooling around down there under the highway, he'll radio it in, figuring they're up to something. But if he sees two white guys down there, he'll go right on drinking his coffee, figuring we're going fishing."

Bonus's Dodge Dakota pickup sits ready in his driveway. Jimmy rides shotgun, glancing back just once at the rectangle of marble carved with a stranger's name. Bonus drives the pickup through his side yard, past his Winnebago, to another gate at the rear of the yard. Jimmy can see that Bonus has already removed the padlock, so he jumps out to open the gate. He has to open it inward. Beyond the chain link is a tangle of green. Stubby hawthorn and crab apple and plum trees, none tall enough to offer shade, poke out above sumac and beautyberry, all woven into an effective fence by cross-vine and scuppernong and Virginia creeper.

Bonus pushes the truck into a part in the greenery, a two-track carved by illegal funeral processions to an off-limits cemetery. "This used to be Butterfly Road," he offers. "Runs along the railroad bed." Bonus extends his right arm in front of Jimmy's face and points toward the pond. "That was Hamilton Street." Jimmy sees an arc of cracked gray curbing, what was once a street corner. Under the elevated ramp that leads to the New Highway, they drive on bare sand where sunlight cannot reach. Here, the two-track turns toward the pond. "Now, we're on St. Luke Street."

"We're on pavement," Jimmy says, surprised to find himself in a ghost town.

At the end of St. Luke Street, eight brick pillars that once supported a house stand in useless rows. A forlorn rose crawls across what had been a yard, throwing red at them unexpectedly.

"Not for long. We gotta turn here and try to get through all this stuff." Bonus stretches to look over the hood of the pickup, watching as the two-track twists around piles of brick and chunks of curbing.

"This was Kimbrough Street. See those cedar posts there? I helped old man Tuffing, Chappy Tuffing, put those in back when I was an E-1, back in the fifties. You can't beat a cedar post. Old Mr. Chappy grew some fine watermelons, and he gave 'em away."

Jimmy sees four cedar posts strung with rusted wire and honeysuckle. The pickup bumps over a curb, onto a few feet of pavement, over another curb. Once again, Bonus's hand floats in front of Jimmy's face, pointing. "That was Tuttle Street. Look down there and you'll see the old road over the dam. Used to have to come down Tuttle to get over the pond."

Past the remnants of Tuttle Street's houses, the ground has been bulldozed smooth. Ahead of them, the New Highway imposes its figure against the sky like a reconstructed *T. rex* in a Smithsonian rotunda. Bonus drives into the shade offered by the four-lane roof and makes a right turn into its dark path. "Now, this woulda been Cemetery Road, or what everybody called Cemetery Road. It really had some other name, something like Jefferson Street, or maybe it was Jackson Street, something like that. But long before that, it was how the black folks got down to the Lamplight Cemetery."

Jimmy had stopped listening to the recitation of dead street names, but the cemetery regains his full attention. From their shaded vantage point, the fenced rectangle is desert-bright, its arches of granite and cement and marble bouncing the sun's light at them. Cedars stand in neat rows marking the lanes among the graves.

Bonus backs the truck to the gate. "Here," he says, handing a tiny key to Jimmy, "you hop out and open the gate, and I'll back on in."

"You've got a key?"

"Yeah, well, the highway department put a padlock on it, expected folks to call them up anytime they wanted to get inside. Me and Osmond—you know Osmond Vause, the county sheriff?—we came down here early one morning and sawed theirs off and put ours on."

"So you let people in?"

"Naw, Osmond keeps the key. I think he was pissed off the troopers didn't give him one to begin with. Anyway, he drops the key off whenever he hears we need it."

It still makes no sense to Jimmy, but he gives up and gets out of the truck to unlock the gate. Bonus backs carefully down the narrow road, brushing cedars. Jimmy follows slowly, looking at the bricks lining the family plots, odd sized and old. When Bonus climbs out of the pickup and puts his cane on the ground before letting his feet support him, Jimmy wonders how they are going to lift a marble marker.

"Don't let this cane worry you none." Bonus answers the unspoken question. He walks to the back of the truck, lowers the tailgate. "I need it to steady myself sometimes. But if I'm holding one-half of this slab of marble, that'll steady me just fine."

Jimmy jumps into the truck bed and slides the slab toward Bonus. Back on the ground, he lifts one end and Bonus, having propped his cane against the side of the truck, has no trouble lifting his portion. They walk the marker toward the array of floral offerings covering the fresh grave, stepping over two older graves to get to it. Someone has cleared and leveled a rectangle, and Bonus and Jimmy drop the marble into the prepared site. Both men realize the moment needs to be marked, and Jimmy is grateful when Bonus speaks. "The stone says this man was in World War II. I like to picture General Eisenhower standing next to St. Peter, shaking hands with the GIs as they come home."

Jimmy goes back to the pickup for Bonus's cane, stepping again over the two old graves, which are littered with broken crockery. Jimmy sees a broken coffee cup, a piece of a plate, the chipped milk-glass base of an oil lamp that still holds a wick, all carefully laid at the headstones, too organized to be vandalism. "What's all this stuff on the graves?"

Bonus puts the cane squarely in front of him and leans on it with both hands. "Thanks. Well, Vodelia says it's what the old blacks do, something they did back in Africa. Put broken dishes and stuff on the graves." Bonus points to the new grave. Scattered among the pots of azaleas and chrysanthemums and wreaths are similar offerings. "Lamps, too, for some reason. Always got to have a lamp, and it's got to be broken." Using his cane, he points to the foot of the new grave, where

Jimmy sees yellow fragments that had been a ginger-jar lamp, neatly broken, neatly placed between a peace lily and a spray of irises.

"That's why it's called the Lamplight Cemetery?"

Bonus grins. "Yeah. Folks used to say you could look down here at night and see the lamps lit up."

# Chapter 5

## *Joelle*

JOELLE IS THE QUESTION GIRL.

"Do you know there are rocks that float?"

The question buzzes mosquitolike from the back deck, through the screen door, into the dark room where Jimmy sits imprisoned within the cone of light that conjoins him to the computer screen. Leaning on the keyboard in surprise, he enters *dfsj* on his spreadsheet and will later find it overprinted on a drawdown diagram.

"Hello?" he asks the night.

"Hello?" echoes Joelle. "I'm Joelle? Me and my grandma live across the street from you?"

Jimmy slides backward in his wheeled chair and hits a light switch. He sees long hair, long legs, blinking eyes set in the round face of a child.

"Are you really a geologist?"

Jimmy doesn't think he should invite a pubescent into his house, so he goes outdoors to meet her. "Yeah, I'm a geologist. My name's Jimmy Steverson." He extends his hand, a gesture new to Joelle, who puzzles it out just in time to put her hand into his and participate in her first handshake. "And how did you know I'm a geologist?"

"One of the ladies Meema, my grandma, sews for, well, she goes to the same beauty shop as that real-estate lady you bought the house from."

The complicated yet simple answer makes Jimmy think of his mother, at the beauty shop every Thursday morning, reporting on beauty-shop news every Thursday night at dinner. "So you live across the street."

"Uh-huh. My grandma's Vivia Wardlaw. I call her Meema. She keeps wanting to come over and say hello, says you're gonna think we're not friendly, but she's really busy right now. She makes pageant dresses? And there's some kind of big pageant deal happening in Florida in two weeks, and she's making seven dresses just for that."

"Well, when she's not busy, I'd like to meet your grandmother."

Joelle has no way to know that Jimmy has just concluded the conversation, so she slides her hands into her jeans pockets and leans against the doorframe. "How come there's a geologist around here? I thought geologists stayed in places like Hawaii, doing stuff around volcanoes and earthquakes."

Jimmy flips on the floodlights, which send a spray of light over the deck and well out onto the pond. "Let's sit down out here," he suggests. "I just got this new furniture for my deck, and we'll inaugurate it." Jimmy sinks into the redwood rocker Sears delivered that afternoon. Joelle perches in one of the two Adirondack chairs that complete the set.

"Cool."

"Well, I'm a groundwater geologist, mostly," Jimmy explains. "Right now, I'm putting in some wells out at the Muldoy Chemicals site. We're pulling out some polluted groundwater. But there are lots of geologists who do what you're talking about, study volcanoes and earthquakes."

"You ever seen any of those rocks that float?"

"Hold on." Jimmy is reluctant to go inside, afraid she'll follow, but he is even more afraid she'll never leave if he doesn't present his credentials, those rocks that float. To discourage her from coming in, he yells from indoors, "It'll take me a minute to find 'em!"

She waits patiently. Jimmy returns with a white cloth bag.

"Let's dump this on the picnic table. I'm pretty sure there's some pumice in here."

Joelle stands at Jimmy's side, silently watching the rocks thump out of the dirty bag onto the table. "All of these are igneous rocks," Jimmy tells her. "I used this when I was teaching. My first year out of college, I taught earth science in middle school. Obsidian," he points out. "Rhyolite. Diorite. Granodiorite." Joelle picks up each rock, runs a finger over it, sniffs it. "And here's what you're looking for." He hands her a gray lump.

Joelle arranges the rocks in a neat row and recites the words he taught her. "Obsidian," she tells the black glass. "Rhyolite," she tells the pink one. "What did he call you?" she asks the black-and-white one.

Jimmy finds the bucket he uses to wash his truck and fills it with water at the hose. He puts the bucket down on the deck. "Here," he says. "See if it floats."

Carefully, she places the pumice in the bucket, and they both watch it float.

"Where did you find all these?"

Jimmy sighs. "Mostly New Mexico and Colorado, I think."

Joelle squats next to the bucket and pokes at the pumice. "Did you go out there just to pick up rocks? I mean, did somebody pay you just to go out there and find rocks and give them names?" She removes the pumice, hefts it, returns it gently to its unlikely flotation.

"No. I picked some of these up while I was at field camp out there. That's like a college course you have to take to learn to be a geologist. And some I just picked up while I was hiking. I don't really collect rocks. Most of the geologists I know do, though. They collect minerals, usually."

"Tell me all the names again?"

"Hold on." Jimmy goes back inside, reappears with one of his rock-

and-mineral guides. "Why don't you borrow this? You can take all these to school, maybe, and show them to your class."

Jimmy holds the drawstring bag open, and Joelle drops the rocks into it. She balances the bag on top of the book in her left hand, gripping the wet pumice in her right. She leaves without saying another word.

Jimmy returns to the humming monitor, now colorful with swimming fish. He clicks *Save* while he scans his open notebook, trying to recall where he left off. The phone rings.

"Hello? Mr. Jimmy? This is Joelle? Meema said to call and say thank you and tell you that I'll bring all your stuff back tomorrow."

☙

One week later, Jimmy has learned to expect the voice from the porch.

"Mr. Jimmy? Did you know that possums are marsupials? Like kangaroos?"

Tonight, he has both computers on, his old Mac and his new Gateway, translating from one to the other. "Gimme a minute, Joelle," he yells. He feeds each machine a disk and uses the minute to reorient himself from spreadsheet to mammals.

"Yeah," he says, opening the screen door. "Yeah, I guess I knew that. Possums have those little sacks on them for the babies." He pulls a cushion from its protected spot under the eaves and throws it into one of the Adirondack chairs. He settles in, listening.

"Well, they're the only ones up here. The only marsupials in North America. Isn't that wild? But I wonder why we couldn't have gotten the kangaroos instead. Possums are ugly."

"And mean."

"Yeah, they snarl."

"Did you take biology last year?"

"General science."

"You interested in science?"

"I guess. I mean, it's all around us, so how can you not be interested in it?" She laughs. "It'd be like being in the Krispy Kreme and not wanting a doughnut."

"How about math? You good at math?"

"Yeah, I guess. I'll be in the advanced class when school starts. Precalculus."

"Hold on. I've got a book you'll like."

Jimmy goes back inside. In the several visits over the week they've known each other, a ritual has been established. Joelle knows, somehow, not to go inside, just as Jimmy knows not to invite her in. She visits on the back deck, and he sends her off with a book or gadget. Tonight, he returns to the porch with *Math Magic*.

"Now, some of this is simple. You know, stuff you're too smart for. But he teaches you some tricks, too, some shortcuts."

She takes the book between her hands, sandwiched, then slides her left hand under the spine as though it's a baby's head. She opens the book like someone about to sing from a hymnal.

"You can't keep giving me books, Mr. Jimmy. This is the third one."

"I think it's 'cause I like watching how you handle books. You hold books like you like 'em."

She looks puzzled again. "How can you not like books?"

"I think you like everything, Joelle. Anyway, I've got tons of books. You will, too, eventually. Go to college and you'll have boxes and boxes of textbooks when you're done. And then I ended up with all the books, somehow, when me and my wife split up. To tell you the truth, I think I gave that book to her, and now it's sitting on my shelf."

"Well, thank you." She closes the book, sandwiched again between her palms. "I better go. Meema will be yelling that I'm bugging you."

"Sorry it's not about possums. I am fresh out of possum books."

Chapter 6

# MaryBeth

MARYBETH IS IN HANDCUFFS when Jimmy learns her name.

Joelle calls his attention to the event. He hears her yell from his front porch. "Mr. Jimmy! You oughta come out here and see this!"

Jimmy has scrambled some of the fresh eggs Fairy Etta sent over, has toasted some of Miz Mayme's bread, and is lingering over his Saturday-morning breakfast. He jumps up to see what calamity has brought Joelle from his back deck to his front porch and has her speaking in exclamatory sentences. By the time he reaches the porch, she has abandoned it for the better view from the street. Miz Mayme stands on her front porch and Fairy Etta on her sidewalk. Everyone stares down the street, at the last house on Jimmy's side of Randleman, where two sheriff's cars are parked, blue lights twinkling.

Jimmy joins Joelle on the sidewalk. "Somebody hurt?" he wonders.

"Do they send police cars when somebody's hurt?" asks Joelle.

Miz Mayme answers before Jimmy can try to explain police procedure. "I don't think nobody's hurt. I think it's just MaryBeth in some kind of trouble again."

A third car pulls up, a Volvo wagon. Its driver neatly parallel parks between the two sheriff's cars. "Damn, that took balls," says Jimmy before he remembers Joelle.

Mayme laughs. "That's that professor lady, leaves her kids there for MaryBeth to mind."

The professor lady, unfazed by the radio cackle and the blue strobe, strides to the door and knocks. Two sheriff's deputies appear on the porch. The three stand and talk until a third deputy emerges, holding the screen door open so that a fourth deputy can escort a young woman. They all stop and let the professor lady talk to the younger woman.

"God, they got handcuffs on her." Mayme speaks softly. "Like that little girl could get away from them big fellas."

The handcuffed girl walks carefully down the stairs, an officer holding each elbow. She looks as though she dressed for jail—loose jeans and a faded blue T-shirt, hair in a ponytail.

"Is it hard to walk with handcuffs on?" asks Joelle. "Does it make you unbalanced or something?" She runs up Jimmy's stairs, places her hands as though handcuffed, and walks back down, answering her own questions empirically.

The deputies insert the girl into one of the cars, then stand talking for several minutes. The professor lady asks questions, nods at the answers, writes notes on a pad. Jimmy stands with his hands in his pockets and realizes that he isn't really interested in this arrest, that it is saddening to see in person, not exciting like a TV arrest. Mayme and Joelle are enthralled, however, so Jimmy works to invent a polite excuse to leave them and return to his toast and eggs. When a third cruiser pulls into Randleman Road, Mayme heads down the block. Jimmy steps onto his porch, grateful for the opportunity to retreat, hoping he can microwave his breakfast back to life.

But Mayme pauses two doors down, at the empty house with the forlorn For Rent sign. "Jimmy. You come walk down there with me. Joelle, honey, go listen for my timer. Take the bread out of the green oven if it goes off." She is already moving again, and Jimmy has to catch up with her. "All three ovens is going," she says to Joelle, "but the green one's done first."

The sheriff leaves his car blocking Randleman Road, sticks his head into a deputy's car, speaks to MaryBeth, pats her shoulder. Watching four deputies and the county sheriff and three Crown Victorias crowd the tiny block, Jimmy wonders if anyone is left to patrol the rest of Osilo County.

The professor wedges herself into the circle of officers. "Why did you send four deputies to arrest one tiny woman?" she demands of the sheriff. "And did they really need handcuffs?"

"No, ma'am, they probably didn't need handcuffs at all," the sheriff answers. "And I sent all four of my deputies because they needed the practice. You ask Miz Mayme here. She'll tell you we don't make a lot of arrests in Osilo County."

When the cars pull out paradelike, the quiet left in their wake is numbing.

Jimmy tries once again to leave, but Mayme stops him. "Let's go see what we can do for Karen."

The professor sees them approaching and politely puts away the cell phone she has just pulled from her shoulder bag. "Morning, Mayme." She shrugs her shoulders. "We warned her."

"Oh, yeah, honey. You couldn't have done no more for her. I was wondering what I could do. This here's Jimmy, Jimmy Steverson. He bought Orene Connell's place, next to me, you know? Jimmy, this is Karen. Well, Karen, I done forgot your last name."

"Karen Knox. Nice to meet you, Jimmy." Jimmy nods, and Karen turns back to Mayme. "I'm about to call her lawyer, but she told MaryBeth last time she'd have to finish her sentence if there was another probation violation. So I'm reasonably sure she'll have to do a little over a year in Columbia. She'll be in county for a while, until the hearing and the transfer. I'm going to pack her some things. They'll let her have them in a couple of days. At least they did last time."

"Oh, yeah, Osmond will let her have stuff in his jail. He'll take care of her."

"What was that about his deputies needing practice?"

"Well, Osmond's an odd bird. He don't like to arrest people. He says he likes to prevent crime, not lock people up. He brags about it

53

whenever the county jail's empty." Mayme crosses her arms over her chest. "What about you? Something I can do for you?"

Mayme's offer takes the focus off MaryBeth and places it on Karen. Karen's efficiency evaporates. Her head drops forward, and she stares downward. Jimmy can see her jaws clenching. He can't tell if she's mad or about to cry. Finally, she looks up.

"Mayme, you're sweet to offer. Can I call you?"

Mayme nods.

Joelle, of course, keeps Jimmy up to date on MaryBeth.

"Did you know," she greets Jimmy from the back deck, "that MaryBeth had her hearing today?" That's her Tuesday question. Wednesday nights, Jimmy doesn't hear from Joelle because she and everyone else on Randleman Road are at prayer meeting. Jimmy has begun to look forward to his Wednesday-night respite from Joelle's questions. On Thursday night, Joelle continues. "Did you know MaryBeth gets transferred on Monday? Up to Columbia?"

Jimmy has no interest in MaryBeth and has lost patience with the neighborhood's fascination. He is at his briefcase, searching through hundreds of loose pages for the one photocopied sheet he needs in order to make a Friday deadline. DEHP expects quarterly reports on the groundwater project he is supervising at Muldoy Chemicals. In those reports, Jimmy has to cite the obscure federal regulations that govern what chemicals may be in groundwater, and in what concentrations. Jimmy can recite the chemicals and even the parts per million, but he can't recall the lawyerly footnotes that the official report requires. He takes the briefcase outside so he can continue his search while Joelle rambles.

"Hey, girl," he offers. He sits at the picnic table with his briefcase before him. "Keep talking. I gotta find something."

Joelle comes to the end of the picnic table and looks into the briefcase. She laughs. "You've got bags of dirt in there."

"Yeah, those are some samples I gotta take up to Columbia, to the lab at my office. But somewhere in here is a list I need."

"If it's a list, don't you have it on one of your computers?"

"You are indeed a child of the information age. Yeah, well, I know for a fact this list is in three places. It's on the hard disk on my new Gateway. That's the one my boss informs me I'm required to use. But Windows seems to have hidden it somewhere in something it calls a folder. And of course, I keep the regs on a floppy, but to use that I'd have to plug the Mac back in, and I just unplugged it yesterday and put it in the closet because I thought that me and the Gateway were getting along. And the third place is somewhere in this briefcase."

He pauses, and Joelle takes the opportunity to return to her topic. "You know MaryBeth will go up there in a bus? Like a school bus? They're painted white, though."

"You know, I like it better when you talk about rocks and possums."

Joelle shrugs. "I better go," she announces.

Jimmy doesn't understand her sudden exit but is grateful. He closes the briefcase, takes it into the living room, and reopens it on the coffee table. Settling on the sofa, he resolves to empty the contents. He stacks papers on one side—papers that might be hiding his list—books and booklets on the other side, sample bags on the floor. Jimmy finds enough trash to justify a trash bag. He is in the kitchen looking for a brown grocery bag when the front screen rattles.

"Jimmy? It's Mayme."

Jimmy freezes and considers not answering. He had not wanted to chat with Joelle, and he doesn't want to chat with Mayme. Jimmy resents the disruption of his work, but he hides his irritation and has a smile on his face by the time he opens the door. "Hey, Miz Mayme. Come on in."

Mayme steps just over the threshold, aware she's intruding. "I heard you and Joelle. I mean, I didn't mean to be listening, but your deck's right out my kitchen window. Anyhow, I had to come tell you. Joelle's mama is in the women's prison up to Columbia. That's why Joelle lives with her grandma. And that's why the little thing's so interested in all this going on with MaryBeth. I know you been letting her talk your ear off, and you been sweet to her, so I thought you'd wanna know."

Jimmy does not want to know. His mind is still within the Windows maze, looking for the file that lists those regs. "Well, I'll keep that in mind when I talk to her. Thanks, Miz Mayme."

"And I'm gonna ask you to help us out this weekend. Down at MaryBeth's house. We're gonna move everything out to the sidewalk and sell it all. Big yard sale."

# Chapter 7

## *Totch*

TOTCH OWNS THE BARBECUE PLACE.

For weeks now, Jimmy has watched the smoke puff and flag, has greedily inhaled the scent of pork when it makes its way across the pond to his deck. Tuesday night, he stops by Mayme's to share a bushel of peaches with her, peaches he picked up at a roadside stand in Trenton, and from that he gets the chance to go to Totch's.

"These is fine peaches. Your mama musta taught you how to pick out good fruit," nods Mayme, meaning thanks.

"The lady at the stand helped me. She said the ones that are too hard should just stand around for a while, and the ones that are too soft could go into a cobbler, and the ones that are just right should go in my mouth."

"And I'll make us a cobbler, too," Mayme promises. "What was you doing up to Trenton? What do you do? You sell?"

"I'm a geologist," he answers. He thinks for a minute, wondering how to explain what he does to someone unfamiliar with terms like *site*

57

*assessment, remediation, well monitoring, pump tests.* "Up at Trenton, there's this recycling plant. They take plastics we throw away and make something else out of them. They have all these wells in the ground to make sure they're not polluting the groundwater with anything they're doing, and my company tests those wells. So I was up there sampling wells. The guy who normally does that is off on his honeymoon, and I filled in for him."

Mayme watches him as he speaks, then nods. "Now I know why I see you muddy. You drill them wells sometimes?"

Jimmy nods.

"My uncle Bud was a well driller, down to Allendale County." Having decided that her new neighbor is a well driller, she goes back to culling, just as the peach-stand owner told Jimmy to do, just as everyone in South Carolina knows to do. "I'll leave 'em out here on the sleeping porch awhile, them hard ones."

A knife of scent slides beneath their noses, cutting powerfully through the sugary fruit smell and even the blanketing bread smell. "Whoa, that barbecue smells good." Jimmy hasn't had supper yet.

"Totch knows how to cook a pig," agrees Mayme, nodding.

"I gotta go over there and try that man's cooking," Jimmy says, looking hungrily at the gray cloud across the pond.

Instantly, Mayme's nodding stops. She looks at Jimmy. He knows he is being sized up, but he doesn't know why. Is she wondering if he can afford to eat out? Is she wondering if he'll fit in with the locals? Does the place have some kind of reputation he doesn't know about?

When Mayme turns her rapid nod back on, Jimmy feels relieved. "I'll get Bonus to take you," she announces. "Totch cooks barbecue on Tuesdays and Thursdays so it's set to serve from Wednesday on. On Saturday nights, sometimes he runs out of barbecue, so he cooks up steaks, and he buys my cloverleaf rolls for Saturdays, them ones I sell to Kountry Kookin. You want barbecue or steak?"

"Barbecue," Jimmy answers. He looks bewildered, trying to figure out how Mayme does so much baking for so many businesses.

Mayme nods. "Bonus comes by almost every day picking up

bolenos, takes 'em down to the Legion post. I'll get him to take you over to Totch."

Jimmy leaves Mayme wondering why he needs an escort.

When he and Bonus make it to Totch's Thursday night, Jimmy learns that he needs both escort and translator, the way his mother required explanation of the Waffle House code. Jimmy has eaten at many a Waffle House at all hours of the day and night and enjoys hearing the waitresses translate his breakfast order and shout it to the cooks: "Order over easy. On two. Scattered and smothered." Totch's is more complicated.

Totch stands behind a counter, one hand resting ready on the cash register.

"Totch, how ya doin'?" says Bonus. "We'll take a coupla teddy bears and a coupla postcards."

Jimmy knows instinctively not to talk. And he does his best not to look confused. He acts just the way he does when he deals with the computer guys back at the office, guys who know what *http* stands for.

Totch punches buttons. "Twenty-two," he says.

Bonus hands the man twenty-two dollars. He then takes two of the small pastel bears from the barrel next to the counter. Next to Totch's register is a rack of postcards, all of them looking like they've retired from careers as bar coasters, all bearing rings that interconnect like the Olympics insignia. Three different scenes are represented—a photo of the old mill, an aerial view of a nearby golf course, and a picture of three fishermen fishing off the bridge that crosses Rosemary Creek, one of the upstream tributaries that helps fill the pond. Bonus studies these choices for a while, glances at Jimmy, then looks back at the postcards. He finally picks up two identical postcards.

"Y'all go on back and say hello to Rhonda," Totch says.

Bonus nods. They push through a screen door and emerge onto a deck sheltered beneath a tentlike roof. Jimmy looks across the pond, wanting to see his property from another angle. His house is easy to spot, the end of the row, the one with the new roof. But it doesn't really stand out from the others, and that disappoints Jimmy. The little mill house on the pond is all his, not bought with the help and advice of his parents like his first condo, not bought as part of a lost dream like the old farmhouse he and his ex-wife had remodeled. The little mill house on the pond was his decision, is his possession, paid in full.

He and Bonus settle opposite each other at one of the picnic tables. Within seconds, a teenage girl places a basket of hush puppies between them, and the fried-corn smell pulls their fingers into the basket.

"How y'all doing?" she asks, leaning over the table, looking at the postcards. She leaves before they can answer and returns in seconds with two Budweisers. Atop each of the postcards, she places a cold, dripping bottle, which explains the circles.

Bonus sips his beer and looks around the deck, nodding at a few people, lifting his Bud as a wave to some. Jimmy drinks his beer and studies his postcard. The inscription on the reverse says, "Dillehay Mill, built 1847, largest textile mill in the South, Osilo County, SC." The old mill stretches across the front of the card, a formidable brick building. Two five-story towers jut outward, each topped with a cupola. Wondering how long the building was, Jimmy counts the windows: thirty-three. An ancient truck is the only evidence of the black-and-white photo's age.

"How old you think this truck is?" he asks Bonus.

Bonus takes the card, holds it at arm's length, squints. "Something from the thirties, probably."

"So what's left on the pond, that's just one of the towers?"

"Oh, yeah. Some of it burned down, some of it got knocked down, people stealing brick."

Jimmy sips his beer, trying to connect the crumbling bricks he can see from his deck—what he knows as the old mill—to this industrial complex. Even more puzzling, he finds no clues on the postcard, no Rosetta stone to decode the Totch's experience. Then Bonus leans forward and taps an index finger on the scratched photo.

"Back in '84, the county-council folks got some kind of grant. Federal money. Supposed to do something to encourage tourism. So they printed up these postcards. Totch has boxes of 'em. Now, what you do when you come to Totch's is, if you want a Bud, you buy a picture of the mill here, and if you buy the picture of the golf course, you get a Coors, and if you buy the picture with them guys fishing, then you get a Miller Lite."

Jimmy can't bring himself to nod, can't even pretend to understand this mystic ritual. At least when the computer guys talk *PIM* and *URL* and *CGI*, he can fall back on the question he asked them that started the gibberish, can put the gibberish into context. Here at Totch's, Bonus's explanations remind Jimmy of spring break after his sophomore year, when he got into trouble in Cabo San Lucas, arrested in Spanish while too drunk to comprehend English.

Fortunately, the teenager brings two platters full of food. Slivers of barbecued pork, cooked right there in that big smoking pit off the deck, fill half the plate. Bonus and Jimmy don't talk for a while. They enjoy the tender meat and the sweet coleslaw and the peppery hash dolloped over rice. The waitress stops by with a plastic bucket, checks their hush-puppy basket, replenishes it with two handfuls from her bucket. "How y'all doing?" she says again, and moves on.

Jimmy studies the activity at the pit, which seems to mostly involve putting out huge volumes of hunger-inducing smoke. A sturdy woman wearing an apron and work gloves moves in and out of the cloud. "That's Rhonda," Bonus tells him. "Totch's wife. She runs the cooking. Totch runs the register 'cause he knows who to let in."

The screen door bangs, and Jimmy looks up to see Totch scanning the deck like someone expecting trouble. He comes to their table.

"So who's your buddy here, Bonus?"

"Totch, this boy's Jimmy Steverson. Bought the house right next door to Mayme. He's been wanting to meet you and Rhonda."

Totch stares at Jimmy, and Jimmy sits motionless, wanting his features memorized so his initiation will be complete. "What you do?"

"Geologist," he answers.

"Geologist," echoes Totch. "At the clay pit? They gonna reopen the clay pit?"

Jimmy shakes his head. "I don't know anything about the clay pit. I'm out at the Muldoy Chemicals site, putting in some wells."

Totch is still not satisfied. "You work for them state people? One of them agencies?"

Mystified by the suspicion in Totch's voice, Jimmy hesitates, so Bonus answers for him. "Uh-uh," he assures Totch, shaking his head slowly for emphasis. "He works for some company up in Columbia."

"Yeah? What's the name of it?"

"KDR," Jimmy answers. "It's a consulting company. We do—"

"What's that stand for?"

Jimmy laughs at that, at the inquisition gone one step too far. "You know, I honestly don't know. It had that name when my boss bought the company, I think, and he just kept it."

Totch likes that answer. "You-all 'bout done with them postcards? Ready for two more?"

When they leave, Bonus carries the two teddy bears and the six postcards they have accumulated. Just outside the door is a wooden box with a slot in it, nailed to the top of a wooden barrel. Bonus drops the two bears into the barrel and the postcards into the slot.

"You gotta bring 'em out," he instructs Jimmy. "So they been sold. You have to take them outside before you can give 'em back."

Back in the pickup, Bonus tries to unravel the Totch's experience for Jimmy. "Totch's used to be a barbecue restaurant," Bonus begins, making Jimmy wonder what it is now. "Now, it's a gift shop," he explains, even though Jimmy hasn't said anything aloud. "Them health-inspector people kept hitting him with regulations, wanting him to buy lots of stuff. They'd put a thermometer in the cooler and say it wasn't cool enough, and stuff like that. So he got into some kind of hassle with the health inspectors, and they turned him in to the tax office 'cause he had people working for him that wadn't on the books. You know, 'cause he couldn't afford the Social Security and workmen's comp and all that stuff. So then he got into some tax mess and what-all. So after he went to jail for tax evasion, he couldn't get a liquor license, so he couldn't sell beer, and any man knows you drink beer when you eat barbecue. But old Totch opened up again anyway, and then the highway people said he didn't have enough parking space to operate a restaurant, 'cause everybody had been starved for barbecue while he was in Atlanta and 'cause he was like a celebrity by then— you know, fighting the IRS and all. I mean, he had big crowds here, and they was parked all over the road. Well, his lawyer finally told him the only way he could serve barbecue was to give it away."

Bonus pauses to enjoy his toothpick.

"So that's what he does. You buy a teddy bear, and he gives you barbecue. You buy a postcard, and he gives you a beer. If you got kids with you or something, you buy one of them yo-yos, and they get a Coke for that. I think you can get iced tea, but I forget what you gotta buy." Bonus screws up his face, trying to recall the iced-tea conversion factor. "Anyway, teddy bears is eight dollars, and yo-yos is one dollar, and postcards is three dollars. That's high for a postcard, but Totch can't get beer from a distributor without a license, so that's what he has to charge. All he's got is a business license to operate a gift shop."

They are on the New Highway crossing Stone Bowl Creek. Off to the left is the dam, and beyond it stretches the pond. "So he checks everybody out, looking for informants?" asks Jimmy.

Bonus laughs. "Yeah, he was checking you out good, wadn't he?" Pulling into his extra yard, next to his Winnebago, he looks over at Jimmy. "So you really ain't got nothing to do with any state agency, do you? I'd hate to have told one to Totch."

Totch grew up working. He learned business skills from his family, learned suspicion early.

His parents owned the only dry-cleaning shop in Walthourville. His uncle owned the Esso station. Totch worked at both places. At the cleaner's, he watched his parents get nervous when a state auditor came in asking about sales tax, saw the fear when the man added up numbers, felt the intimidation when his parents wrote a check for an amount the man quoted. He was at the Esso station that Sunday when his uncle sold a six-pack to two fishermen he didn't know, a mistake that eventually involved a lawyer and a fine and bankruptcy.

His mother was alone at the cleaner's the day the robbery attempt occurred. She pulled a sawed-off mop handle from under the counter and slapped the boy across the nose with it. What she didn't know how to handle was the OSHA inspector. She called Totch. "It's Mr. Osher," she cried into the phone.

Mr. OSHA left behind a sheaf of citations, papers in three colors. "This blue one says you gotta install an air-filtering system," Totch told his mother, who had never been able to afford an air conditioner. "And this pink one says you don't have any records showing how you dispose of solvents."

"I told Mr. Osher we use it all up," said his mother.

"And this yellow one says we're not storing the solvents safely. And here's another pink one, says what will happen if we don't pay the fine."

Totch's mother closed the shop and never reopened it.

So Totch knows he has to check Jimmy out before he can sell him another postcard. He's not about to spend any more time in Atlanta. He knows the sheriff can find out about Jimmy, so he waits until Osmond wants barbecue.

"Totch, I need to feed the boys but keep 'em in the cruisers. Can you put teddy bear on a bun?"

"How many you want?"

"Two each, I reckon. Fourteen. No, sixteen. I guess I better feed Alicia, too, or she'll have it out over the radio that I fed everybody but her."

Totch does the math. Osmond has only four paid deputies, so he must have the volunteer deputies on duty, too. "You-all on the lookout for lottery machines again?"

"I can't tell you 'bout it, Totch. And you can't talk about it."

"Okay, sure. When you want 'em?"

"One of the boys is on the way."

"It'll be ready. Listen, got somebody new eating here. Bonus Wooten brought him in."

"Bonus wouldn't bring anybody that would cause you trouble, Totch."

"I know that. But he's from some company up in Columbia." Totch's intonation makes Columbia sound like a Taliban stronghold.

Osmond smiles at Totch's paranoia. "Gimme his name, Totch. I'll talk to him."

"Steverson. Jimmy Steverson. Bought Orene Connell's old house over there by Bonus."

# Chapter 8

## *Mark*

Mark delivers the bolenos.

Jimmy wonders what else he does, what he does for a living, but Mark explains before he can ask. "I work over to Kaye Clay. Well, I used to. Heavy equipment operator. Got laid off two years ago, and Mayme, bless her heart, started paying me to haul for her. She does the morning run herself, but she don't like to drive at night, so I do the evening deliveries. She's my mother-in-law, you know. Well, I mean, she used to be."

"You divorced?" Jimmy says.

"Uh-huh. But Mayme's still good to me, still family. Might be 'cause she sees more of me than she does Sandra. Sandra ain't one to visit home much. She moved down to Charleston, got a job in a fancy hotel arranging conventions and stuff."

Jimmy has dropped by to deliver a bag of tomatoes to Miz Mayme. He met Mark lounging on her porch.

"You grow them tomatoes?" Mark asks.

"Naw. I pass a place on my way to work every day. Lady puts pro-duce out under a shed, and you drop the money into this metal box."

"I been there. She grows squash and beans, too."

Miz Mayme appears at the screen door. "Mark, you can start load-ing up now."

Jimmy hurries to open the door for Mayme, who dangles bundles of shoeboxes from each hand. Each bundle is two shoeboxes wide and five high, tied with twine. Jimmy takes the bundles from her and fol-lows Mark, who lowers the tailgate so Jimmy can slide the bundles into the truck bed. All business, Mayme heads back in for the next load.

"Listen," Mark says, "why don't you ride around with me while I haul the bolenos?"

Jimmy faces an evening of answering e-mail and printing out a well construction diagram. Driving around the county with Mark and a truck full of bolenos sounds better. "Sure," he answers. He goes back to Mayme's screen door, ready to carry more boxes.

Mark's red Ford Ranger has a large cab with a third seat, air condi-tioning, and a CD player. As they pull out of Miz Mayme's yard, Jimmy glances at his five-year-old Toyota Tacoma, its jade-green paint spat-tered with mud, achieving accidentally the camouflage pattern hunters pay money for. He tries to imagine being out of work for two years and driving a truck like Mark's. "How have you been managing so long without a job?"

"Doing all right. Doing pretty good." Mark has never made a plan, never known worry. Fresh out of high school, he landed a job helping build the New Highway, learned to operate the big orange machines he loves. He knows that if his credit card is declined, a new one will arrive in the mailbox. When his child support is due, somehow a job always turns up. "I do this stuff for Miz Mayme. And I'm in the Jay-cees, so I get to know whenever something's going on at the fairgrounds, and I help set up. Sometimes, I run rides, stuff like that. And I help a fella over in Augusta sometimes. Does repops."

The first stop is the Fill-It-Up station on the highway to Columbia. "I used to pick up bolenos here," Jimmy tells Mark. "Back before I had any idea who made them."

Mark unloads six of the bundles, cuts the twine with his pocketknife, and builds a neat stack of shoeboxes between the door of the convenience store and the row of newspaper racks. He waves at the clerk and hops back in the truck.

"Don't you need to get a receipt or a signature or anything?" Jimmy asks.

Mark is busy backing out, but he hits the brakes, spends a minute looking puzzled. "Oh, I see what you're asking. Naw. See, we ain't really delivering nothing to the Fill-It-Up people. They can't sell bolenos inside the store 'cause of them rules about where things are cooked and how they oughta be labeled. See, Mayme used to sell her bolenos at the farmers' market. God, you could get some good stuff there. There was this lady, I never did know her name, but she made the best soup. Put it in Mason jars. Anyway, some fella from the health department, well, they don't call it the health department no more, they got initials. . . ."

"D-E-H-P," offers Jimmy. "Department of Environmental and Health Protection. They control what I do, too. Everybody I know calls them 'Deep.' You know, as in deep shit."

"That's them. That's them. Them DEHP people came in and said the soup lady couldn't sell her soup because it wasn't made under sanitary conditions or something, and of course they made Mayme stop selling her bolenos. So anyway, now we deliver 'em to places like this, and people pick them up by the box, and they go inside and give the clerk the money, and he just don't ring it up on the register. It'll go in an envelope or a jar or something, and I square it with 'em once a month."

Mark takes shortcuts new to Jimmy, who tries to pay attention, to learn his way around the county that is now his home. They are on a county road tight with trees, and the only thing visible is the yellow triangle of bugs within the headlights, so Jimmy gives up on navigation. Mark pulls into the parking lot of a laundromat.

"You don't work on Saturdays, do ya?" Before Jimmy can answer,

Mark is out of the truck, stacking boleno boxes next to the change machine. Back in the truck he left idling, Mark restarts the conversation as though he left it idling, too. " 'Cause I was thinking maybe you could come out to my place tomorrow and fish. I saw you got a new boat, so I figure you fish."

"At your place?"

"Yeah, I got my own pond. You can't eat the fish out of Dillehay Pond. They got all these signs up, says you can catch the fish but you can't eat 'em, and I ain't one of those guys that goes to all the trouble of fishing and then don't eat what ends up in the boat. We can eat what we catch out of my pond." Before Jimmy can respond, Mark points off into the darkness. "Over there's Kaye Clay." Jimmy looks but sees only a dirt road and a cattle gate briefly illuminated by Mark's headlights. "That's the clay pit, where I used to work." Still driving at well over the speed limit, Mark leans over the steering wheel and stares, wishing the lights back on, his yellow hard hat back on his head.

"Mark, you might want to look where you're going."

"Yeah, sorry. Anyway, I worked there for almost thirteen years. Sometimes, they call me in still. Anytime there's work. It keeps my OSHA papers up, so I can drive all the machinery." An array of colorful neon appears, outlining a building, and Mark turns in. "This is Loop's Corner. We can get a beer here."

Mark opens the tailgate and hands bundles of shoeboxes to Jimmy. "All these go in?" Jimmy asks.

"Yeah. Loop sells more bolenos than anybody around here."

Jimmy is glad to have the cold bottle of Michelob in his hand because Loop's is cooled only by a huge, rusted fan mounted into a wall. Jimmy studies the fan. He has never seen anything like it.

"My daddy built that fan," a man tells him. "Been running since 1955."

"Your name Loop?" Jimmy asks.

Mark's head pops up from behind Loop's counter. "Yeah, Jimmy. This here's Loop. Loop, that's Jimmy. He bought the house next door to Mayme."

Loop reaches over the counter, shakes Jimmy's hand. "Always glad to meet another man who'll buy beer from me. And you watch out for Miz Mayme. She's fine."

"I think she watches out for me," Jimmy says. "She keeps me stocked with that bread she bakes."

Mark chats with two men who sit in folding chairs in front of the cricket boxes, beer cans in hand. To Jimmy, the store looks like a museum display invaded by sportsmen. Dozer caps and orange vests hang on the wall among antique tools. A phone booth with a closet rod stretched across it holds coveralls on sale for $29.99. Fishing rods are propped against a battered red Coke cooler, which looks squat next to the tall chrome-and-glass refrigerated beer display. Over the door is a sign warning, "Beer may not be consumed on the premises."

All the bolenos delivered, Mark begins talking as soon as he turns the key in the ignition, as though he and the engine run on the same battery. "Loop's is kind of a hangout for blacks. But Loop ain't particular. He'll sell us beer, too. Those guys I was talking to? One of them, Calvin, he used to work at the clay pit with me. I keep hoping that big state project will get going, that thing True Padgett keeps talking about. True's that guy that goes to Columbia from here?"

"Our congressman from this district?"

"Yeah, that's it. True's our congress guy. He was at the Jaycees meeting last week. Said he's still working on this big project, something about the pond that would bring in a lot of jobs. Calvin said he's heard about it, too. I figure maybe the clay pit would open again if that state thing comes through."

Mark gets quiet after that, and Jimmy dozes off.

They watch Saturday's sunrise from the earthen dam that is also Mark's driveway. Mark collects people like Velcro collects lint, and he has collected Jimmy, who needs to orbit another man with a divorce behind him. And he is curious about Mark, who describes himself as unemployed, laid off from Kaye Clay, yet lives on twenty-seven acres in his two-story home on his own fishing pond.

"So you and your wife built this place?"

Mark nods over his Coors can. "Yep. And I bulldozed the dam, dug the pond. But Sandra, well, there ain't much around here for a smart woman to do. I mean, if you don't wanna be a flowerpot, you gotta get off the porch, you know? Anyway, Sandra got a job at that Holiday Inn Express they built up where the New Highway meets the interstate, and she kept getting promoted, 'til she got promoted right on down to Charleston."

"My ex-wife just got a promotion," Jimmy says. Jimmy has not heard from Gwen since the divorce fifteen months earlier. "I called her when I heard about it, left a message on her answering machine." Jimmy tells Mark what he has told no one else. He also sent her a birthday card, but she did not reciprocate on his birthday.

"Sandra and I sorta have to talk 'cause of the kids," Mark says. "You know, they come up once a month for a weekend, and all summer. That's why Sandra keeps the place. This is all really in Sandra's name. I couldn't have kept the place after I got laid off, and she wanted the kids to have the place to come back to. So it's in her name, and she lets me live here."

"We restored an old farmhouse in Lexington County," Jimmy begins, then stops to pour coffee from his thermos. "It was hard to see it sold." He empties the Styrofoam cup before continuing. "I heard she bought a condo in Columbia."

"You have to pay alimony?"

Jimmy laughs. "I can't imagine Gwen wanting alimony."

"I got child support to pay. As long as I make just enough to send the child-support checks, Sandra's happy. That's why I have to work off the books. If I had any income on paper, well, the tax people would know first off, and my wife's lawyer would know second off. And then the child support would go up."

The sun that had been a pleasant gift on a weekend morning is now a hot hand on Jimmy's hat. "I think we should give up, Mark. We've been sitting here two hours, and we don't have a thing. You got anything in this pond?"

"Oh, yeah. I take care of my pond. Lime it and fertilize it every spring. Stocked it with bass a long time ago. Pulled an eight-pound bass outta here yesterday. You fish much?"

"I'm just getting into fishing."

"Well, they seem to like the big wiggly lures." He hands Jimmy a package of pumpkinseed lizards. "Try these things. Listen, I got a repop to do next weekend, over in Augusta. You wanna come along for the ride?"

"A repossession?"

"Yeah. Pick up a car some guy ain't paying for. I get a hundred dollars for every one I get. The title-pawn place pays me."

"No thanks. I'll stay out of that one. Is it safe?"

"Aw, I got a gun."

Mark's gun was issued to him by Sheriff Osmond Vause because Mark is a volunteer deputy. Sheriff Vause, who wedged his own way into law enforcement as a volunteer, calls Mark to duty.

"I checked out what you told me," Osmond begins. "Looks like they're planning on bringing them in tonight. Figure they'll catch us off-guard on a Sunday night, I reckon."

"You gonna do like you did last time?"

"Yep. We'll give 'em a couple days. Let 'em get the things delivered and plugged in."

The machines come into Osilo County discreetly, in small, unmarked panel trucks, and are installed during the night. Mark makes his next boleno run the following night and reports to the sheriff as soon as he gets home: "Three places. The Fill-It-Up station on the New Highway. Loop's Corner. And the Food & Fuel over by the SaveMore."

"We'll meet at your place," Osmond tells Mark. "If we meet anyplace else, word will be out before we get there."

In addition to Mark, the sheriff has one other volunteer deputy. The Reverend Mickey Balentine spent twenty years as a police chaplain in Tampa, Florida, retreated to Walthourville as an associate pastor because he could no longer counsel alcoholic cops who abused their wives. Hungry for small-town values, he had found only a small town, until Osmond gave him a mission. When the lottery proposal was put on the ballot in 2000, the Reverend Balentine joined Osmond in campaigning against it. "I've seen addiction," the reverend told people. "Gambling's an addiction. If we let the state sanction it, then that makes it look safe. It's not safe." The lottery was approved by the voters of the state of South Carolina, but Osmond had not surrendered, and the reverend needed a battleground with a tangible enemy.

Osmond won't put his full-time deputies' careers at risk, so he supplements his two volunteers with his retirees. "Got some more lottery machines to deal with," he says, giving them the chance to volunteer.

"Oh, hell yes, Osmond. I got nothing to lose," says sixty-seven-year-old Lowell Biggers.

Paul Gardner, old enough to have trained Lowell, lets out a whoop. "It beats hell out of sitting here watching *Oprah* reruns."

There has been a gas station at Loop's Corner since the forties, back when County Road 11 was a stretch of state highway, part of the Woodpecker Trail that channeled Northerners to Florida. Now, Loop sells bait, fishing and hunting licenses, hot dogs, cold beer, and bolenos. He wants to sell lottery tickets, too, has been licensed by the Lottery Trust Authority to do so, but Osmond Vause has yet to allow a lottery machine in Osilo County. On Friday, when he and Jimmy had stocked Loop's with bolenos, Mark noticed the new electrical outlets and the thick gray cables. They were easy to spot at Loop's, where light bulbs still hung from fuzzy black cords installed by the Rural Electrification Administration. It was three days later, replenishing the boleno supply, when Mark saw the machinery covered in tarp and called it in to Osmond.

"Here's what we'll do, boys," Osmond directs his four volunteers. "I go in by myself. I explain what I'm doing. These machines are wired up like a computer, so I cut the cables. You-all stay outside. You're just crowd control, in case there's some excitement."

They go to Loop's first. Osmond pulls his bolt cutters out of his trunk. He has never needed his gun, but the bolt cutters once freed a starving dog from a tangled choke collar, cut open a padlock that let him into a storage unit where stolen computers were stashed, snipped through an old barbed-wire fence so his men could search for a lost three-year-old.

"Well, Osmond, I thought it was worth a try," Loop tells him. "I thought you mighta eased up some on this."

Osmond hands him a manila envelope. "This is a copy of the county ordinance that prohibits gambling in Osilo County, Loop. There's also a letter in there from me saying I'm the one that cut the cable, in case the lottery folks give you some kinda trouble."

Loop sighs, leans on the counter he has known since he was too short to see over it, when his daddy ran the place and he was Little Loop. "Osmond, why don't you just let the machines come in? It's gonna happen sooner or later. I talked to a coupla folks on the county council, you know. They say they're okay with it." Loop doesn't relate the full conversation. Both council members he talked to want the lottery in Osilo County, know it will happen eventually. But neither Macy Gillingham, who teaches at the elementary school, nor Derrick Ulmer, who owns Ulmer Tool Rental, has any idea how to harness a runaway sheriff. They hope the next election will take care of the problem.

Osmond is in no hurry. He leans on Loop's counter from the other side, pulls two ones from his wallet. "Gimme a Diet Pepsi, Loop." He pops the can, pockets his change. "Most people in Osilo County need to keep their money in their pocket, Loop." He points to the machines. "Those things will take money from the poorest people, from people desperate enough to think money might fall out of the sky and fix their problems, and that money will go to send somebody else's kids to college. People who buy lottery tickets are not people who are going to send their kids to college. I don't want anyone in this county scammed into thinking they might be millionaires, any more than I want True Padgett promising that the state's gonna fill in the pond and make jobs for anybody who can haul dirt."

Loop nods. He has heard it all before. "Osmond, they're expecting you to do this. They told me you'd need a court order, and you don't have one."

"But they won't do anything, Loop. They don't want this to get out. They put lawyers on it or send SLED down here, it'll be in the papers, and they don't want bad publicity. They want people to associate the lottery with education, not gambling. So listen, I'll just snip those cables, and I'll be gone."

Osmond locates the gray cables snaking from the wall and cuts them flush. He wraps crime-scene tape around the machines and adds an evidence seal, something he has just had printed up at the newspaper office.

Loop uses his pocketknife to open the manila envelope, finds a letter typed on Osilo County letterhead with Osmond's signature. He has a hard time reading the ordinance, a photocopy of a handwritten entry on a ledger page dated 1946. Loop chuckles. "Osmond, this thing will never hold up, not against the state. It ain't even done on a typewriter. And it's from 1946."

"It's still the law, Loop. Constitution's pretty old, too, but it's still the law."

Loop laughs again. "Come to think of it, Osmond, it's handwritten, too, ain't it?"

The process goes quickly at the Food & Fuel, but on the way to the Fill-It-Up, Osmond gets a call from the dispatcher warning of two highway-patrol cars parked there. Osmond doesn't want confrontation. He motions to Mickey Balentine.

"Reverend, get the church bus, go out on the New Highway, and have a flat tire. Go down a couple of exits so they'll be gone awhile."

"I'm on it," he tells Osmond. "Probably take me twenty, thirty minutes to get on the highway, a few more to let the air out of the tire."

Osmond nods, turns to Mark. "Mark, go get a load of bolenos from Miz Mayme, head up the other way, toward Columbia, then let the boxes fall out of your truck and block the road." When Mark hesitates, Osmond adds, "I'll pay for the bolenos." He looks at his watch. "It's getting on time to eat. Lowell, you run out to the Chicken Strut, bring back some chicken fingers or something. Paul, you go over to that place across the New Highway from the Fill-It-Up. Call me when you see the highway-patrol cruisers leave."

"Osmond, that's a fabric store," Paul protests.

Osmond knows that Paul and Lowell are counting on the day to produce more than just a few hours' pay. They need relief from the tedium of retirement, something to talk about at the dinner table. "Okay. Pull out your badge and tell 'em you're on a stakeout."

Behind the counter at the Fill-It-Up is an excited teenager who talks while Osmond works. "I knew you got rid of them state troopers, sheriff," the boy says. "Soon as I saw 'em take off, I knew you was behind it. You better hurry. They was suspicious. Oh, and Sheriff Vause? I got some papers I got to give you. Something about how this ain't legal and all."

"Make sure you give that envelope to your boss," Osmond tells the boy.

"That's all you're gonna do?" the boy complains. "I thought you'd smash 'em up or something. Hell, anybody can replace cables."

"I'm not trying to make a mess, son. I'm trying to make a point."

Chapter 9

## *Sally*

SALLY HECKERT KNOWS WHO OWNS WHAT and who pays their bills because Sally is the Osilo County tax collector.

When Sally was eight years old, she earned her first Girl Scout badge, a round patch of fabric with a tree on it, the conservation badge. She absorbed the Girl Scout motto—*Be prepared*—immediately, admiring a motto phrased in the imperative. For this morning's phone calls, she is nervous, but she is prepared.

Sally proceeds in steps, the same way she earned the badges to stitch on her sash. Yesterday, she called the Charleston office of Senator Gibbes Anson, who had promised during his campaign to take care of his constituents in the convivial style of Strom Thurmond and to bring home federal money with the vigor of Fritz Hollings. Carly Albritton, the office manager there, always chats long enough to sift a mutual acquaintance or a shared cousin, whittling the state's population down to a family reunion. Turns out one of Osmond

Vause's deputies is Carly's Sunday-school teacher's nephew.

Having woven her political net, Carly got down to business. "So what you need is a contact? Somebody to call for information about this company?"

"I need to know how to reach them, short of flying to Paris. If somebody in Washington can contact them for us, if there's some business commission or something that handles this kind of thing, that would be great."

"I'll get you some names, don't you worry, hon."

Carly called back an hour later and gave Sally two phone numbers and four names. "And you know, anytime anybody up there in Walthourville needs the senator, you know you just call, don't you, hon?"

Sally left the tax office early enough to get to the Osilo County Library before the five o'clock closing time. She accessed a government Web site and printed out a chart listing the State Department's under secretaries. She checked out a French-English dictionary and a book called *Review Text in French*, both of which she took to bed with her. Before dawn, she was on the Internet finding out what the euro was worth these days.

*Be prepared*. Now, she clears off her desktop, leaving only the phone and her jelly jar of dangerously sharp pencils. She opens the paperback Larousse, finger pressing the spine to make it lie flat. Next to that, she places a sheet of paper on which she has noted the exchange rate of the euro and had conjugated *taxer*, a verb that never came up during her two years of French at Stone Bowl Valley High School. In front of the Larousse, she places a brand-new legal tablet. On one side of the tablet is her chart of under secretaries, on the other the list of phone numbers provided by Senator Anson's ever-helpful office manager.

She dials the French Embassy first because she dreads it the most, practicing "*Allo, je m'appelle Madame Heckert*" as the phone rings. Her silent recitation ends when a sentence spoken in French is followed by its English counterpart: "If you wish to speak English, please press two."

Sally punches two, then listens to complicated voice-mail commands in romantically accented English. She pushes five buttons before she is allowed to leave her message.

That done, she takes a deep breath. Then she dials the United States State Department. An actual person answers the number provided by the senator's office. Sally asks for the first of the three names Carly gave her. Her answer is the seashell silence of a telephonic transfer, a musical interlude, and voice-mail instructions. Sally leaves her message. Then she hits redial, reaches a different actual person this time, but gets the same result. She leaves her message a second time. She repeats the process for the third name and for two under secretaries.

Sally leans back in her swivel chair. The wall clock tells her she has been at work thirty-three minutes. There is nothing written on her legal pad. She has left six messages in the vacuum that is Washington. She has cost Osilo County six long-distance phone calls. That worries Sally. Osilo County often can't afford to send her to the meetings and seminars she is required to attend to be certified by the South Carolina Tax Commission. Sally attends anyway at her own expense because she likes sitting in classrooms, likes meeting people who do what she does.

None of the classes taught her how to get a check out of SBI Industries.

Jimmy meets Sally that Friday, when weather keeps him from the well site. Nobody works near a drill tower in a lightning storm.

He puts together an overdue report and e-mails it to the KDR office, then sits at the kitchen table with an array of receipts until he has his expense reimbursement form ready to fax. He has numbers to feed a hungry spreadsheet, but his data is still in the form of muddy notes in his Rite-in-the-Rain field notebook. Which is in his briefcase. Which is in his truck. Out in the rain.

He decides that if he's going to make a dash for his truck, he might as well run errands. He opens his refrigerator and concocts a mental grocery list. When he pulls into the SaveMore lot, his rearview mirror shows the Osilo County Courthouse. The DEHP report he is working on requires a drainage map and an abandoned-well survey, and for that he needs an aerial photo, which he can find in the county tax office. He backs out and drives across the street, parks as close to the building as he can, still is soaked when he reaches the door.

The Old Courthouse has not functioned as a courthouse for some time. Court is actually held in the new Law Enforcement Building out on the New Highway, built by federal crack-down-on-crime dollars. The old building is now home to various county offices. Jimmy walks down a musty hallway until he finds a door labeled, "Tax Collector, Osilo County." He opens the door to an unlit room and finds himself trapped by a long counter. Behind the counter are three desks and two light tables with maps draped across them. At one end of the room, a door stands open, releasing a shaft of light that penetrates the rainy-day gloom.

"Hello?" he asks.

He hears a movement.

"Hello back," says a woman's voice. Jimmy hears a file drawer close and the plunking footsteps of someone in athletic shoes. Then a tiny woman appears. "Tax office is closed on Fridays," she says.

Jimmy is accustomed to the government offices of Columbia. "You're closed on a weekday?"

She is not quite five feet tall. She does not approach the counter because she has trouble reaching it. "Closed," she repeats. "That's why the lights are out. We're open on Tuesdays and Thursdays from nine to noon."

"Well, how about the planning office?"

"Closest we've got to that is a building inspector. I can give you his phone number."

"Well, is there maybe a form I could just fill out and leave? I need a copy of one of your aerial photos."

"What's wrong with coming back on Tuesday from nine to noon?"

"I'll be at work then."

"What property?"

"The Muldoy Chemicals site."

The short lady flips on the lights. Jimmy sees a younger woman than he was led to believe by her throaty voice and bossy manner.

"You work at Muldoy?"

"Sort of. I work for a company in Columbia, but we're putting in wells out there."

"Well, if you drove all the way down here from Columbia, I guess I can print something out for you."

Jimmy does not plan to correct her misconception, since it's getting him what he wants, but her next question makes him honest.

"So, is it raining this bad in Columbia?"

"Well, actually, I didn't drive here from Columbia. I live here. On Randleman Road."

"You bought Orene Connell's house," she says.

Jimmy nods.

"Come on around here." She lifts a hinged section of the counter that allows access. While Jimmy lowers the gate politely behind him, she types at a keyboard. "First, I've got to get the Muldoy Chemicals tax parcel number because that will tell us what map we want." From a metal rack, she pulls out a sheaf of maps, then throws the yard-wide pages onto one of the desks. Her ponytail flags her every movement, a kinetic exclamation point that makes her appear to be in constant motion.

"I'm Sally Heckert," she says, looking at the maps, not at Jimmy. "I'm the tax collector." With her palm, she smooths the aerial photo draped across the desk like a stiff tablecloth. Lines have been drawn on the photo, turning the black-and-white picture of trees and streets into a giant jigsaw puzzle, each piece a tax parcel.

"Here's the Muldoy site," Sally tells him, pointing a red fingernail at one of the larger polygons. "Parcel 18-044-19. Now, you want a copy with the property lines superimposed, or just the photo?"

"Both," says Jimmy.

"Three dollars each."

Jimmy nods.

Sally warms up the blueprint machine. "This will take about five minutes to get up to speed. And it's smelly, especially on these rainy days. There's no ventilation in this old building."

"Well, I appreciate your doing all this. I mean, you're not even open." Jimmy runs his fingers over the map, feeling the gritty ridges of hand-inked lines atop the smooth Mylar, wondering why the county doesn't use computerized drafting equipment.

"I do most of my work when we're not open. When I'm open, there's always people in here. Lawyers and real-estate people and timber buyers. So I have to come in on the days we're closed to get anything done. Listen, while you're waiting, you want to see the rooftop of your house?"

"Sure."

"I don't have to look that number up," Sally says. "That's the Dillehay Mill property, one of my biggest headaches." She throws another sheaf of maps onto the desk, flips to the one she wants. "Here's you," Sally says, pointing her red fingernail at a tiny rectangle. Jimmy leans close to see his roof, the four inked lines around it defining his property. Five such blocks line his side of Randleman Road, five the other side, like windowpanes puttied into the gap between the curve of the highway and the straight line of the railroad tracks. "Tax parcel 27-409-03," says Sally. "That's the Dillehay Mill property. Well, actually, SBI Industries is listed as the property owner."

Jimmy nods, fascinated by the map, worried about how small the Randleman Road houses look next to the mill parcel, how vulnerable the tiny neighborhood is, erasable by a mere widening of the highway. He realizes he should have visited this office and seen this map before he bought his house. He was too eager to be done with house hunting, too sure of the bargain he found on a scenic pond. And he had assumed the county owned the pond.

"Print me a copy of the map with the pond on it, too."

"Three more dollars," she warns.

"So they own the pond? That SBI company?"

"Yep. The pond, the old mill site, and a bunch of other holdings all around Osilo County, all up and down Stone Bowl Creek. All told, that company owns seventeen percent of the taxable property in this county." Sally feeds the first sheet of Mylar into the blueprint machine. "The Dillehay Pond map is probably the most-copied map I've got, thanks to True Padgett. He keeps calling me for copies, trying to convince the state legislature to fill the damn thing in."

"To do what?"

"To fill it in. You haven't heard about True's plan?"

"He wants to fill it in? Isn't it about three hundred acres?"

"Three hundred and twenty-nine," says Sally. "Every time I send him a copy, I remind him of that fact."

"I've never heard of such a project, and I'm in the environmental reclamation field," Jimmy says.

"There isn't such a project. True Padgett's been running on it for years. He talks about all the jobs it would create."

Jimmy realizes he has bought a house and dock on a pond that might become acres of backfill. What can you build on fill? He has a disquieting image of his dock leading to the curbing around a Wal-Mart parking lot. "That's insane," he says. "First, it's not the way to address the pollution problem. Second, it's just not practical." His mind is calculating cubic yards of dirt, and the figures are astronomical.

Sally puts the next map in. "Don't panic. It'll never happen. Not unless True Padgett can shake enough money out of the legislature to buy a few million truckloads of dirt from Kaye Clay. And I doubt even the South Carolina legislature is that stupid. Wait 'til you meet True, then you'll understand. He's harmless." She copies the last map Jimmy requested. "Nine dollars," she tells him.

Jimmy doubts she has access to a cash drawer if her office is closed, so he manages to pull a five, three ones, and a dollar in change from his jeans pockets.

Writing a receipt, she asks, "You want some pizza?"

"Ma'am?"

Sally doesn't like the *ma'am* but ignores it. She is dying to tell some-one about calling the French Embassy. "The reason you found that door unlocked is I just had a pizza delivered, and it's getting cold. You want to share it with me, that's fine. They'll only deliver a large, and I can just about crawl inside the box it comes in, which means there's a lot more pizza than there is of me. So if you've got the time to eat lunch with me, I'll tell you more than you ever wanted to know about the pond you live on."

In the back room from which Sally emerged is a corner set aside as a break room. A gray metal desk, missing all its drawers and splotched with rust, holds a coffee maker surrounded by mugs and Styrofoam cups and plastic utensils. Under the desk, a mini-refrigerator hums. In front of the desk stands a tattooed drafting table, its top lowered to a horizontal position, making a wide eating area. Sally opens the pizza box there.

"There's Cokes and stuff in the fridge," she offers. "Want one?"

Jimmy nods, so she retrieves a cold red can for him. She fills a paper cup full of water for herself, then peels two thin paper plates from a stack.

"Now, I assume you *don't* want the pond filled in."

Jimmy can only shake his head, his mouth full of cheese and dough.

Using a plastic fork, Sally works to cut her slice into bite-sized pieces. "No sane person would," she agrees. "But it's a hot topic around here. I'm thinking of putting up a chart showing who wants to fill it in and who doesn't. I'll put your name in the *No* column. I reckon all of you folks down on Randleman Road would say no, unless somehow it would raise y'all's property values, and I can't see how living next to a landfill would raise property values. Now, True would be in the *Yes* column." Sally chews and thinks. "And everybody knows Osmond Vause is against it. You know Osmond?"

Having just bitten into a second slice, Jimmy can only shake his head.

"Osmond's the county sheriff. He doesn't even like to hear people talk about filling the pond, says it's getting their hopes up for nothing.

He and True are always going at it. But Billy Kaye's got to be for it, along with everybody he had to lay off from Kaye Clay after they finished the New Highway. But then he'd have to deal with his wife. I wonder where Vodelia Kaye wants her name on my chart."

Jimmy shrugs and picks up a third slice. He thinks he should participate in the conversation, to be polite, so he comes up with a question before taking a bite. "Wouldn't she say yes, too? 'Cause of her husband's business?"

Sally shakes her head. "I might have to make a third column just for Vodelia. She's always got some opinion no one would have thought of. Vodelia is president of the Osilo County Historical Society, even though she's been living in Atlanta for ten years now."

Jimmy nods and chews, thinks of another question. "How about the pond owners? That company? Wouldn't they fight having it filled in?"

"We'll probably never know what they think about anything." Sally pounces on the opportunity to tell her story to a captive audience. "Let me tell you about SBI Industries. That's Stone Bowl International Industries. I send tax notices to them just like I send them to everybody. I don't get a check back. They get a past-due notice, just like everybody else. Then they start getting all those warning letters. Then their property goes on the auction list. Now, the minimum bid is the taxes owed. On every piece of their property, that's several thousand dollars. On the biggest properties, like the pond and the old Dillehay Mill site, it's tens of thousands of dollars. It's taxed as commercial property. But there aren't a lot of folks wanting to spend that kind of money on what looks like useless property. The chamber-of-commerce guys are always showing the mill properties to developers, but there's no reason to build houses and stores because nobody down here has jobs."

Sally pauses to take her second bite. Jimmy compares her consumption to the four slices he has already swallowed. He decides to stop eating and listen.

Sally blots her mouth. "Now, selling the property is complicated by all kinds of environmental issues. The pond, for instance, has got some kind of stuff in it. But the old mill buildings are a problem, too. Asbestos, for one thing. Old tanks buried on the property with God knows what in them. There's even some old metal drums stacked in a building, and nobody knows what's in them. So nobody's likely to buy something the EPA is gonna make them clean up."

"CERCLA," Jimmy says, pronouncing it *sir-kluh*, like those in the business do.

Sally Heckert knows about CERCLA, too. "Yep. The Superfund law. You own it, you gotta clean it up. The EPA says it will take well over a million dollars to clean up what's left of the Dillehay Mill. But nobody can make SBI do it. We can't even make them pay their tax bill. Now, I've been working here in the tax office for twenty-something years. I started out as a part-time clerk, then started drawing the maps. I ran for collector six years ago, when Blue Hardaway died, 'cause I figured it was the only way I'd ever get a raise. When I started rooting through the files, I found out that old Mr. Hardaway had long since quit sending tax notices to SBI. Probably figured it was a waste of postage." Sally licks her lips. "I guess, to me, it's a challenge. I want these people to send in a check just like everybody else that owns property. But first, you gotta find them. Their headquarters are in Paris, but they have mills all over the world, places like Venezuela and Thailand. They sure don't have offices in that little post-office box. I've been mailing nastier and nastier letters and getting nowhere. Then I got that letter on the wall over there."

Jimmy turns and sees a framed letter. Gnawing crust, he gets up and scans the closely spaced page. "This is in French."

Sally laughs. "Yeah, that was the first problem. I got the French teacher at Stone Bowl Valley High to translate it for me. Turn it over," Sally tells him. "The English version is on the back."

Jimmy lifts the cheap frame from the nail that holds it, turns it over to see a typewritten page taped to the back. He reads it twice. "What in hell does this mean? All this about the World Bank and the euro?"

Sally laughs again. "If you send me that kind of b.s. when I mail your tax notice, I get to sell your house. There's a joke around town that the Board of Realtors is going to put me in the Million Dollar Club 'cause I sell more houses than anybody else."

Jimmy replaces the framed letter on the wall.

"Well, anyway, that letter pissed me off," Sally says. "So I called Senator Anson's office and asked for help. They gave me some names at the State Department and somebody to call at the French Embassy."

Jimmy chuckles.

"Yeah, it's wild, isn't it? I'm a little part-time county tax collector, and I'm on the phone to the French Embassy." Sally eats another tiny bite of pizza. "I actually practiced my French before I called." She looks at her watch. "They still haven't called back." She pushes cold pizza around her plate.

"You want a warm piece out of the box?" suggests Jimmy.

"Naw. I'd rather talk than eat."

"Isn't there some legal ramification to all this?"

"I hope so, but I doubt it. I mean, it's gonna take somebody who knows about international law and international banking. We've got three banks here in Walthourville. I thought the bank managers might know something. Well, Jolene Newlin at the Bank of the South got there by working her way up from teller. Mac McAvoy over at Carolina Federal got to be manager because he was a football hero at Clemson. Then there's this young guy, actually has a degree in economics from Furman. He manages the Bank and Trust. He doesn't know anything either, but he didn't want to admit it, so he started dishing out advice. He told me to give up on collecting the taxes and start trying to figure out what to do with the property. So you can see I don't have a tribunal on international law and banking at my disposal. The obvious thing is to accept reality and assume ownership of the land. But let's face it, Osilo County doesn't need to own land it can't do anything with. Osilo County is poor. You can tell where the county line is, can't you? You cross from Richland County into Osilo, and boom, you're in a pothole."

Jimmy puts his hands on the pizza box. It's still warm, so he pulls out a fifth slice.

"Go ahead," Sally tells him. "Help yourself." Finally finishing her first slice, she pulls out a second.

"You think any of the old mills could be a brownfield site?" Jimmy asks.

"A what?"

Jimmy smiles. He might have repaid her for the pizza, given her some hope. "Google it," he tells her, wanting to get back to the pond issue. "So where does filling in the pond fit into all of this?"

Sally is busy forcing the plastic fork to cut her pizza slice into the tiny pieces she prefers. She shakes her head. "That's all it is, just talk. Something for True to use to get votes from the unemployed, something to fill up space in the newspaper. It sounds nutty to you and me, but then we both have jobs, don't we?"

Jimmy stuffs the rolled-up maps under his rain slicker and makes a run for his truck. In the SaveMore parking lot, he grabs a wet shopping cart, having learned there are never any carts in the store. He makes it inside just as lightning cracks the sky, turns to watch the display, notices for the first time the antiquated architecture of the Old Courthouse, a regal building crowned with a cupola, trapped between Valley Video and the Super Soap Car Wash. He wonders if Sally is alone in that big building.

After Jimmy leaves, Sally scribbles a note to herself—"Google brownfield"—then returns to the stack of plats she had been working on. She transfers the changes in property lines—mostly large parcels multiplying by division into many smaller parcels—from each plat to the appropriate tax map. She inks lines and writes tiny numbers within the parcels until her eyes burn. In her classes, she has learned that most counties employ draftsmen to do this work, and that they do it on computers. Here in Osilo County, Sally shares an office with the assessor, who is on maternity leave. The two of them keep the maps up to date, freeing up their one employee to answer the phone and handle tax payments.

Exhausted, she hangs the heavy Mylar sheets back in their rack and files her unfinished work in a limp and mottled folder. Then she tears a big sheet of paper from the roll that feeds the blueprint machine. With her T square and a marker, she creates a three-columned chart. At the top, she free-hands, "Want to Fill in Dillehay Pond?" Under the question, she labels her three columns "Yes," "No," and "Other Ideas."

No one from Washington returns Sally's calls. She has no way of knowing that, to those in Washington important enough to be on Senator Anson's list or the federal government's Web site, Friday is the first day of a three-day weekend spent at second homes in Winchester or Duck. And on Monday when they return to their desks, they won't be in any hurry to return a phone call to someone with an area code they don't recognize.

On her way out, she thumb-tacks her sign in the hallway, gray flecks of paint falling onto her white Reeboks as she does. She glances at her watch: 5:46. *Six heures moins* something. Hurrying to her car, her umbrella providing little defense against the blowing rain, she counts to *quatorze. Six heures moins quatorze.* But then she looks at her watch and finds that it isn't *six heures moins quatorze* anymore, and she laughs.

## Chapter 10

## *Veau*

VODELIA KAYE IS STILL VODELIA to the folks in the Valley, but in Atlanta she evolved into Veau.

This weekend, she is back, baby-sitting Cone Duffy. When she hears a lawnmower start, she pushes Cone's chair onto the porch. Fairy Etta has told her that the sound of a lawnmower is soothing to Cone. She and Cone watch Jimmy mow first his small patch of grass, then Mayme's. When the mechanical drone dies, Cone is asleep. Veau checks the brake on his chair, then walks the short diagonal across the street.

"Mr. Steverson? You home?"

Jimmy is folding laundry when Veau Kaye knocks at his door. He throws towels over the briefs and boxers and T-shirts spread on his sofa. Holding open the screen door, he offers only a reluctant hello, wondering if he has any ones in his pocket to contribute to whatever charity this woman represents.

"Hey, there. I'm Veau Kaye. You're Jimmy Steverson?"

Jimmy nods, trying to place her name. Then he remembers—the woman Mark mentioned, the woman the tax collector talked about, the rich woman who lives in Atlanta.

"Listen, I'm watching Cone this afternoon. We've been sitting on the porch watching you mow. Any chance I can talk you into mowing that little strip in front of Fairy Etta's house? Normally, Bonus does it, but he's off at some American Legion get-together in Orlando, and all that rain we had this week has the grass shooting up."

Jimmy has already pushed the mower under his back deck and covered it with a tarp. Ready for a shower and lunch, he tries to think of an excuse. The only thing that pops into his mind is an empty gas tank, but the five feet of green between the curb and Fairy Etta's porch could probably be done on fumes. "Sure," he says. "Be right over."

"Thanks. I'm gonna run on back now. I'm scared to leave him along too long."

When Jimmy bumps the mower over the curb, Cone wakes. His eyes follow Jimmy as he makes one short swipe, then another.

"Any grass out back?" he asks Veau.

Veau shakes her head. "Out back is the chicken yard." She walks down the three steps to stand next to Jimmy. "How about having some lunch with us? A little picnic lunch here on the porch. Cone seems to perk up when there's another man around." She smiles, then turns to glance at Cone, strapped into his wheelchair. "And I've been wanting to meet you," she says, as though making a confession. "I keep hearing about the new guy who moved into Miz Orene's house."

Jimmy had been trying to decide whether to microwave a frozen burrito or a hot dog for lunch. He is sure Veau will offer something better. "If you don't mind how dirty I am," he answers.

"Cone. Cone. Cone, this is your neighbor Jimmy. Jimmy, this is Cone Duffy."

Jimmy picks up Cone's limp right hand, holds it between his, and fashions a handshake. "Good to meet you, Cone."

Veau unfolds a spare lawn chair for Jimmy. "Fairy Etta is off on what Cone calls 'one of her adventures.' Fairy Etta knows where the fun is, doesn't she, Cone? She's up at that bingo place in Rock Hill, the one the Catawba Indians opened. I knew when I read about the church getting together a bus trip up there that Fairy Etta would be dying to go, so I called and told her I'd come visit with Cone while she went." She smiles at Cone.

Jimmy sits carefully, trying to find room for his feet. Clay pots crowd the porch. Stranded in his wheelchair among Fairy Etta's ferns and pineapple plants, Cone looks like an old car abandoned to weeds. His head twitches, and his eyes blink nervously. Jimmy takes in the surroundings, a view from yet another porch on Randleman Road. He can look directly across the street into Miz Mayme's open front door.

Veau looks at home and out of place simultaneously. Her short hair is the work of a recent trip to an Atlanta stylist. Gold shines at her ears. Her white jeans and blue silk T-shirt and leather sandals are elegant. She has a grace that could not have been contained forever on Dillehay Pond, like the balloon that is more magical when it floats away. Yet she is clearly comfortable here, settled into the webbed chair, patting Cone's hand every so often.

"Iced tea, Jimmy? Fairy Etta makes the best iced tea in the world."

"Yeah, thanks."

Veau goes inside. Jimmy moves over to sit next to Cone in case he is needed.

"Cone, I'm glad we finally met. I live over there in Orene Connell's old house. I've seen you sitting out here lots of times, but I've just never stopped to visit. Your wife's been sending me eggs, leaving them at Mayme's for me. I sure do appreciate those fresh eggs."

Veau has made it back to the screen door but stops to admire Jimmy's effort at a one-sided conversation.

"I work down at the Muldoy Chemicals site," Jimmy tells Cone. "We're putting in some wells down there to clean up the groundwater. I hear you worked at the mill before you retired."

Veau pushes open the screen door, and Jimmy stands to help her. She holds a tray that offers ham sandwiches and potato salad.

Back in their chairs, plates balanced on their laps, Veau helps the conversation along. "Cone started out as a doffer when he was nine, probably around 1915 or so, although we're not sure about his birth date, so we're not sure about his age. You probably got a century under your belt, don't you, Cone? He was a section boss when the mill quit running. They kept Cone on as a foreman in the warehouse, but it didn't pay as much, and Fairy Etta lost her job. She worked in the mill office. When Cone retired, he had sixty-five years in. They wouldn't give him credit for all sixty-five, though. They wouldn't admit to using child labor. Cone's told me a lot about the history of the mill. He was here during the general strike in 1934, when the National Guard was brought in." Cone shows no awareness. Veau holds a paper cup to his mouth and pushes a straw in. He sucks automatically. Then, using her fingers, she spreads moisturizer on his lips. "He gets real dry. He's always breathing through his mouth now. So, Jimmy, you like living on the pond?"

"Oh, yeah. That's why I bought the house, because of the pond."

"Orene and Buddy Connell lived in that house. Miz Orene was the last teacher at the old mill school. I grew up in a house right behind Vivia Wardlaw's, on a street that's not there anymore."

"You live in Atlanta now, I hear."

Veau, who has spent most of the summer at her Jekyll Island home, is sensitive enough not to mention second homes to those whose only homes are the size of her garage. She nods. "Sally Heckert called me this morning. Said she scared you to death."

Jimmy is caught once again with a loose name he has to put into place. "The lady at the tax office?" Jimmy remembers the little lady with the pizza, but he doesn't recall being scared.

"Sally said she told you True Padgett's scheme, that you hadn't heard about it. So she suggested I reassure you. Let you know that the pond will stay just as it is."

"Well, that's good to know." Jimmy has finished his sandwich and is hoping Veau will offer a second helping of the homemade potato salad. He remembers what Sally Heckert said about Veau having an opinion no one else would think of. "You think anything ought to be done with the pond?"

Veau rattles her ice cubes. "I wouldn't fill it in." She rattles her glass again, then blots Cone's mouth. "Dillehay Pond was built in 1847. The dam is granite, brought from farther up Stone Bowl Creek. That building you see crumbling down there, well, that's just a piece of what was. The thing was five stories tall. Brick. It was the largest mill in the South. And it produced yarn and osnaburg and linsey and moved right on into the twentieth century, making woolen cloth for uniforms in World War I and canvas in World War II. It closed down for a while right after World War II, which meant that some veterans came back to find their jobs didn't exist. But then a few years later, it reopened and made sheets and towels, stayed afloat through the sixties by switching to denim. Back in the early 1900s, Osilo County was the textile center of the South. This county had the highest per capita income in the state." Veau stops, takes a breath. "Listen. Monday night, there's a meeting of the Osilo County Historical Society. Now, don't start thinking up polite excuses yet."

Jimmy can't help but laugh.

"True Padgett will be there," she coaxes. "Probably collecting votes in a wheelbarrow."

Jimmy asks his question again. "What would you do with the pond?"

"I'd like to see the state buy it and turn it into a park." Her answer comes so assuredly that Jimmy knows she has a plan of her own, just like True has a plan. "I'd like to see some of the mill houses around it preserved as a historical site. I see it as a smaller version of Williamsburg or Old Salem."

Jimmy can't help himself. "You're kidding," he says.

Unoffended, Veau laughs. She is not ashamed of her vision. She started bucking trends as soon as she had her high-school diploma, refusing to enter the Miss South Carolina pageant, enrolling in college instead of cosmetology school, managing Kaye Clay's office and every man and machine working the quarry, marrying the man she loved in spite of the county-wide gossip that she married Billy Kaye for his money. Veau belongs to Atlanta now, but Osilo County belongs to her, and she plans to renovate it. "No, I'm not kidding. Like I said, a smaller version, much smaller. But I do see a preserved Carolina mill village open to tours, with B&Bs around the pond, and the pond open for recreation." And Veau does see it. She can close her eyes and see charter buses bringing tours to a welcome center at the old mill site, Fairy Etta's house reconstructed with the old fireplaces opened up, a brass marker at the Lamplight Cemetery acknowledging the graves of slaves, ski boats and rowing regattas on Dillehay Pond.

"These little mill towns were the high-water mark of capitalism," Veau says. She knows Jimmy won't attend the historical-society meeting, so she encapsulates her presentation for him. "An industrialist named Hammond Hutto bought this land, dammed Stone Bowl Creek, built a mill, built a whole town to house his workers, had a school operating inside the mill, lured farmers away from their land and into these new towns. Mills and mill towns changed our history." Veau finally notices Jimmy's empty plate. "Did you save room for dessert? Fairy Etta made banana pudding."

Veau returns with two huge bowls of pudding, puts a tiny taste into Cone's mouth, smiles at his loud smacking, turns to see Jimmy smiling, too. "Jimmy, did you know your house was built in 1870?"

"God, no," answers Jimmy.

Veau does not miss Jimmy at her meeting. She has quite an audience without him. In a county with no malls, no movie theaters, no Home Depot, and rare access to cable, Veau is entertainment. Most of the county's politicians are regulars. True Padgett and three county-council members and Walthourville's mayor circulate. Sally Heckert does not consider herself a politician. A member of the historical society, she baked the chocolate-chip cookies and the sour-cream pound cake. Veau counts forty-three of the society's sixty-one members and thirty-odd nonmembers. But her target audience consists of two women from the South Carolina Parks and Recreation Department.

The meeting is held in the auditorium of Stone Bowl Valley Elementary School, built by the WPA in the thirties, abandoned for the consolidated Osilo County Elementary School in the eighties. When the school board auctioned the old school, Veau bought it, telling her husband that the heart pine, old brick, copper wiring, and antique fittings were worth it. The principal's office is now the headquarters for the historical society, and meetings are held in what was the school's cafetorium. The school board had marketed the building to developers as a potential outlet mall and was disappointed when Veau was the only serious bidder. She appeased the board by restoring the playground, then deeding the fenced park back to the county. And Kaye Clay Park's appraised value gave her husband's company a sizable tax break that year.

"Good evening. My name is Vodelia Kaye. I want to welcome everyone here tonight to our meeting. I hope everyone has had a chance to enjoy the cookies and cakes and coffee, and we thank Sally and her hospitality committee for that. We have two special guests here this evening, Joanne Burnham and Amy Miller. I think you all had a chance to meet them. Following my presentation tonight, Joanne and Amy are going to explain the state's new Heritage Highway Project, which will both preserve important sites and encourage tourism to those sites. So let me get my little talk out of the way, and then we can learn something from Joanne and Amy."

True Padgett jumps out of his front-row seat to turn off the lights, to make himself look like part of the program, to focus attention on himself. Veau's first PowerPoint slide appears, showing the title "Mill Houses of Osilo County." "I'm going to talk about some of our old houses," she begins. "This is one of our mill houses, one of so very few left. They were built as part of the vision of the industrialist Hammond Hutto beginning in the 1840s. On nearly twelve thousand acres of land, Mr. Hutto built a dam and a mill and a whole town. He built almost three hundred houses."

She lets that number sink in while her eyes scan the interest of the two women from Columbia. She needs no notes. "Three architectural styles were used. This photo shows the chalet style. You can see the steep roof and the gingerbread trim in the V of the gables that give it that chalet look. The L shape made it a little larger than most of the mill houses. Mr. Hutto constructed these near the depot and the tracks, where visitors would see them. Of the seventy-three he built, fourteen stand, and only this one is still recognizable." Veau taps her keyboard, and Fairy Etta's house appears on the screen. "This is commonly called the shotgun style. It's a narrow house with the ridge line perpendicular to the front and a front porch as wide as the house. Many of these have had additions, making them L-shaped now. This is one of the few without additions or major remodeling. Most of Mr. Hutto's houses were of this style, but even these smaller houses had yards. Part of his technique to lure farm families was to make sure everyone had enough room for a garden plot and their own little yard. I have counted forty-three of these houses still standing, but of those, only nineteen reflect the original simple style. The third style, the least common, is the cottage style. These are wider than the shotgun houses but also small. The ridge line is parallel to the front, and the front porch is just half the width of the house. Mr. Hutto built only twenty-five of these, and most of those were destroyed in a fire during World War I. There are three left. The one in the photograph has been modified, as you can see, but it's the only one in good condition. Most of us are familiar with this house." Veau waves her fingers in front of the screen, showing off coral fingernails. "This is where LizAnne Dilly does our nails."

She clicks to a screen showing columns of figures. "Of Mr. Hutto's three hundred houses, sixty are left, but only twenty-one are still in recognizable or repairable condition. That's seven percent of the houses he built. That means that ninety-three percent are lost to us. And we don't want to lose more. The Osilo County Historical Society hopes to see some of these houses preserved. We want to see an expository museum explaining the history of Stone Bowl Creek Valley, starting with the Native Americans who carved bowls into the granite to use for grinding. Dillehay Pond offers centuries of history. It can be enjoyed as a place to appreciate that heritage, as a place of beauty, as a recreational site."

And then Veau puts her two unprepared guests on the spot. "And I am hoping Joanne and Amy can tell us how their Heritage Highway

Project might help make all that happen."

When everyone is gone, Veau turns out all the lights in the building and stands in the foyer watching moonlight pour in through the transom over the wide front door. She attended school here from first grade to sixth. Into the pine floors, memories have worn their tracks. Teachers hurrying up and down the one wide corridor were announced by their tapping heels. Students and teachers both cocked an ear when Mr. Lamar's leather shoes came squishing down the hall. The day passed not by the clock but by the sounds from the hallway—the patter of the first-graders heading to recess, the marching of the third-graders, the careful steps of the sixth-grade girls out of step with the boisterous stomping of the sixth-grade boys. Hearing Mr. Joe, the janitor, swish his push broom meant that it was almost three o'clock, almost time for the bell.

Veau heads to the room still labeled with a brass 3, once Miss Lemon's third-grade classroom, where Veau opened her first geography text. The remodeled room is now Veau's bedroom, where she stays when she is back home. Few people in Osilo County know about Veau's bedroom in the old school building. They assume she stays with her sister or her cousin or at the Holiday Inn Express on the New Highway. Veau keeps the door to room 3 locked.

Billy laughed uproariously when Veau told him what she was doing with the old school.

"You have your home on the fairway at Jekyll, you have your cabin up at Highlands, and I have my getaway back home." She showed him her calculations, the cost of her staying at the Holiday Inn Express, the tax advantage of restoring a historic building. She could not explain to him the need she has for Osilo County, a place that needs her, enfolds her, in a way that Buckhead and Jekyll Island never will.

"I thought we were gonna tear it down, sell the flooring and stuff like that," Billy argued, just to tease her. Veau fascinated him. None of his friends' wives would ever have thought of living in a school.

"It was built by WPA craftsmen," she told him. "The brickwork alone is art worth saving. Have you ever looked at the brick arch over the front door?"

"Well, I've never made love in a classroom," Billy said.

Veau chose room 3 because it was across the hall from the girls' bathroom, where a garden tub and shower were added and new tile flooring laid. The cloakroom that was shared by rooms 3 and 4 is now a galley kitchen. Her king-sized bed, in the middle of the room, situated so she wakes up with a view through the wall of windows, is dwarfed by the space, by the nine-foot ceilings. What was called "the book closet," where Miss Lemon kept workbooks and smelly mimeographed papers and chalk and the boxes of Animal Crackers she handed out for the slightest achievement, now holds Veau's clothes. Miss Lemon's old desk is her headboard. The blackboard still hangs along one wall. Vodelia sleeps well here.

# Chapter 11

## Cone

CONE DUFFY IS DYING in the house in which he was born, in the town where he worked all his life, in the time allotted for him to die, a time when dying is the job he was assigned.

Seven days old, Cone lay at his mama's feet on a blanket while she put in her hours in the weave room. His developing vision first focused on the warp threads, thousands, laced one by one by his mother, a "draw-in hand," who counted to get the pattern right. This was the sky he knew, occasionally darkened when her foot gently pulled him under her skirt, hiding him from the men who walked through with clipboards. His cries could not compete with the mill noise, so his stomach learned to wait for the subtle changes in sound, when his mama would take advantage of the moment when a harness was ready for the loom, or when she needed more yarn, or when she pretended that she did, so she could button him inside her shirtwaist to nurse. Old enough to walk, he was banished to the spinning room, where his aunt Jolee kept an eye on him, where a little boy could go unnoticed among the barefoot doffer boys paid to climb the looms and change bobbins. The mill school took children at seven. Cone's mama lied and sent him at five. Let out of school, he ran to the spinning room and swept or ran errands, was paid in crackers and pennies. He hoped to look useful enough to get on as a doffer as soon as one of the boys got old enough to move on to creeler or folder or card hand or got hurt. When he was nine, the McElveen family moved to Burlington to work in the mill there, vacating eight positions and leaving the spinning room short two doffers. Cone brought home two dollars and fifty cents every week. He didn't mind jumping into a barrel to hide when the child-labor people came through. He was used to being hidden.

Then he had to figure which job he wanted because where you started was where you ended up—picker room or weave room or finishing room. His hero was his cousin, muscular six-foot-one Glad Duffy, Aunt Jolee's youngest, who taught Cone to play football by tossing wooden bobbins at him, who taught him to swim in the pond, who had his own rowboat and took Cone fishing. Glad was a loom fixer, so Cone wanted to become a loom fixer. He got his chance when Glad went off to fight in the Great War.

Cone was the youngest loom fixer anyone could remember, though he had lied about his age so many times no one believed him now. He just wanted to hold the spot for Glad. When he heard Glad was back, Cone went right to Aunt Jolee's house on Cemetery Road.

Glad was sitting on the front-porch steps framed by Aunt Jolee's hydrangea bushes, a beer bottle in his hand in broad daylight. He did not recognize Cone but shook the hand Cone extended.

"I just come by to tell you welcome home. And to tell you Mama wants you over to dinner on Sunday." Glad wasn't looking at him. Cone turned to see what he was watching, caught a glimpse of Dillehay Pond between the houses. "We can go fishing maybe, after dinner," Cone went on. "I took care of your boat. I got it chained to a tree." Cone sat down next to the silent man, trying to narrow the mysterious distance between them. "You glad to be back?" When there was no response,

Cone nodded in answer to his own question. Then he made his announcement. "You know, I been holding your job for you." Glad pulled in a deep breath but said nothing. "That's all I been doing all this time. Just holding it for you. It's yours."

Glad finally turned to look into his face, and Cone was sorry when he did. Cone had never seen a face so void of expression, a face that was not happy or sad or bored or exhausted or angry. "So you're Cone, I guess," the face said. "You want a beer?"

Cone was shocked. Glad's beer might be excused, an indulgence granted to a returning war veteran, but if Cone were to be seen drinking a beer right here on Cemetery Road, it would cost him his job, the job he had saved for Glad. Cone could not imagine not caring about rules, so he assumed that Glad had just forgotten, that maybe army rules were different. Cone stood. "I guess I'll just get on back home. I just come by to, you know, to tell you that."

A few seconds passed, long enough for Cone to reach the sidewalk, before Glad spoke. "To tell me what?"

"About the job. Your job. I just been holding it for you. There ain't a lot of jobs, you know. It's hard to get on, even for the soldiers coming back. So I wanted you to know that your job—"

"I ain't staying here." Glad did not get up and go inside, just looked into his brown bottle. But it was as though he left.

Cone stayed on at the mill. When times got bad, when they made people handle more than one machine, sometimes more than one job, he did whatever there was to do. A couple of times, he had to work in the spinning room, even though that was just for women. During the general strike in '34, when the National Guard encircled the mill, Cone and his widowed mother were not only out of work with no income but put out of their home with forty-eight hours' notice, since it was mill owned and they were not mill employees when they were on strike. The only good that came out of the strike, that Cone could ever see, was that people pushed to own their own houses. Cone bought the house where he was born.

He had moved up, to homeowner. He moved up within the mill,

from job to job, willing to change when ownership changed but never leaving. Now, unable to swallow solid food, anchored to a wheelchair, Cone feels he is still moving up, moving up now to a life beyond this one. His job now is to be patient, to wait for the good Lord to relieve him from this job he's been holding.

Unable to speak, he has tuned out the voices around him, ignored like buzzing flies, and instead lets his mind receive a broadcast of memories. He remembers his little girl, her third birthday party, relishing it over and over because she never had a fourth, dying of diphtheria. Cone relives the party, tastes the cake, hears the new baby doll cry. He never relives the funeral. He pictures Glad in uniform in the Christmas parade, hears the marching band. He pitches baseball games, sees the chalked numbers on the scoreboard, waves at Fairy Etta so the other girls will know the star pitcher is hers. He turns the ignition of his brand-new '55 Chevy, takes Fairy Etta to the Hilltop Drive-In Theatre, hears the movie through the speakers hanging in the car's windows. When Jimmy Steverson introduces himself, Cone looks at the young man on his front porch, and then there are several men on the porch, and the Philco is turned up loud for the fourth game of the World Series, and they let out a whoop when they find that Fairy Etta is pouring beer out of her iced-tea pitcher, and she winks at Cone and goes back in to fix ham sandwiches.

Only Fairy Etta knows he can still communicate. He can look into her eyes and make her smile, just as he did all those decades ago. Cone and some of his friends had heard of the dances put on by the mill in Augusta, where a boat took the mill workers up the long Augusta Canal to a dance pavilion. Cone and his buddies managed to crash the party, pretending they knew everyone there. Cone sat next to Fairy Etta, still pretending, saying, "So, how are you doing? Haven't run into you in a while."

Fairy Etta looked at him, a challenging look right into his eyes, and Cone was sure she was going to give him up. After letting him suffer for one long second, she couldn't help smiling at his eager face. "We'll have to make up for lost time, won't we? You'll have to promise to dance every dance with me."

When Cone could talk, he liked to say that the good Lord had treated him well. "He led me right to Fairy Etta, you know. The good Lord thought I had waited too long to get married. I was thirty-nine, you know, and Fairy Etta not even twenty. See, I won this contest, won five dollars. So me and my buddies decided to have a big time, to take the trolley over to Georgia, to the King Mill over in Augusta, so we could ride that canal boat and go to that dance we had heard about. Now, I couldn't of gone without that five dollars, and that five dollars was put right into my hand. It wasn't money I worked for, it was just put right into my hand."

When Fairy Etta is changing him, bathing him, putting food into his feeding tube, she does not look at what she is doing but right into his eyes, and he speaks right back into her eyes. The last thing she does every night, after checking his oxygen tank, is to take his face in her hands, let him look into her eyes, let him say good-night to her.

Jimmy is climbing into his truck when he hears his name called. He looks toward Mayme's house, remembers that she's not home, that she's off at the VFW fish fry with Bonus. Then he sees Fairy Etta in front of the abandoned house that stands between her home and Bonus's extra lot, down in the dirt, on her knees.

Jimmy jogs the short distance. "You okay?"

"I'm okay. A couple of my girls got out."

Jimmy peeks under the house, spots two of Fairy Etta's chickens pecking at the ground. "Want me to crawl under there?"

"No. You'll just scare 'em. They'll come to me in a minute. But I need you to go in and sit with Cone, case I have to chase 'em."

Jimmy does not want to sit with Cone, but Fairy Etta keeps him supplied with fresh eggs. "Well, I was just heading to Columbia. But I can stay a little while."

Jimmy doesn't mind the first hour. He parks Cone's wheelchair in front of the TV, and they watch the last few innings of the Braves game. Jimmy offers Cone water every few minutes and is surprised each time the inert man pulls liquid through the straw. "Had enough there, Cone? What you wanna watch now? How about the news?" Jimmy would like to know the time but doesn't want Cone to see him checking his watch, so he lets *Headline News* tell him the time. He has been sitting with Cone for over two hours when finally he hears Fairy Etta in the backyard fussing at her bad girls.

Jimmy will be late for Lakeishia's party, and Lakeishia doesn't want her guests fashionably late, she wants them on time. He speeds to Totch's, worried because it's Saturday afternoon and Totch is usually out of barbecue by now. Jimmy forgets to speak the language. "Totch, you sell just the meat?"

"Teddy bear weighs a pound," Totch tells him. "You figure a pound for a guy, probably half a pound for the ladies."

Jimmy leaves juggling two five-pound Styrofoam containers of barbecued pork and ten teddy bears. He drops nine of the bears into Totch's barrel, decides to keep one. At Lakeishia's, he presents her with the bear, hoping to distract her from commenting on how late he is. It doesn't work.

"And where have you been? We're on the second batch of Margaritas, and you missed Will teaching Mike how to do a cannonball."

"Sorry. There's this old man lives across the street. His wife asked me to sit with him for a few minutes."

Lakeishia leads him to the kitchen, puts a drink in his hand. "Some emergency?"

Jimmy smiles, knowing how his explanation will sound. "Her chickens got out."

"Her chickens?"

"Yep. She keeps chickens. Brings me fresh eggs. So I thought I should help her out."

Lakeishia leads him onto her deck. "Jimmy's here!" she announces. "He was held up by a chicken emergency. Time to eat!"

Lakeishia puts the teddy bear into a casserole dish and adds a serving spoon. "That's bear," she explains deadpan. "They eat bear down in Osilo County."

Later, they inaugurate Lakeishia's new hot tub, the reason for the celebration. One-hundred-and-two-degree water gurgling around him, tequila gurgling within him, Jimmy becomes talkative. He explains the teddy bear terminology. Lakeishia is enthralled, Margaret Mead discovering the Samoans. "And what's iced tea?"

"Key chain."

"Bottled water?"

"Totch doesn't stock bottled water. A Coke is a yo-yo."

"Diet Coke?"

"Can't get it at Totch's."

Carl is slowly sinking into the foam. Jimmy sits on the edge of the hot tub, gets a grip on Carl's biceps, and pulls him up until his nose is above the surface.

"You have rescued me," Carl says, though he remains limp.

"I'd be unemployed without you."

"And I do not want a body in my new hot tub," Lakeishia says.

"I am way too hot," Carl complains. "I need to get back in the pool."

"It's too damn hot for a hot tub in July, anyway."

"You get Carl in the pool, Jimmy. I'll get you another drink. What is that in Osilese? A postcard?"

Jimmy helps Carl stand. "A postcard's a beer. I don't know what they'd call a Margarita."

"That would be a report card," Carl announces. "No, a punch card. Get it? Punch?"

Jimmy and Carl float side by side in the pool. Lakeishia executes a perfect jackknife, comes up between them.

"Lakeishia, how can you afford a hot tub and a pool?" Carl asks. "Embezzlement comes to mind."

"Were I planning a career in embezzlement, I would be working for Bill Gates, love, not KDR."

"Good point," Carl concedes.

"The pool was here when I bought the house. A pool adds no value to the sale price," Lakeishia says, beginning a tutorial. Carl looks at Jimmy, rolls his eyes. "Which means it's a freebie when buying. When

I sell, it will add to the appeal of the house, and it will give me plea-sure in the meantime. Jimmy, you need to rent out your little house and buy a bigger one. I've already explained to you that you need a mortgage deduction."

"Yes, ma'am. What's the tax advantage of a hot tub?"

"None. I just needed to spend the money I siphoned out of the payroll escrow before Carl noticed it."

"Would Carl ever notice it?" Jimmy asks.

"Actually, yes, he would," Lakeishia answers. "He's like a lizard. He looks like he's asleep, but then the tongue comes out and snares a bug." Carl obligingly extends his tongue. Lakeishia grabs Jimmy's float to hold her audience in place. "Jimmy, I'm worried about you living down there. I heard you telling Jamil about the guy with the gun? Doing a repop?"

Jimmy looks away, lets a few beats pass before answering. "I had the good sense to decline the invitation."

Carl speaks, sounding surprisingly sober. "You shouldn't be the object of such invitations, Jimmy. Rent that wigwam out, leave your boat at the dock, reserve yourself fishing rights, get back up here in time for the Carolina-Clemson party." They stop to applaud Mike's cannonball. "Do fresh eggs taste any different?" Carl asks.

# Chapter 12

## *Vivia*

VIVIA WARDLAW SEWS.

Jimmy walks across the street to the Wardlaw house to deliver a gift for Joelle. He is pleased to find a sturdy metal door to knock on, tired of rattling Miz Mayme's screen. Joelle opens the door, releasing crisp, cold air and a mechanical hum.

"Are you coming to visit us, Mr. Jimmy?"

"Well, yeah. I was hoping to get to meet your grandma."

Over the hum, a smooth, mature voice invites him in. "Come on in, Jimmy."

Jimmy steps into an interior that does not match the mill-house exterior. He finds himself in a living room converted to a business, a room as unexpected as Miz Mayme's giant kitchen with its bubbling sourdough jars. He stands within a U-shaped counter. From the smooth Formica surface rise walls of shelves where bolts of fabric stand upright like giant books, a library of color.

Within her U-shaped work area, Vivia Wardlaw is a pale gray dot, almost invisible until she swivels on her wheeled stool and offers her hand to Jimmy. "Well, I am sure glad to meet you. I hate I haven't had you over yet."

"Joelle told me you were in the middle of a big project. And I won't stay. I just brought something for Joelle." He holds up a small gift bag. "I think I might have hurt Joelle's feelings the other day, and I didn't mean to. So, anyway, I thought I'd come by and apologize."

Vivia stands and motions toward the sofa, neatly positioned at the opening of the U, its striped blue-and-gold damask matching the drapes at the window behind it. "Sit down, sit down," she insists. "Joelle, honey, what do you say?"

"Thank you, Mr. Jimmy."

Joelle perches on the stool and peeks into the bag, rooting through the ribbon curls supplied by the Hallmark store. Jimmy tries to make sense of the marvelous machinery arrayed behind her. At the top of the U, a Packard Bell monitor sits beside a Pfaff sewing machine, linked by a spool rack spitting colors at the beige plastic surrounding it. The shelves of thread lead Jimmy's eyes hypnotically left to right, as though reading a line of type—a row of reds arranged from the darkest wine to baby-girl pink, a row of greens from magnolia leaves to watery mint, a row of yellows from sunflower to butter. The left arm of the U is Vivia's cutting area, draped now with a stiff see-through fabric weighted with a T square. On the right arm of the U, Jimmy recognizes a scanner, though he has never seen one with a Singer label. Jimmy has used scanners hundreds of times to make computers swallow maps and well logs and pictures, but how this technology relates to sewing machines he has no idea.

Joelle removes each item from the gift bag individually. She positions the box of stationery on her knees, and on top of that she places the pen and the book of stamps. Then she folds the gift bag and slides it beneath the stationery box.

"I thought you might have somebody to write to," Jimmy says. "And I'm sorry if I hurt your feelings."

Finally, Joelle smiles. She doesn't look at him when she speaks. "Well, you didn't know."

"No, you didn't have any way of knowing, Jimmy," Vivia adds.

The teal blue screen on the monitor and the columns of icons taunt Jimmy. "You good with Windows?" he asks Vivia. "I just got a Gateway, and I keep losing things in Windows. I'm used to a Mac."

"Folders," says Vivia. She bounces off the sofa and clicks the mouse a few times. "It puts things in folders."

"That's what it's done, I think. When Joelle came over the other night, I was going crazy looking for a list, and I'm still looking for it."

"Use this Explorer thing. You probably don't know if you're looking for a file or a folder. It'll name a file after the first word you type, if you don't remember to give it a name."

Jimmy shakes his head. "I thought Explorer was a game."

"Well, no, the games is under Accessories."

Joelle giggles. "It's got some card games. Did you ever find your list?"

"Not on the Gateway," he admits. "About one in the morning, I admitted defeat and dragged the Mac out of the closet. So, Vivia, is all this stuff in the manual?"

"Well, now, I don't know. I think you have to be on that Internet thing to get the manual. I wish it come with a manual. Shoot, even a microwave comes with a manual."

"What does all this do?"

"Well, now, I print out my bills with the computer. I found out that people will pay a bill and won't argue if it's all printed out and looks real, like a bill you'd get in the mail. I used to hand people a dress and say, 'Three hundred dollars,' and they'd try to jew me down. Now, I hand them this printed-up bill with 'Invoice' in bold sixteen-point at the top, and folks just write a check. But the computer's mostly to get the embroidery and the monograms on." She opens a disk tray. The labels on the floppies look like coloring-book pictures of ABCs and farm animals and flowers, showing the designs they hold. "And the scanner, well, now, it lets me take a picture and turn it into embroidery. Then the machine can do the design."

Jimmy is ready to leave then, ready to say he has to get back to his supper, ready to escape a household where "jew" is a verb, but his eyes snag on the garment rack. "Did you make all those?" he asks Vivia. "Is that what you do?"

"Yes, that's what I do. Joelle, honey, hold one up for Jimmy to see."

Joelle balances her stack of gifts on top of the computer monitor and pulls a dress off the rack, child-sized but adult-styled, stiff with ruffles. To Jimmy, it looks as comfortable as papier-mâché, and he pities the child who has to wear it. But the bolts and the cutting table and the machinery make him appreciate the labor involved. The dress is lavender, but lavender cut from three different bolts, cuffed and collared in white and shiny with beads the size of birdseed.

"Pageant dresses, mostly," Vivia explains. "Right now, I'm up to my elbows because of this thing coming up in Florida, the Little Miss Orange Glow and the Littlest Miss Orange Glow."

Jimmy has witnessed two beauty pageants. In high school, he was in the audience to encourage a friend competing for the title of Miss Jaycee County Fair. And he endured the entire Miss America pageant one night to keep his mother company while she recovered from a hysterectomy. He cannot picture children in pageants. "These are for little girls?" he asks, just to be sure he understands.

"That's mostly what I do for."

"Meema made Miss South Carolina's dress two years ago," announces Joelle.

"Well, now, that was a pretty one." Vivia pivots on the sofa, points to what little wall space is left in the room, where framed photographs of her successes hang. Three-by-fives and five-by-sevens of little girls crowned with sparkling plastic tiaras surround a ten-by-twelve portrait in a gold frame. "That's the one," Vivia says.

Jimmy looks up to see a model-quality beauty whose thick brunette hair seems grown purposely to nestle a crown, her sculpted body crossed by the Miss South Carolina ribbon, in what looks to Jimmy like a plain white dress. "I made it so's to show her figure," Vivia says. "She's a tall girl, and she's real athletic, so she's got these pretty little muscles. And of course, to make her coloring stand out. She's part

Cherokee, and I wanted that beautiful skin to shine." Jimmy looks again at the photo and realizes that Vivia's dress has done those things. He has looked at the girl, not the dress. "So I used all white, and I made the dress in a stretch fabric with no sheen to it, so her skin would shine by contrast. It's just a sheath, really. I pulled in a pleat right at the hipbone sarong-style and put a white satin rose there."

When Jimmy leaves, he still doesn't know if he should address her as Vivia or Mrs. Wardlaw. He avoids calling Mayme by name because he doesn't know whether to put the Miz in front of it or not. While he heats his bottled spaghetti sauce, he makes the decision to address his neighbors by their first names. They are all adults.

Jimmy is astounded that people will come out so early for a yard sale. Mayme shows him the ad she ran: "Yard sale. 610 Randleman Rd. Sat. 7-noon. No early birds."

She has him hauling furniture onto the street at five in the morning. "Oh, they'll be here. They'll be here early. They was here yesterday knocking on the door of an empty house. Dealers. I saw 'em down here, and I let one of 'em have the stove."

On MaryBeth's porch sits the upholstered furniture—a sofa, a glider rocker, one armchair. The pieces seem to match, all faded to a sad beige. Yet piece by piece, they sell. At six, the kitchen table and chairs are sold to the first early birds. At nine forty-five, Jimmy loads the last heavy piece, the glider rocker, into the back of a Suburban. He hands Mayme the twenty dollars it brought and begs for a coffee break.

"Honey, you run on if you need to. We can handle it from here," answers Mayme.

"I'll be back. Just let me get some coffee. And I don't think I ever ate breakfast."

At home, he checks his answering machine, knowing it will bark a reminder: "You promised you'd be in this game. You're the quarterback, and you haven't made a practice yet."

The KDR staff is playing a team of DEHP staffers on a field at the university campus. He pours coffee into his travel mug, puts two Nutri-Grain bars in his shirt pocket, and heads back out the door, where he is greeted by a vision. Vivia's porch is crowded with little girls. Actually, it's crowded because of their pink dresses. The five girls stand apart, spaced like open umbrellas. They seem to be dressed to match until the details of lace and beads and seaming become apparent. A woman comes to Vivia's door and calls one child in, for a fitting, Jimmy guesses. He remembers Vivia's offhand mention of a three-hundred-dollar charge and realizes that at least fifteen hundred dollars in gross income stands between Vivia's porch swing and her rocker. Jimmy waves at the little girls. They don't wave back. All of them watch him suspiciously as he makes his way back to the yard sale at MaryBeth's house.

"Your meema's busy this morning," he greets Joelle.

"Do you think they'll ever learn to be nice?" asks Joelle. "They are all little witches. They get in there and insult each other. They whisper? Stuff like, 'Her knees are bony' or 'Her ears stick out.' And they talk bad about the dresses, too, even though Meema is right there. Stuff like, 'Did she pick that out?' or 'Is she for real in that?' Like they don't all look like they're from another planet, you know?"

Jimmy is chuckling. He pays for a lasagna pan and two James Patterson novels he had told Mayme to set aside for him.

"Jimmy, I'd give 'em to you, but this ain't my stuff. You know that?"

Jimmy nods. "Doesn't MaryBeth want to keep any of this? For when she gets out of jail?"

"No place to keep it, I reckon. Karen owns the house."

"They sisters?"

"No. MaryBeth baby-sat Karen's kids for years. When MaryBeth lost the house, Karen bought it back for her, let her keep living here. But MaryBeth's one of those that can't get their act together, you know? Here, she got this house free, inherited from her granddaddy and grandma. They was mill people, the Boatwrights. Then she borrowed on it, couldn't pay, lost the house, ended up paying rent to the bank for a house she should of owned. But MaryBeth can't hold onto nothing. She couldn't keep a job. Worked at the laundromat. Lost that 'cause money was missing from the machines. Waitressed at the Kountry Kookin. I heard she got fired from that 'cause she kept calling in sick. Then she started keeping kids here. And she was good at that. You'd hear 'em laughing down here. You'd hear 'em singing. She'd put a wading pool out back and have the sprinkler going. Then she started them parades. Every Friday. Had a parade down the block. Had them beating on coffee cans like they was drums, and marching. Everybody came out on the porch to see. God, they was cute. Fairy Etta would even get Cone on the porch in his wheelchair to watch ever' week. MaryBeth had a way with kids. But she kept on getting in trouble. God knows, Karen's the best thing ever happened to her."

"So Karen will rent the house out now?"

"Well, I don't wanna speak for Karen."

Jimmy smiles at Mayme's downshift from between-you-and-me to evasion.

"Jimmy, there's two things left I need you for. You ain't gotta do 'em today. I bought the refrigerator, and Vivia bought that funny-looking table." Mayme points to a tiny piece of mahogany, its tabletop just a foot square.

Jimmy sighs. "I'm supposed to be in Columbia in two hours for a football game."

"Football game? In the summertime?"

"People I work with. It's just something we do for fun. We play football 'cause all you need is the ball. Anyway, I can't haul stuff right now. But I'll take Vivia's table down to my house and bring it to her when I get back. And I'll take care of your refrigerator tomorrow."

Mayme nods. "Bonus got a dolly. I'll get him to put it up on the porch here."

Jimmy picks up the table and runs.

"What do we do? Can we tackle her?"

"If she's gonna play, she must know she'll get tackled." Carl voices the obvious.

Jimmy stays out of the conversation. The DEHP team includes a woman, and the KDR team doesn't know what to do about that. They huddle around the boxes of bolenos Jimmy has provided.

"I ain't playing tag football. I hate tag football. We always tackle."

"She's an athlete. Runs marathons. Runs that thing in Charleston where they go over the Cooper River Bridge."

"She's probably gonna be wide receiver then."

"That's fine with me." Jimmy finally enters the conversation. "I won't be on the field when she's out there, so I won't have to worry about her."

As it turns out, no one has to worry about tackling Jana Hardaway. Twice Jana catches the ball lobbed by DEHP's quarterback, and twice she runs faster than anyone else, straight over the pale chalk line that marks the end zone. DEHP wins 18 to 6, which means that KDR has to buy the beer and burgers. They fill up five tables at a Five Points restaurant.

"Somebody needs to learn how to kick," Carl points out.

"Maybe Jana kicks like she runs," suggests Jimmy.

"Jana can't kick too well," says Jana herself from two tables down.

A couple of pitchers later, the talk finally leaves football.

"But the plane of the fault we can't define, not without some seismic, and we don't have the money for that. But we wrote up a paper about it."

"We got the first samples in from those USGS wells down on the coast. We got the contract for the palynology."

Following a conversation means changing tables. Jimmy ends up talking to Jana across a pitcher. "What do you do at DEHP?"

"I head up the Water Quality Division."

The two KDR guys on either side of Jimmy whistle. "In deeper," one says.

"That's an expression," Jimmy explains. "All you guys at DEHP, we say you're 'in deep.' For the bosses, the division chiefs, we say you're 'in deeper.' "

"Inside DEHP, we say the same things," Jana admits. "I'm new at the boss stuff. I transferred up from the coastal office."

Pitcher number three has Jimmy speaking candidly. "That's unusual, the transfer thing. Most everybody I've ever known at DEHP leaves and goes into consulting before they have a chance to get promoted."

Jana nods. "Yep. We're the training ground. We're a government agency, can't compete with the big consulting companies. Lower salaries. No fancy equipment. So we get somebody with a B.S. or M.S. in geology. They work for us and write their dissertation on the weekends. Then they take their Ph.D. and their three years of DEHP experience and all the contacts they made and go to work for you guys at twice the salary."

"So how come you didn't do that?"

"Got a child to take care of. I need to be home at night. I know about the consulting world. I worked it for a while. Saw more of airports and highways than I did my little girl. DEHP will never pay me well, but I'm home at six." She changes the subject. "I hear you're running the show at the Muldoy drill site."

Jimmy nods. "We're still pulling up data now. Once we've got the plume defined and the models ready and get squared away with you guys on the remediation program, then I'll still be down there to see about the monitoring wells. So I'll be there two, three years. I bought a house down there."

"I heard. Right on that old millpond."

"If you know about Dillehay Pond, then maybe you can help me with something. I've been hearing this rumor going around Osilo County. Something about some state project having to do with the pond, maybe filling it in."

Jana lets out a whoop. Two DEHP guys at the next table overhear and chuckle. They explain to the next table, and pretty soon three tables of DEHP geologists are laughing. One raises his mug. "To True! To True and his rumors!"

Jimmy looks at Jana. "So it's just a rumor?"

Jana sighs. She puts down her mug. "Damn if I'm drinking to True Padgett. My boss insists that I handle the man's calls personally. And he calls all the time. And drops in." She shakes her head. "As for your pond, Jimmy, you need to get the DEHP report and read it. Come to think of it, didn't you guys at KDR do the field work for us on that?"

Carl answers. "Jimmy did most of it. But he won't read anything unless it's written in the mud on his truck."

"Well, unfortunately, it's that report that put fuel into True's fire," Jana says. "Basically, we concluded that there isn't anything practical to do. A bunch of heavy metals are there, all right, in a two-foot-thick layer of sediment, but they're already covered by clean sediments, and they aren't going anywhere. Most of the mills shut down in, what, the forties? We recommended that fish from the pond not be eaten, that the water be monitored. Signs went up about the fish. We sample the water every six months." She takes a swallow from her mug. "Now, our mistake was that we wrote a very thorough report. In saying there isn't anything practical to do, we talked about the options. Now, do you remember that Carolina bay out at the Nuclear Dynamics site? The little one where the alligator lived?"

"Oh, yeah," Jimmy nods. "Full of some kind of solvent, but that alligator sure liked it."

"Well, that little bay was actually filled in. Clay-capped, then mounded over, so rainwater runs off, doesn't infiltrate. So, anyway, that was cited in the report as one way to treat such a site."

"But that was a tiny pond. The pool at the gym is bigger. Dillehay Pond is over three hundred acres."

"Thank you." Jana salutes. "But True didn't read it that way. In the report, we brought up the little bay mostly as an example of an impractical option. True Padgett decided to consider it a suggestion. And when he comes by my office and I explain how it's impractical and unnecessary, he wants to know why we don't just vacuum up the pollutants."

Jimmy has to laugh at that.

Someone says, "Why don't you, Jana? Sounds like woman's work to me!"

"I'd fire you," Jana tells him, smiling, "but I know you're quitting in two months anyway. The only fun in being a boss is firing people, and nobody stays around DEHP long enough to get fired." She takes another swallow. "True Padgett picked out that one stupid paragraph that I wish to God we had never put in the report," she tells Jimmy. "You ever met him?"

Jimmy shakes his head.

"That's the bad part. He drives me nuts, but he's the nicest guy in the world. What other state legislator drops by the DEHP office? To my knowledge, not a single one has ever set foot in the place. But True sent me flowers when I got promoted. And when he comes by, he asks about my daughter by name, and brings me my favorite candy."

"What's your favorite candy?" Jimmy asks.

"Snickers bars, the little ones."

"I'll start dropping by with Snickers bars," promises Jimmy, "and pictures of my dock."

"Jimmy, tell her about that rich lady, the one who wants to build Colonial Williamsburg on Poison Pond," Carl says.

Jana fakes a look of alarm. "There's another nut down there? Please don't give her my name."

Within her Formica U, her sewing machine humming, Vivia is comfortable. She has always sewn. Her grandmother taught her how to sew, on the front porch of this house, sitting in rockers hand-stitching seams. When Vivia was eight years old, she asked Santa to bring her a pair of pinking shears. They were under the tree on Christmas morning, between her Tiny Tears doll and her stocking filled with oranges and ribbon candy and the big, oily nuts her daddy called "nigger toes" and cracked for her.

She made her wedding dress, real white silk from Chinese mulberry worms and lace tatted in France and Cuba. She and her husband moved to an apartment in Columbia, near Fort Jackson, where he was in training. He had to stay on base during maneuvers, and she was alone a lot.

The apartment complex was not like Randleman Road. Seventeen duplexes meant thirty-four apartments. Every day, someone moved in. Every day, someone moved out. Vivia watched from her window, saw other people's sofas and tables come and go.

She walked up the sidewalk to the corner, where the street of duplexes met the four-lane, a river of trucks. She walked back, wondering why it was so muddy here, wondering why there were no flowers anywhere. On Randleman Road, marigolds would be blooming out front and tomatoes would be growing out back.

One morning, she heard the mailman clang shut her mailbox. She stepped onto the stoop of the duplex, hoping to say good morning, but the mailman was already at the next duplex. Vivia pulled two envelopes from the black metal mailbox. Her neighbor's door opened. A man came out wearing jeans, shirtless. Rolled magazines were jammed into his mailbox. He tugged at them to get them out, said "Aw, shit" when an envelope sailed to his feet. He picked it up, glanced at Vivia, and went back indoors.

Having seen the man who would not speak to her, Vivia began to worry about the wall that separated them. She stayed away from it. Touching the wall was touching him. She could hear his movements, hear him close his refrigerator door, hear him flush the toilet. He was so close. She tried not to listen to his sounds. Then she realized that he could hear her sounds. She closed cabinet doors carefully. She dreaded flushing the toilet. She stepped into the closet to blow her nose.

She didn't realize how long she had stayed in the apartment until her husband came home from his field exercise and found her. No groceries, mail spilling from the tiny box, her face pale and her hands shaky from a diet of tap water and vanilla wafers. "What's wrong with the goddamn toilet?" he yelled. He bought groceries, arranged for milk to be delivered, told her about calling cabs, left her a map of the city, wrote a list of neighbors he knew from the base. The next time he came home, she was under the desk, asleep. He took her picture before he woke her. He brought her home to her family, to Randleman

Road, and showed her parents the picture of their daughter in her knee-hole bed. After the baby was born, checks started coming, U.S. government allotment checks, a percentage of his pay. They always came, but he never did.

Vivia is easing the fabric through slowly. Netting will pucker if she goes too fast. When she hears the knock on the door, she opens her mouth to call Joelle. Then she remembers that Joelle is at Sunday school.

Vivia doesn't like to open the door. It's a solid door, steel, fireproof. There is a peephole through it and a deadbolt on it.

She finishes her seam, smooths it, weights the tiny petticoat with her pinking shears. Then she goes to the door and peers through the peephole. She sees a man standing on the other side of her door. She will not open the door to a man. She goes back to her netting. She puts satin binding on the hem. Otherwise, it will scratch the little girl's knees.

Jimmy hears Vivia's sewing machine, but no one comes to the door. He leaves the mahogany table on her porch.

Front porches are a new phenomenon to Jimmy. He is just learning to make use of his. He can take machinery apart for cleaning and oiling and leave it there for days. He doesn't have to worry about things getting stolen. Today, he is cleaning his logging unit. Veneered in dried mud, it looks like a piece of square pottery. The clasp is completely hidden. He had logged a just-finished section of well Friday when a piece of drill stem fell into the slurry trough, sending a mud shower in all directions. Jimmy is glad he ignored the computer guys at KDR, who wanted his laptop hooked up to the logging unit, so the well logs would go right into the computer, bypassing the scanner. Mike Livingston, KDR's computer guru, attended a conference and found out about the software and has been after Jimmy ever since. Mike, though, has never been to a drill site and doesn't understand that the software is for use by oil companies whose equipment is safe inside air-conditioned trailers. Jimmy knows better. He can get the dirt out of this gadget, but he can't rescue a Pentium chip from drilling mud.

Joelle asks her question from the sidewalk: "Do you know there are fractals?"

Jimmy laughs. "I've heard of fractals. I didn't know I'd be talking about them today, so I haven't read up."

Joelle sighs. She bites her lip. "Well, it's like a shape. It's like the world is broken into funny pieces."

Jimmy nods.

Joelle sighs again. "Well, I think that's all I know."

"Well, I think that's all I know about fractals, too, Joelle."

Joelle nods. "I've got a book from the library. But anyway, Meema wants you to come over for dessert. She made a cheesecake. She puts walnuts in the crust."

"Sounds good. When?"

"Now, I think."

"Let me wash my hands. Can I look at your fractals book?"

"Oh, yeah."

Vivia keeps her dining room uncluttered. Her business stays in the living room. The three sit around a lace-draped table, Vivia's cheesecake in the center between silver candlesticks.

Vivia cuts a generous wedge for Jimmy. "I'm glad to finally get you over, Jimmy. It's nice having you for a neighbor. And I wanted to say thank you for bringing me the table down from MaryBeth's."

"That was no problem."

"It's over there in the corner. I bought that fern at the Winn-Dixie to put on it."

Jimmy turns and admires the table, cleaned and polished, the brass pull on the drawer shiny. "There's a Winn-Dixie store around here?" he asks.

Joelle answers. "Meema likes to go to that new one, on the Columbia highway."

"That's a long way to go for groceries."

"Well, it's just over the county line." Vivia feels safe in grocery stores.

She can push her cart for hours and encounter few men. "That table belonged to MaryBeth's grandma and grandpa. I knew them growing up. They was mill people. Her grandma was my mama's best friend, and I spent a lot of time over there. They went to the mill school together, and they was both in the weave room. MaryBeth's grandma, Miz Boatwright, always kept candy in that little drawer, just for me. It was like our little special secret, you know. Sometimes it was Mary Janes, and sometimes it was silver bells. That's what we used to call Hershey kisses. There wasn't no air conditioning back then, so usually it was silver bells in the wintertime and Mary Janes in the summertime. And sometimes, even the Mary Janes would have melted to the wrapper, and I'd have to peel it off. But anyway, I did want to save that little table of Miz Boatwright's."

"It looks good there with the fern on it," Jimmy comments. "And this cheesecake is great."

Joelle walks him back to his porch, where they sit on the top step and turn pages in the book about fractals. "I think this book is too complex for both of us, Joelle. This is a topic that's sort of theoretical."

"I shouldn't try to read it?" Joelle is disappointed. She hoped the book might explain why everything around her seems to be a jagged piece of something broken.

"Sure. You gotta stretch your brain like it's a muscle. But sometimes when you're learning something, you have to start with the basics. Next time I'm in Columbia, I'll root through the bookstore and see if there's something simpler. Something I can read without getting a headache."

"Meema was home when you brought the table."

Jimmy tries not to show his surprise at the change of subject. He listens.

"She won't go to the door if I'm not there." Joelle stands suddenly and takes the book from Jimmy's hands. "I mean, she really appreciated you bringing the table. She thinks you're real nice. But she just can't open the door."

Joelle stares at Jimmy, waiting for something. He has already failed the fractal quiz and feels he is now failing another test.

" 'Night," she says.

Jimmy is unaware of what Joelle really wants. Approval or disapproval of her grandmother's behavior. Either one.

## Chapter 13

## *Karen*

KAREN IS THE COLLEGE PROFESSOR.

To others, Karen seems to have a lot of loose parts. A tote bag weighs down one shoulder, rattling mysteriously, occasionally emitting the muffled ring of her cell phone. Sandals slap her feet, and jewelry clinks like wind chimes. Her skirts are long and don't seem to have straight hems, and her shirts are loose and hang over the skirts, so it's hard to see where one ends and the other begins.

But with her children, she has clear control. They flow around her like her long skirts, flapping away and returning. Karen knows they will return to her side, like a magnet assured of its eternal attraction to tiny metal filings.

She takes full control of the conclusion of her marriage. "Because you have allowed me to assume all the responsibility for Camilla," she tells her husband. "Because you went about your life, flying to conferences, going in on weekends for grand rounds, running for president of the county medical association, in perfect confidence that I was here taking care of Camilla. Because you have treated me like a baby-sitter, completely unaware of how I was managing to pursue my career."

He sits across from her at the dining-room table, where she asked him to. He listens, impatiently at first, ready to clear up whatever problem she is presenting and move on, right hand resting on his pager, eager to feel its vibration. He assumes he will hear about some new problem with Camilla, a new doctor, a new medication, a new therapy, a new round of seizures. When he realizes he is listening to his wife's plan to move out, his hand leaves his beeper and folds with his other hand on the table before him. He displays the professional calm he perfected in medical school.

"Camilla is stressful to both of us," he begins. "Perhaps more for you. The maternal bond. But I give as much of my time to Camilla as you do."

Karen cannot suppress a laugh, a short, sad laugh. She shakes her head.

Martin pulls out his Day Runner. "I am president of the state ARC," he reminds her. "I helped raise forty thousand dollars for them last year. I am on the UCP board. I am on the County Disabilities Awareness Council." At each assertion, he points to an entry in his calendar—a monthly meeting, a weekly meeting.

"Those things take you away from Camilla, Martin. Those things mean I am here with her, or looking for a sitter to be with her."

"These things are for Camilla. I have to make time for these things. I miss every other oncology symposium because of the UCP meetings. I miss the medical alumni meeting because of the Awareness Council meetings. And Special Olympics, for God's sake. I'm on the national board."

"And when do you wipe her butt, Martin?"

He leans away from her. He closes his Day Runner.

"When do you change her underwear after one of her seizures? Do you line up the M&M's and try to teach her to count? Do you arrange your afternoon schedule around her speech therapy and her physical therapy and her occupational therapy?"

Silence sits on the table between them like a too-big centerpiece. Both are thinking of an interval in their lives, a time they have never talked about, never will. A day that was a clear ancestor to this day. Camilla was just five. Bryan was not yet born.

Karen sat on her haunches, immobile, staring at Camilla. During the half-hour Karen had spent punching holes for daffodil bulbs, Camilla had stabbed futilely at one spot with a plastic spoon. Karen continued to stare at her five-year-old infant until her damp knees and fingers chilled her to awareness.

"Come on, Camilla. Let's go inside now." Camilla did not respond to Karen's soft voice. "Come on, Camilla. Get up and go inside with Mommy." This time, Karen spoke peremptorily, in a drill sergeant's voice. She knew that would not work either, but she felt obliged to try, as though she got points for effort.

Karen picked Camilla up and carried her inside, each struggling against the other. In the bathroom, Karen removed her own mud-caked jeans and threw them in the tub. She lay Camilla on the bath mat and began the ordeal of undressing her. In a sad silent movie, Karen pulled socks from kicking feet, peeled the diaper from the arched body, stretched a shirt over flailing arms.

In the kitchen, both mother and daughter in clean clothes, Camilla sat in her vinyl-cushioned chair with raisins and banana slices before her while Karen listened to the ugly quiet of the house. When the finger food was gone, Camilla's hands continued to search. Karen directed her to containers of poker chips to pour from bucket to bowl to box to floor.

With Camilla momentarily safe, Karen hurried to the mailbox. She returned to find Camilla knocking cans from the pantry shelves. Karen made the mistake of trying to pull her away from the mess. A can flew at her cheekbone. Resenting another bruise to explain, Karen's sole reaction was a sigh.

She placed Camilla back among the poker chips, put the cans back on the shelves, sorted the mail. She set aside her husband's mail, a bill, a stack of junk mail. A brochure invited Karen to attend a chemistry symposium. As though it were a dessert menu, she scanned the titles of the papers to be presented. She read aloud: "Anomeric. Dissociative electron transfer. Cooxidation reactions."

Karen watched Camilla for signs of the lull that came on sometime during the afternoon, a low-tide quiet that was Karen's only period of escape. Instead, she heard the quickened breathing that signaled a tantrum. She pulled Camilla into the carpeted, unfurnished dining room and let the tantrum take its course. Karen called the hand-flapping, kicking, screaming roil a tantrum, trying to avoid the word *seizure*. Patronizing doctors informed her that there was no evidence of seizure activity on Camilla's EEG, implying that Karen's description of the episodes was not evidence. Karen watched over her child until the tantrum subsided, then placed Camilla again among the red and black chips.

The phone rang. Karen stared at it as though an alarm had sounded. Camilla cocked her head to one side. The phone was an enemy in this house. When Karen was tethered to the phone, Camilla was free and uncannily aware of that freedom, a freedom to chew on the fringe of a rug and gag, to empty the Tide box onto the floor. An answering machine to screen the calls had seemed to be the solution, but Camilla had broken two, swallowing a button off the last one. She had been in the ER for an endoscopy because of it. Now, there was just the wall phone that Camilla could not reach. Karen counted nine rings. Both mother and child were relieved when the ringing stopped.

The lull came. Camilla's mouth dropped open, her head lolled forward, poker chips still clasped in her fist. Karen went quickly to the phone. She had three calls to make and, at most, thirty minutes in which to do it.

"Dr. Pinner? This is Karen—"

"Yes, Karen," he interrupted too quickly, too affably. "How are you?"

"Fine. I'm calling to find out if you've decided about the instructor for the evening course. Chem 101."

"Well, yes, Karen. We filled that position with one of the scientists working out at the Nuclear Dynamics site. You know, there's an intern program at NDS, and this fellow can help our students have access to that." Karen didn't respond, and Dr. Pinner poured more words into the phone. "And I think he'll stay with us for a while. He seems to need the extra income."

*Need?* It boiled up out of the sentence like a filthy word. What did this man know about *needs?* She was embroidered with needs—to talk to people, to calibrate equipment, to smell a chem lab, to crawl back on shore. "Thank you, Dr. Pinner."

Her index finger trembling, Karen cautiously punched the second number on her list, a long-distance number. She was still trying to erase the echo. *Needs? Needs? Needs?* "Dr. Shu? This is Karen Knox." A pause indicated he was trying to place her. Karen closed her eyes and swallowed stomach acids. *Needs?* "I'm returning your call."

"Oh, yes, yes. I am sorry to not place you."

Karen didn't remind him where they had met. She was having trouble hearing him, his carefully spoken English keeping time with the *needs? needs? needs?* in her ears.

"Well, I have a proposition for you," he went on. "Actually, I had hoped to run into you at the conference last month."

Conference? Karen could recall when her pocket calendar kept track of conferences and symposia and seminars. Her eyes traveled to the calendar on the refrigerator, its large squares dotted with Camilla's routine.

"Here is the situation," he said. "I am putting together a research team. I have a major grant that should support us for five year. From the work that you've published, your molecular modeling studies, it looks like you would fit it nicely. I wondered if you could send me your C.V., then fly up here to see the lab and talk over what we're planning. Should be a good post-doc position for you."

Karen's eyes were on Camilla. Camilla was drooling and falling forward. Karen wanted to pick her up and tuck her in bed, but she knew from experience that the slightest touch would turn the stupor into a frenzy of clenched-teeth screaming.

"I don't have my Ph.D. yet, Dr. Shu," Karen answered.

"No degree yet? I thought you be finish by now. Well, you must be close to your defense date. I mean, if you could join us within, say, the next twelve month, that would work. We have informal meeting here in two weeks."

"I really don't think I'll be able to, no."

"Travel money is available."

How do I get out of this? thought Karen. How do I explain that I am nowhere near completing an abandoned dissertation? That my lab equipment has been pushed into a corner and covered with a black tarp? That day-care centers won't take my child?

Finally, Dr. Shu said something else, and Karen said something else, though she had no idea what. She pushed the disconnect button and called the last number on her list, that of Camilla's physical therapist, to reschedule an appointment. Lately, Karen had begun to envy the therapist her dangling earrings, her polished nails, her orderly appointment-oriented life.

Karen changed Camilla's diaper, put a sweater on Camilla and herself, and herded the child onto the front porch to sit in the swing. Motion soothed Camilla, and the two could sit side by side for long periods of time. Karen liked to think they were sharing something.

The street of two-career families was busy with people returning home from work. Karen did not answer the waves of neighbors. Returning the empty gestures seemed to her like waving at TV characters. These same smiling people did not invite Camilla to birthday parties, did not include the family in cookouts or pool parties.

"Camilla, come hop into the car. You and Mommy will go get Daddy." She carried Camilla from the swing to the car and put her into the backseat among soft toys, things that would not hurt when hurled. They still owned just one car, although they could well have afforded two. Karen kept the car on the days Camilla had therapy and picked her husband up at the hospital. Martin could not understand why Karen didn't want a car of her own. Karen knew that a second car would sit accusingly in the driveway, a large metal monument to no-where-to-go.

At a stoplight, she found herself focusing on the windshield instead of through it. Glass. Glass had always fascinated her, had probably lured her to chemistry. In the sixth grade, the teacher had told the class that glass was really a liquid, very viscous, flowing so slowly humans couldn't perceive it. A car honked.

She pulled into the faculty lot, parking in sight of the door from which Martin would emerge, if he remembered they were waiting. She looked in the rearview mirror to check on Camilla. Camilla tore pages out of a book, a catalog kept in the car for this purpose. In the tiny mirror, Karen saw a portrait of a pretty child with brown eyes and hair cut too short. Karen pulled her eyes away from the reflection. Watching Camilla always gave her a haunted feeling, like watching wind blow an empty swing in a playground.

After fifteen minutes, Karen knew she would have to take Camilla from the car and find Martin. She took a deep breath, dreading the effort.

"Camilla, let's go on inside and find Daddy."

Karen pulled Camilla from the backseat and carried her to the door of the building. She was grateful when the double doors swung open automatically. She put the child down, positioning Camilla in front of her. She grasped Camilla's shoulders, firm enough to restrain, loose enough not to bruise, and moved Camilla through the tubelike hallway. When Camilla's arms floated up like wings, Karen folded them back down, bending to hold Camilla's arms in place, knowing that this fluttering would go on and on, feeling a pain form in her lower back from the forced stoop.

Karen straightened to ease her back. The little arms went up. Karen saw Camilla's hand brush the orange-and-black-striped lever that was the fire alarm. The lever moved. Camilla's arms went down.

Karen reflexively pasted Camilla's arms to her side, stopped still, held Camilla still. The lever was not flat against the wall, but had Camilla activated it? Shouldn't there be a noise, bells, a siren? Maybe there was. There was a *whoop-whoop* in Karen's ears, but she thought it had been there awhile.

The two waded toward a closed door. The corridor walls were painted gray up to a height of about four feet and above that were white. Karen's eyes followed the high-water mark created by this institutional two-tone. She tried to concentrate on the door, their goal. But when she turned around for a moment to make sure they weren't blocking anyone in a hurry, she became disoriented. Which way? She suddenly had a desperate fear of meeting someone, of having to function, to talk.

When she reached the door and opened it, the cold metal of the handle brought back some clarity. Shock therapy, she thought. She used her body to hold the heavy door open. Her thumbs pressed Camilla's shoulder blades, pushing the child ahead of her. The door closed behind them with a choking sound. Karen looked up into a man's face. His mouth was moving.

Was there an alarm going off? She could ask him if he heard the *whoop-whoop*, too. No, she cautioned herself.

Karen took a deep breath. She told herself to talk. This man is talking to you, she explained to herself. She felt the tendons behind her knees tighten, felt a stripe of muscle on her neck, felt breath leaving her mouth.

Talk.

But she was under now. She couldn't breathe, certainly couldn't talk. This man would understand. I'll talk when I get to the surface. Gulping, engulfed, she moved on, dragging the anchor that was Camilla.

What's that word? she wondered. One of her chemistry terms. *Immiscible*. I'm immiscible. It's okay.

Martin is thinking she has fallen back into that well. Karen grew strong climbing out of the well but will always be aware of its existence.

"We're parents, Karen. We can't just end this like you can turn in a leased car. Have you thought that this might confuse Camilla? Have you thought about how Bryan will handle this?"

"As long as you continue to coach his soccer games, he'll see you just as much as he ever has."

"That's why I block out that time, Karen. That's time devoted to Bryan."

"Then continue to devote it."

"And why are you moving the children out of this house? This house was built for you and for the children. If you insist on this, this separation, I'll move out temporarily. That would be simpler."

"No. I'm moving to the Randleman Road house."

"To where?"

This surprises Karen. That he does not even know where the house is. That he does not know where his children spend all those hours with their baby-sitter. That he does not know she now owns the house.

He catches up quickly. "Isn't that where the sitter lives? Mary? Beth?"

But his ignorance sparks an anger, an anger Karen has no time to deal with. "It's on the chalkboard in the kitchen. The address. The phone number."

Twenty-five hours pass before Martin checks the chalkboard. He gets home about nine. Having eaten supper in the hospital cafeteria, he has no need to go into the kitchen. So it is the next morning, as he grinds coffee, that he thinks about the chalkboard. He is astonished that the list includes the name and phone number of a lawyer. While the coffee brews, he adds the lawyer's number to the list in the back of his Day Runner.

Mayme has volunteered his services. Jimmy is uncomfortable doing this chore, and he is pretty sure it shows.

It does show. Karen apologizes. "Look, I'm sorry. The movers took everything else, but I left the computer there until Martin could get what he needed off the hard disk."

"Well, I don't really mind. I guess it's just awkward."

"Oh, yeah. No doubt about it. Divorce is awkward as hell."

They are in a neighborhood of luxury homes backed snugly against a private golf course. At the end of a cul-de-sac, they pull into a driveway that curves toward a three-story brick home. Jimmy glances at Karen, wondering why a woman would leave this landscaped home with the blue of a pool peeking through the shrubbery to live in a mill house on Randleman Road.

"But there's really nothing awkward about this particular errand," Karen reassures him. "My husband knows I'm coming to pick up the computer." She smiles a businesslike smile at Jimmy. "Both our lawyers know it." She doesn't like it that her life looks like a soap opera, even to this stranger.

Jimmy expects an empty, echoing house with abandoned picture hooks here and there on the walls. Instead, he walks into the kind of room he usually glimpses only in magazine photos. Two plaid sofas face each other, a huge, round coffee table between them. A fat chair holds a pillow covered in the sofa plaid. Baskets of dried flowers. Tiny, framed pictures on shiny tabletops. Jimmy wonders what Karen has taken from the house, what her movers have moved, because nothing seems to be missing. Still, the place reminds him of the vacant houses his realtor walked him through.

"The office is on the other side of the kitchen." Karen leads him across the hardwood floor of the living room, into the den, across a wide brick hearth, between the kitchen islands, through French doors, and into a large room with floor-to-ceiling bookshelves and built-in Formica desks on two sides.

"Great office," Jimmy says.

"It's Martin's. I try to keep my work at the university." She unplugs cables as she speaks. "The box for this thing is in the attic."

They climb a hardwood staircase. It occurs to Jimmy that her ex-husband should have brought the box down for her, should have disconnected the hardware, should have boxed it up for her. But no courtesies or customs or ceremonies mark divorce. Divorce is paperwork, business, legality.

"Right here." Gwen pointed. The lawyer squinted. "I know it's just a typo, but it's describing the acreage, so I want it correct before I sign it."

Jimmy flipped through the fourteen pages of the divorce agreement, looking for some reference to acreage. He found it. Their farmhouse sat on 14.7 acres of land, and someone had typed 12.7.

When they had bought the two-story house, built before anyone knew what insulation was, built when coal stoves and fireplaces provided heat, they had purchased an adventure. They camped around a kerosene heater in one of the four high-ceilinged rooms downstairs, cooked on a Coleman stove on the back porch. They started with the necessities. They reroofed. Jimmy installed a new pump, and water flowed reliably but noisily through pipes that intruded from walls and floors.

Then County Road 12-301 was paved, and the dirt road that had cut across a corner of their land suddenly became a line dividing it. As they knelt on their roof, feet wedged against nailed boards, they could see the glint of cars taking this newfound shortcut to Lake Murray. So they sold the cutaway 3.4-acre triangle to a developer.

At the closing, a lawyer had flipped to the last page, the signature page, and showed Gwen where to sign. "Here, and here, and initial here."

Gwen turned back to the first page and began reading. The lawyer, the two realtors, the developer, and Jimmy waited through the long minutes, all of them wanting desperately to look at their watches.

Gwen let the little finger of her left hand mark a place. With her right hand, she pulled another paper toward her. She compared the two pages. "Here," she told the lawyer. "The tax-parcel number is typed in wrong. I want it correct before we sign it."

The closing had been postponed, and Jimmy was pissed. He wanted the check, wanted to get the new septic tank installed, wanted to get the electrician out to put in new wiring so he could start repairing the walls, wanted to fill his pickup with PVC pipe and two new toilets and an acrylic shower stall. The correction had been made, and Gwen read the newly printed pages, and her signature atop Jimmy's made their 18.1-acre property become 14.7 acres.

Seven years later, Gwen once again read each word and once again found a typo, and Jimmy watched her end her marriage with the same businesslike precision with which she had sold the 3.4 acres. The documents reprinted, Gwen's signature atop Jimmy's made the divorce a fact and caused the 14.7 acres to be sold and the proceeds divided. For Jimmy, it was the typo, not the signature, that marked the occasion. One digit, two sets of initials marking the correction, the moment when Jimmy understood that his marriage was over, that Gwen wasn't just having an affair she would get tired of, wasn't going to change her mind.

As Karen pulls down the attic ladder, Jimmy looks through the open doors on either side of him. One room is wallpapered in football helmets and baseball caps, the other in ballerinas. Both rooms are empty. He realizes then that the children's furniture has been moved, nothing else.

She climbs into the attic and tosses the boxes down to him. From the landing, he drops each box harmlessly to the carpeted floor of the den. He is already boxing the tower when she returns downstairs.

"Does the printer go, too?"

She hesitates. "Yes."

Jimmy bends into a box to hide his smile.

Back in the car, without Styrofoam and cardboard to keep them busy, they have a harder time with conversation. After a few minutes of silence, Jimmy finally thinks of something to say. "Did you get the cables?"

"Yes."

That exchange takes them to the neighborhood's gated entrance.

Karen tries. "Mayme says you're a well driller."

"Sometimes. Well, legally I am. I have a driller's license. But I'm actually a field geologist for KDR. We're an environmental consulting company out of Columbia. I'm assigned to a groundwater remediation project at the Muldoy Chemicals site."

Nodding, Karen keeps her eyes on the road, though she wants to look at him again, to reassess him, because it is as though she has just met him. He is reassigned from the "Blue Collar" column to the "Educated Professional" column. That knowledge makes her more comfortable with him but less comfortable with herself. Am I a snob? she wonders.

Unaware of his change in status, Jimmy forces himself to study the scenery, hoping to see something worth mentioning.

Karen continues to ponder her character flaws. Is it a character flaw to find him more interesting because he is more educated? She knows that if she had been introduced to Jimmy on the USC-Osilo County campus—"Dr. Knox, I'd like you to meet the geologist in charge out at Muldoy Chemicals, Jimmy Steverson"—she would have reacted to him differently. She wonders if she reacts differently to people she meets on Randleman Road. And now she lives on Randleman Road.

"I assume it's a long-term project, then, if you've moved here from Columbia."

"Um, probably three years," Jimmy answers. They pass a field where goats nibble grass. Jimmy is about to say "Look at the goats" when he recognizes that her statement was an effort at conversation, a much better effort than his goat topic. He adds to his answer. "I had to move somewhere. I was sort of in the same boat you are, just divorced. We had restored this huge, old farmhouse out in Lexington, west of Columbia. Fourteen-plus acres and a pond. The wiring was antique, light bulbs hanging from the ceiling. So we couldn't have an air conditioner. We had one of those little refrigerators like in a dorm room, and even that was always blowing fuses. And you can't even find fuses anymore, so we had to get the place rewired. And there's building regs about that. It has to be a licensed electrician, so we had to spend money on that. But I did the plumbing. Gwen's very exacting, so she was good at cutting Formica and wallboard. Man, when she cut it, it fit." When Jimmy realizes he is praising his ex-wife, he stops. "Anyway, when we sold it, we made a fortune because we had paid almost nothing for it. So I had all this cash sitting around, and I needed some kind of tax break, so I was looking for a house."

"But Randleman Road?" she asks.

"It was the pond, not the house. Two or three years ago, I worked on the pond. KDR had a contract to provide DEHP with data for some kind of environmental assessment. I took water samples and core samples."

"So is the pond really polluted?"

"You're a chemist, right?" Jimmy asks. When she nods, he continues. "You know how it is, then. Most people see the names of those chemical compounds and freak. Heavy metals, mostly in the bottom sediments. Probably gonna stay there."

The conversation does not require enough of Karen's concentration. A few synapses are busy circulating thoughts about the house she has just been in, a house that was her design on graph paper turned into a contractor's blueprint, part of her recovery therapy. She had caught herself trying not to touch anything, skirting the furniture, walking through the house like she had walked through Ripley's Aquarium down at Myrtle Beach, seeing a self-contained world behind glass. It surprised her, bothered her, that Martin had not moved anything, that nothing in his life had moved. She had stood in the hallway between the children's bedrooms looking at the emptiness, looking at the vacuum tracks in the carpet, looking for Martin's footprints. He had not been in the children's rooms. He had not missed them.

Accidentally, because they match, they become a couple, like two bricks might become bookends. Jimmy delivers three loaves of Miz Mayme's bread to Karen's new home and is invited to share chili.

"Mom makes good chili," says Bryan. Jimmy knows he will disappoint Bryan if he doesn't stay.

The house has been transformed. Jimmy was aware of the hectic remodeling, has seen the crews working late. The new kitchen, a shiny palette of white cabinets and baby-blue countertops and new appliances, is defined by a lunch-style counter. In front of that sits a round table painted white and four chairs, each a different color.

"The red chair's mine," Bryan tells Jimmy. "Purple is Camilla's. Mom gets the blue one. So I guess the yellow one's yours."

"We painted it ourselves," Karen says from the stove. "It was a beat-up old table, used to be my grandmother's. I spent a lot of time sitting there eating her good cooking, so I wanted it here. I let the kids paint their chairs whatever color they wanted. Man, that bread got here just in time. What would we do without Miz Mayme?"

Karen places bowls and plates and silverware on the counter. "Jimmy, would you set these out? Bryan, would you get Camilla to the table?"

Both males do as they are told. Jimmy is placing a paper napkin at each place when he first sees Camilla. Bryan holds her hand, leading her to the table. She seems unaware of Jimmy's presence.

Jimmy greets her anyway. "Hello, Camilla. I'm Jimmy."

Camilla sits in her purple chair. She picks up her spoon and puts it into her empty bowl. She places her fork atop her plate. Bryan brings her a glass of milk. She puts it between her bowl and her plate.

"She probably won't say anything," Bryan says.

"That's okay by me," says Jimmy. "The less said about my table manners, the better."

Karen is looking into the chili, stirring unnecessarily. Her emotions are afloat on her face, and she is waiting for them to submerge. Jimmy spoke so casually to Camilla, so comfortably. He has no idea what a remarkable thing he has done. Camilla is commonly ignored, asked about, stared at. Guests often act annoyed around Camilla, move away from her, like people react when cats rub against their legs. Karen turns around and sees Jimmy seated at her table, between her children. She watches him. There is a man in her house, at her table. That highlights the changes she has made in her life. And that man has done an uncommon thing, which highlights him.

Finally, Jimmy turns to her. "What's up? Something you need me to do?"

Karen shakes her head and turns back to the stove. She decides to pour the chili into a pottery casserole instead of just putting the saucepan on the table.

"Want a tour?" she asks him after supper.

"Of your renovations? Yeah. I've listened to all the buzzing and hammering for two weeks now. I think I deserve a tour. And I can't help but wonder what's behind all that plastic in the living room." He stands, begins removing plates and glasses from the table and placing them on the counter.

"There's a big hole in the living-room wall," Karen explains with the glee of a child. "Eventually, it will lead to the addition, but right now it makes me think of Alice's rabbit hole."

❧

"You were smart to have a lawyer early on," Annie Gramling tells her. Annie, the wife of a physics professor at the university, is the only lawyer Karen knows. "He moved early. He's asked for custody."

Karen's eyes close in a slow-motion blink of disbelief. "Martin wants the children?" She leans back into Annie's sofa. "Martin wants custody of the children," she repeats.

"That's what his lawyer is saying."

"Maybe the lawyer got it wrong. Martin can't cope with the children. He doesn't have any idea about Camilla, about what she needs. And he's never home."

Annie gets up from behind her desk and sits at the other end of the couch. "This is maneuvering. What your husband wants is not to have to pay child support. That's mandated and court-ordered and a set amount, and daddies in general do not like that much control over their lives."

"He wants the children so he doesn't have to pay child support?"

"That's what he thinks he wants. Right now, he and his lawyer are thinking in checkbook mode. Let him get over it. Let's figure out what you want. You could ask for full custody or joint custody, or you could let him have full custody."

"I want Camilla and Bryan with me," states Karen. But as she says

139

it, a montage flits across her mind, vignettes of a child-free life. What would it be like? She would be free to go anywhere at any time without planning ahead. No canceled trips because the sitter's mother died or the sitter has an abscessed tooth or the sitter goes to jail. No missed symposia because Bryan breaks a collarbone or Camilla has the flu. She could chair committees, present papers at conferences, get stranded in airports, work all night in the lab. She could go shopping for clothes and maybe have the time to try them on without Camilla there pulling sweaters off counters and blouses off hangers. Still, she says it again. "Camilla and Bryan are with me."

That night, Karen lies in her new double bed with only the just-textured ceiling to look at, a bumpy background to her worries—legal documents to file, financial records to locate, exams to grade, a grant application due. Her temporary bedroom is the living room, one wall of which is a black plastic tarp protecting the house from the sawdust of the addition that will become a family room, an office, her bedroom, two new baths. The tarp draws breaths from mysterious currents. Karen finds the plastic sighs and rattles comforting, finds the construction process appealing; if it's not right, you just start over.

It is a comfort to know that she does not have to start tomorrow with instructions to the yardman, who showed up twice weekly in a pickup truck, honked, then sat and waited for orders. Karen pretended an interest in the yard, guessed what needed to be trimmed or mowed, and put him to work. It is a comfort not to have to start the day apologizing to the housekeeper for what Camilla had smeared on the carpet or thrown against the kitchen wall. Often, Karen hid Camilla's laundry rather than explain the soiled blue jeans and wet underwear. It is a comfort to know that Martin will not be at the breakfast table, his cell phone at his ear. Martin always ignored the ringing of the household phone, answering only his cell.

Karen likes what is not here, what has not contaminated the little mill house. She is learning to like what is here.

## Chapter 14

## *Gwen*

GWEN IS THE EX-WIFE, the ex-life against which thoughts echo.

She is enjoying her freedom. She attends more meetings, flies to the national Geological Society of America meeting in Denver, no longer limited to the regional meetings in Winston-Salem and Atlanta. She buys a kayak and joins a group that spends weekends on whitewater rivers in Georgia and North Carolina. Free from picking up deadwood on all those piney acres, from reporting deer-hunting trespassers, from classes on laying tile, she can work late on weeknights and save her weekends for trips down the Chattooga and the Neuse.

She was surprised at the profit realized from the sale of the farmhouse. With her half, she made a sizable down payment on a condo with a twelfth-floor view of the Broad River entering Columbia. Gwen likes to get up early, likes finding the newspaper right outside her door, not at the end of a quarter-mile gravel driveway. She reads *The State* on the balcony, then brings her laptop out to work on an abstract due

Monday. She bikes to work these days, looks forward to it, no longer has a time-wasting commute to dread.

Today, she is making the ninety-minute drive to Osilo County, to the university's branch campus there, to head up a seminar. In a wicker trunk stored on her balcony, she finds her nail polish and sets about painting her toenails a deep color called Sandstorm. Her fingernails are short and neat and natural, but she likes to see her toenails gleam.

In charge of the deep-drill project in Florence, she spends days on the road, occasional nights camped out at a motel near the well field. At the office, there is no one senior to her. Her boss is in Washington. Lately, she's begun keeping cut flowers in a crystal vase on her desk. Gwen is in charge and in control and does not miss Jimmy, who was never easy to control.

The first time Jimmy calls Karen, he has an excuse and a plan. "I'm on campus, at a seminar. Can I take you to lunch?"

Karen is caught off-guard. For Jimmy to call her here, at her office, takes him out of context. Jimmy is part of the new house in the Valley, of home. She can't picture him here on campus.

"I teach until twelve-thirty." It's a statement, not a response to his question.

"I'm done at noon. Can I come to your office?"

"Room 202, science building. The door's always open, so you can wait here if you beat me." Directions, but still no answer to his invitation.

He feels comfortable in her office. Two computers, both up and working, face each other with a swivel chair between them. Tossed over the chair is a grayed lab coat, sat upon so many times that it has taken on the shape of the chair and is now upholstery. A pair of safety goggles sits on top of one of the monitors, floating above a cloudy-sky screen saver, staring at the relentless display of data on the opposite monitor. Lines of numbers appear, reappear as graphs, reassemble as numbers when new data flows in, cycling back to graphs, as mesmerizing as the sailing clouds of the screen saver.

"Is it still churning?" Karen asks.

Jimmy nods.

"Damn thing is so slow." She tosses the Chem 101 textbook onto her desk but opens the file cabinet to carefully store her transparencies. "Where would you like to eat?"

"I was hoping you'd know. This is your stomping ground."

She points to a brown paper bag. "I don't usually eat out. No time. But the nearby choices would be the student union, the sub shop at the gas station, or the Kountry Kookin."

When Karen calls attention to her lunch bag, Jimmy notices her other provisions—a jar of peanuts, packages of raisins, little cans of orange juice. She could hole up here for a while. "I'll settle for getting to visit your office," Jimmy offers, "and leave you to brown-bag it, if you're busy."

She shakes her head. "Next thing I've got is a lab at three. The summer schedule is grueling—class all morning, lab every afternoon. I need to get off campus. I just rarely give myself the luxury."

"Then I vote for the sub shop."

Jimmy leads her to his pickup. "I've never been to this campus before," he tells her.

She smiles, finally. "I like it here. Most of the buildings are new. And the satellite campuses tend to get the kids who couldn't quite make it, financially or academically, to Columbia. So they work a little harder."

She looks around his truck the way he looked around her office. He has cleaned up the cab in her honor, but the mats are stained with red clay, and stashed behind the seats are rubber-band-bound tubes of maps. As he pulls out, a screwdriver rolls from under the seat. "It's obvious you work for a living," she comments.

"Well, the truck does, anyway."

The screwdriver tumbles back and forth, making a rhythm as Jimmy stops and starts. The noise is comforting and makes talk optional.

He is well into his meatball sub before she has her waxed paper arranged properly in front of her. She smooths the paper and empties a bag of barbecue-flavored chips next to her turkey sub. "So what's this seminar you're attending?"

"A conference on current research in the state. It'll give me some CEUs to apply toward keeping my registration current."

"Did you get anything out of it?"

"Yeah. A couple of CEUs." He puts his sandwich down. "It's aggravating, coming to these things. I went into geology because I like being outdoors, and because everybody in geology seemed, well, they all seemed like free spirits or renegades or something. You know, climbing mountains and hiking deserts and stuff. Next thing I know, you have to have a certificate from the state saying you're a registered geologist. Then people start having these conferences and seminars and symposia to hand out these CEUs, just so the state will let you keep your registration." He takes another bite.

"You don't see the point?"

"No. It's a waste of my time. There are some people that like coming to all these meetings and eating doughnuts and networking. I just want to work. I mean, I can kind of see the point about having a driller's license. That's kind of like a business license, so if you hire somebody to drill you a well, you're sure the guy knows how to set pipe. But this geologist registration stuff is just some excuse for people who like to talk and lecture to get up there and make us pay to listen to them." He takes another bite.

He has eaten a half-dozen suppers at her house by now, but he has never talked this much, never spoken about anything of particular interest to him, never expressed an opinion. Karen lets him set the conversational pattern, tries to keep it going.

"Any interesting speakers so far?"

With a mouth full of food, he is at a disadvantage. All he can do is smile and hope it holds the situation until he can swallow the meatball in his mouth. "The keynote speaker is my wife."

She has finally put food in her mouth, so all she can offer is an attentive face.

He eats one of her chips. "My ex-wife, I mean. She's one of the organizers of this thing."

Karen quits eating but doesn't talk. She just nods.

"I knew this was a USGS-sponsored seminar, so I guess I should have figured she'd be part of it, but I just wasn't thinking. My boss back at KDR signed me up because he knows how bad I am about letting my registration lapse."

"So you were surprised to see her?"

Jimmy shakes his head. "I haven't seen her at all. I mean, to talk to her. She's in charge of the thing, so she was running around all morning setting things up and putting out fires. She did the keynote talk, like I said, but I was late, so I missed that."

Karen is amused and hiding it. Then she pictures herself running into Martin at a chemistry symposium, having to deal with him professionally, and her amusement dissolves. Martin would be patronizing and overbearing in such a situation.

"It must be awkward," she suggests.

Karen's brown hair has crept over her shoulders. With both hands, she gathers it at the base of her neck, pulls it over her left shoulder, and curls it around her index finger until it becomes a corkscrew. Jimmy has noticed that Karen's waist-length hair demands attention, one minute draped smoothly down her back, the next gathering electricity or coiling itself around moisture pulled from the air. Watching Karen manipulate her hair, Jimmy tries to recall any interaction between Gwen and the reddish cap that topped her head. He cannot remember seeing her brush it. She kept it pragmatically short, razored at the neckline, trimmed above the ears, so he assumed someone cut it, but he never heard Gwen say so. Jimmy liked the coppery color, liked the way sunlight bounced from her head, liked calling her "Red." Jimmy realizes he is comparing his wife to this woman sitting across the table, realizes he has done that a lot recently, most commonly as he watches Karen with her children. He and Gwen never even talked about having children.

"Yeah," he says in answer to nothing, just to bring himself back to conversation, away from wondering how significant it is that he is comparing Karen to Gwen. "Well, I'm used to it. She was always the ambitious one. It was one of the things that stretched the marriage apart. I'm happy doing what I do, but she's ambitious. I liked it at first. I was proud of her. It's still not easy for a woman to be a geologist, and she just keeps climbing that USGS ladder."

"A lot of us—women, I mean—feel like we have to push, to keep climbing. Like you said, it's still hard for a woman in some professions."

"Yeah, I tried to keep that in mind. But she started pushing me to climb. If there was an opening at one of the big consulting outfits, she'd want me to apply for it. She'd point out some buddy of ours who had discovered a fault, and she'd remind me that I never published. For a long time, I just told her that I was happy doing what I do. I mean, for a *long* time. I'm slow, I guess. And then I realized she wasn't happy with me doing what I do."

And that hurt, Karen thinks. She almost says it aloud but catches the words. Anger is more socially acceptable than hurt. "Well, the seminar got you on campus and got me a lunch date."

Jimmy has finished his sandwich. He balls up his wrapper and takes it and her empty chip bag to a trash can. That gives him a few seconds to decide to make his admission.

"I should have called you before today. I mean, they signed me up for this seminar a month ago, and I knew it was on your campus. But I kept putting it off."

He does not put off finding Gwen. As the breakout sessions convene following lunch, Jimmy spots her with a clipboard and a Palm Pilot gripped in one hand, pointing directions with the stylus, held in the other. She glances up at Jimmy, then pokes at her Palm Pilot.

"You're in room 132, Jimmy." She points down the hall.

"I know. I just wanted to say hey."

She looks up at him then and smiles. "Hey. You doing okay?"

"Pretty good."

"I heard you have a couple of those wells in at Muldoy."

Jimmy nods. "Yep. It's moving along. Got here late, so I missed your talk. How'd it go?"

She looks surprised, then concerned. "If you missed it, you ought to go see the core samples. We're down to Triassic red beds in well field 4, so I brought along some of the core."

"Jesus, Gwen, I hadn't heard that." But he would have eventually, he knows, in a USGS professional paper, as good as it gets for geologists. "That's cool. You going deeper?"

"Oh, yeah. Still good recovery." She already has more Triassic core than any previous project has recovered, but she'll keep the core coming up as long as the bits will penetrate.

Walking to room 132, Jimmy glances back to see Gwen pointing out directions with her stylus while punching at her Palm Pilot with her thumb. Gwen is always doing more than one thing at a time. To her, impatience is a virtue, preventing the waste of time. Jimmy looks at his thumb, wonders how she does it.

He invites the whole family down for a cookout.

"I've eaten I don't know how many suppers at your house," he tells her. "So it's my turn."

"Yeah, well, my setting one more place at the table isn't quite the same as your fixing a meal for a whole family."

"Hey, it's just a cookout."

Although a complicated one, he admits to himself. He is cooking rib eyes for the two adults, but Bryan doesn't like steak, and Camilla doesn't chew food properly, so burgers are on the grill for the kids. He bought Cokes for the kids, but it turns out they don't like Coke. Bryan drinks only Dr. Pepper, and Camilla drinks only fruit juice.

Bryan climbs into Jimmy's boat, causing Karen a moment of panic until she reminds herself that the boat is tethered to the dock, that Bryan can swim, that he's just yards away from two adults. She limits herself to a warning. "Be careful, Bryan."

Camilla is happy on Jimmy's back porch. She has her tackle box, the plastic treasure box that she always carries. From it, she removes magnetic letters, big wooden beads painted bright colors, crayons still sharp and clean, sticks of gum. She aligns them into patterns, then puts them back.

Karen offers some explanation. "Every now and then, I replace the gum, although she never seems to chew it. She likes the different colors, so she's got all kinds in there. There seems to be something about things that are alike but different in color." Her eyes are locked on Bryan in the boat, but she is trying to relax, sunk into an Adirondack chair, a glass of zinfandel in her hand.

Gwen never liked zinfandel. "Trash wine," she pronounced. "Something for people to ask for who don't want to study wines." She drank dark red wines. "Wines that are full of history," she said. Putting the zinfandel into his grocery cart, buying something Gwen did not like, something he knew Karen did, made Jimmy very aware of his new situation. He flips the burgers, tests the steaks with a fork, wonders when he'll buy Pop-Tarts, a food Gwen refused to have in the house.

"You like bratwurst?" he asks Karen.

"No. Well, yes, but I try to avoid it. High fat."

"Chicken? On the grill?"

"Oh, yeah. I love grilled chicken."

"The kids?"

"Yep. They'll yum that right down."

"Next time, we'll do that," Jimmy decides. "Something everybody likes."

Jimmy is learning to settle for the locals. When Mark brings over a cooler full of fish and offers to fry them up, Jimmy gets out beer and calls Bonus. The three men and Pontoo are eating on the screened porch when the commotion begins.

Mayme emerges from her back door, in a hurry. She walks through

Miz Charlie Mae's backyard into Karen's and right into Karen's back door. A few minutes later, the men see her emerge with what looks like a bundle of laundry. Back in her own yard, she throws the quilted comforter tentlike over her clothesline. Among the red-and-white figures of Mickey Mouse are splotches and chunks of brown.

"Yuck," says Mark. He leaves Jimmy's porch and goes to Mayme, who is stretching her hose to the clothesline. "You want some help?"

"I'm just gonna hose it off and leave it here for now."

Jimmy follows Mark. Bonus, leaning on his cane, watches from Jimmy's porch.

"Something happen down at Karen's?" Jimmy asks.

Mayme fires the hose at the comforter. "Camilla had one of those things that happens to her, bless her little heart." Mayme turns toward Jimmy's house and yells at Bonus. "Bonus, I need you to run over and sit with Cone. Fairy Etta's gonna go help Karen get Camilla into the bathtub. Jimmy, Karen's gonna send Bryan down here 'til we get everything all cleaned up. You'll have to feed him some supper."

Mark takes the hose from Mayme. "I'll finish this. You run on back and help." He covers his nose with his free hand.

Bryan saunters into the yard, his hands in his pockets. "Hey," is all he says.

Mark winks at Jimmy. "So, Bryan, you want a beer?"

"No, thank you."

"There's some Dr. Pepper in the fridge," Jimmy tells him. "Go on in and help yourself."

Bryan runs in and opens Jimmy's refrigerator, which is always more interesting than the one at home. Jimmy keeps his butter bin full of Snickers bars; he calls it his "stash." Bryan opens several Styrofoam containers but can't recognize the contents, so he settles for his Dr. Pepper, a drumstick from a KFC bucket, and a Snickers bar. On the kitchen table sit small plastic bags of wet dirt, mysterious writing on each one. Next to the back door is a mound of denim splotched with red clay and streaked with axle grease, muddier than Bryan's soccer uniform ever gets. And in Jimmy's dish drainer is a turtle shell.

Bryan settles in between the two men, pushing aside a jumble of paper plates and empty Corona bottles to make room for his Dr. Pepper can. "Jimmy, why'd you put a turtle shell in the drainer?"

" 'Cause I washed it. Pontoo brought it to me."

Bryan is happy to be here, eating fried chicken and chocolate for supper, trying to figure out what Jimmy and Mark are saying about an old Ford truck for sale somewhere. He stands to throw his chicken bone into the pond, the way he saw Mark do, but his eye catches Camilla's stained quilt dripping on Miz Mayme's clothesline. He had forgotten why he's here, had forgotten that he should not be having a good time, that his escape is because of something bad happening to his sister.

Bryan's face changes so suddenly that Mark looks around to see if something is happening behind them. "Hey, kiddo, what's wrong? You got a stomachache?"

"No. I'm okay."

For his first date with Jana Hardaway, Jimmy chooses a benign setting. In Columbia, people whose work paths cross often meet at lunch anyway, which lessens the importance of the event. Within the downtown area, dozens of lunch spots are within walking distance of the Capitol, the university campus, and the office blocks, so the noon crowd is a mix of students, professors, legislators, state employees, business types.

"You can always spot the students," Jana says. "They can have beer with lunch."

"And it seems like they can afford it. When I was in college, beer was a luxury reserved for game weekends, and then we pooled our resources and bought a keg."

"The olden days?" Jana teases.

"Not that long ago," Jimmy smiles, "I got my master's in '91. But it seems so different now. Now, the kids have credit cards and cell phones and laptops."

"So you're jealous?"

"Hell, yes. Grad-school life was great. Just enough money to live on, no responsibilities."

They eat moussaka, dip crusty bread into olive oil, and share a rectangle of baklava. The lunch date is easy because eating fills the time, because work limits the date to an hour, because Jimmy never met Gwen for lunch during the workday—she was always too busy— so there are no reminders, no restaurants to avoid.

The second date is more complex. Jimmy has to issue an invitation, an invitation that might be declined. When his boss throws a party, that provides the event.

"You need to leave any particular time?" Jimmy asks. "To relieve your sitter?"

Jana shakes her head. "My mother's baby-sitting."

To escape the crowd that stays inside with the air conditioning, they are sitting on Carl's deck, watching the sky, hoping for a meteorite. Jimmy risks another question: "Doesn't your ex-husband help out?"

"There is no ex-husband."

Jimmy doesn't know what to say next, so he just nods.

"Lara's adopted. From Russia. My sister's a pediatrician, does volunteer work over there, and I went along once. She and I both came back with little girls. I named my daughter Lara, after the *Zhivago* character, because it's Russian but it's something Americans can pronounce. Lara's five now."

When Jimmy drives Jana home, he realizes he has to drive home, too, all the way to Osilo County. He likes her and wants to see her again, but he learned tonight that she is a complete picture, framed, and needs no one else in her landscape. He would have to be wanted, and he would have to put in miles.

Karen is right down the street, no driving required, and has regular emergencies.

# Chapter 15

## *True*

IF YOU'RE WHITE and live in Osilo County, True Padgett has buried somebody in your family.

When True inherited the business from his father, he wanted to expand, so True tried for the black business as well, the only customers left to seek. He couldn't see what difference color made to a dead man. Because he had the contract with the county for indigents and prisoners, Padgett's Funeral Home had embalmed a few blacks, and the procedure was the same. True approached black people wherever he found them—the manager of the South Carolina Electric & Gas office, his bank teller, his son's football coach—and solicited their business with his ivory-and-silver-engraved business cards. Coach Lehigh chuckled and returned True's card. "True, you start burying black people, the white people won't be caught dead in your embalming room."

When his sons began to take over the business, True was free to enter public life, something he had always wanted to do. He had been put into a suit and tie at ten and taught to usher mourners to their pews. At hundreds of funerals, he had observed that the dead body was not the center of attention. The hush and the awe were extended not to the mystery of death but to the arrival of the preacher. Nothing could begin without the pastor or the reverend or the priest. Only the preacher had a reserved parking spot, on which True had been told to stencil "Clergy." Ten-year-old True looked the word up, found the definition magical—"an ordained group charged with pastoral duties." The preacher spoke in a low voice, and everyone quieted and leaned forward to hear. The preacher was everyone's friend, a member of everyone's family. True, always set apart as the boy whose bedroom was above the embalming room, wanted to be everyone's friend, part of every family. He studied the preachers, asked his father how one became a preacher, how one became "ordained."

"Preachers?" his dad had asked. "Well, some of 'em go to school. Some of 'em just declare themselves preachers. They're parasites, if you ask me."

Trudell Padgett, Sr., known as Dell, had also noticed the attention lavished on preachers. Dell Padgett drove to the hospital and retrieved the dead body, stayed up all night at a stainless-steel abattoir undoing what surgeons or disease or an eighteen-wheeler had done, arrayed borrowed floral displays around a poor man's coffin. Then the reverend walked in, spoke words that Dell had heard him say the week before, and left with a fifty-dollar bill that some family member tucked into a handshake.

"What's a parasite?" True wanted to know.

"Means they don't make an honest living. They live off other people's sorrows, other people's loneliness."

"How can you make a living off loneliness?"

"People join a church just so they'll have at least one person visit 'em when they're in the hospital." His father had lost patience. "Don't think I'm letting you turn into a preacher," he told True.

Because he owned a business, True was asked to sit on boards and head commissions. He served two terms on the county council, and then the Democratic caucus drafted him to run for the state legislature. True had discovered politics. Wearing a suit and shaking hands and talking seriously to total strangers were required, and he had been trained for that all his life. Every white family knew him, and blacks remembered him as the friendly guy who didn't think color made a difference, so he easily defeated the Republican barber who ran against him.

When election time rolled around, True drew on his advertising skills, dormant while he ran the funeral home. His slogans, visible in kitchens on refrigerator magnets and on billboards throughout his district, were popular. "If it's True, it's the Truth." "True is true to you!" "Execute TRUE judgment (Zechariah 7:9)." The Republicans searched the district and offered their best. One by one, the principal, the bank manager, and the car-lot owner followed the barber in defeat.

True is entrenched in his seat in the legislature. Now, he upstages preachers, though he is one of their breed, living off a handshake and a smile and a promise. Now, he is the one people strain to hear. Now, he has a county-wide congregation.

Jimmy is happy to open his door to the face he recognizes from billboards. To Jimmy, True Padgett is a cross between Colonel Sanders and Strom Thurmond. He walks True through the kitchen to his screened porch. "Sit down out here with me, Mr. Padgett. Want a beer, a Coke?"

"I'd like a Coke, thank you, Jimmy, and I'd like you to call me True."

Settled in the Adirondack chairs, True with a Coke, Jimmy with a Corona, the two watch the pond and let it start the conversation. Totch's cooking sends a smoke cloud upstream.

"Don't that smell good?" True opens. "Makes you want a teddy bear, just to smell it."

"Totch can cook, all right. I've never had better barbecue, and I drive all over the state."

"I hear you're a geologist."

"Yes, sir. I work for KDR. That's a consulting company in Columbia. I'm based at Muldoy Chemicals right now."

True's "Uh-huh" makes it clear that Jimmy's profession is important. "That's why I'm here to see you, Jimmy."

"I thought you were knocking on doors looking for votes. I didn't know you were here to see me."

"Well, I'm always looking for votes. You registered?"

Jimmy drinks from his Corona bottle while he tries to remember. "You know, I don't think I ever did register here in Osilo County."

True pulls a printed form from the handkerchief pocket of his sports coat. "Fill it out. Mail it in. You're registered."

"Thanks."

"So, I read that report you did on the pond here."

"No, sir, I didn't write that report," Jimmy corrects him. "My company, KDR, got the contract to pull up the samples and analyze them. I did the sample recovery. We sent the results to DEHP, and they wrote the report."

"Uh-huh." True nods. "So you pulled up all that mud, with the cadmium and the chromium and the PCBs and the lead and the mercury? I hope you wore some of that protective gear."

"I wasn't in any danger." Jimmy wants to clarify but decides to let True lead.

From the same pocket that held the voter registration form, True pulls a three-by-five index card. He reads, " 'Warning. Fishing advisory. Do not eat fish pulled from Dillehay Pond. Fishing permitted but fish not to be consumed! Swimming and boating allowed.' " True puts the card back in his pocket. "That's what all those red-and-white signs all over the pond say."

Jimmy nods, tilts the Corona back for a sip.

"You disagree with that?"

"No, I think it was a good idea to post the pond. I wouldn't eat anything from the pond."

True settles back into the cushioned Adirondack chair. "Then you can see why I'm concerned. My constituents live around a poisoned pond with poisoned fish."

Jimmy empties his bottle, places it on the porch floor.

True continues. "I think the state of South Carolina, maybe even the federal government, should step in and address this problem."

"Well, True, the state has stepped in. They studied it very thoroughly—that much I can vouch for. They published a report, and they posted the pond."

"Action," says True. "They haven't taken any action."

"I'm gonna get another beer, True. Can I bring you something?"

"No, thank you, Jimmy. I'm fine with this Coke. They make these Cokes bigger now, takes me awhile to drink 'em." When Jimmy comes back with his second Corona, True continues. "When I was a boy, Cokes came in glass bottles. And when I was a boy, we fished in Dillehay Pond and ate the fish. And I know there are people here still catching fish and eating 'em. I know my constituents. They don't put gas in their motor and go out on the pond and catch fish and throw them back. They like to take something home, have fish fries."

"You could suggest to the county sheriff that he patrol the pond, give people warnings."

"Ticket people for catching something to eat?" True shakes his head. "No, like I said, Jimmy, I want some action." True leans forward, elbows on knees. "What action would you recommend, Jimmy, you being a professional in the field?"

Jimmy recognizes the corner before he backs into it. "There is no suitable action, True. No remedy."

"Oh, but there is, there is. There's always a remedy, always a solution. I like to find solutions and answers. And I'm here to see if you'll help me find the answer to this one. Now, in that report you-all did, you said that the pond should be filled in, didn't you?"

"DEHP did the report, True, not me or my company. And DEHP did not suggest filling in the pond." Jimmy is half amused, half impatient.

Out of the sports-coat pocket comes a photocopy, and True reads again: " 'Management solutions in such situations include infilling and capping.' And they go on to talk about this Carolina bay that was filled in and covered with clay."

"True, that bay was tiny. I've seen that bay. It was maybe half an acre. Now, look out there at Dillehay Pond. It looks small because it's only about twelve hundred feet at its widest point. But it extends up Stone Bowl Creek for two miles. You're talking over three hundred acres, True."

"Three hundred and twenty-nine, I'm told," True corrects. "What I see happening begins with draining the pond, laying pipe in what used to be the creek bed. At the bottom of the pond, according to that report, is a two-foot-thick layer of polluted sediment. We bring in truckloads of clean fill, and we cover that. Terrace it, not fill in the Valley, just terrace it."

"Why?"

"To protect my constituents from this pollution, that's why."

Jimmy does not explain to True that his vision will not work, that preventing water from infiltrating the covered sediments would require a mound to divert it, that groundwater would be imperiled, that True's plan would allow the disturbed pollutants to be washed into Stone Bowl Creek, into the Savannah River. Jimmy does not explain because he understands that he is talking to a zealot, like the Jehovah's Witnesses who come to his door and want to recite but will not listen.

"Well, you won't get my support on that plan, True. You're describing a massive operation against a threat that's dormant."

True allows a dramatic silence to follow. Jimmy is uncomfortable now.

"Jimmy, do you know the unemployment rate in my district? Almost nineteen percent. Do you know how many truckloads of fill this project would take? How many people it would employ? How many dollars would flow into this district?"

"Wasted money, True."

"I don't let tax dollars get wasted, Jimmy, I can tell you that. Protecting my constituents from poisoned water and poisoned fish, that's a good use of tax money." True is not angry. Padgett's Funeral Home was a training ground for dealing with people in every imaginable circumstance—parents bitter because their two-year-old was killed by a drunk driver, elderly women staring in confusion at their dead husbands, adults relieved at the death of a helpless parent. So he recognizes Jimmy's exasperation and tries another approach. "Well, you don't have to agree with me, Jimmy. I'm used to people not agreeing with me. I just wanted your professional opinion. To be frank, we don't have a lot of educated professionals here in this district. Not many people I can call on and say, 'How does this work?' So I was just picking your brain."

"No problem, True."

True leaves Jimmy a refrigerator magnet cut in the shape of his district, all of Osilo County except the Columbia suburbs that spill over the county line, like a cracker with a bite taken out of it. On it is printed, "TRUE or false? TRUE Padgett is the answer." Jimmy adds True's magnet to Camilla's tackle-box collection.

# Chapter 16

## Osmond

OSMOND VAUSE IS THE COUNTY SHERIFF, so a typical day might involve dead goats and might start at five in the morning.

"Who would shoot my goats is what I wanna know."

"What I wanna know, Robbie, is why you were out here this early looking for your goats."

"I feed 'em before I go to work, Osmond." Robbie Taylor spits the words. "Not that it's any of your damn business. They're my goats, and this is my property. What is your business is who the hell shot my goats."

"What you know, boys?" Osmond calls out to the two deputies wading in the creek around the goat carcasses. Brice Bedenbaugh is twenty-two years old and was a stock clerk at Wal-Mart before becoming a deputy. Lanny Graybill is one year older and opted to be a deputy after trying to teach seventh grade. Neither has ever seen anything like this. "Find out anything?"

"I don't think they was shot, Osmond," Brice says. He plays his flashlight over the pile of bloody goats that almost dams the tiny creek. "They're all torn up."

Osmond walks sideways down the creek bank and beams his flashlight on the scene. "Jesus, they been chewed on."

"Chewed on? What are you talking about?" asks Robbie Taylor. Robbie sells goat milk to a processor in Columbia and farms soybeans and works full time at a paper mill outside Augusta. He got up at three to feed the goats and looked for them in the dark until four. When he found the pile of dead goats in the creek, he ran back to the house and called the sheriff's office. "What's big enough out here to chew up eleven goats?"

"Nothing!" shouts Osmond. It's a time of day Osmond calls "quarter to dawn," when darkness makes people think crazy things. He is not going to let it get started. "Nothing chewed up your eleven goats. Something chewed *at* them, that's for sure. Probably dogs, Robbie. Dogs. A pack of dogs. You hear dogs barking around here?"

"Oh, yeah. Hunters come across my place, let their dogs get lost, and never come back for 'em. There's a pack of 'em out here."

"Yeah, well, those deer dogs found some goats." He climbs the creek bank back to where Robbie stands. "Robbie, go on to work. Ain't no sense you losing a morning's pay."

"Well, I gotta get 'em out of the creek and bury 'em, Osmond."

"Well, yeah, I reckon you do. We'll start hauling 'em out. You go get your tractor."

When Robbie leaves, the two deputies stand in the creek bed looking up at Osmond.

"We gotta pull these goats out?" Brice asks. His pants are already muddy and wet. Goat blood will ruin his uniform for sure.

"No, goddammit, you don't gotta pull goats out. It ain't in your job description. But it seems like we could help the man. Now, go on to the cruiser and get us some rain gear and some gloves, and let's start the official goat recovery process." The two young men splash out of the creek, glad to be out of the water. "And I'll buy y'all breakfast at the Kountry Kookin soon as we get done."

Osmond beams his flashlight into the trees that line the creek. Then he turns the light off, saving his batteries. In the dark, the creek is loud, trickling merrily around the dead goats. He sniffs. The goats still smells like goats, not dead goats. They haven't been dead long. When he hears the boys coming back, he turns his flashlight on again.

"We'll just pull 'em out of the creek, up to where it's level," he instructs. "Robbie'll dig a trench with his tractor and push 'em in, I reckon. Save one of them goats out. We'll put it in a Hefty bag and take it to the vet, just to be sure it was dogs."

After breakfast, Osmond sends the deputies back on patrol to finish their shift and heads to the office. He doesn't make it. Instead, a radio call herds him to LizAnne Dilly's nail salon, where a snakebite has been reported. The location doesn't surprise Osmond. LizAnne, in addition to running her nail salon and doing taxes, is one of Osilo County's EMTs. Osmond finds an ambulance idling in LizAnne's gravel parking lot. On the porch stands Johnny Plante, the EMT who drove the ambulance from the rescue-squad garage, who tosses away the cigarette he's not supposed to be smoking on duty, and Bridget Mooney, waving her hands to dry her nails. The back doors of the ambulance are open, and Osmond sees Teeter Thibault sitting up on the stretcher, his right pants leg split up the side.

Osmond nods toward the porch, speaks to Teeter. "How you doing there, Teeter?"

"Damn moccasin bit me, Osmond."

"You'll be all right. You've got LizAnne taking care of you. She inside?"

"Yeah, she's waiting on the snake."

Johnny speaks up from the porch. "LizAnne said to tell you to come on inside, and she'll fill you in."

Osmond finds LizAnne calmly gluing acrylic nails onto Shirley Grooms's fingertips. Shirley is talking when Osmond comes in and doesn't stop when she sees the sheriff.

"And they were both covered in mud. They scared me to death

when I looked up and saw them standing there in the door. I thought maybe they were robbers or something. Osmond, you should have seen her. She knew just what to do. She took her scissors there and cut Teeter's jeans right up the side, then started squirting something on the snakebite. She told me to call for the ambulance. And I did. Johnny got it here pretty quick, and LizAnne got Teeter right into it."

LizAnne manages to interrupt Shirley. "Shirley, you sit here and let that glue set up, and I'll go talk to Osmond." LizAnne motions Osmond through the hallway of the old mill house and into the next room, where she runs her tax business.

Osmond speaks softly. "LizAnne, shouldn't that ambulance be screaming down the highway?"

LizAnne chuckles. "Probably not. He won't need to go anywhere unless the snake was poisonous."

"Teeter said it was a moccasin."

"Those boys will call anything a moccasin. Rudolph Lunt brought Teeter in, so I sent him back out to Two Mill Pond to find the snake. He told me they killed it."

"You don't think we ought to send Teeter on to Augusta, just in case?"

LizAnne shakes her head. "It's not a bad bite. There's no swelling. I've called Augusta, just in case. They've got the antivenom, if he needs it. But I'm waiting for Rudolph."

Osmond nods. LizAnne knows how to manage time and people, and she doesn't panic. Osilo County has no hospital, just a clinic in Walthourville for flu shots and stitches. Everything else requires a one-hour drive to Augusta or an even longer ride to Columbia in one of the county's two ambulances, so LizAnne treats the vehicles as critical equipment, not to be dispatched unwisely. LizAnne is one of the few people in the county Osmond would hesitate to overrule. "I'll go out and keep Teeter company while we wait for the snake."

Osmond climbs into the ambulance with Teeter. "So what happened, Teeter?"

"Moccasin bit me."

"Tell me about it," Osmond says.

"Rudolph was pulling the boat out of the water. I was backing the truck down. When I got out, this big old moccasin bit me. I think I stepped on him."

"And where were y'all when this happened?"

"Out on some pond."

"Which pond, Teeter?"

"We was out on Two Mill Pond."

"So what were you and Rudolph doing out there, Teeter?"

"We was just out in the boat."

"You two were fishing?"

"Naw."

"You wasn't fishing?"

"Well, sorta."

"You were trapping turtles, weren't you, Teeter? You and Rudolph?"

Teeter scratches his head. "Osmond, there ain't no law against it. We called Fish and Wildlife, and they say there ain't no law against it."

"Well, call 'em again, Teeter. There's a list of endangered turtles that you can't pull out. And now you've got a snakebite. So you might want to find some safer way to make a few bucks. How much you get for turtles? Is it really worth it?"

Teeter doesn't answer.

"And you were on private property, Teeter. That's mill property. It's posted. There's signs everywhere."

"Well, hell, they ain't around, Osmond. They're in France. How are they gon' know me and Rudolph are out there? And shoot, they'd probably be glad we got some of them turtles out of there anyway, don't you reckon?"

They both hear the noise of Teeter's pickup speeding toward them. When Rudolph brakes, gravel peppers LizAnne's porch.

"God, she'll be pissed," says Teeter.

Rudolph has a cardboard carton that once held twelve Michelobs. "Here it is, Osmond."

"Show it to LizAnne," Osmond tells him. Osmond knows the snake has been shot, knows that neither Teeter nor Rudolph has a permit for a gun, or even a hunting or fishing license.

LizAnne appears on the porch. "Rudolph, the gravel is supposed to stay in the parking lot. Bring that box up here." Rudolph carries the carton as though it contains a religious relic, places it gently on the porch floor in front of LizAnne. She squats, pulls the cardboard flaps back, sticks her hand in to turn the snake over to look at its belly. "Banded water snake," she announces. "Nonpoisonous." She starts issuing instructions as she's springing to a standing position. "Teeter, you'll be fine. Johnny, drive Teeter over to the clinic, make sure he gets a tetanus shot. Rudolph, you drive Teeter's truck over there and meet them. Don't either one of you spray any gravel when you pull out."

"You sure, LizAnne?" asks Teeter.

LizAnne comes down the steps, puts her head inside the ambulance. "It's a big snake, Teeter, but it's not poisonous. The only thing you got to worry about is getting back here to see me about your taxes. Remember, I got you an extension, but August 15 is coming up."

"Can I have the snake?"

"I'll put it back in your truck."

Osmond shakes his head in admiration at a woman who can identify snakes, insert IVs, handle the IRS, and deal with women who think the color of their nails is a critical decision. LizAnne reminds Osmond of the wife he left behind in Georgia. She was a bookkeeper, did the books for the contracting business Osmond abandoned, did taxes, too, like LizAnne. "LizAnne, can I buy you some lunch?" Osmond asks.

Knowing she has two more nail customers and three tax clients due this afternoon, LizAnne is already on her porch. But she hears something in Osmond's voice. She hears loneliness. LizAnne is the only person in Osilo County who knows about Osmond's wife, knows because she files his taxes. "I don't have time to go out, Osmond, but if you want to bring something back, we can eat in the kitchen."

"I'll be back at one," he tells her.

She throws him a quick wave as an answer. When Osmond backs the cruiser out, his foot on the brake, mindful of the gravel, he hears

LizAnne fussing at Bridget: "Bridget, your nails are long since dry. You can head on home anytime."

Osmond won't date because he is still married, still believes in marriage, can't bring himself to divorce the mother of his boys, can't forgive himself for leaving them. But he misses the company of women. LizAnne is safe company, happily and securely married. Every woman in Osilo County is delighted to have car trouble, giving them an opportunity to pull into Dilly's Auto Repair and spend a few minutes with LizAnne's fine-looking husband, Boone. Every man in the county, including the sheriff, knows he's no threat to that union, so Osmond can sit at the kitchen table with LizAnne for a little while and remember what his other life had been like.

❧

From his kitchen, putting away groceries, Jimmy hears the radio crackle that announces the sheriff's car. Osmond knocks on Jimmy's back door, making Jimmy wonder how the sheriff knows he's in the back of the house.

"Hello, Osmond." Jimmy has met the sheriff twice now at Totch's.

"How ya doing, Jimmy? See you got this screened in."

"Just last week."

Osmond steps inside the screened enclosure and looks up at the aluminum roofing. "I like this aluminum stuff. Nothing to paint."

"They did the whole thing in less than three days. Wanna sit? Want something to drink?"

Osmond scratches his face. "Naw. Can't stay. You the one that called about the car?"

"Yeah. Last night. A car drove along the pond, right through my backyard."

Osmond is looking at the Adirondack chairs, permanently cushioned now that a roof protects them. He sits. So Jimmy sits, too.

"It was a Taurus, dark green, I think. The plates weren't South Carolina plates, but I couldn't read anything in the dark."

"You know Miz Fuller, don't you? Charlie Mae Fuller?"

"Not really. She's that real old lady lives next door to Karen."

Osmond nods, leans back in the cushions to tell his story. He sighs. "Miz Charlie Mae was a kindergarten teacher. She's outlived two husbands. She had a boy by her first husband, and that boy died in Korea. She had two boys by her second husband. Jack Fuller died in Vietnam. That's what everybody says, anyway, but I was in Washington chaperoning the senior class on their field trip, and we never did find his name on the Wall. We were gonna make one of those tracings, like everybody does, and bring it back to Miz Charlie Mae. Then there's the other boy, L. O. Now, L. O. kinda comes and goes."

Jimmy wishes he had never dialed the sheriff's office, never reported the green Taurus driving through his backyard. He interrupts. "Listen, Osmond. Excuse me a minute. I was putting groceries away when you came by, and I still got meat to put up. You mind talking in the kitchen?"

"Sure, sure." Osmond jumps up and follows Jimmy into the tiny rectangle that is his kitchen.

Jimmy wiggles a pizza into the narrow freezer compartment of his side-by-side Kenmore refrigerator. "So what's Miz Charlie Mae got to do with a car in my backyard at two in the morning?"

Osmond scratches his face and tucks in his shirt. "L. O. Fuller, Miz Charlie Mae's boy, well, there's a warrant out. Back child support. Lots of back child support. Kids are grown now, but the warrant's still active, and the wife won't back down. If I lay eyes on him, I got to put him in jail."

"He didn't support his own kids. Maybe he *should* be in jail." Jimmy tosses two packages of ground chuck and one of boneless chicken breasts into the freezer.

"Well, yeah, that's a school of thought, all right. But if I put him in jail, that still won't get the wife no money. And Miz Charlie Mae won't get to see her boy. Now, what I heard is, L. O.'s working at that Toyota plant up in Kentucky. He gets down here every couple of months, and he kinda scoots through the backyards and drops in on Miz Charlie Mae."

"Osmond, he drove through three backyards to get there. Just barely got between my deck stairs and the dock. Left tire ruts in my yard. Had no headlights on. I imagine he took out Mayme's clothesline." Jimmy stacks two cans of tuna on a cabinet shelf.

Osmond takes whole-wheat bread and Rice Krispies and paper towels from a plastic bag and arranges them on the white countertop. "Well, Miz Mayme took down the line."

Jimmy slams the cabinet door and lets the wooden *whack* replace the "Shit!" that would normally have erupted. "So everybody on the block knows this guy's coming, this guy who wouldn't take care of his kids, and everybody knows he's gonna drive through backyards."

Osmond sees a Raisin Bran box on a shelf, so he puts the Rice Krispies box next to it. "Well, I think Miz Mayme woulda told you, if she had a chance."

Jimmy opens a Coors. He isn't going to offer beer to a uniformed sheriff, but he can't ignore him either. Jimmy holds open the refrigerator door and waves an invitation.

"Naw, thanks, Jimmy. Can't. I'm still clocked in. But God knows a postcard would taste good about now."

"Look, Osmond. I just don't like somebody cruising through my yard, just missing the deck, no lights on. So whoever plans this conspiracy, well, ask them if they can reroute L. O. so he doesn't go through my yard."

Osmond nods. "You don't approve of me ignoring a deadbeat dad, do you?"

Jimmy offers no answer.

Osmond scratches his face, sighs. "Jimmy, I do look at things a little different, I guess. I think my job is to take care of people, to protect them, even if it means protecting them from the law. So, mostly, I rank things. There's big stuff, and there's everything else. Now, back last summer, there was some big stuff. I saw something I hope you'll never see. I saw this little baby strapped into the backseat of a car, left there. Left for five, maybe six hours. It hit ninety-eight that day."

Jimmy puts his beer can on the counter.

"She wasn't six months old, I bet. Turns out the daddy, along with some buddy of his, decided to go steal some copper wire out of the old Munsching Mill building up the Valley. Parked the car in the parking lot. Went in, pulled out some wire, did some drinking, apparently. Probably did some drugs, too."

Jimmy has been slouched against the counter, but his body pulls erect and his hands fold in autonomic respect for what he is about to hear.

"That little girl cooked alive. Pulled out what little hair she had. There was a wad of hair in her little hand. And her tongue. Well, that baby's tongue was sticking out of her mouth like a big cigar."

Osmond stops abruptly. He walks back onto Jimmy's newly screened porch. Jimmy follows.

"The mama was working an extra shift at the paper-cup plant just this side of Columbia. So I drove up there. I got her off the plant floor. I told her. Well, anyhow, I guess I take some things serious. And some things, you know, I just look the other way. So if L. O. wants to come see Miz Charlie Mae a few times before she's gone, and he don't cause trouble in Osilo County, then I'm not gonna know he's here. And if some geologist wants to float his bass boat in the pond and look at the stars and smoke some weed, well, I ain't gonna see that either."

Calling out, "See ya later, Jimmy," Osmond steps down the three treads off the deck. Back in his car, his dispatcher is reporting some loose cows blocking traffic on County Road 314. There's also a call about some teenagers racing motorcycles on the dam. Osmond calls in. "Alicia, I'm near the dam. I'll take care of the motorcycles. Send the boys out to 314."

Jimmy stands at his back door looking at his green metal boat with the trolling motor, bouncing against his dock. He turns back to his kitchen cabinets. From the Raisin Bran box, he pulls a Ziploc bag that cost him fifty bucks. He flushes the leaves and rinses the plastic bag, just to be sure, before he throws it into the trash can under the sink. He doesn't know what to make of a sheriff who thinks he should protect people from the law.

Osmond Vause is a native of Osilo County, but he was living another life in Georgia when Hurricane Hugo brought him back to South Carolina and a bullet made him stay. He walks and rewalks the path of that bullet, weaving his way among pine and sweet gum and water oak, trying to see how that bullet made its way through all those trees that could have stopped it. He walks right up to the garage, wondering how the bullet found the one window, missing the brick wall that could have stopped it. He looks through the garage window and imagines a car, imagines a man, wondering how that bullet angled itself just so, through the open car window into the brain of Alexander Ducasse.

Those walks are the only crack in the concrete he has poured around his secret. Those walks are the reason he became Osilo County's sheriff, which gives him carte blanche to patrol the Ducasse property, looking for clues where there are only memories. Osmond pictures his memories in a jar, like the jar full of nails he kept handy back when he was a builder. He fumbles through that nail jar, shakes it, hoping to stir the right memory to the top. He does not remember the victim, Alexander Ducasse. To a ten-year-old boy, he had been old Mr. Ducasse who lived up the hill, the man who owned the land behind his house, the acres of trees where Osmond and his brother Billy built tree houses, forts, camps, tents, dams. He does remember the gun, remembers comparing it to the shiny six-shooters pulled from holsters on *Bonanza* and *The Wild Wild West*. Uncle Will's World War II relic was heavy and square in his hand and is cold and gray in his memory.

Osmond knew that Billy was sneaking the pistol out because he overheard their father lecturing him about it. Billy lost his bike privileges and his allowance for a month, but that didn't cure him. Unable to imagine Billy's rebellion, their father simply put the gun back into Uncle Will's unlocked footlocker, stored in their garage while Uncle Will served his final tour overseas, at the same base in Germany where Elvis had been stationed. Once, their daddy and Uncle Will took them into the woods on the Ducasse property and let them fire Uncle Will's pistol. They aimed at a sheet of plywood propped against a pine. Osmond remembers painting the target onto the plywood, how much fun it was to be allowed to get paint on his clothes, to paint the white circles.

Old Mr. Ducasse died in 1968, the year Osmond's family moved to Athens, Georgia, where he and his brother went to the University of Georgia, Billy becoming a dentist, Osmond a builder. Osmond didn't hear about the shooting until 1989, when he returned to Walthourville to rebuild the Marbury home, one of the many damaged by Hurricane Hugo. Osmond encountered Bruce Marbury, known as "Berry," at a meeting of the Greater Athens Chamber of Commerce and learned they were both from Walthourville. They were about the same age, but Berry had gone to the Catholic school, so they had never met. Osmond had no interest in taking a job back home, in a state where he wasn't licensed, but Berry talked him into a reconnaissance trip by throwing in the promise of a fishing weekend on the boat he kept at a Hilton Head marina.

Osmond sucked in his breath when he saw what Hugo's winds had accomplished. Tree trunks lay on the nearly flattened house, thick oaks and long pines parallel to one another, pointing the way Hugo had gone. One pine had been forced horizontally through a front upstairs window, skewering the house, its root ball now obscuring the porch roof. "Hugo picked that tree up whole," Osmond marveled. "Your insurance man was right, Berry. You gotta raze the house and start over."

Berry nodded in agreement, unsurprised. "The problem is my folks. They don't want a new house. They want the old one back."

"Ah, yeah." Osmond understood then. Berry had already tried the local contractors, modern contractors building modern homes. Berry was hoping that Osmond could figure out a way to re-create an eighty-eight-year-old house quickly enough so that his seventy-something parents would be around to move back in. "Labor's in short supply, Berry. Half the houses from Charlotte to Charleston need reroofing."

"Can you salvage anything?"

"The front door looks okay," Osmond said. He was joking, but Berry took him seriously.

"Actually, it's the kitchen door Mama really wants saved. She notched us all growing up there, on the doorframe, and the door itself was like a bulletin board. She had pictures of the grandkids all over it, seventeen of them now, and pictures they colored, stuff like that. When you walked in the house, you always went right to that door first, to see what was happening, 'cause that's where the graduation invitations would be, or the vacation pictures, or whatever."

It was like having Grandpa Walton ask you to rebuild that house on the mountain. Osmond was hooked. The kitchen door was at the end of the central hallway, which was also the foyer. It still hung true, and its many coats of enamel—the good, old lead-based stuff—had protected it from the elements. Several thumbtacks were still there.

"We can save the door, Berry. And there are probably some other removable things, like that mantel in the living room, maybe the oak flooring in the dining room. I can get it done, but it's gonna take money, and time."

"Daddy likes to say he hopes he's got enough time left to spend all his money," Berry laughed. "It'll do them good just to watch the reconstruction."

The deal having been struck, Berry drove through Walthourville to show Osmond the rest of the damage. Osmond was curious to see his boyhood home, and Berry obliged. "Looks pretty intact," Berry commented. "The yard's a mess."

Osmond was looking at the changes, not the storm damage. The curving brick walkway that made skateboarding a bumpy adventure had been replaced by a more utilitarian concrete strip. The driveway, which had been pleasantly noisy gravel, was now concrete also. The house itself was still painted white, just as Osmond remembered it. His eyes traveled to the wooded acres stretching behind the house, what had been to him a vast playground. The pines all leaned in one direction, wind-whipped, and the less supple hardwoods showed wounds where limbs had been yanked away. Through the thinned greenery, he saw a fence. "What's fenced off back there?"

Berry leaned forward to get a better look. "We're behind the Ducasse property," he answered, as though that explained it.

Osmond was looking at a six-foot height of chain link topped by strands of barbed wire. "What on earth made them fence it in?"

Berry looked surprised. "Well, the shooting."

When Osmond looked blank, Berry continued. "Mr. Ducasse was shot and killed. Must have been after you-all moved, otherwise you'd have known about it. Summer of '68. Hard to forget that year. King was shot, and Bobby Kennedy, then Walthourville had a murder." Berry accelerated, pulling away from the curb where Billy and Osmond had waited for the school bus. "He was in his garage, in his car, and the shot came through the window. They never did find who did it."

Osmond knew. He knew in that moment. He knew why they had moved, knew why they had been hustled off to summer camp. And he knew not to ask Berry questions. Instantly and instinctively, he became protective of what he knew.

"Everybody knew Mr. Ducasse was rich, so the police figured it was supposed to be a robbery. Walthourville had never had a murder, so the local cops probably didn't know what to do."

Osmond knew what to do. His mind had already digested the central fact and now craved more information. He stayed quiet so Berry would keep talking.

"The state sent some cops down from Columbia to help out. Mr. Ducasse owned lots of buildings and rented them out. The hardware store, the drugstore, all that stuff downtown was his. But they couldn't find anybody who didn't like him." Berry stopped then, concentrated on driving through a slew of teenagers crossing the road between Stone Bowl Valley High School and the Burger King.

Osmond craved details about the shooting but was now tooled for discretion. "New stadium," was the only comment he could manage.

He was lucky because talk of the stadium boomeranged back to the shooting. "Built it about five years ago. Every civic organization in town had some kind of fund-raiser. Daddy said the town was determined to build it without tax money. Old Mrs. Ducasse, as a matter of fact, donated some land that they auctioned off."

Osmond managed not to swivel his head toward Berry, managed

to formulate a safe half-question: "So she must still live at the old place."

Berry nodded. "Yeah. But she's kept that fence up all these years. And I've seen her get out of her car to close the gate across her driveway. You ready to eat?"

Osmond pretended to be interested in his business, in getting the Marbury house rebuilt, in his kids. The secret became a wound, a weakness to protect, to hide, something to live with that couldn't be talked about, like his colon polyps.

He became a researcher. He told Audron Meese, owner of the only newspaper in Walthourville, that he wanted to look through old copies of *The Voice*. "I'm rebuilding the Marbury house," he told Audron. "I thought while I was here, I'd put together a memory book for my mom. Birthday surprise. She'll be sixty-five this year."

"I don't remember anybody named Vause," Audron said. "When did you-all move to Georgia?"

"In the sixties," Osmond hedged.

"Well, I didn't start up until '68. But you go on and look. Help yourself to the copy machine if you find anything. Make some copies for your mama."

Osmond found a box labeled "1968-1969, Editions 1-78" on the bottom of a stack of four cartons. The first two issues were one page each. Osmond knew that the first multipage issue was the one he needed. It told him a story he already knew, seemed to have always known. It was like watching a rerun.

The first thing he recognized in that front-page story was the date—the first Friday in June, when he and Billy were at home because school had just let out, Daddy was at work, and Mom was at school packing up her classroom. Billy got the pistol out of the garage and went off in the woods. Billy was the big brother, so he didn't invite Osmond, didn't want to include him in his disobedience. Osmond remembered hearing the popping of the pistol, off in the woods. He probably heard the shot.

In July, weeks after the shooting, *The Voice* ran a headline announcing the caliber: "Bullet Was 9MM." Audron Meese knew his readers would understand what bullet he was referring to. Osmond didn't know the gun's caliber, but he knew the make, his boy-child brain having absorbed Uncle Will's history of the pistol: "It's a Walther. Took it off a dead German somewhere in France, just three, four days after D-Day."

For all of 1968, it was rare for *The Voice* to publish an edition without some reference to "the Ducasse murder." A guest editorial demanded more deputies. All the letters to the editor were about fear, about locking doors and guarding children. The town council declared it illegal to use firearms within city limits. A new fellowship hall at the First Baptist Church was named after Mr. Ducasse.

In June 1969, on the anniversary of the shooting, the front-page headline complained, "Still No Suspect." Just one month later, the moon landing seemed to cure the town of its interest in the death of Mr. Ducasse. On the front page of *The Voice* was a photo of a fifth-grader with the caption, "Young Mike Sikes vows to become an astronaut," a paragraph about the Ladies of Galilee prayer circle, which was meeting daily to pray for the moon mission, and quotes from local politicians about the importance of the event.

At the Osilo County Library, Osmond was surprised to find half a shelf of books about guns. He took them one at a time, concealed inside an open *Road Atlas of North America*, and studied them at a table with his back to the wall, learning that Walther manufactured several pistols used by the German army, and that some of those used nine-millimeter ammunition.

As he studied, he realized how odd it was that he knew nothing at all about guns. Looking through *The Voice*, he had come across half a dozen photos of boys with their first buck. But after Uncle Will's Walther, Osmond's father had never again shown them a gun. There were lots of fishing trips on charter boats out of Savannah, on ponds all over Georgia. The garage in Athens had a wall rack for all the fishing gear. Osmond realized he owed all those wonderful weekends to the shooting. Everything after that, everything his daddy did, was just caulking a hole.

Osmond took his research back to Athens and interrogated his mother, his brother.

On Mother's Day, he exploited a memory. He gave his mother a cedar wren house.

"Mama, do you remember that bird nest in the blue jeans?"

"In blue jeans?"

"Yes, ma'am, in Billy's blue jeans. You had hung them on the line, at the old house, back in Walthourville."

"In Walthourville?" She laughed. "You're asking me to remember a bird nest from twenty years ago?"

"Well, I remember it. You called us out to the backyard to show us. And you wouldn't take the jeans down, even though we were headed to that summer camp in Blowing Rock." He let the camp reference hang there for a minute, hoping she'd say something, but she just shook her head, bemused. Osmond didn't give up. "You left them hanging there, and we had to stop in Greenville, at Sears, to get Billy a new pair."

"I do remember that. Those brand-new jeans went right into the duffel bag for camp, unwashed, and I was worried he'd have to hike or something in those stiff things."

"Seems like we had to pack for camp in a hurry."

Mama smiled the way she always did when she talked about Daddy. "Your daddy wanted to surprise you-all with that trip to camp."

Osmond's theory was that his mama had been surprised, too. "And then there was the move to Athens. So I guess you had to yank those old jeans off the line anyway."

"Probably did," she said agreeably.

"That must have been a hard time for you."

She looked puzzled. "Moving to Athens?"

"Well, that whole summer. Getting us ready for camp, then moving. Everything was so rushed." Osmond took a chance. "Did Dad get fired? Or something?"

"Lord, no, Osmond." She laughed. "Dad got a better job here in Athens. We put the house in Walthourville on the market, and it sold almost immediately. Now, that caught me by surprise, how quick it sold. We had to pack up and move."

"And you didn't mind?"

"Honey, it was a step up for your daddy, and we bought a bigger house. And we figured the schools in Athens would be better than the schools in Walthourville."

Osmond could hear his daddy making those arguments to Mama. "But you had to change jobs, too."

"Teachers can teach anywhere, Osmond. So, will you hang this birdhouse for me before you go?"

Osmond approached Billy by bringing up camp.

That Jimmy Carter grin of his split Billy's tanned face, and he laughed. "Oh, I loved that camp. Remember the *Playboy* magazines?"

Osmond had to laugh, too. One of the boys had brought a knapsack full of *Playboy*s, probably leaving all his underwear at home. They spent every night eating melted Hershey bars and looking at breasts by flashlight.

Billy went on, distracting Osmond from his mission. "Do you remember what happened when you got hold of that bow and arrow?"

Osmond had forgotten. "The string popped! I had a blood blister on my finger and a God-awful bruise on my cheek."

"You looked like hell. You'd hold up that blood blister and scare the younger boys at campfire time."

Osmond tried to get him back on track. "Don't you wonder why that happened? Why we got sent to camp?"

"Same reason all kids get sent to camp. So moms and dads can have a few weeks of peace and quiet. Maybe you and me and the wives should pack off our five and charter a big boat and fish the Gulf."

"But Mama and Daddy didn't have a vacation while we were gone. They moved. Sold the house and packed it up."

"Well, maybe that's why, then. So we weren't in the way for the packing and moving. Or so we wouldn't be concerned about it."

On the way home from camp, their daddy had announced the move with questions: "How would you guys like to have your own rooms? What would you think about going to some UGA football games?"

That first summer had been a good time. Their mother kept them busy, taking them on tours of Athens, getting new library cards, visiting her new school and their new school, buying brand-new three-speed Schwinns at the Western Auto. The news from Walthourville never reached them. It never occurred to the boys to ask to telephone their abandoned buddies. Long-distance calls were luxuries reserved for Grandma on holidays, timed with an egg timer. They did not know they were fugitives.

But Osmond knew now, and the knowledge made his life a puzzle jumbled in the box. He took courses in firearms. He bought land in Osilo County, began a house there as an excuse to return, to listen for answers to questions he couldn't ask. He volunteered with the sheriff's department, went from volunteer deputy to part-time deputy, which made him eligible for courses at the SLED Academy. Then he ran for sheriff. The election and the final move from Athens to Osilo County cost him his business, his marriage, custody of his boys.

For Osmond, the county border is a cofferdam, something he built to drain the truth from that day in a long-ago June, something he meant to be temporary. Worse than the nightmare of Billy in handcuffs are the long nights of heartburn, when Osmond lies awake belching fear, fear that he's wrong—that he gave up his home, his wife, his sons, the brother he thinks he's protecting, for nothing, for his own sick delusion—fear that the cofferdam is his prison. He is walking the path of the bullet.

## Chapter 17

## *Bryan*

BRYAN HAS SPENT HIS SIX-YEAR LIFETIME being no trouble at all.

He was born into Camilla's world, and he attends her life. During her speech-therapy sessions, Bryan fills coloring books. He is allowed to watch her physical-therapy sessions, is encouraged to clap when Camilla balances on one foot. But he is puzzled when he grows old enough to easily mimic what Camilla does with so much effort, so much praise. For waiting rooms, he invents a game. He first lists all the magazines he finds, patiently writing out the titles in block letters, then sits down with his pad and pencil and tries to predict what publication the next patient will choose, scoring himself with a complicated system—one point if he guesses their choice, two points if he predicts they won't pick up anything, two points if he suspects they have their own book. He records his points in one column, the time he has waited in another, his score in the third, unaware that he has taught himself ratios while still in kindergarten, fortunately never thinking to add together the minutes waited, to compare the totaled hours to his age, to resent the proportion.

On the first day of first grade, he was given a big manila envelope with his name written on it, a brown rectangle that sat on the kitchen desk unattended for days. On Monday morning, he pulled it out from under the journals and bills that had accumulated on top of it and handed it to his father.

"I think there's something in there you have to sign," Bryan said.

Martin made his way through the sheaf quickly, shaking his head impatiently, wondering if the teachers thought the parents were children, too. Each 8½-by-11 sheet announced just one fact, in thirty-six-point type—a PTA meeting, a book sale, a parent-teacher conference schedule, a school fund-raiser. Each sheet was a different color, and Bryan watched as yellow and pink and orange were slapped onto the table. But his father held onto the blue sheet.

"Bryan, do you have any interest in soccer?" Martin asked.

Bryan did not know what soccer was. He did know that his father was interested in that blue sheet of paper. "Yes," he said.

Martin had a pen in his shirt pocket, and he completed the short form in seconds, adding a note above his signature that he would coach if his schedule permitted. That blue sheet of paper was the magic passport that let Bryan emigrate from Camilla's nation, that gave him access to his father, who now saw Bryan as the tool he needed to make his escape.

The campfire pit is Bonus's idea. "We always have a fire at the campground, all us RV people," he tells Jimmy and Mark and Bryan. "We just sit around the fire and bullshit."

"We're sitting around the dock bullshitting now," Mark points out.

"I wouldn't mind a campfire," Jimmy says. "Is it legal? Don't we need some kind of permit for a fire?"

"Is anything really illegal in Osilo County?" asks Mark.

"It's fine unless there's a ban on outside burning," Bonus says. "We need a pit, though. Bryan, you've got the youngest eyes in this crew. Scout Jimmy's yard and find us a safe place."

For the next few minutes, the three men shout directions at Bryan as he points out possible sites in Jimmy's dark backyard. "How about here?" he asks.

"I want it closer to the lake," Jimmy says.

Bryan scurries to another spot. "How about here?"

"It oughta be within reach of the hose, just in case," Mark points out.

Bryan finds Jimmy's hose and stretches it out on the ground. The men look at one another, impressed that the boy thought of that on his own. "How about here?"

"Is it kinda flat?"

Bryan nods vigorously.

"Then that's it."

For the next three weeks, Bonus and Bryan work on the campfire pit. Bonus talks to Karen to work out a schedule around Bryan's softball practices and his own responsibilities as a Meals on Wheels volunteer. "Make sure he's in old clothes," Bonus reminds Karen. "This is dirty work."

Bonus pulls his pickup onto Randleman Road and blows the horn. Bryan has never been summoned by a car horn before, but when he hears the honk, he runs. "I gotta go," he hollers to the sitter. He doesn't bother to ask her approval, thinks of her as Camilla's sitter, doesn't even remember her name. Every week, there's a new sitter, a student his mother taught, or a Burger King employee she recruited while waiting for their order, or a teenager who put a flier on the grocery-store bulletin board hoping for a summer job. Though he couldn't have articulated it, Bryan recognizes the phases—the compassion when they first meet Camilla, the fatigue of the second day, the disgust they no longer hide as they clean Camilla on the third or fourth day, the boredom of Friday that leads to his mother's desperation when no one shows up on Monday.

Bonus and Bryan spend the entire afternoon in the True Value hardware store. "I already got bricks we can use," Bonus tells him. "They're old bricks, used to be the pillars under the old houses that got torn down. But we need mortar mix." The bag of mortar mix is loaded into Bonus's pickup and paid for, but still he leans against the counter and talks to the other men.

Bryan examines tiny drawers filled with screws, nail bins, pipe, dowels, fencing. Occasionally, he brings an item to Bonus and waits for a pause, never interrupting. "Mr. Bonus, what's this?"

"That goes inside the toilet tank. Makes it flush." A few minutes later, Bryan is holding a small piece of metal that is surprisingly heavy. "That's called a joist hanger. You'd use it if you were building a deck." Bonus uses his hands to make a right angle. "Holds one piece of wood onto another." Bryan almost has the next object figured out before Bonus tells him. "That's a hinge. Like on a door."

Bryan wanders the hardware store, where all the things that make up the world wait on shelves, wait for people who know what they are and how to put them together. He is a scientist discovering atoms.

Bonus drops him at home just in time for supper. After supper, Bryan lifts the heavy lid on the toilet tank, examines door hinges and knobs, unscrews the pulls on cabinet drawers and screws them back in.

"We gotta load the bricks into the truck," Bonus tells him. "You'll have to do most of the heavy work. Just toss 'em up there."

Bryan picks up one brick, walks to the truck, stands on tiptoe to drop it gently into the bed.

"You'll be forever doing that. Just throw 'em."

Bryan picks up a brick, looks toward Bonus, then lobs it into the truck. When it lands with a *thunk*, he says, "I'm sorry! Did it hurt your truck?"

"Kiddo, that's a pickup truck. It's required by law to be dented and dirty. Throw those bricks in there."

Bonus maneuvers his pickup into Jimmy's backyard. Bryan stands in the bed of the truck, feeling tall and powerful, tossing bricks onto the ground.

"Now, see how Jimmy's yard slopes down toward the pond? Well, what we gotta do is dig us out a level spot." Bonus uses his cane to draw a semicircle among the weeds. "Get the shovel from the truck and dig this out." Bonus perches on the tailgate and watches Bryan dig. "It'll end up being like half a circle," he explains. "We'll curve a little retaining wall along the uphill side, about three bricks high. Then we'll lay bricks in the flat part to pave it."

Bryan wants to know what a retaining wall is, what it means to "lay bricks," but he doesn't ask. He knows that Bonus will let him build the wall and lay the bricks. On the days scheduled for work on the campfire pit, Bryan is glad to get on the day-care bus, no longer dreading the afternoon hours, no longer imprisoned with Camilla and the sitter of the week.

Bryan sits on the tailgate watching Bonus, who is using a board to scrape the work area flat. "Now, you gotta dig us a trench around this half-circle. That's where we'll build our little wall. Now, if we were building a bigger wall, we'd have to put in a concrete foundation, but we're gonna lay these bricks right on the ground." They trade places. Bonus gets on the tailgate to supervise, and Bryan begins to dig the trench. "One brick wide, one brick deep," Bonus tells him. "That's it. That's good. Lay a brick in there, see if it fits."

The next day, Bryan mixes mortar. "Little more water," Bonus instructs. "That looks right. Now, pick up a brick. Use your trowel there and slather some mortar on the end. More than that. Like you're putting peanut butter on a cracker. That's got it. Now, drop the next brick in the trench right in front. Put your level on top. I can't see that little bubble from here, kiddo. If it's level, keep going." The trench is filled with the bottom layer of bricks. "Now, pick up a brick, but this time put mortar on the end and the top. Then lay it down, mortar side down."

Bryan has a hard time holding a brick with just one of his small hands, so he balances each brick on his knees while he dollops mortar. Using both hands, he settles each brick gently into place. "The mortar's all squishing out, Mr. Bonus." Bryan's jeans hang heavy with mortar, and his face and hair are splotched.

Bonus coughs to hide a chuckle. "That's okay. Scrape it off. Just keep going. It's looking good."

Bonus ultimately lets the wall become four bricks high because Bryan is having so much fun and because he is getting better with each brick. "Look at that, kiddo," he says. "You have laid brick. You're a bricklayer."

Bryan's old home was brick, and he knows that a brick wall should be smooth, shouldn't have those scallops of mortar, shouldn't look like a layer cake with too much frosting. But it is a brick wall, it is standing, and he built it.

The next day, they ready their semicircle for brick pavement. "Smooth it out with the board, like I did. Now, put the board down and put your level on top. All right, now we gotta arrange these bricks in here. Then we sweep dry mortar and sand in between the bricks and sprinkle water on it."

Bonus settles on his tailgate with a Bud while Bryan spends the rest of the afternoon arranging the rectangular bricks to best fit inside their semicircle. "How about this, Mr. Bonus? It looks kind of like a rainbow."

"That looks good, looks real good. Put your level on it. Then we're ready for mortar."

They finish on a Thursday. On Saturday evening, they build their first fire. Jimmy stops at a Wal-Mart in Columbia to find skewers for their hot dogs and marshmallows.

"Bryan, this is a fine campfire pit."

Mark agrees. "Listen, I thought you guys were gonna dig a hole and put a rock circle around it. This here's like something you see in a state park."

"I think you've upped my property value, Bryan," Jimmy tells him.

"He gathered all this firewood, too," Bonus points out.

"I think he's gonna have a permanent job keeping us a pile of firewood handy," Jimmy proposes. "How 'bout it, Bryan? We'll make you the fire marshal."

"I'll bet your mama is proud of what you built," Mark says.

Bryan doesn't say anything, but when Mark looks at him, expecting an answer, he nods a lie. Bryan won't trouble his mother, can't imagine how she could come down here to admire the campfire pit while encumbered with Camilla, doesn't expect anyone to clap when he stands on one foot.

Bryan keeps the campfire pit swept clean. Every afternoon, weather permitting, he searches the wooded area behind Bonus's house, gathering deadfall. Limbs that are too big he drags into Bonus's yard. When enough accumulates, Bonus hollers, "Chain-saw time, I reckon!"

When the men gather at the fire pit, Bryan knows he is included. They expect him to get the fire going. When Mark hires him to help deliver the bolenos—" 'Cause that way, I don't even have to get out of the truck," he says—Bryan begins to look forward to both afternoons and evenings.

Every Monday around four-thirty, Carl yells, "In the conference room!" to announce the weekly staff meeting. Every Monday, his crew yells back, "We don't have a conference room!" then heads to what everyone but Carl insists is the copy room, which houses not only the copy machine but also the refrigerator, the microwave, and the conference table.

Carl settles into a chair at one end of the table and starts the meeting as he always does: "We by God do have a conference room, and this is it. Now, Lakeishia, tell us what the hell we need to know."

Louis and Mike sit on one side of the table. Will gets a Mountain Dew out of the fridge and settles next to Jamil on the other side of the table. Lakeishia, at the end opposite Carl, is busy inserting pages into folders. "Jimmy's on his way," she tells Carl.

"Like how close?" Carl asks.

Lakeishia smiles. "He called from the parking lot."

Jimmy straggles in, drops his briefcase on the floor, goes to the refrigerator, and sits down with a cup of yogurt. "Whose yogurt am I eating?" he asks.

"Mine," says Lakeishia. "I'll put it on your tab." She scoots folders down the table, three for each person. "Okay, Carl's put together an overview of the gold-mine site reclamation. That's the red folder. I want your input on that. It's too big a project for us, but I think we could bid on some aspects of it. Then we've got a chance to buy up the business from Goddering because they're selling out to some big company, and the big company doesn't want to do the South Carolina stuff. Too small-potatoes for them."

"Isn't it small potatoes for us?" asks Jamil. "It's just well sampling."

"More like bread and butter for us," answers Lakeishia. "These permanent contracts keep us going between the big jobs. Anyway, that's the yellow folder. I think we'll need more people, maybe another truck or two, so look it over, throw out your thoughts. Then there's the green folder. That's the bucks. I'll go over that when we've done the other two. Carl?"

Carl takes over, asks for progress reports, leads them through the blue and yellow folders, lets Lakeishia take over at the green folder. "That it?" Carl asks. "Anybody got anything else we need to know? Or don't want to know?"

"I do have one more folder," Lakeishia says, sliding purple folders down the table. "This is something we all need to study." Jamil and Louis open theirs first, start laughing, recognizing one of Lakeishia's practical jokes. "And there will be a quiz."

Jimmy is her favorite target, and he is her target for this one. Behind him on the wall hang the results of one of her ongoing jokes, a chart tallying the gadgets Jimmy has lost—four GPS devices, seven shovels, three hard hats, a pair of hip waders, a tripod—and tracking the betting on what he will lose next.

The purple folder makes Jimmy laugh, too. On the title page is "The Accidental Geologist, or How to Survive in Osilo County." Page two is a "Glossary of Osilese," which defines *teddy bear* as barbecue. A footnote clarifies: "Except on Saturdays, when teddy bears are unavailable and calendars are served, known to foreigners as 'steaks.' " The last page is a passport application.

"I like the last page best," Jimmy says. He reads aloud: " 'Travelers to this remote region must be vaccinated against Osilocution, a virus that results in estivation of the male human.' " As he reads, two words stand out as though highlighted in yellow: *remote* and *estivation*.

"Is there a cure?" Carl asks, flipping pages as though searching.

They adjourn for beer and ribs at their usual Five Points hangout, Lakeishia buying Jimmy a beer "because it's a known antidote to Osilocution."

On the drive back to Randleman Road, Jimmy finds that he forgot to put CDs in the truck and has nothing to play, few stations to choose from beyond the city limits, too much time to think. At one time, he liked driving, looked forward to the downtime as an opportunity to play the Elton John CDs that he loves and his ex-wife hated. Now, he mulls the purple folder, the phone call from Carl insisting that he start showing up for the weekly staff meetings, Carl's closing comment about a cure.

When he pulls into Randleman Road, he sees flames illuminating the faces of Bonus and Mark, wishes he could turn around and go back to his friends, wishes he didn't have to sit around a campfire that reminds him of those fireplace evenings with his wife.

# Chapter 18

## *Martin*

MARTIN IS THE EX-HUSBAND, the solid surface against which Karen pushes to propel herself in a new direction.

Martin is noted for his ability to focus single-mindedly on a problem, on one patient at a time. That skill makes him an excellent oncologist. His focus now is on his wife, another problem requiring a solution. Martin thinks she has fallen back into the pit, the deep hole that had required him to take a leave of absence for four weeks because she had been hospitalized for four months.

At the beginning of that four-month nightmare, he recruited a full-time Irish au pair to care for Camilla, picked her up in New York, and escorted her to their home, the perfect solution to a temporary problem. Martin came home every evening to find the au pair waiting at the door, desperate for him to relieve her. She scurried to her room, locking the door. He let her get away with it for one week, thinking she had to adjust.

On Sunday evening of the second week, he knocked on her door and asked for a conference. "Tierney, I expect you to feed Camilla supper, to put her to bed. I bring home work to do in the evenings. You have your days off."

"No one said there'd be diapers to change, diapers on such a large child."

"I thought the agency told—"

"No one told me what she would be like."

That statement froze Martin. No one had told him either. "I was under the impression you were told to expect a special child."

Tierney looked frightened then. She wouldn't look at him. When she realized she had to answer, she finally spoke in a whisper. "I thought *special* meant something else."

"I'll get additional help."

On Monday, Martin's appointment schedule suffered while he spent several hours on the phone, shunted from agency to agency. Finally, he arranged for aides from AtHome Health Care, Inc., for the housekeeping services of Dust Bunnies, Inc., for meals to be delivered by Casseroles and Company.

"You'll have to coordinate these things, Tierney," he told her.

He expected her to feel promoted, but the twenty-year-old was intimidated. On her day off, while Camilla was cared for by an aide, Tierney disappeared. The New York agency was defensive when Martin called, pointing out that Tierney's contract had not specified dealing with a profoundly handicapped child, that she had offered to repay her airline ticket, that they had no one available who could handle such a situation.

Martin called Camilla's neurologist, who referred him to the county's Department for Special Needs Citizens. DSNC sent a caseworker, who filled out nine pages of forms during a ninety-minute interview. Three weeks later, Martin received a letter informing him that the household did meet the requirements for their respite-care services. A list of "Qualified Respite Care Service Providers" was attached.

Martin telephoned the caseworker. "Which one of these providers is assigned to Camilla?" he asked.

"Well, we don't assign them. You call them and make arrangements. DSNC reimburses you whatever it costs. You're qualified for up to forty hours of respite service."

"All you do is pay for it? I don't need you to pay for it. I need you to provide it."

"We train all our providers, in CPR, for instance. We run a check for criminal records, and we do a drug screen."

He called all seventeen names. Only one provider was available.

"Why, I know Camilla," she told Martin. "Mrs. Knox calls me sometimes, like when she has a dentist appointment or something, someplace she can't take Camilla."

Martin was annoyed to learn that he had retraced Karen's steps. "Well, Mrs. Knox is sick and hospitalized right now, so I need considerable help with Camilla. When are you available?"

"Well, I am so sorry to hear about that. I can sit on Monday afternoons, Tuesday mornings, all day on Fridays, and sometimes on Saturday mornings. Mrs. Knox used to have my schedule stuck up on her refrigerator, so she'd know when she could schedule her doctor's appointments and things like that."

"Mrs. Dunaway, can you quit your other job? I'll pay more than DSNC."

"Oh, I don't have another job. I'm retired, and I just do this when I'm not busy with my other activities."

Martin pasted Mrs. Dunaway's hours in among those of AtHome Health Care, Inc., added the services of one of his file clerks who needed extra money because she was saving for a trip to Hawaii. But he still found himself called home at least twice a week because of a crisis, because of a no-show, once because two caregivers showed up at one time. During the four months of Karen's hospitalization, Camilla was never taken to a therapist, Martin turned away new patients, his parents sent flowers, Karen's parents stayed in a hotel near the hospital.

When Karen came home, full of insight and plans and Prozac, she kept Casseroles and Company and Dust Bunnies, Inc., on the payroll but gradually dismissed the caregivers until she was back down to Mrs. Dunaway's schedule on her refrigerator. Whenever Mrs. Dunaway was at the house, Karen was at the university completing her dissertation. As soon as her defense was scheduled, she spread grid paper on the dining-room table and drew up plans for their new home.

Martin watched her for weeks before approaching her with the directory he had downloaded, residential schools for the mentally handicapped.

"There's one in Florida that looks good, and one near Atlanta. There are two in Pennsylvania. We could take a trip, go visit some of these places."

"Martin, don't you think I've researched this?"

"You have?"

Karen looked astounded. "Yes. And apparently you haven't. Camilla's too young for most of them." She pointed at the schools on his list. "The one in Florida will take them at twelve if they're ambulatory and toilet trained. The one near Atlanta takes them at eighteen, same conditions. The only one I could find that would take someone requiring the level of care Camilla needs is Swan River in Pennsylvania. It costs forty-five grand a year, Martin. And even if we could afford it, well, I can't do it yet. I can't send my helpless, nonverbal five-year-old child to another state. Do you not know that? I wish there was such a place just down the road, I admit that." She was not looking at Martin as she spoke. "I could see her when I wanted, visit her, take her out for ice cream. But that's a daydream. There is no such place. When she's older, she'll have to be placed. That I understand. And I have learned to let myself look forward to that time." She turned toward her husband. "But I need to live now. And now, Martin, I want another child."

Martin has learned to cherish silence, to enjoy the moments of stillness between the shrieking outbursts. After Karen and the children move out, the house is backfilled with silence. He looks forward to walking into it at the end of the day, like stepping into a hot shower. He is able to work, to read. Eventually, he realizes that silence is not a presence but the absence of voice and movement.

On his first attempt, he cannot locate Randleman Road. The second time, he has a map, but when he locates 610 Randleman Road, he finds it hard to believe that Karen and his children are living in such a house. Martin cannot imagine what the interior might look like, how it could hold more than one room. He drives to the end of the block, turns around, and returns to park in front of 610, feeling free to stare because he has chosen a weekday, knowing Karen is at work. He assumes his children are in day care somewhere.

Someone taps at the passenger-side window. Martin presses a button to lower the glass. A man leaning on a cane says, "Hello, there. Something I can do for you?"

Martin decides that honesty is the simplest solution. "My name is Martin Knox. I'm trying to locate the house where my wife moved."

Bonus nods. "Want me to tell Karen you were here?"

"No."

Bonus nods.

Martin picks Bryan up every Friday afternoon for softball practice, then supper. If a Saturday game is scheduled, Bryan spends Friday night. Martin recognizes this arrangement as precarious, since softball peters out at the end of July.

"Why don't you plan on spending every Friday night?" Martin proposes.

Bryan has waited for that question and has practiced a cautious answer. "My bedroom's empty," he offers. It's an excuse if his father needs one, a starting place if he doesn't.

Martin is confused for a second. He has forgotten that Bryan has been spending Friday nights in the guest room, his bunk bed and toy shelves having been moved to Randleman Road. "Why don't we refurnish it?"

Caution gone, the six-year-old's too-loud voice says, "If I stay over tonight, we could buy all that stuff tomorrow."

Martin pulls out his cell phone and calls Karen. She agrees easily to the arrangement. "Of course. Every Friday night. But you'll have to take Camilla, too." Karen has been ready for Martin's request, has practiced her demand.

Martin is enduring the Golden Corral, which he hates but Bryan loves. He checks to make sure Bryan is still at the dessert buffet before answering. "I can't spend time with Bryan if I have Camilla."

"I do it all week. I would love for you and Bryan to have time together. But frankly, I'm in favor of the plan because it'll give me a night off. And I don't have a night off if Camilla's here, so it's both or none."

"Okay."

"Okay? What will you do with her?"

"I'll see that she's taken care of."

The plan is too vague for Karen. "So you won't be taking care of her. Who will? Have you hired someone? Have you forgotten how hard that is?"

"I've been anticipating this, Karen. I've done some research. I've found a respite facility. It's operated by UCP. I'm surprised you don't utilize it."

"The Rodale Home in Columbia."

"You know about it?" Martin was sure she would protest putting Camilla into the hands of strangers.

"Of course I know about Rodale. I had a conference in Tucson last month. Where do you think she went? But it's just too far to get her there too often, and too much trouble to round up prescriptions and clothes and such. If you want to take her there once a week, do it, but you're in charge."

Bryan appears with a mountain of soft-serve ice cream topped with hot fudge sauce and sprinkles. Martin looks at it with distaste but says nothing. Bryan rearranges his ice cream, listening raptly but discreetly to his father's conversation.

"I'll arrange it. We'll start Friday. I'll have Camilla's meds ready if you'll pack suitcases for the two of them."

"Done. What time?" She is determined to pin him down, knowing that if a time and date are fed into his Day Runner, it will happen.

"Five o'clock."

"Fine. And I want an agreed-upon return time. How about Saturday evening after they've had supper?"

Martin hesitates. He knows Camilla will have to leave Rodale by three, and he was hoping to return her immediately to Karen. "Will Camilla eat in a restaurant?"

"I don't recommend that. But you do what works for you."

What works for Martin is delegating. He knows of a medical student in Columbia whose Egyptian wife is looking for undocumented work while waiting for a green card.

After Martin drops his cell phone into his pocket, Bryan builds shapes with his ice cream for several seconds while he gathers the nerve to ask for details. "So Camilla's gotta come, too?"

"I'll pick the two of you up. Camilla will stay in a facility in Columbia."

"Up at Rodale?"

"Yes, Rodale."

Bryan is grinning. "I can show you how to get there."

"Not necessary. I've hired someone to take her and pick her up. It'll just be us guys."

Martin has harvested the healthy organ.

Jimmy is a beneficiary and a prisoner of this complicated arrangement. He now has someone to wake up with on Saturday mornings, now has a weekly commitment. He and Karen carry their coffee mugs outside, sit on the back steps watching the pond.

"I shouldn't feel so good about the absence of my kids," she tells Jimmy. Then she tells herself that she can, that it is allowed, repeats mantras learned during her four months of inpatient therapy. "But I do," she admits out loud, to herself.

Jimmy watches the mist crawl over the pond, a gift from last night's thunderstorm, watches as veils twirl into funnels, admires Gaspard Coriolis's ability to recognize a phenomenon and devise an explanation, to feel the earth turn beneath him, air rise and expand and sink around him, to recognize that all the motion was related to the mystery of the clockwise swirl before him. He puts both hands around his hot mug, studies a plume of steam rising from his coffee, wonders if the ability to discover is a rare gift.

"You want some more coffee?" Karen asks. "I need some." She has not slept well. Several times during the night, she had awakened, panicked, wondering if Camilla was alone, neglected, abused.

"I'm ready for breakfast," Jimmy announces. He has slept soundly.

# Chapter 19

# *Audron*

AUDRON MEESE OWNS THE NEWSPAPER.

The business began as a print shop. Audron printed church bulletins, sales circulars, notices, business forms, whatever he was paid to produce. The Walthourville Ladies League published a cookbook in 1964, and he printed and bound a hundred copies of that. The league ladies were excited about their success and decided to start a newsletter so they could share recipes more often. The *Ladies League Monthly Newsletter* began a three-year run that ended when all the ladies had jobs and no one had time to track down birth weights and bowling scores. Even Audron missed it. When SaveMore ordered a weekly ad, Audron suggested they turn it into a fold-over and include a recipe and the Little League scores. He called it *The Voice of the Valley*.

Computers and printers and copy machines took away Audron's customers, but *The Voice*, the only advertising outlet for Walthourville businesses, prospered. Overwhelmed with being owner, editor, reporter, photographer, and sales manager, Audron finally quit printing his own paper. Now, he clicks *Send*, and his copy goes to a Columbia firm that prints, labels, and mails *The Voice*.

When Audron stops by the Old Courthouse for the legal notices, he passes Sally Heckert's "Want to Fill in Dillehay Pond?" poster. He immediately pulls his notebook out of his bag, glad to see something that might be news. No one has merely voted yes or no. Everyone has explained. Seventeen people have written their names under "Yes" and added notes: "Need the work"; "Kaye Clay might reopen"; "Jobs"; "Need to bury all that pollution stuff." Under "No" are thirty-three names with their reasons: "I swam there as a child"; "It's too pretty to fill in"; "Where would we fish?"; "I'd have to sell my boat." No one has ventured an entry in Sally's last column, "Other Ideas." Audron copies all the comments, photographs the poster, then hunts for its creator.

The front-page above-the-fold article that results is the first thing Jimmy ever reads in *The Voice*. Like a lot of other people in the Valley, Jimmy subscribes to the Columbia paper. Karen, who received a free one-year *Voice* subscription because of her perpetually running ad for a baby-sitter, never reads it, but Bryan loves it. Unlike the paper his daddy reads, full of bad news from Washington and Wall Street, this one has pictures of kids playing softball or running through sprinklers or eating watermelon at day camp.

Bryan shows up at the campfire pit with something to show Jimmy. "Jimmy, look. You're in the paper."

"Oh, yeah?" Jimmy assumes it's about his project at Muldoy Chemicals. "Listen, let's go inside so you can call your mama and tell her you're gonna eat some man-food with us."

Bryan walks into a kitchen smelling of beer. He hands Jimmy the newspaper and looks into a steaming pot. "I thought you cooked these on the grill," he says.

"Brats get soaked in beer first."

Delighted by the concept of beer-drenched food, Bryan forgets about *The Voice*, so he is startled when Jimmy whistles.

"What in the hell?"

Mark appears at the kitchen door. "Grill's fired up. Bring 'em on."

"Mark, listen to this crap." Jimmy reads the headline aloud: " 'Vote on Pond Filling.' "

"Vote? We get to vote on it?"

"He's talking about this poster somebody put up down at the courthouse."

"Oh, I saw that. Sally put that up. She's just having fun."

"Well, it's not fun now. My name's in here."

Mark forks brats onto the grill. "Bryan, you want two or three? Jimmy, just read the damn article to me."

"Well, he talks about the pollution and True Padgett, then he has this paragraph with me in it. 'Sally Heckert reports that a newcomer to the area, Jimmy Steverson, purchased an aerial photo of the pond. Nancy Auerbach, business manager of Muldoy Chemicals, confirms that Steverson is a geologist overseeing a project there contracted to KDR, a Columbia firm.' "

Mark laughs. "Well, damn, now you're famous." He opens his mouth to jokingly ask for an autograph but closes it when he sees that Jimmy is not amused.

"Where do I go to find this Audron Meese guy who wrote this?"

"Go to *The Voice* office, down by the depot. It's the only two-story building in town, 'cept for the courthouse. It used to be a store, the old mill store."

Through one of the plate-glass windows flanking the door, Jimmy studies a display of old store fixtures. Atop the red Coca-Cola cooler stands a row of glass cracker barrels advertising Lance cookies. Propped against the cast-iron stove is a sign offering, "Biddies 5¢." Through the other window, Jimmy sees a man working within a modern U-shaped desk between two monitors. Behind the man, mounted on the wall like a painting, is an old screen door, a double door with "Colonial Bread" printed on the mesh.

Jimmy taps at the window and then walks through the recessed door. Audron stands and extends his hand.

"Afternoon," says Audron. "Audron Meese. What can I do for you?"

"I'm Jimmy Steverson, Mr. Meese. You mentioned my name in an article this week."

"I sorta did, you're right. I tried to call you a couple of times, but all I got was your answering machine."

Jimmy remembers the messages. He thought they were sales calls. "Well, your article implies that I'm somehow involved in this pond-filling idea. I don't appreciate being misrepresented like that."

"Well, sit down here and we'll get it straight."

"I don't think I want to do that. I want to talk to your manager or editor or whoever's in charge."

"If you look through my little paper there, you'll see that my name is on the masthead as the owner and editor. And I write every news article in it except the church news and the school news. Reverend Balentine does the church news for me, and during the school year I get the editor of the high-school paper to do me a column on school news. Except for that, I'm the culprit. So fire away."

Jimmy flips through the twelve pages of *The Voice*. "You didn't write this recipe for broccoli casserole."

Audron smiles. "No, sir, you caught me there. I forgot about the recipes. LizAnne Dilly owns the manicure place, and she collects recipes from the ladies who come in, and she puts that column together."

Jimmy looks around, trying to get his bearings. Behind the old store counter looms printing equipment that looks long unused. Between the machinery and the brick wall is an open area with a long folding table engulfed in paper and books. There is no noise, not even a radio, and the quiet absorbs Jimmy's anger. He has been concerned that his involvement in this pond-filling nonsense will somehow reflect on KDR, but now he thinks he's overreacted, that assuming an article sandwiched between a broccoli-and-noodles recipe and a story on Vacation Bible School has significance is like taking a comment in a high-school yearbook seriously.

"Listen here," offers Audron. "Sit down and talk to me and I'll get it right."

"I don't want you to get it right. I don't want you to use my name in any connection at all with this pond-filling crap. I work for a company that does environmental cleanup, so if I'm trying to create a cleanup job, well, that's unethical, maybe illegal. Makes me look suspect. And it could make my company look bad."

"Why'd you need an aerial photo?"

"I needed an aerial photo of the Muldoy Chemicals site. I got one of the pond, too, just because I live on the pond."

"Oh. Well, didn't you talk to Sally a long time about the company that owns the pond?"

"I don't want to be interviewed, Mr. Meese. I just want to tell you not to use my name in your paper." As soon as he speaks, he realizes he probably can't tell a newspaper what to print.

But instead of invoking the First Amendment, Audron apologizes. "Well, I'm sorry. I'll leave your name out from here on in."

"You will? What if I get arrested?"

Meese chuckles. "Well, I do print the police blotter, but I've been known to edit that a little bit. Listen, around here, most everybody wants their name in the paper. That's why they buy it. I try to put as many names in as I can. My wife reminds me if there's somebody I haven't talked about in a while, and then I'll try to think of some reason to print their name."

"What do you know about this pond-filling rumor?"

Audron shakes his head. "It's nonsense. Something True Padgett dreamed up. I talked to some folks up in Columbia, and there's nothing to it."

"That makes this article kind of misleading, doesn't it?"

"Look, I gotta have something for the first page. The first page is stuff people talk about. It's gotta be a question, like who to vote for, or some controversy, or some bad accident or something."

Audron gained his knowledge of journalism from a one-day course, self-taught. He drove around the state buying up newspapers. He brought them back to his print shop and spread them out on the floor. The big-city dailies—those from Columbia and Spartanburg and Florence—didn't help him much. But the smaller towns—Edgefield and Barnwell and Saluda—gave him a template.

Audron made notes. He listed what he found in Edgefield's weekly—the front-page news, the second-page calendar of events, an editorial page, two pages for obituaries and new babies and weddings and parties, two for high-school football and Little League, the back page for the police blotter and the jury list and a few classifieds. He noted what he didn't find—comics, weather, news that wasn't local. Then he listed what he found in Barnwell's and Saluda's papers, and the lists were almost identical. Audron had found his formula.

Everything after page one he could handle. He studied the front pages again, making another list. He recognized two categories. Car wrecks, storm damage, gas-station holdups—those were bad news. The other articles on the front pages had to do with whether or not to do something—build a new school, widen a road, raise taxes.

A death was the birth of his business. While Audron was printing four hundred copies of his third edition, Alexander Ducasse, a prominent businessman, was mysteriously shot and killed in his own garage. Everyone in the county knew Mr. Ducasse, and everyone wanted details of the shooting. Audron went to the sheriff's office and was surprised to be given copies of official reports. He made himself knock on Mrs. Ducasse's door. He took photos of the garage. He reprinted the third edition, this time on a full-sized sheet of newsprint folded around what he had already printed. The four hundred copies sold. He printed six hundred more. His wife helped him handle the subscription orders as they came in.

In the one thousand eight hundred and twenty-two editions published since then, front-page news has been hard to come by.

"The other pages are easy," Audron tells Jimmy, "but I gotta root around for something to print on the first page. Especially in the summertime. With school out, there's not much going on in Walthourville. Now, if I could write about Osmond and the lottery machines, well, I'd have a headline."

"You mean the sheriff? What does he have to do with lottery machines?"

"He won't let the state put 'em in. Not in Osilo County. Anytime they get installed, he clips the wires."

"Why can't you print that?"

"Well, we're trying to keep it quiet. If it gets to be known state-wide, well, the Lottery Trust Authority will have to do something about it, and then Osmond will be in trouble."

Jimmy gives up trying to understand Audron's plan to protect the sheriff, goes back to trying to understand Audron. "And you do it all? You're the reporter and the photographer and everything else?"

"I farm out a lot of it, like I said. The preachers love to do editorials. The kids at the high school like to write up the football games and school news. And if somebody's got a wedding or something, they'll bring me the details. Sometimes, Vodelia Kaye e-mails me articles. She writes stuff about historic places in the county. Everybody likes those. They're kind of like ghost stories." Jimmy is silent, so Audron continues. "So, anyway, I do the front page and take the pictures and fit it all together."

Jimmy feels like he has yelled at a child. "Yeah, well, listen, I just don't like my name being attached to this pond-filling nonsense, okay?"

Audron is nodding. "Oh, yeah, sure."

"Stone Bowl Valley High School principal Wallace Bliven was killed Friday night in an accident on the New Highway involving a school bus. The bus was bringing the football team home from their game in North Charleston. Mr. Bliven's Cherokee swerved into the path of the bus. Seventeen athletes were injured."

The number of athletes varies from dream to dream. Audron worries about the number, about what it might mean. Each time he has the dream, he jots the number down on his calendar, hoping to detect a pattern. The worst part of the dream is that the article is read to him by Wallace Bliven, who then screams, "But I'm not dead! I'm right here!"

Audron is full of all the secrets he keeps. Each time he empties the trash-can icon on his computer screen, he wishes there were a way to empty his head of all the words he doesn't print. He doesn't think anyone needs to know that Walthourville's only doctor was arrested with a prostitute in a Columbia hotel, that a middle-school teacher was caught shoplifting in a Charleston mall, that Sheriff Vause owns a contracting company in bankruptcy in Georgia, that the high-school principal regularly appears before the magistrate on DUI charges.

What he doesn't print is a burden, and what he does print terrifies him. What if he gets it wrong? The first name Audron left out of the police blotter was that of Vann Smalley, high-school quarterback, scouted by Georgia Tech and Clemson and Alabama, picked up for beating another boy. Three years later, Vann was back in town, no longer wanted by the Crimson Tide, married to an Alabama girl. He was arrested again, for beating up another man. Audron looked at the name for a long time, called Osmond Vause for more information, was told that Vann Smalley seemed to be attracted to other men, got disgusted with himself afterwards, then beat up his partners. Audron printed the name and the charge. He had acted the first time to protect a boy with a career ahead of him, the second time to protect others from him. When the Alabama girl left Vann Smalley the day *The Voice* arrived in mailboxes, Audron was hit in the face with his own power, something he didn't want.

He can make people laugh or cry or leave their husbands or lose their jobs, when all he ever wanted was to make a living with his printing equipment, machines he cannot bring himself to sell, nuts and bolts and cylinders and fluids he can manipulate and fix, constant movement and an enveloping racket and an income based on the simple paradigm of cost per page, spewed as he watches, *puck-puck-puck*.

Now, before he sends his copy to Columbia, he e-mails it home to his wife, who proofreads it for him. "It's okay," Shelley tells him. "You got it all right. All the names are right."

Only Shelley knows of the dream. Shelley is a fixer. She talked to Osmond Vause, who talked to Wallace Bliven, who stays off the road. The principal rides the bus now, with the team, instead of driving. Then she told Audron, "You can quit that dream. You never write about anything that happens on the New Highway anyway, because it's always people from somewhere else."

As soon as Jimmy leaves, Audron hurries back to the bathroom, a walled-off corner of the old store, four feet by three feet of floor space with a twelve-foot ceiling, a silo with a toilet and a sink. Audron can never bring himself to close the door. He once considered installing a phone in the bathroom in case he got locked in, but he didn't want to explain a phone in a bathroom. As soon as he heard of cell phones, he bought one.

He throws cold water on his face and leans on the sink, sucking air, listening to his heart thump, waiting for it to slow, shivering. Jimmy had stood in front of his desk just like Wallace did in the dream. Jimmy had brought Audron's nightmare to life.

Audron had caught himself before telling Jimmy that True Padgett regularly sends him handwritten articles. Audron never uses True's contributions, long exhortations bristling with numbers, but he does carry them home to his wife. Shelley loves to read them aloud.

"Oh, Audron, this is a good one."

Shelley put in her twenty at the Nuclear Dynamics site and took early retirement so she could care for both her mother and her mother-in-law. After a day of feeding and bathing and entertaining two Alzheimer's patients, Shelley finds Audron's problems refreshingly solvable. For her, True's writings are entertainment.

She stands behind the island in her kitchen, pretending to preach. She reads, " 'It has seemed good to love our Pond, where we are suffered to enjoy the Glory of the waters, to fish and to boat. Yet a Plague of Pollution was visited upon our Pond. Eleven signs on the shore of our Pond stand as Testament to this Pollution. We are enjoined not to eat of the fish, not to partake of the Bounty of our Pond. Salvation lies in the hands of our one hundred and seventy legislators. But Redemption is in our own two hands. We must tear the signs from the earth, bear them to the State Capitol, take to Caesar that which is his. We must seek an Answer. We must enter into a Covenant among ourselves, to redeem three hundred and twenty-nine acres of God's Earth, to resurrect the company that once offered ninety-four jobs.' "

"Why does he capitalize all those words?" Audron asks.

"You know how every word referring to God is always capitalized?"

Shelley says. "You know, how they'll capitalize *He* and *His* and *Him*, every little word that means God? Well, True's trying to make his stuff look like that, so he's got to have some words with capital letters here and there."

Audron nods. "How do you know so much?" he asks his wife. "You always know these things I can't figure out."

True Padgett sends a clipping of the article to Columbia's newspaper, *The State*, which uses it as filler about three weeks later in its "News from around the State" section. "Pond May Be Filled," says the headline. "Walthourville's *The Voice* reports interest in a project to fill the polluted Dillehay Pond. Geologist Jimmy Steverson, associated with Columbia consulting company KDR, obtained an aerial photo of the pond from a county office. Congressman True Padgett, a vocal proponent of this remediation project, commented, 'It's up to the scientists to figure out how to do this thing. I've talked about it in the House for years, but sand gets put on Myrtle Beach instead of being used to bury this scourge that's endangering everyone in my district.' "

Lakeishia is the only KDR employee who reads the newspaper closely enough to notice the tiny story, wedged in among accounts of a school-bus driver in Barnwell arrested for indecent exposure, a fire on a Coast Guard vessel off Beaufort, and a new runway under construction at the Greenville-Spartanburg airport. Always alert for new sources of income for KDR, Lakeishia circles the one-paragraph article with a blue highlighter and puts it in front of Carl. "Is there such a project, Carl? Should I be researching it?"

Carl is already dialing Jimmy's phone as he answers. "Lakeishia, you're supposed to be the brains of this outfit. That pond's big enough to show up on the state highway map." Lakeishia retreats when Carl begins growling into the phone. "Jimmy. What in the hell is this thing about? This article?"

"Is this Carl? What article?" Jimmy is at the well site, sitting on his haunches labeling core, trying to minimize contact between his cell phone and his muddy gloves.

"There was some article in that little paper down where you live, and now *The State* is talking about it."

Jimmy stands. "Oh, shit."

"What the hell were you doing?"

"All I did was go into the tax office to get an aerial photo."

"What did you do that for?"

"I needed a photo of the Muldoy site, to do the drainage map. I just went ahead and bought the map with the pond and my house on it, too."

"Did you talk to anybody about filling it in?"

"It comes up sometimes down here, Carl."

"Quit talking about it. Don't ever talk about it again."

"What does it say in *The State?*"

"I'll fax the damn thing to you. But it says you work for KDR, so now the company's associated with this damn stupid scheme."

"True Padgett must have planted that article, Carl."

"Jimmy, why don't you move someplace where the politicians are just plain old crooked, like we expect them to be, instead of schizo-phrenic, okay?"

Jimmy doesn't know what to say. He looks down at the ten feet of core his boots straddle. "I've got that purple clay in a core here. The contact. Hit it at three hundred and ninety-four feet." Carl doesn't re-spond, so Jimmy adds details. "It's tight, so I don't think we'll find any contaminants below it, but we're pulling up samples just to be sure."

Carl sighs. The contact, the base of the aquifer they are trying to protect, has been found on time and under budget because Jimmy knows what he's looking for and how and where to find it. "Jimmy, God knows you're the best at what you do. But I'm up here in the big city trying to make people hire us. And if KDR is associated with a crackpot, then we look crackpot, get it?"

Jimmy gets it.

# Chapter 20

## *Camilla*

CAMILLA IS ELEVEN GOING ON TWELVE but will always be two.

She lives within a kaleidoscope. Reds and yellows glow and pulsate. Greens and blues have depth, concavity. In Camilla's world, there are green holes and blue pools punctuated by vibrating neon lights of red and yellow, all seen against a flat white sheet that she has to push out of her way as she walks. Her field of vision is limited by a dark ceiling. There is no *up*, nothing above eye level. Anything appearing from above her head is terrifying in its suddenness. A ceiling light clicking on is a lightning bolt. A balloon settling to the carpet is a meteor.

Sometimes, too many things happen at once. Sometimes, Camilla is squinting into a green hole and is confronted by a lightning bolt and jolted by a meteor, one blaze merging with another. Then her mind folds itself up and rolls downhill into a shady puddle, dousing the flare but convulsing her little body. For a while, there is blackness and softness.

On top of a bag of cloverleaf rolls left in his mailbox, Jimmy finds a note from Miz Mayme: "Need a favor."

Jimmy rattles her screen and walks on in. "Miz Mayme? What you need?"

"Jimmy, somebody's got to drive to Augusta for the lottery tickets. Bonus always does it, but he's at Fort Jackson at a reunion."

"Mayme, that's an hour from here. I've got to e-mail data to DEHP tonight."

"Jimmy, the Powerball's up to fourteen million. Somebody's gotta go. And you ought to take little Bryan with you."

"Well, I don't have to go to Georgia for lottery tickets. I can pick some up in Columbia. I have to run up there anyway to drop off some core samples."

Mayme is shaking her head. "It's not right to do that to Osmond. He's fighting the state lottery, so we don't like to buy tickets in South Carolina. Bonus always goes to Georgia for tickets."

"So because you've got a sheriff tilting at windmills, you guys drive all the way to Georgia? How 'bout just not buying lottery tickets at all?"

Mayme doesn't understand the windmills allusion, yet she recognizes the sarcasm in Jimmy's voice. She forgives the challenge to her logic, but she doesn't appreciate having her loyalty to Sheriff Vause questioned. "Well, Jimmy, if you don't want to go, just say so."

Bryan chatters all the way there, taking advantage of having an adult's undiluted attention. "We had a soccer game in Augusta. Then we all went to the Sonic for chili dogs. And I've been there to that museum, with my school. And some of Camilla's doctors are there." He tells Jimmy about his best friend's broken leg, about the new bunk bed his daddy bought him, about a food fight at day care. "It was girls doing it!"

Crossing the Savannah River into Georgia, Jimmy is reminded of Columbia's bridges across the Broad. He crossed that river at least twice daily, going to and from work, for all the years of his marriage. The Broad pushes hurriedly through Columbia, jostling over rocks, but the muddy Savannah below him now seems not to be moving at all. He pulls into the parking lot of Marvin's Market, where a sign welcomes them to Georgia and advertises cigarettes, beer, and lottery tickets. Inside the crowded and tacky store, Jimmy has the odd sensation of wrongdoing. Standing in the long line, he has time to realize that he was talked into doing something he doesn't approve of. Bryan appears next to him with Doritos, a Dr. Pepper, and a MoonPie. "Bryan, put all that junk back. We're gonna eat some Mexican, so this trip won't be a total waste."

In the restaurant, full of enchiladas and waiting for sopapilla, Bryan asks for the lottery tickets. He produces envelopes from his jacket pocket and begins labeling each with a name, stuffing one ticket into each envelope. "This is how Mr. Bonus does it," he explains. Bryan prints "Camilla" on the last envelope.

"Doesn't Bonus get a ticket?"

"No. Mr. Bonus doesn't buy tickets for himself. He says if he doesn't buy a ticket, he's got a dollar more than somebody who did buy a ticket. He says it different, though. It sounds funny when he says it."

Jimmy is ashamed of himself for having bought a ticket. "How 'bout you? Is one of those tickets for you?"

Bryan shakes his head.

"You want mine?" Jimmy offers.

Bryan shakes his head again.

Jimmy admires the patience Karen exhibits around Camilla and enjoys watching her interact with Bryan.

"You keep 'em in line, don't you?"

"I haven't always been that way," she answers, shaking her head for emphasis. "When you first have kids, it's scary. And especially a child like Camilla. You know, I'll always have to watch after Camilla. She'll always be pretty much like she is now, kind of like a giant toddler."

"Did having a handicapped child . . . Did that have anything to do with your divorce?"

She nods. "Sure." But she doesn't add anything else. Jimmy figures he has walked into posted territory, but then all of a sudden she continues. "At first, I thought it would actually make the marriage stronger. You know, the facing-a-crisis-together scenario. But we faced it differently." She is putting away groceries. When Jimmy saw her drive up, he walked down to help her with the bags. Putting cans on shelves, she talks without looking at him. "He got really into it, sort of like he did with coaching Bryan's teams, softball and soccer. He got himself elected president of the state ARC. He's on the Special Olympics Board of Directors. He started a newsletter about special education. He's a good fund-raiser." She closes the pantry door and turns to her countertop, colorful with bananas and tomatoes and oranges and cantaloupes. She drops the tomatoes into a colander, rinses them at the sink, talks a little louder over the noise of the water. "What he didn't do was sit with her while she had her annual EEG, brush her teeth, follow her to the bathroom to clean her up."

Jimmy has settled at the round table. Karen arrays the tomatoes on a towel to dry, puts the bananas in a basket and the cantaloupes in the fridge, and sits down across from him. "Sorry. I got too graphic, didn't I?"

Jimmy shakes his head. He doesn't speak. He wants her to continue, wants to know more about the end of her marriage, wants to know more about the end of his.

"I needed a lot of help with Camilla. My parents live in Indiana, so they're too far away to help. His parents live nearby, but, well, they play bridge every Thursday, and they go on cruises twice a year, and they're on this and that church committee. I used to joke about forming a grandparents' committee so they'd have to join. Anyway, I put an ad in the paper, and MaryBeth responded."

Karen tells him MaryBeth's story, tapping her kitchen table to point out where it started. "MaryBeth lived here, in this house, at that time. She kept kids here, in her home. Camilla didn't faze her at all. She kept Camilla and Bryan both, after school, overnight, when I went away to conferences, anything I needed. I couldn't have survived without MaryBeth. And so I got involved in her complicated life. MaryBeth wrote some bad checks. 'Bad paper,' she called it. She spent six months in the Richland County Jail and was on probation. So she couldn't get a job in a licensed day-care facility. And she had a lot of debt, which was a mystery to me because she had no car or anything else that's normally debt-encumbered. She had lost this house, was renting her own house from the bank, and was about to be evicted. So I bought the house."

Karen gets up from the table, sets out a row of cans—two cans of stewed tomatoes, a can of beef broth, a big can of hominy, a little can of green chilis. "Open these cans while I chop up an onion," she directs.

Jimmy knows which drawer holds the can opener. "What are you cooking?"

"Posole."

"What in hell is posole?"

"It's a Navajo dish, I think. I got the recipe out of a newspaper when I was presenting a paper in Tucson. This is one of those quick cheater recipes, but it's good."

"This is a meatless night, then?"

"God, no, I gotta have my meat. I got chicken left over, and I'll chop that up and drop it in after everything's in the pot. Think of it as a kind of chowder," she suggests.

Jimmy wants to steer her back to the husband and the house and MaryBeth, but he doesn't want to appear rudely curious. So he opens the cans and gets out a saucepan for her.

"Well, so, then I ended up renting MaryBeth's house back to her."

And then Camilla howls. Karen does not leave the kitchen, has trained herself not to reward Camilla's outbursts, but the noise invades the senses and is as impossible to ignore as rap music. Karen opens her recipe book, a three-ring notebook of clipped and copied recipes encased in plastic pages, like a photo album. She hands it to Jimmy, who flips through the alphabetical arrangement until he finds the ragged piece of newsprint titled, "Posole—Quick!" He scans the directions, or tries to, but is amazed at how difficult it is to read with Camilla's barked, "Dut! Dut! Gah! No! No! Not! Dut! Dut! Dut! Dut!" shooting into their ears, relentless, like a rogue smoke alarm.

Jimmy puts the opened cans next to the stove. Karen browns onions and garlic. Bryan appears at Karen's hip, faking an interest in the pot. Karen puts her arm around his shoulder and continues to stir.

"Dut! Dut! Dut!" screams Camilla.

Karen gives Bryan the spoon. Using just one hand so her arm never leaves Bryan's shoulder, she pours the beef broth into the pot, then the hominy. Bryan stirs, and the two of them sway with the motion. "Dut! Dut! Dut! Nah!" continues through the long minutes of simmering. Gradually, the *Duts* are replaced by a nasal sound like a baby's sneeze. When only the soft sneezes can be heard, Bryan moves away from his mother and begins to set the table, and Karen reaches for the can of chilis. Jimmy has been watching them intently and knows they are responding to a familiar signal, a subtle change in sound that marks the end of Camilla's rage, recognizable to them in the way that Jimmy recognizes the tonal change between a potato chip commercial and the return to an NFL game.

"Bryan, you wanna chop the chilis? Put them in that little green bowl? Jimmy, we have to add the chilis at the table 'cause the kids don't like them. Will you take over stirring here? I'll go change Camilla. She always wets herself after one of her Dut Dut episodes."

As he stirs, Jimmy tries to listen to Karen's voice, the soothing voice of a mother changing a baby, but Bryan turns on the television, to the Disney Channel. And so Jimmy watches the big corn kernels and wonders how you can live with something like that, something so awful and yet so frequent that you give it a name.

Camilla appears at the doorway, wide eyed, open mouthed, her hands held in front of her like a chipmunk's paws. When she sees Jimmy, her eyes close and a big, mobile smile takes over her face. Her eyes open and the smile disappears. Her eyes close and the smile returns.

Bryan takes over. "Go on and sit down, Camilla," he instructs, and she does.

Karen, having dealt with the soiled clothes and towels, returns to the kitchen. In seconds, she has a cantaloupe halved and the seeds removed. She puts cantaloupe half-moons on a platter next to the bowl of chilis while Bryan spoons posole into bowls. "Are we all set?" she asks, scanning the table as she sits. "Bryan, tell Jimmy your joke about my cookbook."

Bryan drops into his red chair and grins. He looks into his bowl of posole as he talks. "Well, Mom had these little pieces of paper with recipes on 'em? And she said she was gonna have 'em laminated. And I said she should have 'em eliminated."

"Don't you love it?" Karen asks Jimmy.

After supper, Bryan works on a poster for his softball team while Camilla removes and sorts and replaces the treasures in her tackle box. Jimmy and Karen clean up, talk about the cost of the new transmission in Karen's Volvo, speculate about the rumors of a Publix store being built on the New Highway, smile sadly over the latest Miz Charlie Mae episode.

"She was at that empty house?" asks Jimmy, who has heard an outline of the incident from Bonus.

"The house between hers and Mayme's, the one with the For Rent sign," Karen explains. "Like anybody's going to rent a house with half the roof missing. Anyway, Miz Mayme says Charlie Mae was on the back porch, knocking on the door. Mayme called Bonus, and they got her home, but she went right back. And she kept saying something about boiling peanuts."

"Alzheimer's?"

Karen nods. "Bonus got me the name of her granddaughter in Spartanburg. He says Miz Charlie Mae practically raised her. I talked to her, a girl named Geneva. But she doesn't want to give up her job at KFC to come live with her grandmother." Karen rolls her eyes at the young Geneva's priorities. "I told her if her references check out, I'll pay her to keep my kids. And she can look after Miz Charlie Mae at the same time."

The return to the subject of Karen's marriage surprises both of them.

"The day I told Martin I was leaving him," she begins as she closes the dishwasher, "I told him that he didn't help with Camilla. And he opened his Day Runner. And he showed me all the things he did for Camilla. All the board meetings and conferences." Isolated from the world of adults, Karen had envied Martin his Day Runner, would open it while he was in the shower, run her fingers down the pages, imagining the conferences and luncheons and meetings. Envy became resentment as she noticed the orderly entries increasing, past seven o'clock, past eight o'clock, into weekends, until finally she hated the sight of the black leather book. As she sat at their dining-room table telling him she was leaving him, wondering if she could do it, wondering if she would do it, he had given her a focal point, an inanimate object to talk to. He had opened the book that recorded the life she wanted.

The dishwasher begins its noisy work, and she says no more.

# Chapter 21

## *Sandra*

SANDRA OWES HER CAREER TO HER MOTHER'S BOLENOS.

At sixteen, she began making deliveries. On the way home from the motor-vehicle office, Sandra behind the wheel with her glossy new driver's license, Mayme made her case: "You can start doing deliveries now."

Sandra expected this and was ready. "The homeroom bell rings at seven forty-five," she said, assured that this would excuse her from morning duties. Her real reason was embarrassment. She did not want to drive around the county with a car full of bolenos, did not like to be associated with them, had even altered the pronunciation of her surname, saying it like her French teacher did.

Mayme, who got up at three-thirty to start the baking, had no qualms about waking her daughter. "You'll have to leave by five then."

Sandra hated the chore only one morning. Her first delivery was to the old Ramada Inn, which had stood empty for three years but was now reopened as the Woodpecker Inn. At the reception desk was a thin man wearing what looked like a long vest, his skin a color Sandra had never seen before. "Good morning," he said in very British English, and Sandra looked at the first foreigner she had ever seen. Instantly, Sandra reinvented herself, hiding the sulky teenager who had walked in the door ready to throw the two shoeboxes of bolenos on the counter, revealing instead a young woman with a mission.

"Good morning to you," she smiled. "I've brought you a dozen of our bolenos, made just this morning."

She soon knew every member of the Kurunji family, four generations of whom lived and worked at the hotel, a family that expanded occasionally as a nephew or cousin arrived from India. Every weekday morning, Sandra loaded thirty-seven shoeboxes of bolenos into Mayme's station wagon, left earlier than necessary, hurried through the first five drop-offs, saved the Woodpecker's two shoeboxes for last, lingered with the Kurunjis until she had just minutes before earning another tardy slip.

One day, one of the grandparents was operating the desk and was on the phone, so he motioned her through the swinging gate. A man walked in the door and looked around the empty lobby. "Don't y'all have a breakfast in here?"

He was addressing Sandra. Being behind the counter gave her definition, she realized, like putting on a uniform. Since Mr. Kurunji was still on the phone, Sandra answered, "Not until six-thirty." The man looked at his watch, let out a sigh. "But there's coffee ready," she told him, pointing out the coffee urn. Sandra liked being the person behind the counter, the person with answers, solutions. "And I guess I can go on and put out these bolenos."

After that, Sandra helped set up the breakfast buffet in the mornings, then went through the little gate that marked the border, fascinated with the mechanics of checkout and credit-card imprints and ordering supplies. She had tea with the family before leaving for school, studied them, wondered why they had crossed an ocean to be where she was, absorbed a new concept, moving on to move up. Sometimes she was giddy, amazed to be talking to people born on another continent, sometimes jealous of their extended-family cocoon.

A Holiday Inn Express went up on the New Highway, and Sandra had another stop on her daily list. She liked the crisp newness of the place, the clientele in their business suits. She studied the women she saw there, women with briefcases, calculators, credit cards, destinations. She offered to spread the bolenos out on trays, soon was hired to oversee the breakfast buffet, soon was filling in at the reception desk. The day after her high-school graduation, she became a full-time employee. The owner of the franchise also operated two motels in Charleston, and Sandra took over managing one of those, commuting back and forth to Mark and the children until she was asked to manage the second as well, then announcing to Mark that she was leaving, moving on, moving up.

Bored with motels, ready for resorts, she sidestepped to the downtown Hilton, where she began helping with conventions and receptions and meetings and found herself without a title but de facto in charge of the events office. When she learned all she could at the expense of the Hilton empire, having attended all their seminars and retreats and training sessions, she offered her services to the Peronneau Inn. As she updated her résumé, she realized that a Boulineaux would fit in nicely at the Peronneau, so she dropped Mark's last name and became again Ms. Sandra Boulineaux.

The Peronneau is small but has a distinct advantage in Charleston—it is over one hundred years old. Near the Peronneau, painted onto the brick wall of another old building, is The Hat Man, a ghostly advertisement for a hat store closed in the early part of the twentieth century. A city ordinance protects the useless picture, requiring not only that it not be painted over but that it be repainted and preserved. When Theodore Roosevelt stayed at the Peronneau, there was an engagement broker responsible for dances and teas and banquets. There is, therefore, still an engagement broker at the Peronneau instead of an events manager, just as there is still a Hat Man. Sandra loves the way the title looks on her business cards, loves the way she can go in any restaurant and be waved at by someone for whom she has planned a wedding reception or a Citadel reunion or one of those annual occasions so long running that no one remembers what they commemorate. She is wise enough to appreciate the niche she has found, safe from ambitious college graduates waving degrees in hospitality administration or marketing or English literature. The owners, three ancient gentlemen who spend their time playing golf on Kiawah and drinking at the Yacht Club and in the Peronneau's own High Tide Bar, treat her like a granddaughter. She loves the small staff, which has become her family.

Since school ended, the kids have been reminding her that they spend the summers with Daddy. She reminds them of the Fourth of July fireworks over Charleston Harbor, stalls them after that with beach picnics and water-park excursions, finally can no longer postpone the drive to Osilo County. She delivers her children to Mark, to the house he lives in but she owns. She inspects the house, makes sure there are groceries for the kids, endures the usual questions about child support.

"So you want me to keep sending you the support checks? Even though the kids are here?"

Sandra shoots Mark a look she learned from her first boss and uses effectively to indicate that a stupid question will not elicit an answer. Sandra keeps up the house payments, pays the taxes, renews the insurance, so the kids will have a place to vacation outside the city and a place to spend time with Mark. She insists on child support, a monthly connection between children and father, something she never knew.

She found her father fairly easily, when she finally made the effort. At the age of ten, she asked Bonus Wooten a question: "Mr. Bonus, is my daddy really dead?" Sandra was perceptive enough to notice that her mother lived in a state of expectancy—looking out the front window when a car went down the street, hurrying to the mailbox, grabbing the phone—and intelligent enough to observe that there was no grave to visit, no talk of cancer or car accident, no talk of her father at all.

"No, honey, he's not. But he's sure enough gone. To your mama, that's dead, so let's leave him that way, okay?"

Bonus, too, had located him easily, asking a buddy at Fort Jackson to check the military-benefits records. Bonus had found Royce Boulineaux, had talked to him on the phone, in Albuquerque.

"I ain't ready to come back, Bonus," Royce Boulineaux had said, as though he were late returning from a ball game.

"That's your business, Royce. But you left a wife over there in that house and a little girl, and they got to eat and pay the light bill."

"I'll send 'em what I can."

Sandra, too, utilized her father's army background when she Googled him. SSgt/Ret Royce Boulineaux was mentioned on a VFW Web site. He and three other members of his post had organized a rodeo for handicapped kids. That was in Dallas. He had gone from there, but Sandra tracked him to Galveston and Mobile and Knoxville. He seemed to be getting closer until he turned up in Baton Rouge.

He has a phone number in the book, so he isn't hiding. Sandra never tries to contact him, just wants to know where he is, like an astronomer keeping track of an asteroid.

Mark has never been late with child support. He knows he can go two months without paying on his truck, then send in one payment and a late fee and a note saying he's working again. He can get three months behind before Bell South cuts the phone off. But he knows that an empty beer can rolling around in his pickup might cost him a four-hundred-dollar open-container fine, and he knows that Sandra offers no grace period.

"Well, okay, Sandra, I was just wondering."

"You wonder that every summer," Sandra says. She smiles, amused, like when the kids ask if they can have a dirt bike, or ice cream for breakfast.

Mark smiles, too. "You know I gotta see what I can get away with. You know that about me."

That's what she likes about him still. It's something she can't do. It makes him a great playmate for his kids.

Jimmy has grown accustomed to Mayme calling him through her kitchen window to let him know Fairy Etta left him some eggs, or from her front porch to thank him for cutting her grass when he cut his, but he is surprised to hear her voice on the phone.

"I'm wanting you to come to supper," Mayme says. "Tomorrow night. Friday night. Seven o'clock."

Jimmy can't recall seeing a table in Mayme's kitchen, but he has no doubt her cooking will surpass a basket from the Chicken Strut. "Sure. Yeah, thanks, Mayme. I'll be there." Mayme hangs up before he can ask what he might bring to the meal. He can't picture a bottle of Shiraz in Miz Mayme's kitchen, and bread and desserts are obviously not needed, so he picks up a dozen tulips at the SaveMore.

Mayme has never been given flowers. She looks at Jimmy's green-wrapped bundle for a long time before extending both her hands, handling the bouquet as though holding an infant. "Why, these is the most beautiful things I've ever seen," she says, then disappears into a back room, presumably to find a vase. Jimmy is left to navigate Mayme's completely rearranged front room, the rocking chair and coffee table moved out to accommodate a shining mahogany drop-leaf set with bone china and sterling silver and linen napkins for four.

Mayme reappears with a vase and a young woman. "Jimmy, this here's my daughter, Sandra. Sandra, this here's Jimmy, that bought Orene's house."

Sandra does not belong here, not in this room, not in this house, not in this county. Her pale green business suit, a lustrous silk, is mockingly out of place, worn as a statement in the pointed way of a Moroccan ambassador wearing his djellabah in Manhattan. Below the short skirt, runner's muscles bulge, hard brown knots contrasting with the fragile fabric. Jimmy is instantly uncomfortable, partly because he assumes that Mayme is setting him up with her daughter, mostly because Sandra herself is rigidly uncomfortable, an Episcopalian at a talking-in-tongues service.

Sandra's left hand is wrapped securely around a large crystal vase. She offers her right hand to Jimmy. "Jimmy." When she takes his hand,

219

her manner changes, as though Jimmy has telegraphed some message through his right arm: *I don't belong here either. We're both from the outside world*. She smiles, nodding in agreement to things that have not been said. "Thank you for the lovely flowers."

"Sandra give me this vase for Mother's Day," Mayme says. "She lives down in Charleston. Jimmy, you go on and sit down."

Jimmy squeezes past the table and sits on the sofa, not sure if it is appropriate to sit at the table yet. He watches the show Sandra performs with the tulips. She drops them into the vase, where they spread into an artistic display as though ordered to do so. Then she stretches over the table to position the vase in the dead center of the table, skillfully avoiding contact between her silk suit and the chairs. She reminds Jimmy of his mother on vacation in Belize, afraid to touch anything, afraid to drink the water.

"So you grew up in this house?" he asks.

"Yes," she laughs, "I did!" Like a laser pointer, her eyes shoot around the room, to the chenille bedspread on the sofa, to the Last Supper print above it, to the plastic pot on the window sill, to the metal TV stand, each an illustration of her unspoken caption: *Hard to believe, isn't it?*

When Karen appears at the screen door, Jimmy almost says "Thank God" out loud. With Karen at the table, he is relieved of being coupled with Sandra and can enjoy Mayme's cooking, a whole roasted chicken and freshly snapped green beans and potatoes mashed with buttermilk and scratch biscuits and peach cobbler.

Dinner conversation is Sandra's bread and butter. She tells herself that this meal, in this house, is practice, training; she doesn't like to think of wasted time. "Karen, you have done wonders with your house. It's a transformation. How do you visualize it in the end?"

Karen, who faces a roomful of strangers at the beginning of each semester, has no trouble talking to one new face across a table. "Comfortable. Just enough room for me and the kids. I'm doubling the size, adding a master suite for me and a home office. Until that's done, I'm actually sleeping in Bonus Wooten's RV."

"Sounds like an adventure. I'm in a townhouse, in a restored warehouse in downtown Charleston."

"Close to work?"

"I can walk to work, although actually I run."

While Karen and Sandra use their professional skills to bounce the conversational ball across the table, Jimmy and Mayme simply eat.

Mayme is spooning a second helping of cobbler into Jimmy's bowl when Karen asks, "So, with all that catering responsibility, do you keep a standing order here for Mayme's bolenos?"

Jimmy's attention is pulled vacuumlike from his steaming cobbler into the vibrating silence. He looks up into each face, wondering if someone asked a question he did not hear. Karen instinctively knows that she has pulled a forbidden bell cord. Behind Jimmy, Mayme stands motionless with the pan of cobbler.

Finally, Karen says, "No more cobbler for me, Mayme. I'm way too full for seconds."

Sandra does not eat desserts. She adjusts the napkin in her lap, sips from her glass of water, and clears a space on the table for the cobbler pan before responding to Karen's comment. "I wouldn't dare import bolenos," Sandra says. "The pastry chef would probably resign."

"Well, Charleston has enough good stuff, like those pralines you can buy at the Old Market. We don't want to give them Mayme's bolenos anyway," Karen says. "And I've had something called Charleston cannonballs."

"Now, those we do serve occasionally," smiles Sandra. "At some of the more casual functions. And I'm working to resurrect peach leather. Nobody makes it anymore, so I've talked one of our suppliers into trying to adapt the old recipe to something they could produce. I think it might become a sort of trademark item for the Peronneau. A treat to leave in guests' rooms, maybe, a garnish for sorbet, that kind of thing."

"You'll have to tell me what peach leather is," Karen says.

"Essentially dried peaches. The old method was to sun-dry the fruit. It's pounded into sheets, or maybe rolled out, I don't know, and sugared. Then the sheets are rolled up, finger-sized."

"I'm thinking of dried apricots."

"Something like that," Sandra agrees. "But very distinct to Charleston."

"Murdis Grandberry, colored lady who took in laundry, used to bring us peach leather," Mayme says. "You don't remember that, Sandra? Murdis used to tell me her mama made it."

"No, ma'am, I don't remember that." She does remember Murdis, remembers being embarrassed that her mama handed her a cardboard box of dirty clothes out the front door when everyone else she knew had a washer and dryer.

"You was real little, I guess. When the laundromat opened downtown, I quit using Murdis."

*And then I bought you a washer and dryer*, Sandra adds silently. Resentment was the ugly egg tooth that let her break out of the shell she was born in, but she has not been able to shed it.

Mayme sends the leftover cobbler home with Karen. Karen puts it in the fridge so the kids will have it when Martin returns them on Saturday, then turns on her porch light, her signal to Jimmy. She waits for him in the RV. Her contractor built a connecting ramp between the RV and the house, a short hallway of plastic tarp and two-by-fours.

It is after midnight before they open the bottle of Shiraz Jimmy brought with him.

"This was the only thing missing from Mayme's table."

Karen, full of Mayme's good cooking, content to have Jimmy filling her bed, a night free of children, thinks that nothing is missing from her life. "That was a fine meal. Although conversation with Sandra turned out to be a chore."

"It was? You two chattered all through supper."

Karen laughs. "You didn't notice anything that wasn't on your plate. That woman acted strange." Jimmy rolls over, ready for sleep, but Karen finishes her description of Sandra. "Like a cat around water."

# Chapter 22

## *Geneva*

GENEVA'S LIFE IS A SERIES OF ACCIDENTS, and the latest accidents send her to Randleman Road to become Karen's sitter.

In Charlotte, North Carolina, the Board of Directors of Southeastern Dining, Inc., meets and decides to buy all the KFC franchises in Spartanburg, South Carolina. Geneva is cleaning up one night when her manager tells her there's a new owner, that there might be some changes. Never having known who the original owner was, Geneva cannot imagine how it could bother her any. A week later, the manager tells Geneva she is being laid off because the new company is shifting people around.

For a week, Geneva enjoys being laid off. She sleeps late, or pretends to, until her two roommates are off to work. Then she can shower as long as she wants and fry bacon and bake brownies and click the remote. Geneva has been the third roommate in a two-bedroom apartment since April, when her boyfriend disappeared, stranding her in a duplex she couldn't afford by herself. She moved in with Vonda and

Jackie, but most of her things went into storage. They set up her bed in the living room, pushing the couch alongside it like a fence.

Then Mull, Jackie's boyfriend, begins showing up every afternoon.

"I ain't got cable," he explains. He settles in on the sofa, a little too close to Geneva.

Geneva watches Mull drink her Cokes, fix a sandwich with her pimiento cheese, and take over the remote. Right in the middle of *One Life to Live*, he switches over to ESPN. She can't complain too much. If she makes Mull mad, then Jackie will get mad, and they'll want her to move out. And until she pays the back rent at her old apartment, she can't rent a new one.

Just to get out, to get away from Mull, she decides to go down to the Employment Security Commission, sign up for unemployment. That's when she finds out it will be thirty days before her first check comes.

Trying to hide from the heat radiating from a half-acre of asphalt, Cotton Carruthers has spent most of the day inside the prefab metal building that serves as his office. He catches up on sending out late-payment notices and has a stack of tag-and-title forms ready to take to the Department of Motor Vehicles the next morning. By the time Geneva drives onto the car lot, he is flipping through TV channels, bored and ready for distraction. He recognizes the '90 Escort, remembers selling it to a dumpy little girl whose hair needed washing, knows that she's a couple of payments behind. He doesn't recall her name.

"Hey, hon," he greets her when she walks in.

"I brung it back," she announces. "I got laid off. Ain't no way I can pay you. And I had to jump-start it to get it here, and the man who jumped it says it's leaking outta the water pump, so I'm just turning it back in."

"Well, sweetie, it ain't a library book. You can't just turn it back in 'cause you'll still owe on the note."

"I just told you I got laid off."

Before Cotton can sell her on repairs and refinancing or title pawn or check holding or any of the other schemes by which he keeps people sending him money, Geneva asks, "Can you give me a ride home?"

That breaks his heart, the thought that she has no one to drive her home. He turns off the TV set. "Lemme have a look at it, hon."

When he slides into the driver's seat of the still-running car, Geneva yells, "Don't cut it off!" When he turns the key, her face wrinkles up, ready to cry. It is ninety-nine degrees, and she is a long way from home.

Cotton pops the hood. "You don't need no water pump, hon. Who told you that? Just a leaky hose. But you probably do need a new battery." He slams the hood, ready to get away from the hot engine. "Let's go on inside, work something out."

In the air conditioning, Geneva feels better. She stands right in front of the window unit.

Cotton pulls her file. He still can't recall her name and doesn't want to ask her, so he looks through his sales records until he finds the Escort. "Geneva Ann Fuller," he says. "You're two payments behind, got another one due on the first."

Geneva pulls herself away from the air conditioner, sinks into a chair in front of Cotton's desk. She doesn't say anything. She has already told him twice that she got laid off.

"Hon, you know what refinancing is?"

Geneva nods. She doesn't know what refinancing is, but Cotton's tone tells her that whatever it is, it might fix her problems.

"Well, I can refinance your car, give you enough to buy a battery and get that little piece of hose fixed. But I gotta know you've got money coming in. You been looking for work?"

"I'm gonna get on at the Waffle House down in Clinton, just as soon as they call me. It's whenever the girl goes out on maternity leave."

And she will need a car to get there, Cotton knows. Cotton doesn't make his money selling cars. Cotton sells credit. He lets people stretch money over time, and most of the people he deals with stretch a little money over a lot of time, like pantyhose on a fat lady. And he makes interest on all that time.

"Lemme update your file here, hon. What's your address?"

"I'm staying out at Colonial Apartments."

Cotton hears a lot of that. His customers are never living any-where, just staying there, and they never offer a complete address. "What's your apartment number, zip code?"

"It's number 12-D. I don't know the zip code."

Geneva drives away with a battery from another car on Cotton's lot, a replacement hose he scrounged from a box in his storage shed, copies of all the papers she signed, and a new lower payment not due for forty-five days.

The sun is going down and the heat has relented, so she drives to Stow-It-All Storage to visit her things. Geneva likes punching the code number into the keypad and making the mechanical gate go up to let her in; it makes her feel like she belongs here. She drives to her unit, unlocks the padlock. As she slides the garage door up, hot air pours out as though she has opened an oven. In the back corner of the five-by-five box stands her Christmas tree. Between her and the Christmas tree are boxes of all sizes. On top of the boxes are throw pillows, a giant teddy bear, a plastic pumpkin, a melting shower curtain, a TV, a toaster oven, a laundry basket filled with towels. The only piece of furniture she was able to get into the storage unit is her gold velour swivel rocker. Geneva's favorite boxes are the ones marked "Kitchen." She finds one and pulls it over to the swivel rocker. She sits down and rummages through the box, checking on her dishes and her mugs and her dishtowels that match her oven mitts.

She hopes that someone is home because she doesn't have a key, and she can't ask the manager to let her in because she isn't supposed to be in the apartment, isn't on the lease. Jackie and Vonda are both at the mall, but Mull is there watching something on E! and lets her in.

Geneva puts together a grilled cheese and watches through the glass door of the toaster oven as the cheese melts. Vonda always tucks the bills behind the blender, and Geneva sees a new one there. On top of the South Carolina Electric & Gas bill, which has already been there awhile, is the phone bill. On the envelope, Vonda has done a lot of arithmetic in pencil and concluded, "Me $21.04. Jackie $24.56. Geneva $19.18." Geneva gets a Mountain Dew and wanders into the living room with her sandwich. She watches TV with Mull, wishing he'd leave. Geneva doesn't like Mull. She is pretty sure he knows where her boyfriend Tad is because Mull showed up one day with Tad's Jet Ski trailered behind his pickup.

The next day, Geneva stays in bed while Jackie and Vonda get ready for work. She pretends to be asleep, which is hard to do with the *Today* show on so loud. As soon as they are out of the parking lot, Geneva packs her clothes, using suitcases she finds in Vonda's closet. She has to get out before Mull appears, but she grabs what she can. She takes her comforter and pillows but has to leave her bed, her striped sheets, her pole lamp, her shoebox of word-find books.

All she can think about is the first of the month. If she leaves now, leaves like her boyfriend left her, Geneva will not have to pay her part of the phone bill or the light bill or the rent. At Stow-It-All, she has to decide what to take, what will fit in the trunk of the Escort.

Some three weeks after Karen's call suggesting that Miz Charlie Mae needs her granddaughter, Geneva mysteriously appears on Randleman Road. Karen is taking advantage of Charlie Mae's backyard, rolling a ball to Camilla on the lush grass. Her peripheral vision catches a young face looking out a back window. After walking Camilla home and asking Bryan to look after her, Karen knocks at Charlie Mae's front door, and the young face answers.

Karen has to speak, since the younger woman says nothing. "I live next door. My name's Karen Knox. I'm just checking on Miz Charlie Mae."

"Nanny's fine." Geneva walks away from the door. "Nanny! Somebody at the door."

Back home, Karen finds Bryan at the computer and Camilla lying on her side with her cheek on the cool flooring, watching Bryan's feet jiggle. Karen returns a phone call to a student anxious about a reference letter arriving on time, checks her e-mail, then telephones Mayme.

"I don't know if she's helping or not," Mayme complains to Karen. "Every time I go over there, she's watching TV or sleeping."

"How old is she?" Karen asks.

"I ain't sure. All that fat on her makes her look old, but when she talks she sounds fifteen."

"Well, just having somebody in the house is probably all Miz Charlie Mae needs at this point," Karen assures Mayme.

"I ain't sure who's taking care of who in that house."

Jimmy's answering machine repeats a message from True: "Jimmy, how you doing, this is True Padgett. I'm hoping you'll help me with some research I'm doing. I know when we're working up highway budgets, they always say that fill costs about three dollars a cubic yard, and I'm hoping you might spend a few minutes figuring out about how many cubic yards we'd be talking. Or you could tell me who would know how to do that. That's your line of work, not mine, so I was hoping you'd help us out here. I thank you."

Jimmy finds a message from True waiting for him almost every evening. Yesterday's message was argumentative: "Jimmy, how you doing, this is True Padgett. I was thinking. In your line of work, you probably know all about what they call beach renourishment. Well, I didn't know nothing about it until I got to Columbia. But almost every year, we vote on how much money to spend trucking sand onto Myrtle Beach. Now, if we can spend tax money doing that, then we can sure spend tax money trucking some sand around Osilo County to protect us from poisons. I was hoping you'd think on that, Jimmy. I thank you."

Jimmy has not responded to any of the messages. Thanks to True, he is now reluctant to answer his phone and is forced to let his machine screen calls. He has no way to screen out Joelle, though. While he erases True's message, she sends the evening's question sailing from the back door: "Jimmy, did you know we're moving slower here than they are down at the equator?"

"Hey, Joelle." As usual, it takes him a second to decipher Joelle's question. Jimmy pictures a globe, pictures it spinning. "Yeah, I reckon I knew that." He found her amusing at first, but now her intrusions have become annoying. He would like to be able to sit in his living room in his briefs and not worry about a girl peeking in his back door. "Listen, honey, I gotta run down to Karen's. Talk to you later, okay?"

Lately, he has been hiding at Karen's, but tonight Jimmy makes the mistake of getting to the house before Karen is home. That means he has to deal with Geneva.

"Can I go now? Or do I have to wait for Mizzus Knox?" she demands.

"Dr. Knox," corrects Jimmy. "You have to wait for Dr. Knox." Jimmy doesn't like Geneva, doesn't want her around, but he's unwilling to deal with Camilla, so he isn't going to release her.

Geneva sighs and continues what she considers her job—shadowing Camilla and stopping her from doing anything dangerous or messy or noisy. Camilla moves about in her erratic way, oblivious to the trailing Geneva, like a kite unaware of its tail. Jimmy watches until he grows impatient. It annoys him that Geneva offers no direction or distraction to Camilla, that Camilla leads and Geneva follows.

Jimmy knocks on Bryan's bedroom door. "Hey, guy, it's me." Jimmy knows that Bryan avoids Geneva, too. When Bryan appears, Jimmy holds up the video he rented.

Bryan grins. "Cool. I'll make us some popcorn."

When Karen comes in, the house is warm with the smell of popcorn and filled with zooming and zipping sounds from a science-fiction movie. Geneva scurries out.

"God, it seems like she could chat a minute, tell me how the afternoon went," Karen says. She comes up behind Bryan on the sofa and kisses him on the head. Camilla looks content lining up crayons on the coffee table, so Karen lets her be.

Jimmy gets up to help Karen with supper. "I think you should find a new sitter," he comments as soon as they are in the kitchen, where the kids can't hear.

"Jimmy, I've been running an ad in the classifieds since MaryBeth went to jail." Karen is annoyed. "It's not exactly a glamour job I'm offering. Nobody wants to be stuck in a house with Camilla all day—no one to talk to, messes to clean up. I can pay more than McDonald's and places like that, but I can't offer benefits."

"Okay, okay. I'm sorry."

Karen has taco shells and grated cheese and shredded lettuce lined up on the counter and is getting out the skillet to brown the ground beef. She is silent for long minutes, finally speaks just as the meat begins to sizzle. "I don't like her either, Jimmy. I don't like that I'm forced to hire someone I don't like to deal with a situation I don't like having to deal with. I'm always making adjustments I don't want to make, compromises. Like living here. I don't want to be here."

Jimmy has never understood why Karen is where she is, why she left the two-story house with the pool for this. "You miss your old neighborhood?"

Karen smiles as though amused. Jimmy missed her point, and she is disappointed. "No. Let me tell you a story about my old neighborhood." She stirs the meat and talks. "Camilla wandered away one day. I got a phone call from a lady down the street telling me Camilla was down there. So I walked down there, and there was this lady standing on her front steps with Camilla. She hadn't even let Camilla into her house. So now we end up here."

Karen's *here* makes Jimmy picture Randleman Road, an ugly little street with dislodged curbs, cracked asphalt, two vacant houses.

"But here, there's Mayme, who brings me bread every day and always squats down on the floor to visit with Camilla. There's Bonus, who offered to park his Winnebago over here so I can use it as a bedroom while they finish the work on the house." Karen shakes her head, bewildered herself at where she has ended up. "I had a therapist once who told me I have a hard time dealing with Camilla because I'm goal oriented. I had plans, and Camilla interrupted them. And I look on Camilla as a problem to be fixed, and she can't be fixed. But here, on Randleman Road, these people don't fix problems, they just survive them. Look at Fairy Etta, over there putting mush into tubes to feed Cone. She just does what she has to do, like everybody on this block. Camilla isn't seen as a problem here. She's just here."

She pours tomato sauce over the meat, busily stirs, trying not to look at Jimmy. She covets his simple life, his freedom. It occurs to her that he can live anywhere he chooses.

In KDR's conference room, two printers spit pages, the copier is rhythmically collating, and most of the staff members sit around a table covered with open pizza boxes, Coke cans, and Evian bottles. Mike is the only one not eating; he's asleep on the carpet, hugging the wall so no one will step on him. Carl learned of a request-for-proposal issued by the EPA, an invitation to bid on the cleanup of an old lumberyard where poles had been treated with creosote. The RFP had been sent to most of the major environmental consulting companies but not to KDR. Carl got wind of it on Tuesday afternoon, and the deadline is nine on Thursday morning. He called everyone in.

Jamil did the research, Will and Louis designed a technique, Jimmy translated that into a work site of labor and machines and their costs, Lakeishia computed FICA and overhead and turned Jimmy's lists into totaled columns, and Mike's software produced charts and graphs and spreadsheets. At two in the morning, Carl ordered three large pizzas.

"It always comes down to the copier," Carl says. After every bite of pizza, he turns to watch the copy machine, hoping not to see the little green rectangle flashing the mysterious *Call Key Operator* signal.

"If the copier breaks down," Lakeishia assures him, "we're headed to Kinko's. We are getting this job."

Jimmy can't remember eating anything but potato chips since lunch yesterday, so he concentrates on finishing off the last two slices of the Meat Lover's. "I could use a cold postcard with this," he sighs.

Focused on work, fueled by adrenalin and dollar signs, Jimmy's coworkers are not in a frivolous mood. Normally, they chuckle at Jimmy's tales of Osilo County, make jokes about Jimmy speaking Osilese again, but tonight a look passes around the table. Silently, Carl is elected spokesman.

"Jimmy, you gotta leave that crazy place."

Jimmy is slouched in his chair, dreaming of beer and barbecue. Carl's words are out of place, like a personal announcement made at a staff meeting, and Jimmy finds himself sitting upright, no longer relaxed. He says nothing, too tired to think. He assumes that Carl's remark is the result of fatigue as well.

But Carl goes on. "You've got a crazy congressman starting some kind of cult down there about filling in that pond. Which is just some kind of urban legend, or the rural version, or whatever, but he's got you running around asking everybody about it, which makes you look crazy, too. There's that street you live on, full of nut cases. And you've got a crazy sheriff, which means it won't help to call 911 when one of the nut cases goes crazy."

Jimmy is too tired to defend himself. The word *crazy* worries him. Jimmy has heard it a lot lately. His father regularly uses it. "How are your crazy neighbors?" he asks in his weekly phone call. Jana Hardaway used it when he told her about his lunch with the tax collector: "She tried to call the embassy? That's crazy." Even Karen used it, when Jimmy told her about Vivia. "There are degrees of craziness," Karen said. "Vivia's harmless, and she's functioning."

"For my master's degree, I did a study of currency exchange in the Middle East," Lakeishia begins. Jimmy is grateful, thinking that she's deliberately changing the subject. "I went to bazaars in Pakistan where you could see currency from all over the world, and people sat on rugs and traded money and magically sent it all over the globe. I couldn't figure out the rules, or who made them, or who enforced them, or how one shop knew what the exchange rate down the street was. I was thinking in complex terms, New York Stock Exchange terms. And I finally realized I was looking at a simple barter system. They were just bartering money." Lakeishia holds her hands palm up, like balanced scales. "Rupees for dollars, pigs for cows. You're in a barter economy, Jimmy. They're not using currency down there. That lady brings you eggs, so you baby-sit her husband. Now, the nice thing about currency is that it's impersonal and it completes a transaction immediately. With the egg situation, you're in debt until the egg lady needs you. Everyone on that block is for sale, you included."

Mike is awake. He props himself against the wall, stretching. "What's she talking about? Did you guys save me any pizza?"

Lakeishia looks at Mike. "We're telling Jimmy that he needs to relocate."

Mike circles the table, gleaning the last of the pizza slices. "What was that about the pigs and the cows?"

Lakeishia smiles. "All economies are based on pigs and cows."

Carl lets his head fall into his hands. He speaks into his empty coffee mug. "Dammit, Lakeishia, I was counting on you, and you're talking about Pakistan and pigs." He lets out a big sigh and looks up. "Jamil, put some paper in the copier. Jimmy, move back into the United States. And speak English."

Chapter 23

## Charlie Mae

FOR MIZ CHARLIE MAE, time no longer flows.

She does not need an alarm clock. She wakes up every morning at five, by habit. Then she checks the calendar thumbtacked to the back of the bedroom door, a fourteen-year-old calendar, and she decides that it is December 12. Time has left its orderly channel and flooded Charlie Mae with eighty-seven years of again and after and before.

"December 12 already," she announces to the empty room. "And that list has to be up at the mill office by this afternoon."

She puts on a long-sleeved dress and a sweater, but she cannot find her coat.

When Geneva shuffles by, on her way to Karen's house, she looks in to see a pile of clothes on her grandmother's bed. "Whatcha doing, Nanny?"

Charlie Mae has forgotten that Geneva is living with her, has forgotten that Geneva exists. Her arms full of clothes, she turns suddenly and almost loses her balance. Charlie Mae leans against the closet door for support and studies Geneva.

"I ain't cleaning that up," Geneva says. "You gotta sleep there, you know, and I ain't clearing all that off."

"You remind me of my granddaughter," says Charlie Mae. "She spends almost every summer with me. She likes to get on her inner tube and float in the pond." Geneva's flip-flops and baggy T-shirt indicate summer, but Charlie Mae does not notice, so she continues to look for her coat, and she continues to talk even after Geneva has slammed the front door. "She's a cutie pie. One time, her mama just forgot all about school starting up, I guess, 'cause Geneva stayed on here with me until Thanksgiving." Charlie Mae empties her closet, then wanders into the kitchen.

The kitchen appliances supply her with purpose. She fills the percolator and plugs it in. She puts bread into the toaster. She sets a bowl of milk on the floor for a cat that disappeared during Hurricane Hazel in 1954. Geneva has left dirty dishes in the white enamel dishpan, so Charlie Mae fills it with soapy water. When the toast pops up, the sound startles her, but the warm smell makes her hungry. She spreads margarine on the toast, puts grape jelly on top of that. She puts the margarine tub back into the refrigerator, closes the door, and leaves the kitchen, forgetting her toast.

She passes Geneva's bedroom and is confused by the closed door. She opens it and is surprised to see an unmade bed surrounded by puddles of clothes, above which rise islands of cardboard boxes. Three sons were raised in this house, so a messy room is a familiar sight to Charlie Mae, comforting. "The boys musta been in a hurry, I guess," she tells the room. She tries to make up the bed but is thwarted by the boxes. She tries to bend and pick up the dirty clothing, but she can't reach to the floor. One pile is tall enough for Charlie Mae to reach. She grabs a handful of Geneva's panties and bras. That evidence does not convince her that the room is no longer occupied by her sons, nor do the framed photos on the wall of the three grown men, two now dead, who were the boys in this room.

The laundry gripped in her hand is a tangible reminder of where she is going, so she makes it all the way to the washing machine out on the sleeping porch. When she opens the washer, she finds it already full of clothes. She drops the wet clothes item by item into the wicker basket behind her, tops that with Geneva's unwashed underwear. "Now, where are the clothespins?" she wonders, ignoring the dryer standing ready. A search of the porch does not produce the flowered clothespin bag she is picturing, a homemade gift from one of her kindergarten students. "I bet I left 'em in the kitchen," she tells herself.

In the kitchen, Charlie Mae sees her forgotten toast, and a smile fills her face. Her first husband, Arlie Tomlin, worked at the mill until a truck pinned him against the loading dock. Before he left in the mornings, he had the coffee perking and made toast for Charlie Mae, until the day he did not come back. "Arlie," she whispers. "Arlie, I wish you would come back." Crying now, she goes into the living room and sits in her chair. She has to pick up the remote to sit down, so she presses the button and a soap opera appears, lulling her to sleep. Near the end of that episode of *Guiding Light*, Dr. Bauer's beeper goes off, and the sound startles Charlie Mae awake. "Was that the whistle, I wonder?" she says. She pushes herself up out of the chair and goes to the sleeping porch. From there, she can see the mill at the end of the pond. Squinting, she can just make it out. "Well, I don't see nobody leaving," she says. "Must not have been the whistle."

Passing the kitchen, she sees the toast, and the sight makes her hungry. She takes the plate to the porch. Sitting in her porch swing, she can see down the street to Vivia's house, where four young girls are lined up waiting for their fittings. "Oh, look at that, getting ready for the Christmas pageant." Then she sucks in her breath, remembering the list. Charlie Mae, in her thirty-two years as kindergarten teacher, had been responsible for the Christmas list. Each child was asked to name one thing for Santa to bring, one gift that would appear at the mill's Santa Claus party. She spent months on the list, quizzing each child, turning them away from inappropriate demands, suggesting things, making substitutions if she had to. Girls who needed shoes would always ask for dolls. Boys who needed coats would always ask for base-ball gloves. She whispered to the girls that Santa would fill their new shoes with candy, told the boys that Santa would tuck a ball into the pocket of their new coat. "I have to get the list there to the office before the whistle." Charlie Mae stands too quickly, the swing drifts away, and she drops to the floor. The swing returns, smacking against her shoulder blades. For long minutes, Charlie Mae sits, overwhelmed by the pain in her coccyx, her shoulders, her legs. Finally, she is able to crawl. Using the porch railing, she pulls herself to a sitting position again, then leans back, exhausted.

When Fairy Etta pushes Cone onto the porch that afternoon, she sees Charlie Mae slumped against the porch railing. She fixes the brake on Cone's wheelchair and runs across the street, yelling for Bonus. "Bonus, get on over to Charlie Mae's. Bonus!"

Fairy Etta is relieved to see Charlie Mae's eyes open. "You okay, Charlie Mae? What happened?"

"Did the whistle blow yet?" she asks. Bonus and his cane clump up the stairs, and Charlie Mae turns to ask him, "Did you hear it, Bonus?"

"I have not heard the whistle yet today, Miz Charlie Mae," he an-swers. Bonus hands Fairy Etta his cane, then straddles Charlie Mae, pulling her up with a hand under each arm. Once they get her inside, Bonus turns to Fairy Etta. "I'll get her something to eat and sit here until that granddaughter comes home. You go on back and sit with Cone."

"I think she needs cleaning up, Bonus."

"I think so, too. But I don't think I should do it, and I think you do too much already, so I'm thinking I'll tell that girl to do it. You go on, now. I'll get some food in her. Nobody ever died of dirty underwear."

"Dirty underwear?" asks Charlie Mae. She leans toward Bonus, and he helps her by pulling her head to his shoulder. She whispers into his ear. "Sometimes, the little ones have accidents. You tell them it's okay. You look in my desk. I always keep spare clothes on hand for accidents."

"What you want to eat, Miz Charlie Mae?"

"I want Arlie to fix me some cinnamon toast." When Charlie Mae smiles, her cheeks balloon and push her glasses up.

"Cinnamon toast coming up," Bonus promises.

Geneva has spent nine hours following Camilla. She fed her lunch and changed her clothes twice. She opens Nanny's front door wondering what she can get on TV, since Nanny doesn't have cable, and if there's anything to eat in the kitchen. Camilla's mother comes in every day and immediately starts supper, and every day Geneva hopes to be included but hurries out, avoiding the disappointment of not being invited. When the smell of urine catches her, she first looks down at her own clothes, thinking Camilla wet her. Voices lead her to the kitchen.

Bonus is seated across the table from Charlie Mae, who is eating cinnamon toast and scrambled eggs as though starved. Geneva stares. No one has sat at the table in years, so the simple meal looks oddly festive, disconcerting to Geneva. The cinnamon smell masks the urine smell, and Geneva's mouth waters. She looks at the stove, hoping there are more eggs, but the skillet is already soaking in the dishpan.

"Geneva, honey," Bonus begins, "I need you to get your nanny into the bathtub, soon as she's finished here."

Geneva nods.

"She had a fall on the porch. She'll be sore and bruised, but I think she's okay. But when you get her in the bathroom, you look her over good."

Charlie Mae stands suddenly, her plate in her hand. Bonus takes the plate, and Geneva takes Charlie Mae's hand, leads her from the kitchen. When they reach the hallway, Geneva turns to Bonus, who is washing the dishes.

"Mr. Bonus?"

Bonus continues scrubbing the skillet, assuming something will follow his name. When he realizes Geneva is still standing there, he turns around. "What?" he asks.

Geneva swallows. "Mr. Bonus, could you make me some eggs, too?"

Then she hurries her grandmother down the hall, not waiting for the answer.

❧

Bearing focaccia bread from Columbia's Gourmet-on-the-Go, Jimmy shows up in time for supper.

Karen meets him at the door. "Stay with the kids," she tells him. "There's a crisis next door, and I need to go help with Miz Charlie Mae."

Jimmy finds Camilla on the sofa tossing sticks of gum from her tackle box to the floor. "Hey, girl," Jimmy says. Camilla does not respond. Jimmy puts the bread on the kitchen counter, looks around for signs of meal preparation, sees none. "Camilla, I'm gonna go see what Bryan's up to, okay?" Camilla pauses for a moment but does not look up. Jimmy knocks at Bryan's door. "Bryan, wanna come help me fix some supper?"

"Why can't we go get pizza?" comes through the closed door.

Bryan stalls for several seconds before opening the door, but Jimmy waits him out. When Bryan finally appears, sullenly clinging to the doorframe, Jimmy answers. "We can't go out for pizza because we've gotta watch Camilla."

"We can take Camilla with us."

Jimmy doesn't know why that's impossible, but he knows that it is. "Ain't gonna happen. Let's go see what we can put together to eat."

Bryan and Jimmy discover ground chuck thawing in the fridge, several vegetables in the crisper. "Burgers?" Jimmy suggests. "We can grill 'em out."

"Down at your place?"

Jimmy hesitates, glancing at Camilla. "No, we'll use your mama's grill. Did she buy any charcoal?"

Disappointed again, hoping for an evening at the campfire pit, Bryan doesn't answer.

"Well, I'll go look outside. You make the patties."

Karen's grill and a bag of charcoal are tucked under the back stairs,

239

the only place she has to store them until the contractor finishes her bedroom and has time to build peripherally important things like a deck. Pouring briquettes into the grill, Jimmy hears the back door open at Miz Charlie Mae's and looks up to see Geneva. She sinks down onto the landing, leaning her back against the door, making Jimmy think of a doorstop. Jimmy watches her reach under her belly to find the pockets in her shorts, where she finally finds a pack of cigarettes and a matchbook.

"Geneva," Jimmy calls. "Things settled down over there? Your grandmother okay?"

Geneva lights her cigarette before answering. "You-all gonna cook out?"

"I'm cooking burgers, yeah."

"I wish you'd cook me one," she says.

Jimmy stops what he's doing and stares at the girl. He is too young to have seen despair, but he recognizes it in the pitiful statement that holds no hope of invitation. "Why don't you come over here and watch the kids?" Jimmy suggests. When she doesn't answer, he adds, "It looks like you're not doing anything over there."

"So, am I back on the clock if I come over there?"

Jimmy squirts lighter fluid on the charcoal, clicks the starter he bought for Karen, finds himself staring at the flames but talking to the girl. "I'll cook you a burger. Consider that payment in full." Geneva uses the rickety stair rail to pull herself up, puts both feet on each step as she makes her way down. "Put the cigarette out," he tells her. The distaste that Geneva seeds blooms into resentment. Jimmy does not want to be here, does not want to sit at a table with Geneva, does not want to be baby-sitting and feeding two children. "Geneva," he begins, then stops himself. He had been about to use the word *waddle.* "Geneva, go inside and check on Camilla."

"You're scared of her, ain't you?" Geneva asks as her bulk brushes by him. "I am, too."

# Chapter 24

# *The Baby*

THE BABY IS NOT OFFERED A NAME, lives on lips only as one-syllable pronouns reluctantly spoken.

Geneva has never held a baby and never holds this one. She wakes up early, hurting, grunts all day as she shadows Camilla. Geneva is accustomed to stomach pain, to gas cramps that make her double over as much as her bulk allows, to the girdling discomfort of too-tight waistbands, even on those 4X's she just bought at Wal-Mart. She lives with her hand in a bag, of bite-sized cookies, chips, M&M's, those little powdered doughnuts she loves, small things that don't need to be un-wrapped. Geneva has no experience with the standard meat, starch, and vegetable flanked by silverware, learned her definition of *meal* work-ing at KFC, has attended no picnics or banquets or luncheons.

Geneva escapes from baby-sitting even more quickly than usual, puts on a nightgown as soon as she gets home, glad to be relieved of the elastic that has etched a red equator around her body. She climbs into bed with a liter of Dr. Pepper and piles several crisp new bags around her, enjoying the rattle and crunch. At every commercial break, she gets up and sits hopefully on the toilet. Nothing happens, and finally she wonders if it's cramps. She never unpacked the boxes and suitcases she brought with her to Nanny's, but she knows there's Kotex in one of them; she pretty much cleaned out the apartment bathroom, gleefully depriving her former roommates of toothpaste and shampoo and Daisy razors and mousse. She uses two pads and puts on an extra pair of panties because she always has heavy periods. She falls asleep with her hand inside the doughnut bag, resting among the soft, sugared pillows, the never-ending supply reassuring to her.

A belt of pain wraps her, yanks her from sleep. Animal-like sounds of panting fill the room, scarier still when she realizes she is the one gasping for air. She struggles to the kitchen, hunched over, her hands walking the walls for support. Geneva swallows some of Nanny's Tylenol, gags on Pepto-Bismol, goes back to bed with some cheese slices and a can of lemonade. An hour later, her knees pulled up, her ankles dug into the mattress as she pushes against the pain, she knows it isn't a stomachache and it isn't her period, but there is no one to call for.

She is certain that each round of pain has to be the last because it's worse than the one before. She just keeps pushing because it feels good to push, like going to the bathroom after being constipated, until she's pushing against a slick lump down under the sheets. Her feet shove it out of the way, and she drops into a well of sleep.

The cold and spongy mattress wakes her. In the shower, Geneva holds her mouth open, lets the warm water gurgle down her throat, surprised at her thirst. When she looks down, she sees swirling red water. Dizzy, she sits suddenly in the tub, cries in hiccuping gasps. Fear and fatigue rattle her with shivers, and she sobs louder, hoping someone will hear and come and know what to do, the way things are supposed to happen, the way things happen on TV. Geneva knows that when a girl cries, a hand appears and strokes her hair, pulls her head to a shoulder. But those TV girls are always skinny and pretty, and Geneva's loud sobs become silent tears squeezed from the reality of knowing that she is not skinny and not pretty and no one is coming. When the water runs cold, Geneva pulls herself out of the bathtub.

Back in her room, naked, her hair dripping, she wants to crawl into bed, but the sight of it—the knot of percale and chenille slick with jellylike stuff and scurfy with dried blood—makes her nauseous. Leaning against the doorframe, wondering if she can go lie on Nanny's sofa without messing it up, too, she sees it move, sees the blue chenille moving. Geneva takes one unsteady step toward the bed, stands rocking back and forth, sees it again, tentative pokes, like popcorn when it first starts popping inside the microwave bag. But silent. She holds her breath, listens.

Geneva's world has introduced her to two kinds of babies. Soap-opera babies smile and wave their little feet in the air and sleep in lacy bassinets. Real babies cry. Real babies howled from the KFC bathroom, meaning another diaper in the trash can Geneva had to empty, sniveled while their mothers ate chicken and biscuits, made a mess in the high chairs she had to clean. Real babies are pushed around Wal-Mart in shopping carts, the tired ones whimpering, the hungry ones bawling. A real baby lived in the duplex adjoining the one Geneva had shared with her boyfriend, who rolled over every night muttering about "that damn screaming baby."

There ain't no real baby, Geneva thinks, 'cause ain't nothing crying. She sucks in air and turns away.

Charlie Mae giggles when she sees the sleeping form on her sofa. One of the boys, she thinks, sneaking in late, probably L. O. She checks the boys' room, conjuring teenagers, expecting to find Jack still asleep, discovers the soiled bed. Retreating into the comfortable ritual of housework, Charlie Mae peels off the bedclothes.

She notices the heaviness, a mass within the darkened linen, and the baby becomes weight. She puts the messy laundry back on Geneva's bed, fingers until she finds a soft lump, pulls away the chenille, gently squeezes the sheets, and the baby becomes a shape. Charlie Mae pulls away the wet sheet, and the baby becomes an image, something familiar, something she smiles at, something to clean and dress.

Charlie Mae knows what to do with a baby. She even knows what to do with a dead baby. Like everything else on Randleman Road, the baby is something that has to be dealt with. Geneva's baby is stored in the closet until Miz Charlie Mae can find someone to help her bury it.

※

Miz Mayme dials Jimmy's number just before two. "I gotta come over there, Jimmy. I need you to help with something."

Jimmy worked ten hours in August heat and is pulled unwillingly from a dead sleep. Mayme's words are annoying, not alarming. He tugs jeans over his boxers and steps out his front door to find Mayme already on his porch.

"Jimmy, we need you to do something, down at Miz Charlie Mae's."

Jimmy knows Miz Charlie Mae only to wave at, a frail figure in the shadows of her porch, in the house next door to Karen, where the baby-sitter lives. Her name reminds him of the visit from Osmond Vause, when he made the mistake of thinking that a car driving through his backyard in the middle of the night would be of interest to the county sheriff.

So Jimmy resents yet another intrusion into his sleep caused by Miz Charlie Mae. Grudgingly, reluctantly, he follows Mayme down the sidewalk, past the boarded-up house at 606, on to number 608. Jimmy's eyes travel to 610, Karen's house, dark for the night. He pictures Karen sleeping, cocooned in her yellow sheet.

Mayme does not knock but walks right into the house. Miz Charlie Mae stands in a bedroom doorway but moves aside like a curtain. Once in the bedroom, Jimmy's curiosity wakes. A smell drapes the room, one of those smells tangled in memory, like clip art embedded within the printing that explains it. And his nose turns curiosity into unease, into suspicion.

What is it? Just the mustiness of a closed-up room? He looks around, sees a four-poster bed with a bare mattress, its faded blue cover showing a darker blue stain, a big delta-shaped splotch starting at the center of the bed and widening to the base. No, it isn't the sharp smell of urine; it's heavier. He watches Mayme slide a cardboard box out of the closet, a Vidalia onion box with a black garbage bag draped over it. Jimmy inhales quietly, giving his nose more to go on. The ocean? Salty? Like the air at the beach?

Mayme slides the black plastic off the box.

Like a wet boat?

In the box is a quilt.

Jimmy's nostrils spread wide like those of an angry horse, pulling in data to send to his brain. A picture surfaces, that clip art he was looking for. A trash can. A trash basket, actually, white wicker, back in the farmhouse bathroom that he and his wife had tiled and painted, the bathroom with the tub that sat on legs. A white wicker trash basket holding discarded tampons. That's the smell, what he remembers, what he inhales now.

Mayme pulls the quilt away. When Jimmy sees the tiny feet, his body flexes backward. Next, he sees a miniature pink-and-white dress, ruffled at the hem, beneath the gray face of the dead baby.

It does not look real to Jimmy. Babies are pink and soft. The thing in the box looks hard, gray, cold. Like limestone, he thinks. Like a baby carved from limestone, a cemetery angel.

Miz Charlie Mae stares at the gray baby. Miz Mayme keeps her eyes on Jimmy, who takes one step backward. She holds the black garbage bag in one hand and the quilt in the other, and she waits. "We need help burying the baby," she tells Jimmy. She turns, puts the black bag onto the stripped mattress behind her. She folds the faded patchwork quilt and holds it draped over her arms. "Bonus is off at that Legion convention in Myrtle Beach, and I can't bend to shovel 'cause of my back. And Miz Charlie Mae can't dig no holes, that's for sure."

Jimmy stands motionless, but his eyes dart around the room in a desperate search for explanation, for a caption that will explain this picture, for subtitles that will translate.

"We want to bury her out in the azaleas, in front of the red tips. So first you gotta dig up some of the azaleas."

Miz Charlie Mae speaks. "Probably just two or three of the Red Ruffles," she says, still looking at the baby in the box.

"They don't have no deep roots, azaleas don't, so that won't be hard," says Miz Mayme. "But under that, the ground turns to clay, and it's like digging into a brick. So we need you to dig the hole."

Jimmy remains silent.

"I wasn't gonna ask you to dig no hole and not tell you why we needed a hole dug, Jimmy. I had to show you."

Jimmy's eyes finally leave the baby and look at Miz Mayme.

"Miz Charlie Mae's granddaughter had the baby," Mayme tells him. "Geneva. She's the one's been keeping care of Karen's children. Hadn't told nobody she was pregnant. Probably didn't know, herself. Anyway, she had the baby right here."

"I heard water running in the bathroom," Miz Charlie Mae says, nodding, her right hand massaging her left. "I thought it was time to get up. It's not, though," she adds quickly, proud of her moment of lucidity. "I found her in the sheets, down to the bottom of the bed."

"Jimmy," says Mayme. "Jimmy, listen to me. If they take Geneva away because of this baby, then there's nobody to take care of Charlie Mae, and nobody to take care of Karen's little girl."

Jimmy feels the muscles at the back of his neck tightening, pulling his chin up, waits while his back muscles shiver, feels it in his sphincter. He walks two steps to the onion box and squats. He studies the puckered plaster that makes up the small face. He looks among the pink cotton folds of the dress and sees a perfect miniature of a hand, the color of pearl. He is very conscious of standing but is unaware of walking through the house. He finds himself on Miz Charlie Mae's front porch, quietly closing the door behind him.

He turns on no lights. On his screened porch, he rotates an Adirondack chair so that it faces his neighbors' backyards. He sits, watches, waiting to see what will happen, knowing what will happen.

He sees silhouettes, dark cutouts distinguishable against the backdrop of shrubbery only by movement. He hears metallic sounds ringing cold in the humid night. He hears voices, women's voices, and he closes his eyes, filtering out Karen's voice, listens again to be sure. And when he is sure, he opens his eyes and watches until there is nothing left to watch.

# Chapter 25

## *LizAnne*

LizAnne is a certified nail technician, a certified EMT-paramedic, and a tax preparer.

She was disappointed to learn that neither the IRS nor the state of South Carolina cared to certify her as a tax preparer. She had to settle for a business license. Every one of LizAnne's certificates, diplomas, and licenses is professionally matted and framed, even her high-school diploma, which she considers useless. LizAnne left high school with good grades but no skills. Only the Rose Garden Health Care facility offered her a job.

LizAnne had a strong gag reflex, and when she pulled a soiled diaper off a patient or emptied a bedpan, her face drew up as though there were a drawstring around her lips. Ninety-two-year-old Mrs. Showalter saw the revulsion on LizAnne's face and began to sob. "I'm sorry, LizAnne. I'm so sorry. I wish I could help it. I'm so sorry."

LizAnne jumped. She did not expect the patients to speak any more than she expected the pillows to talk. "You know my name?"

"You've been here longer than most of them," Mrs. Showalter said.

LizAnne had worked there only seven weeks, and she did not know Mrs. Showalter's name. But once she learned that the people in the beds had names, that almost all of them knew her name, she straightened her eighteen-year-old shoulders and stretched her face into a smile to hide her nausea.

She had been there three years, longer than any other employee, and had worked her way up to activities director when Rose Garden Health Care was sold to a company called Continental Facilicare. No one could pronounce that, so in spite of the new sign at the entrance, the place was still called Rose Garden. Facilicare brought in people with degrees. Staff members, all strangers to LizAnne despite her time there, wore neon-orange ID tags printed with their name and a jumble of letters: OT, RN, LPN, CNA. The new human-resources manager, Lindsey Chandler, MBA, explained to LizAnne that the position of activities director had been eliminated. "We have an open slot for a director of recreational therapy, but we'll be looking for a CRT, someone degreed and certified." LizAnne, back to changing sheets, back at minimum wage, was given a black tag with white letters that said only "Housekeeping."

LizAnne was there to greet the new patients arriving by ambulance and learned what EMT stood for. She sterilized Rose Garden's bedpans during the day and went to Osilo County Technical College at night. In less than a year, she was riding in the back of an Osilo County Rescue Squad ambulance. She loved the stethoscope curled around her neck, loved knowing what to do when everyone else was screaming and crying, loved having doctors call her by name and wait for her to recite BP and pulse, but most of all loved having that certificate to frame and hang on her wall.

She continued to visit her friends at Rose Garden, now behind a new sign because of its sale to Regional Medical Solutions. The old ladies loved to have their nails painted, and the men laughed and joked when she trimmed their toenails and rubbed lotion on their feet.

One of the new Regional staffers, Jennifer Key, PT, told LizAnne she would have to stop doing that unless she was certified.

LizAnne thought the woman was joking. "I'm just cutting toenails," she said.

"You have to be a certified nail technician to do that here. We're liable, you know, for anything that happens to our clients."

LizAnne's interest was up. "You can get certified to do nails?"

For six months, LizAnne worked the night shift for the Osilo County Rescue Squad so she could commute to Columbia for classes at the Pretty-As-a-Picture Hair and Nail Institute. Passing the South Carolina Board of Cosmetology's exam earned her another certificate. She set up a booth in Walthourville's only beauty shop, painting nails by day, performing CPR at night. When her W-2 form from the county came in the mail, she added it to the box with her nail-booth receipts and went to the H&R Block office next to the SaveMore store.

"How 'bout your quarterly taxes?"

"What are quarterly taxes?"

"Your estimated taxes, what you pay every quarter when you're self-employed."

"I didn't know I was supposed to."

"Well, you're gonna owe penalties then."

"But I didn't know about it," LizAnne protested.

"That doesn't matter."

The penalties wiped out LizAnne's profit from her nail-care booth. She got a book from the library and read about taxes when not answering 911 calls or trimming nails at Rose Garden. She went back to the H&R Block office and enrolled in their tax course, then got an associate's degree in accounting from Osilo County Tech, giving her another certificate, a degree, and a business license. Now, she wanted a place of business, walls on which to display all those frames.

The three tellers at Carolina Federal had standing lunch-hour appointments for acrylic nails, and from them LizAnne learned about the backlog of foreclosed houses. She looked at four of the old mill houses and picked the one with the least structural damage. Every contractor in the county came to LizAnne's kitchen table for their taxes, and from sorting through their receipts, she knew who had dissatisfied customers balking at payment and who bought shoddy materials. A new roof went on the old house, the front porch was rebuilt with a ramp for wheelchairs, the living room was turned into a nail salon with a Pergo floor and floral wallpaper, and a bedroom became a carpeted tax office, its bright white walls serving as a backdrop to her array of credentials, which now included a Certificate of Occupancy. The sign hanging from the porch rail said simply, "LizAnne's."

In the nail salon, the topic of conversation is always men.

"Well, I threw him out," Laura announces, her fingers splayed for their weekly twenty-dollar paint job.

"Jerry? Why?"

"All those weekends he claimed he was helping his brother build a garage? Well, he wasn't. But I can't say I'm gonna miss him. He never liked my kids. And anytime their daddies came around, he'd get all, like, 'Don't be hanging around here,' you know?"

LizAnne doesn't know, but she nods. To LizAnne, her marriage license is like her other certificates; she worked for it, prepared for it, and she's proud of it.

When Laura's fingers slide under the nail dryer, she finally gets around to asking LizAnne how she's doing.

"I'm good. Busy with some new classes."

"Classes? Like in school?" Laura is disappointed that LizAnne's life doesn't follow a soap-opera script.

LizAnne nods. "Yep. I wanna be a CPA. I'm taking classes at USC-Osilo."

"I hope you don't quit doing nails," Laura says. "Did I tell you they took me off Zoloft?"

To LizAnne, it seems that her salon customers move from crisis to crisis, from marriage to marriage, zigzagging like balls across a pool table. LizAnne herself moves in a straight line. Now, she has a new highway to follow. *Certified public accountant* is the destination.

LizAnne talks one of her USC-Osilo instructors, Carmen Fenzel, into her partnership idea. "I have to work under a CPA for five years," she tells her.

"Yes, LizAnne. I believe I'm the one that told you about that requirement."

"So here's what I'm thinking. You come work with me, at my tax office."

"Then I'll be working for you. You would have to be working under me."

"Well, I own the place, but I'll be working under your supervision."

"Why do you want to be a CPA anyway? You've already got a good tax business going down there, and you don't need to be a CPA to do that."

LizAnne scribbles in her spiral notebook, trying to think of a concise way to explain her need to be certified. "Nobody certifies tax preparers, but they might one of these days," she hedges.

"And why would I want to be in Walthourville doing books?"

LizAnne has prepared for this one. "Because you could bring your little girl to work, Carmen. I have this whole house where my office is. We could put a swing set in the backyard, get a sitter."

The look on Carmen's face changes. She considers the proposal seriously for the first time.

LizAnne reels her in. "I need to work under you for five years. By that time, your little girl will be in school, and it'll be easier for you to work at some big company up in Columbia. This way, you'll be your own boss, so you can stay home with her when she's sick. You'll get to eat lunch with her, hear her play while you work."

The big sign hanging from the porch rail still says "LizAnne's," but new signs go on the wall. On the left side of the door hangs a pink sign: "LizAnne's Nail Salon—11-3 M-F, 10-5 Sat." To the right of the door is a black-and-white sign: "Tax Preparation and Accounting— Carmen Fenzel, CPA, LizAnne Dilly, Tax Preparer—10-4 M-F or by appt."

Everyone's secrets are offered to LizAnne. In the girls-only nail salon, confidences burble out and are dissolved in the cloud of acetone. In her EMT uniform, she can run into a house filled with fear and desperation and ask questions no one else can ask: "What drugs are you on?" "What did you swallow?" "What did you hit her with?" "How long was the baby underwater?"

But within the file cabinets are the real secrets, life histories recorded on receipts and canceled checks and Visa bills, distilled onto 1040s. LizAnne has known Dr. Peterson, the town's only dentist, all her life. She played in his waiting room at the age of three while her grandmother had casts made for dentures. Like everyone else, she thought of him as stingy Dr. Peterson, the man who wouldn't even buy Girl Scout cookies. LizAnne knows that stingy Dr. Peterson is stingy because thirty percent of his income goes to keep his mentally handicapped son in a private facility in Pennsylvania. Twice a year, he closes his office for a month, leaving Walthourville without dental care, causing those with toothaches or loose crowns to picture him heartlessly vacationing in Hawaii, while he is in fact visiting his thirty-five-year-old four-year-old.

When LizAnne tells Dr. Peterson that his trips are tax deductible, she feels the same sense of power she experiences when she jabs a needle into a muscle. LizAnne files his amended return. When he gets the refund check, he comes by her office.

"Is this right?" he asks, showing her the check.

"It's right, Dr. Peterson."

"Are you sure?"

LizAnne wants to smile, but she knows that Dr. Peterson needs to see a face of businesslike composure. "I am sure," she tells him.

He sits down then. "Do you know what? I'm going to go get my boy and take him to Disney World. I'm going to hire an aide to help me take him down there."

LizAnne knows that Bray Barker keeps most of his income off the books not to evade the IRS but to hide it from his wife, to keep her off the gambling boats in Pascagoula. LizAnne knows to keep a slot open for Veau Kaye's manicure on the first Saturday of each month, when the historical society meets, knows not to ask about Veau's sister because she has driven the ambulance taking the sister to rehab. She knows that the geologist who lives on Randleman Road doesn't need to live on Randleman Road because he has more money in the bank than his house is worth and owns part of the company he works for, but she keeps that secret, like all the others, even when Sheriff Vause asks. LizAnne knows that Sheriff Vause is faking his good-old-boy twang, knows he has an engineering degree from the University of Georgia, that he has three boys and a wife he left back in Athens but never divorced. When she asks how his boys are, Sheriff Vause takes the hint and quits asking questions about the geologist.

And she knows that a 911 call from Fairy Etta Duffy means that Cone has pulled his tubes out again. An ambulance leaving the rescue-squad garage, part of the Law Enforcement Center on the New Highway, takes twenty-one minutes to reach Randleman Road, and that's when there is no train on the tracks. LizAnne solves the problem by giving Fairy Etta her beeper number.

The beeper vibrates across LizAnne's desk like a June bug. She pushes aside the returns she is staying all night to complete, the same returns she works on every year at this time, because people who can't make the April 15 deadline can't seem to make the extension deadline either. Her April rush is organized. On roll-around metal carts purchased as surplus from Rose Garden, neat stacks accumulate under signs made from tent-folded four-by-six cards. LizAnne pulls one of the carts next to her desk and works through the stack labeled "Building Contractors," computing seven-year and five-year and Section 179 depreciations for backhoes and reciprocating saws and panel trucks. Then she reaches for the stack labeled "Farmers" and completes their Schedule F's. The six folders under the "Ordained Ministers" sign require Schedule A's for mileage deductions.

But this is the "August 15 Extension" stack, messy paperwork dropped off by people who expect LizAnne to get them a reprieve from the April 15 deadline. They are a prolific breed prone to filing paperwork in toolboxes, depositing business checks in personal accounts, paying cash, saving receipts from McDonald's while losing those for diesel fuel. When LizAnne sees Fairy Etta's phone number glowing on her beeper, she leaves without turning off her monitor. Six minutes later, she opens Fairy Etta's screen door and lets herself in, but she can see instantly that Cone is fine, asleep in the hospital bed that fills the front room, his oxygen machine producing a reassuring steady sigh, his sheets white and crisp from the clothesline.

"We're back here," she hears Fairy Etta say.

LizAnne faces a messier bed in Fairy Etta's bedroom. Sprawled on the bed is a fat girl, a towel stuffed between her bare legs.

"I cleaned her up, but I don't know what else to do," says Fairy Etta.

Activated by the sight of blood on the yellow terry cloth, LizAnne throws her case on the floor, opens it, snaps on a pair of latex gloves. She pulls the towel away, pushes the girl's legs apart. "Gimme some more water, Fairy Etta. I gotta clean her up some more so I can see. Fairy Etta, you called for an ambulance?"

The girl's eyes do not open, but she shakes her head.

LizAnne addresses the girl. "No? No ambulance? Why not? Did you just have a baby?" She wraps a blood-pressure cuff around the soft flesh of Geneva's upper arm. As soon as the stethoscope is out of her ears, she asks again: "Girl, did you just have a baby? Where's the baby?"

"I didn't know it was a baby," the girl says, her eyes still closed.

"Fairy Etta, where's the baby?"

"That little baby's dead, LizAnne."

LizAnne rips open sterile packages, pushes Geneva's legs wide apart, swabs her clean. "Fairy Etta, when?"

"Awhile ago. It all happened at Miz Charlie Mae's. This here's Charlie Mae's grandchild, little Geneva. Mayme's over there taking care of everything, and she sent little Geneva over here."

LizAnne grabs her medical kit and runs across the street. When she returns, she watches the sleeping girl for several minutes before shaking her shoulder. "Wake up, girl. Geneva, wake up. Talk to me."

Geneva's eyelids lift slowly, revealing a sharp gaze already directed at LizAnne.

"Tell me about the baby."

"Hit just happened. During the night. I was asleep. I woke up hurting."

LizAnne does not blink.

Geneva tries to look away, but LizAnne shakes her again. "Look at me. Talk to me."

"I didn't know it was a baby."

LizAnne's stare has the intensity of a medical probe. She doesn't think that pretty little girl was born dead, but she can't know for sure without an autopsy, and Miz Charlie Mae doesn't need to deal with the coroner and an autopsy and a granddaughter in a courtroom. Finally, she turns to Fairy Etta. "Fairy Etta, go on outta here now."

LizAnne sits on the bed and takes Geneva's face in her hands. "Now, you listen good, stupid girl. And I know you're stupid because it doesn't take a rocket scientist to squirt foam up your twat or peel the foil off a Trojan. Now, everybody across the street is working to make like that little baby girl never happened 'cause they think you're taking care of Miz Charlie Mae. But listen here, stupid girl. I know you're not taking care of Miz Charlie Mae. She's taking care of you." LizAnne knows that Charlie Mae, even with Alzheimer's, is more competent than the girl splayed on the bed, is a natural caretaker the way some people are natural cooks.

"So here's what's gonna happen," LizAnne tells the expressionless face gripped in her latex fingers like a ball she's about to toss. "I'm gonna take care of Miz Charlie Mae. And you're not gonna be in that house the next time I drive down this street. And you need a doctor. You understand that? If you don't wanna go to a hospital, that's just one more sign of how stupid you are. But this isn't something you can hide. You're gonna let down milk. You're gonna bleed for a while. And one of these days, you'll go to a doctor, and he'll know you had a baby. So you think about that."

LizAnne pulls her hands away suddenly, letting Geneva's head loll forward. "Fairy Etta, I'm gone. She won't bleed to death. She might get an infection, run a fever, but that's her problem."

When LizAnne turns on her headlights, the light bounces off the Road Ends sign in front of her and illuminates Jimmy sitting on his porch steps. She knows that 602 Randleman is one of those in her delinquent stack, whose signature will have to be affixed to a 1040 and postmarked by midnight. She gets out of her car, having changed instantaneously from medical savior to tax adviser, like Superman in the phone booth.

LizAnne calls his name: "Steverson!" Jimmy doesn't look up, so she walks toward his porch. Standing on the sidewalk, she asks, "You're Steverson, aren't you? James L.?"

Jimmy looks into the darkness, sees a shiny badge clipped to a woman's collar, squints at it and manages to read the reflective letters *EMT*. He does not recognize her as his tax preparer. He stands, assuming she's here to ask him questions about the dead baby, hoping that someone on Randleman Road has reported a dead baby, hoping Karen made the call.

"Yeah, I'm James Steverson."

"I've got your return ready," she tells him.

He looks perplexed.

"I'm LizAnne Dilly," she reminds him. "I'm doing your tax return. It's ready. You gotta sign it today. I've called you a couple of times."

Jimmy says "Okay" to her, but he is not processing her words.

LizAnne points to the phone clutched in Jimmy's hand. "Who you planning to call at this hour?"

Jimmy has been wondering that himself. He could call his father, ask what to do, but he knows what his father's answer would be. He could call Carl, but he knows what Carl would tell him to do.

"Are you here about the baby?" Jimmy asks.

"What baby?" says LizAnne. She lets the two sharp words slice into the darkness before adding, "I was across the street checking on Cone." LizAnne climbs one step, and Jimmy leans forward to hear, still thinking she will tell him about the baby, but she lays her index finger on the phone in Jimmy's hand and speaks very softly, delivering bad news. "You can call the sheriff if you want to, Steverson. But that man invented secrets."

Weeks later, LizAnne's paperwork catches up with Jimmy. He pays taxes plus a penalty.

## Chapter 26

# *Fairy Etta*

FAIRY ETTA TAKES CARE OF CONE and her chickens.

Her tiny backyard is fenced to contain her flock of barred Plymouth Rocks, ten hens and two roosters. Bonus built the enclosure she designed, roofed it with chicken wire to keep out predators. The gate is right at the foot of the back stairs, so she can slip in to visit her flock whenever Cone doesn't need her.

When the New Highway was built and houses disappeared, Fairy Etta was asked to take in chickens. She fried up the Bantams and Wyandottes and even the White Rocks. And a few of the barred Plymouth Rocks brought to her did not make her cut. She knew who had let their birds wander to cross-breed, who had dirty coops, who had healthy flocks. Fairy Etta loved her black-and-white birds and allowed only the pure breed in her coop. Last year, a fellow from Clemson showed up, a graduate student who had heard about her flock at the feed store. She let him look, let him take pictures, let him weigh and measure her birds, listened to him explain about looking for old breeding stock, explain that the White Rocks had taken over and the barred Rocks were harder to find.

"And the ones I've seen aren't as sturdy as your birds," he told her.

"I take care of my chickens," she said.

"And you started this flock during the war?"

"The Second World War," Fairy Etta explained. "The mill had a truckload of 'em and drove through town giving the little chicks away. It was part of the war effort, trying to get people to have victory gardens and grow food and like that. Everybody got four chicks."

"Would you let me buy one of your birds?"

Fairy Etta motioned him out of the enclosure when he said that and locked the gate. "I don't sell my birds, son."

"It's for a research project. How about that really old hen? She can't be laying anymore."

"Marigold quit laying years ago, but she gave me plenty of eggs, and I'll let her live out her time."

"Any idea how old she is?"

"She's nineteen years old. You'll have to go on along now, son. I have things I need to do."

"May I buy some eggs from you, Mrs. Duffy?"

"I don't sell eggs. I give 'em out to the neighbors when I have 'em to spare, most every day. I get about six most days, ten sometimes. They all save them egg cartons from the store for me, those Styrofoam things, and I put eggs into 'em and take 'em all up and down the street." Fairy Etta glared at the boy for a few seconds before continuing. "I reckon you're just gonna study it, not eat it, which is a waste, so I'm only gonna give you one." She returned from the kitchen with an egg carton containing one brown egg. "Here. Patsy Cline laid that one this morning."

The flock is more than food to Fairy Etta, more than that Clemson boy could know. Fairy Etta worked in the mill office, never on the floor, so she did not work among her neighbors. The brown eggs had let her into their kitchens. Patsy Cline and Marigold and her eight other hens and the two roosters named Willie and Merle are her children. She and Cone lost their only little girl, tried to have more, but it never happened. When Fairy Etta finally got up the nerve to ask Dr. Pratt about it, he told her she'd have to go to the hospital in Columbia for tests, pointed out that Cone was two decades older than she was, that maybe Cone might need tests, too. Fairy Etta couldn't imagine letting a strange doctor in the city do what Dr. Pratt did, and she didn't want Cone to have to endure what she pictured as horrendous medical procedures, didn't want him to think he wasn't the strong man that she knew he was, didn't want him to imagine babies that she could have but he couldn't, so she accepted it as God's will.

They traveled instead. Every summer, they spent a week at Savannah Beach, doing the same things, looking forward every year to another tour of Fort Pulaski, another seafood platter at Ma Williams, roller-skating on the pier. They saved money for a big trip every other year, to Nashville and Stone Mountain and Weeki Wachee Springs, even out west. The trips had given them memories, happy moments to relive with Cone.

Bathing him, she asks, "Cone, you remember when we was at the Alamo? And that little boy was shooting that cap gun at you? And you bought one yourself at the gift shop so you could shoot back at him. You were like a little boy yourself that day."

Trimming his nails, she says, "Cone, that trip to the Grand Canyon was the best one, wasn't it? Remember when we first drove up to it? And we was both just quiet."

Sitting beside him on the porch, the radio on, she suddenly recalls Opryland. "I wonder if the new building they put up is as nice as the Ryman was. I still can't believe we got Porter Wagoner's autograph that time." She pats his hand. "It's still in the cedar chest. I'll run get it."

She puts Cone to bed and falls asleep holding Porter Wagoner's autograph. When she hears Mayme knocking on her front door, she first checks on Cone, then goes to the door. "Put her to bed, Fairy Etta," Mayme tells her. "I need her out of the way so I can take care of the rest of it."

Fairy Etta walks Geneva to her own bed, pulls the covers back, and helps her lie down. She cleans her up and gets her to drink some water and eat some Campbell's chicken noodle soup. Fairy Etta is uncomfortable having Geneva in her house, but not because of the birth, not because of the mess in her bed. For years, Fairy Etta watched Geneva's mother drop the child off at Charlie Mae's, abandon her for long periods of time, show up unannounced to take her out of school to some new house with some new boyfriend. Fairy Etta looked through her curtains as the child came and went, wishing the child were hers, wishing she could go to PTA meetings, read Dr. Seuss books, buy the tiny Easter dresses she saw in the JC Penney catalog. Stuffing a towel between Geneva's legs, she wonders again why God and all his angels let babies come through the wrong door. Fairy Etta knows her lost little girl is an angel now because the preacher explained it, and she tells Geneva what the preacher told her.

"Your little baby girl's an angel now, honey. You don't have to worry about her. The little ones, they're planned all along to be angels. Preacher Oldham explained it to me. See, we all have to jump out of heaven. That's when we're born. And most of us, we're scared to because we don't know where we'll land. But the ones that smile and jump right out, knowing all along that God will catch 'em, well, they have the most faith. And because they have so much faith, they go right back to heaven, and they're angels."

Jimmy has less than an hour of jerky sleep sitting upright on the sofa, clutching the phone, before Mayme's yeast lures him into the still-dark day. He brushes his teeth and puts on clean jeans. He drives his truck around to the lake side of his house, the blind side, and lowers the tailgate. He starts with his Weber grill, first disconnecting the propane tank, then wheeling the grill up a sheet of plywood serving as a ramp. He rolls up the Pawleys Island hammock and wedges it in front of the grill. Next up the ramp is the lawnmower. Jimmy slides the plywood back under the deck.

He packs his duffel bag with jeans and underwear and a tooth-brush and deodorant and his razor; the duffel goes into the cab of the truck. From his closet, he pulls an armful of clothes and tosses them onto his bed. He wraps the top sheet around them and hauls them out to the truck. Each drawer of the three-drawer chest is hauled out one at a time, full. Then Jimmy carries the chest to the truck and replaces the drawers. He fills his one suitcase with shoes.

The Gateway computer goes out wrapped in his plaid comforter, the Hewlett-Packard printer in a blanket, the Brother fax in a towel. Around the TV, he arranges bed pillows. In the extra bedroom, he finds the plastic file box labeled "Important Papers" and puts that in the truck cab with his briefcase.

From the kitchen, he takes the toaster oven. He opens a black plastic bag and empties the refrigerator into it. He unplugs the refrig-erator and props the doors open. He sets the thermostat to *Off*, then flips the main circuit breaker. The last thing to leave the house is a laundry basket into which he has thrown computer cables, surge pro-tectors, a box of Nutri-Grain bars, scissors, pens, two phones, a brand-new copy of *The Blake Compendium* still in its Borders bag.

Finally, he hitches the trailer to the pickup, backs into the water, and hauls his bass boat out. Pulling forward, Jimmy can feel the mo-ment the boat loses its buoyancy, surrenders its weight to the trailer. Checking his mirrors, Jimmy watches the wheels of the trailer emerge, can see no sign on the pond's smooth surface that his boat was ever there, worries that he would not have recognized something as simple as displacement, would never have predicted the buoyant force, some-thing Archimedes figured out while taking a bath.

Jimmy buckles the tie-downs and secures the hitch chain just as one of Fairy Etta's roosters crows. Jimmy recognizes Merle's plaintive crow, halfway between a quail calling and a cat mewing. Later, Willie will start up, a hoarse sound like an old man clearing his throat. Driv-ing up Randleman Road, Jimmy wonders when he learned to tell Merle from Willie, when he learned their names.

Joelle watches Jimmy leave Randleman Road. Only Joelle knows that Jimmy leaves his house some nights, for sure on Friday nights, just before Letterman comes on, and quietly walks the sidewalk to Karen's house. Her lights out, her eyes focused between the slats of her blinds, Joelle is watching to see if tonight will be one of the nights Jimmy walks to Karen's, so she sees Mayme at Jimmy's door, giggles when she notices how unhappy Jimmy is at following Mayme down to Miz Charlie Mae's house. When Jimmy emerges just a few minutes later, Joelle is still watching, and only Joelle sees what the porch light reveals, Jimmy's lips sucked tight against his teeth. Joelle mistakes the disgust so clear on Jimmy's face for nausea. She wonders what made him sick, why he hurries home.

Joelle is the only one on Randleman Road unaware of what goes on in Miz Charlie Mae's backyard. Her eyes are glued to Jimmy's house. She sleeps some, falling back onto her bed, which is pushed up against the window to allow her to keep watch at night. When a metallic *clink* wakes her, her digital clock says 4:42. When she sees Jimmy's truck backed up to his deck, Joelle knows he is leaving. She doesn't wonder why. She has always wondered when.

At seven-thirty, with Vivia intent on making a puckerless seam in tulle, Joelle leaves the house. She heads across the street, right through Jimmy's unlocked front door. She is not fooled by the furniture, by the towels still hanging in the bathroom, not even by the books still on the shelves. Joelle's life has trained her to sense absence. She lets her fingers slide down the spine of each book, all those lining the five-shelf case, all those stacked like end tables, all those scattered around the bed. Finally, she chooses one, *Littoral Processes*. The black-and-white photos of faraway coastlines excite Joelle, who has never seen even the beach just three hours from her door. Joelle writes Jimmy a note, using his abandoned printer paper and one of several pens left on the coffee table: "Thank you for the book you left for me, the one about beaches." She tucks the note inside the front cover of another book and returns home to tell her grandmother that Mrs. Connell's house is vacant again.

Fairy Etta syringes Cone's sleep meds into his feeding tube. She gives him long hours of sleep, fewer hours of daylight to endure, which means fewer hours of care for her. Before she wakes him to bathe him, change him, empty the urine bag, she feeds her chickens. They listen for the door every morning and gather sociably at the gate, scratching optimistically. Later in the day, Fairy Etta will fill their food and water dispensers, rake out the coop, find the eggs. Now, she's visiting, scattering her homemade "goody"—bits of banana peel and apple and table scraps added to scratch and grit—from the pockets of a vinyl apron she made just for this.

"You-all sleep good?" she asks them, throwing a handful here, a handful there. "Let's eat some breakfast." She wades through them to scatter goody where shy Dolly hides. "Eat up now, Dolly. I sure did name you wrong, didn't I?"

When Fairy Etta hears the front door open, she explains to the chickens, "That's Geneva. She spent the night here last night. That baby had a baby. I reckon she's headed on back over to Charlie Mae's now. Probably wants some clean clothes to put on."

Then a car door opens and quickly closes. Fairy Etta pauses, her hands in her apron, as Geneva tries three times to start her neglected Escort. It cranks on the fourth try, and Fairy Etta listens as the car leaves Randleman Road. "Well, now, she's gone, too, I guess. That boy over in Orene's house left this morning, pulled outta here with everything he owned in this world, didn't even see me picking up the paper. So now Orene's house is gonna be empty again. And now that girl's gone. I wonder what she's got between her legs. I hope she found the Kotex LizAnne left here. That LizAnne is something. She come by again and left a bag of stuff for that girl, some Kotex and some little booklets to read and all like that. I'll have to go on over later and check on Charlie Mae, I reckon. First, I'll get those sheets and towels on the line. It's gonna take some sunshine to get the blood off those sheets."

# Chapter 27

## *Teeter*

TEETER THIBAULT BECOMES JIMMY'S TENANT, a new name on Randleman Road.

Teeter painted 602 Randleman Road back when the bank renovated it. He is in demand as a painter but often turns down painting jobs to trap turtles. This morning, he is anchoring some new traps in Mark's pond. At dawn, Mark drives his golf cart down his gravel driveway looking for the morning paper out of Columbia, sees Teeter backing his bass boat into the water.

"You're here early," Mark says.

"Yeah, I got a lot to do today."

"Did you spend the night out here, Teeter?"

Teeter connects the trolling motor to the battery, stalling. For several months after Teeter's girlfriend threw him out of her apartment, Mark let him stay at the house. When Sandra brought the children for the summer, Mark explained to Teeter that he'd have to move out.

"I ain't found another place yet, so I just been sleeping in my camper," Teeter says.

Mark parks the golf cart and climbs in the boat. Teeter lowers the trolling motor into the water and twists the tiller, and they glide away from the edge, water gurgling around the bow.

"Listen, you can fish my pond anytime you want, but you gotta find another place to stay, Teeter. Sandra'd have a fit if she knew you were sleeping out here while the kids are here."

Teeter nods vigorously, and the boat bobs in agreement. "I know, I know. I gotta drive down to Hilton Head today anyhow. Got a painting job down there." He stops the boat and lowers the first trap into the water. "This one's gonna float better," he tells Mark.

"Shit, Teeter, that last batch you left here didn't float at all. Now, I got wire baskets with dead turtles down in the bottom of my pond."

"That ain't gonna hurt nothing. Next time you drain the pond, I'll come clean it out."

"Well, you know the kids are around now, and I don't want them watching turtles drown. It's one thing if you catch 'em and carry 'em off, but just drowning 'em don't seem right."

"These here will work. I figured out the chicken wire ain't as heavy as the rabbit fence, and I used a lot more Styrofoam." Teeter backs away, admiring his trap, then pivots the boat in a full circle. "Which way's the dam?"

"You can't get lost on a six-acre pond, Teeter. I can see my kitchen light up that way." Mark points.

"Kids still asleep?"

"They'll probably sleep 'til noon. We stayed out here most of the night watching shooting stars and eating popcorn."

Teeter drops his last trap with a splash that seems to turn on the morning light. Pine trees appear, stripes against a pink glaze. A startled green heron rises from the water, complains noisily, disappears among the stripes.

"Look how good that floats."

Teeter has forgotten his appointment with LizAnne and is on the New Highway before he remembers. He drives for a few more miles, wondering if there are any more extensions after August 15, then finally turns around.

He tells LizAnne that he's a trapper. "Turtles," he explains.

"Well, let's start at the beginning here. I can't even remember your real name, Teeter." LizAnne has his extension paperwork on her desk, but she has learned that making people recite their full name gets them down to business, probably from a memory of Mama's voice.

"Cordell Tyler Thibault. It was the boys on the football team started calling me T-Bone. I don't know how I got to be Teeter."

LizAnne puts down her pencil and leans on her elbows. "We had a special cheer for you, remember? 'T-Bone is sizzlin'! T-Bone is rare. T-Bone can take that ball. Way down there!' Man, we spent hours just writing that little cheer."

"I always used to wish I could see y'all, but I was running whenever you'd be doing it."

LizAnne jumps up from behind her desk. Hands on her hips, legs spread wide, she hollers, "T-Bone is sizzlin'!" She waves her arms overhead, pretending she has those orange-and-purple pompoms. "T-Bone is rare." She points to a fifty-yard line. "T-Bone can take that ball." Her arm shoots up to point at the sky, then arcs toward the end zone as she kneels. "Way down there!" LizAnne bounces back into her hands-on-hips position. "It looked good, T-Bone. It looked better with all six of us doing it 'cause we'd go down on one knee one at a time. We were lined up by height, you know, and by the time little-bitty Sally was down on one knee, you were in that end zone."

"I wish I'd seen it."

"You shoulda come to cheerleading practice, watched us do it."

"I never thought of that."

"You know what? My mama took movies of me cheerleading. I'll see if she's got one of us doing that."

"Lord, LizAnne, I'd love to see that."

LizAnne is screening it already, the six of them in those purple leotards with gold fringe flashing, six girls who don't exist anymore. Margaret Altman is now the principal of the middle school, Livvy Enfield teaches third grade, Judy Rettig is a veterinarian taking care of racehorses in Aiken, Sally Heckert is the tax collector, Jeannette Blum is a lab technologist at a hospital in Columbia. They were the closest of friends during those cheerleading months, but they drifted away from LizAnne when they went off to college and she was left behind.

"Teeter, didn't you get a football scholarship?" she asks him.

He nods, looking down at his lap. "Yeah. Got two offers, actually. I went to Georgia, but they never let me play, so I come on home."

Back in her desk chair, LizAnne picks up her pencil. "So you're trapping? Not painting? What all are you trapping?"

"Turtles," he tells her again. "I still paint, too. But I been making a lot of money trapping."

"How do you make money on turtles?"

"This guy in North Carolina buys 'em off me. Pays me by the pound. I figure I'm getting about two bucks a turtle."

"What does this guy do with turtles?"

"He sells 'em to China. They eat a lot of turtle over there, is what he says."

"Okay, so how much did you make last year selling turtles?"

"Well, I went up there twice. Had a trailer full each time. He pays by the pound, after they're cut up. I got about eighteen hundred that first time. Then I got over two grand the next time."

"So you made three thousand eight hundred dollars?"

"I get paid to pull 'em out of ponds, too. People call me to come clear their ponds. They pay me. So I make money that way, too."

"How much did you make clearing ponds?"

"Well, let's see. You know Mrs. Ducasse? I cleared two ponds for her, out back of her house. She said the turtles was eating the baby wood ducks. And I cleared one at Shadow Hills, that golf club up toward Columbia. I charge by how many turtles I pull out."

LizAnne interrupts him. "You've got a big envelope there, Teeter. You got any receipts or anything in there?"

He hands the envelope to LizAnne. "Well, that's mostly from the painting. All them real-estate ladies give me them letters. Them ladies love paper. But I ain't got much on paper for the turtles. That man in North Carolina pays me cash money. Now, Shadow Hills gave me a check."

"You got your bank statements? Checkbook? Anything I can use to total all this up?"

"I don't put money in banks." Teeter makes the statement with conviction, as though declaring his political party.

LizAnne empties his manila envelope and flips through page after page of letterhead, some from builders, most from real-estate agents— "Enclosed check for $800.00 is payment in full for painting of property at 404 Meadow Circle."

"So it looks like most of your income still comes from painting, though, Teeter." She catches his disappointed look. "And it seems like everybody I talk to is waiting on you to do some painting for them." LizAnne does not have to lie. Teeter is an exacting painter. "Shirley Grooms was in the nail shop the other day. She told me how you painted her baseboard molding after she had that hardwood floor put in. She was going on and on about how shiny white you got it, how you didn't get a drop on her new floor. And she said her little girl wanted every wall in her room a different color, and you did it just like she wanted it."

Teeter nods. Painting is a job. He knows he's good. But *trapper* has a ring to it.

"So I think we'll have to call you a painter on your 1040. Plus, you can take off your expenses. You run an account somewhere?"

"The True Value store."

"Okay. You go down there and ask them to print you out a statement, what you spent there last year. We can take all that off."

"I got expenses trapping, too."

LizAnne doesn't want to get him started again, but she is thorough. "What kinds of expenses?"

"There's my boat. Trolling motor. Traps."

"Any receipts?"

"Well, I bought the boat off this man I was painting for down in Hilton Head. He just took it off what he owed me for the painting. I don't know if I could find him to get a receipt from. He lives in New York or someplace. And I build the traps myself."

"How about a license? You need some kind of license to harvest turtles?"

"No. I checked with them Fish and Wildlife people. They got some kind of list about the turtles you can't catch, but there ain't no license."

"You probably should have a business license, Teeter, if you're selling them. I'll ask around about that. How about bait? You buy bait somewhere?"

Teeter perks up. "Naw. Catfish backbones. That's all it takes."

Teeter leaves LizAnne's office and merges onto the New Highway, headed to Hilton Head, having already forgotten his errand at the True Value store, the midnight deadline. Teeter likes painting on Hilton Head. Those houses are easy to paint, most of them just a few years old with good paint on the walls but with new owners who want the yellow bedroom white and the white kitchen yellow. He's pulling his trailer with his boat and traps, hoping to get hired to clean out a golf-course pond.

Jimmy makes it to the Muldoy site by eight, pulls up with his boat still dripping water from Dillehay Pond. When the drill crew breaks for lunch, he sits in the cab of his truck with his plastic file box on the seat next to him, the box his mother put together for him when he first left home, labeled "Important Papers" in her handwriting. Jimmy flips past his birth certificate, vaccination records, college transcripts, divorce decree, finds the file given to him when he closed on his house. The real-estate agent's card is stapled to the front of the file, her phone number in raised gold numerals that could be read by the blind. He calls Carolyn Day and leaves a message on her voice mail: "This is Jimmy Steverson, Mrs. Day. I bought the house on Randleman Road. I want you to sell it for me. If you can't sell it, rent it out."

While he recites his cell phone number, his mind automatically catalogs the contents of the house he left behind—pancake mix and cans of soup still in the cabinet, a box of Tide next to the washer. "The keys are on the back porch, under a chunk of pumice," he says, having no idea that he has not locked his doors, has lost the city instinct to do so, as he has lost the habit of setting an alarm clock, relying on Mayme's yeast to wake him, as he has lost the habit of eating out, waiting instead to see if Mark shows up with fish or Karen sets a place for him, as he has lost the habit of turning on the TV for company, knowing that Bryan will start a campfire and Bonus will show up with postcards. Jimmy recalls nothing else he wants, no photos on the walls, no attic treasures, not even the load of laundry in the dryer, not even his books. "It's furnished," he concludes.

Carolyn Day organized her Bible-study group and suggested its name, the Gemstones, but she is not its leader. At one end of the table sits Mrs. Ducasse, to whom leadership falls automatically, by some undefined birthright. She moderates this meeting in her customary terse manner, opening with "Who wants to start?" and moving things along with "What next?" Her style has replaced *Robert's Rules of Order* throughout the First Baptist Church of Walthourville, at Civitan meetings and garden-club gatherings, at all the civic organizations she controls. Mrs. Ducasse stubbornly remains alone in the house where her husband was shot. Carolyn keeps an eye on Mrs. Ducasse and her forty-three acres.

Carmen Fenzel sits directly across from Carolyn. When Carmen discovered that her husband's golf weekends at Kiawah did not involve golf, she packed her bags and moved out of the house. Carolyn, amazed that a CPA could know so little about property, talked her into moving back into the four-bedroom French Colonial. "You have to maintain possession," she informed Carmen. "Make him move out." Once the divorce was final, Carolyn sold the house and found Carmen a patio home, pulling in full commissions as listing agent on both.

Carmen is reading from the twelfth chapter of Genesis. "So first God says, and of course He's speaking to Abram, 'And I will bless them that bless thee, and curse him that curseth thee; and in thee shall all families of the earth be blessed.' That's verse three. Then verse ten says, 'And there was a famine in the land.' So that's what sent Abram to Egypt. So what I don't get is, first God says that good things are coming and then, just seven verses later, there's a famine."

Bridget Mooney, whose widowed father lives alone in a classic and restorable Sand Hills cottage on almost five acres, sits next to Carolyn. Bridget has learned to respond quickly, before Mrs. Ducasse can insert a "What next?" "So you're thinking what, that God broke His promise?"

"Yeah," snorts Carmen. "I mean, isn't that what verse three says? So what happened to that promise?"

Carolyn throws a private rueful smile across the table to Carmen before answering. "Well, if Reverend Balentine were here, he'd say that it was part of God's plan, that it was what sent Abram to Egypt."

"Why didn't God just tell the man to go to Egypt?"

No one knows the answer to that, and after several seconds Mrs. Ducasse asks, "What next?"

Lynda Short speaks up. Carolyn attended Lynda's wedding just a year and a half ago, at the new wedding chapel where most of the second and third marriages take place. She located the new couple a house under construction, so Lynda could choose her carpet and cabinets, then found financing so they could buy. "I don't really understand all that stuff that comes next. Did Abram really let the Pharaohs have his wife? I mean, to sleep with?"

Mrs. Ducasse checks the text. "Yep. That's what it says. Says she was pretty, then Abram told her to claim she was his sister, not his wife, then he let the Pharaohs have her."

" 'And the woman was taken into Pharaoh's house,' " reads Lynda. "That's in verse twelve. So Abram just gave her away?"

"He thought they would kill him, then take her anyway," Carolyn points out.

"So he gave them his wife to save his own sorry self," summarizes Carmen.

"What next?"

Lynda goes on, still perplexed. "Well, then it sounds like Abram got all kinds of stuff for her, like he sold her. But then it says, 'And the Lord plagued Pharaoh and his house with great plagues, because of Sarai, Abram's wife.' But Abram got to leave with all that stuff, the oxen and stuff, even though he's the one that sold his wife? Am I reading this correctly?"

Once again, Mrs. Ducasse slides her finger down the column of tiny print. "Yep. Verse twenty says Pharaoh sent them both away, I guess to get rid of the plagues, but Abram went with his stuff—'with all that he had,' it says. What next?"

"In chapter thirteen," Carolyn offers, "it says that 'Abram was very rich, in cattle, in silver, and in gold.' So it does sound like he profited, even though he did something wrong."

"Well, I know that Reverend Balentine warned us we'd have a hard time understanding the Old Testament, so I'm thinking it must mean something else. Something other than what it says."

Carmen interprets. "It says that Abram sold his wife. That makes him a pimp."

Bridget adds, "And then the Pharaohs got blackmailed—they had to give her back or get all those plagues."

Lynda sighs. "It can't mean that. It sounds like a movie I wouldn't rent."

Mrs. Ducasse scans the text. "That's what it says. What next?"

"Has anyone gotten to chapter sixteen yet?" asks Carmen. "It gets better. Abram sleeps with Sarah's maid, Hagar. He gets the poor girl pregnant, then some angel appears to her at a well and tells her what to name the boy. To name him Ishmael. And the angel says he'll be a wild man. Then there's a whole verse telling us the name of the well and where the well is. Like that's important." Carmen shakes her head.

"I suppose the well was important because the angel appeared there," suggests Carolyn.

"Okay, but it seems like that angel might ought to have a chat with Abram, not the girl he got pregnant."

" 'Wherefore the well was called Beer-la-hair-oh,' or something like that," reads Mrs. Ducasse. " 'Behold, it is between Kay-desh and Be-red.' That's verse fourteen. What next?"

Carmen is not ready to move on. "And chapter seventeen says God talked to Abram and called him 'a father of many nations.' " Carmen sniffs. "It's like biblical approval for cheating on your wife, getting girls pregnant."

"I think the guys get it in chapter seventeen," says Bridget.

"That's where God changes Sarai's name to Sarah and Abram's name to Abraham," begins Carolyn, knowing that's not the part that interests Bridget.

"Verse ten and verse eleven," Bridget continues. "God invents circumcision. Makes Abraham get circumcised, and he's ninety-nine. And Ishmael, and he's thirteen."

"Ouch," grins Carmen.

Bridget's brow is furrowed. "So is that supposed to, like, make it even? The guys get circumcised, and we have the babies?"

"I'd like to renegotiate that deal," says Carmen.

"What next?"

Carolyn has a closing scheduled for twelve-thirty and is bored with Sarah and her travails. "Abraham did at least try to bury Sarah properly," she offers. "In chapter twenty-three, he tries to buy a burial plot for her, worth four hundred shekels. 'And I will give thee money for the field,' he says. Now, why don't we page Reverend Balentine, and he can join us for coffee and bolenos."

"Breaking for bolenos," announces Mrs. Ducasse.

Carolyn uses her cell phone to page the minister, punching in her number, which she knows he will recognize, to alert him that the Gemstones are ready for his closing prayer. She keeps her eyes on the door, eager to see how the Reverend Balentine will handle this hornet's nest, a room full of bitter women with lots of questions. Mickey Balentine was a police chaplain a lot longer than he has been their associate pastor, and he is still more comfortable around men in uniform than women in heels. When Carolyn proposed the idea of this Bible-study group to the new minister and rattled off the names of the women she thought would be interested, he blurted, "Those are all women I've counseled recently."

"You and I have the same pool of customers, buddy," Carolyn bluntly told him. "They need you when they get married, when they have kids, when they find themselves alone again. And that's when they need me."

Mrs. Ducasse doesn't let the reverend get a boleno to his mouth. "We're reading up on Sarah and Abraham, Reverend Balentine, and the ladies want some explaining."

"It makes no sense at all," Carmen challenges him. "Seems to me Abraham should have been shot."

"I interpret it as the history of an old way of life," he fumbles. The Reverend Balentine is rusty with scripture. As police chaplain, he attended seminars on drug addiction and post-traumatic stress, but decades have passed since his seminary classes on the Pentateuch. "When we read the Old Testament, we see man in the past making laws and rules, sometimes making the wrong laws. Paul's second epistle to Timothy contains a chapter on the importance of scripture in modern times. Second Timothy three-sixteen says, 'All scripture is given by inspiration of God, and is profitable for doctrine, for reproof, for correction, for instruction in righteousness.' I'd say your discussion of the material you've read falls under the *instruction* category."

Bridget learned to be assertive when fighting for child support and now enjoys aggression. She wants to continue arguing, and the reverend is a safe target. "Well, God seems to be approving of all this stuff. I mean, it seems that way."

"Do you think God approves of the way we live today?" asks the Reverend Balentine, hoping to change the subject to something he can palliate with a Proverb or a Psalm or a maxim from Ecclesiastes, his favorite book.

"Compared to selling wives?" asks Carmen. "I'd say we're an improvement."

The reverend retreats into scripture. "I offer you Ecclesiastes chapter three, verse seventeen," he says in a solemn tone. " 'God shall judge the righteous and the wicked; for there is a time for every purpose, and for every work.' I think we have to let God be the judge, and to understand that Abraham lived by the laws of Abraham's time." He opens his mouth to speak as pastor, to recite a spiel comparing the law of Moses and the laws of man, but he can't do it. He opens his mouth again, this time to speak from his years in law enforcement, wanting to tell these women what he thinks of laws in general, that a library full of law books won't stop a suicidal woman from letting her newborn starve, won't stop the cop who found the baby from drinking to forget what he saw, won't protect the cop's wife from his alcoholic rages, that laws on stone tablets won't do it either. But again the Reverend Balentine closes his mouth, swallows the cynicism and the acid reflux that comes with it, turns away.

"I have a favorite from Ecclesiastes, too, Mickey," says Carolyn. "Chapter six, verse one: 'There is an evil which I have seen under the sun, and it is common among men.' " In public, she acts as though annoyed by the Reverend Balentine. In private, they meet regularly at his condo. Carolyn finds it a handy arrangement. Because she sold seventeen of the forty units, including the reverend's, the developer offered her a desk in the lobby sales office, so her car in the parking lot and her presence in the elevator arouse no suspicion among the reverend's congregation or Carolyn's customer base.

Mrs. Ducasse never eats bolenos, distrustful of their lumpy shapes, so she is hungry. She decides to adjourn the meeting. "Cleanup time," she says. "Then the reverend will lead us in our closing prayer."

The women put away their Bibles and go to work cleaning the coffee maker, wrapping up leftovers. Carolyn wipes the table with one hand while checking her voice mail. Between a call from the lawyer's office reminding her of the closing and a call from a seller wanting to know the status of his buyer's mortgage application is a call from Jimmy Steverson about a house on Randleman Road. As she listens to Jimmy's depressing message, Carolyn is grinning at Mickey's discomfiture. He manages finally to get a boleno in his mouth, but Mrs. Ducasse is ready for prayer.

"Time to pray, reverend," she tells him. "Closing prayer," she announces to the room.

The women join hands. They do not include the reverend in their circle. Heads bowed and eyes closed, the women hear the rhythm of the prayer, not the words, and are soothed as by a lullaby. "Lord, these fine women have come together today to try to understand the words of the Bible, words written long ago and in another language. Help us, Lord, to understand what we need to understand, to let you handle what we can't understand, and to do what we need to do. Help us be able to say, 'I have fought a good fight, I have finished my course, I have kept the faith,' as Paul said in his letter to Timothy."

Carolyn shakes her head at the arrogance of Mickey citing the Bible to God and of Jimmy Steverson thinking she'll put her sign in front of a house on Randleman Road. She conducts a mental inventory of the paperwork needed for the twelve-thirty closing. There was a last-minute problem with the termite inspection; she needs to call and check on that. Carmen squeezes her hand, and Carolyn in turn squeezes Lynda's.

Carolyn has no intention of trying to market Jimmy's house. There isn't enough commission in it. But Teeter Thibault, who paints for Carolyn whenever a property needs refurbishing, has gotten hard to find lately, so Carolyn will put Teeter in the Randleman Road house. She will offer to handle the rental, meaning she will know Teeter's whereabouts and will get a percentage of his rent as well. *And I will give thee money for the field* is the verse Carolyn adds to her memory collection today.

"Amen," says the reverend.

The women do not echo his amen. Instead, they repeat the handclasp that passed from woman to woman. "We're done," says Mrs. Ducasse.

The house is empty, the owners at their summer home in Blowing Rock, the key left with the guard at the neighborhood's gatehouse. It's late afternoon, and all Teeter expects to do is unload and set up. He goes in the kitchen door, punches the buttons to disarm the security system. On the kitchen counter, he finds his instructions, which rooms get which colors. He carries tarp up the stairs to the master bedroom, which is to have Adobe Sunset walls.

Teeter stops in the doorway, his "Jesus Christ" loud in the empty house. The room has a wall of windows displaying the Atlantic Ocean. He slides the glass doors aside, and the silence of air conditioning is replaced by the noise of sea gulls and waves and children. Teeter has spent time at Myrtle Beach in motels, at Hunting Island in his camper, at Folly Beach on day trips. He did not know that houses exist right on the beach, that people can lie in their own king-sized beds and look out the window at the ocean.

Teeter pulls his cell phone from his pocket. "Mark, it's Teeter. Boy, you gotta come down here where I am."

"I got the kids, Teeter. You know that."

"Can't you give 'em to Mayme for the weekend?"

"Well, yeah, Mayme always wants the kids. What's up, boy? You need some help with that house?"

"Mark, you gotta see this house. It's right smack on the beach. There's four bedrooms. The people that own it are gone."

"Teeter, there's security down there. They're liable to run you out."

"You ain't coming?"

Mark hesitates. "Can't do it, boy. Can't risk getting in any kind of mess while I got the kids."

"Well, you're missing something."

Teeter makes a food-and-beer run, ready to settle in for the night, and once again has to stop at the gatehouse. "I'm doing painting at the Monahans', on Heron Loop."

The guard recognizes the patched-up camper and rusted boat trailer. Waving a Lexus on through, he leaves the gatehouse and bends to talk directly to Teeter. "Sir, the owners have let me know that they don't want anyone in the house at night. So how 'bout you come back in the morning, get started on your painting then?"

"I was planning on painting all night," Teeter lies.

The guard doesn't mention the two six-packs visible through the thin plastic grocery bags on the seat next to Teeter, but he makes a show of staring at them before answering. "Well, sir, you'll have to take that up with the Monahans. They left instructions that we're to check the house at night, make sure no one's in there."

Teeter drives the island, finds no place where he can park his camper. He pulls into the outlet-mall parking lot, wondering if he can get away with parking there overnight, decides he should drink some of his beer while it's still cold, reaches for his phone to tell Mark that he was right about being run off by security. His cell phone shows an unanswered call, so he redials out of curiosity. Carolyn Day answers.

"I'm kinda backed up on painting right now, Miz Day."

"You're always backed up, Teeter. It's because you're the best. But that's not what I called about. I heard you're looking for a place to stay."

Teeter is focused on his dilemma of the night, having forgotten that he is without a permanent address. He wonders how this real-estate lady found out about his run-in with a Hilton Head security guard. "Well, yeah," is all he can say.

"So I have a rental that just came up. Furnished. Available immediately."

"Tonight?"

"Tonight?" Carolyn thinks for a minute. She certainly hadn't meant tonight. She meant for Teeter to sign a lease, to produce a deposit, and she hasn't talked to that Steverson boy about the details. On the other hand, Carolyn likes the idea of having the county's best painter in her debt, and she likes being in control. "You can move in tonight, Teeter, since you and I know each other so well. Four, uh, four-fifty a month, includes utilities." Carolyn scribbles a note in her monogrammed leather notebook: "Tell Steverson to leave utilities in his name." "It's that house you painted on Randleman Road."

Teeter is slouching but sits up. "That one with the dock?"

"The one with the dock, yes. Listen, Teeter. I'll let you move in tonight, but you have to meet with me tomorrow to sign a lease. And

I'll have to have one month in advance."

Teeter keeps most of his cash under the floor mat of his truck, and he knows there's at least that much there. "Okay. No problem."

Carolyn makes another note to herself: "Pick up deposit at 602 Randleman." Then she crosses it out. She does not want to drive down Randleman Road again. "There's a key on the back deck under some kind of rock. Teeter, you meet me at Totch's tomorrow at noon. I'll treat you to a teddy bear." Carolyn knows that a free meal will lure Teeter. She will take care of the lease and deposit and talk him into painting the exterior of a two-story traditional that needs some curb appeal.

Teeter makes it back to Osilo County in a little over two hours with his second six-pack still untouched. It's dark, almost midnight, but he backs his boat right into the water, sits on his new dock working on the second six-pack. He finds the gray rock, hefts it up and down, finally decides that it must be fake because it doesn't feel like a rock, finds the key beneath it, finds that the back door isn't even locked. Flipping the switch produces no light, so he uses his flashlight to find the breaker box. In the bathroom, he notices toilet paper still on the roll, towels draped over bars, figures whoever lived here was evicted. The bed still has the bottom sheet on it, and he finds a box in the extra bedroom full of blankets, uses a sofa cushion as a pillow.

The next morning, hauling his TV in, Teeter finds a loaf of Mayme's bread on his front porch.

At the Holiday Inn Express on the New Highway, Jimmy is at the breakfast buffet. When Carolyn Day calls him, he is squirting coffee into a Styrofoam cup. "I've rented your Randleman Road property," she tells him. Carolyn peppers Jimmy with numbers, giving him no opportunity to object, then throws in some questions to appear accommodating. "Do you want any special provisions in the lease—use of the dock, maybe? And do you want the property to stay on the market now that you have a tenant?"

"No special provisions," Jimmy says. He puts his coffee down on an empty table, picks up a copy of *The State*, wondering how this woman managed to rent out a house he vacated just twenty-four hours ago. "And see if you can sell it as quick as you rented it." He drops the newspaper next to his coffee cup, then pries a paper plate from a stack next to an array of cereal boxes. "Do you handle property in Colum-bia?" he asks, empty plate in hand, cruising the buffet. He passes a tray of Krispy Kreme doughnuts, a dome covering hot biscuits, finds him-self standing in front of a shoebox of bolenos. He moves on.

# Acknowledgments

Cora Sharpton McElveen, my grandmother, left her father's dairy farm at the age of twelve to work as a weaver, lived until the day she died in the same mill house in which she raised six children through depression and war, told me stories that helped me weave this one. To make sure that I correctly recalled the terms Miss Cora told me, that I was spelling *doffer* right, I consulted an excellent book about the Southern textile industry, *Like a Family: The Making of a Southern Cotton Mill World*, by J. D. Hall et al (University of North Carolina Press, 1987). I also visited the Augusta Canal Interpretive Center, located inside the venerable Enterprise Mill in Augusta, Georgia.

My husband, John, came running each time I cursed the silicon gods, resurrecting material the deities had tried to destroy, once pulling thousands of words from a hard drive gasping its death rattle, never once reminding me of the concept of backup.

My friend in the big city graciously offered advice and expertise.

Carolyn Sakowski took a chance that a geologist might have written a novel.

Steve Kirk polished the manuscript like a magic genie, letting the story out of the bottle.

ml

12/05